NEVER END

Åke Edwardson was born in 1953. He has worked as a journalist and as a press officer for the UN, and has written books on journalism and creative writing. Now a professor at Gothenburg University, he also is a prize-winning author, both for his best-selling detective novels and for his books for children. He has on three occasions been awarded the Swedish Crime Writers' Award for best crime novel.

Laurie Thompson was the editor of the *Swedish Book Review* 1983–2002 and has translated many books from Swedish, including novels by Henning Mankell, Håkan Nesser and Mikael Niemi.

ÅKE EDWARDSON

Never End

TRANSLATED FROM THE SWEDISH BY
Laurie Thompson

VINTAGE BOOKS
London

Published by Vintage 2007
6 8 10 9 7

Copyright © Åke Edwardson 2000
English translation copyright © Laurie Thompson 2006

Åke Edwardson has asserted his right under the Copyright, Designs
and Patents Act 1988 to be identified as the author of this work

First published with the title *Låt det aldrig ta slut* by Norstedts,
Stockholm, 2000

First published in Great Britain in 2006 by
Harvill Secker
Random House, 20 Vauxhall Bridge Road,
London SW1V 2SA

www.vintage-books.co.uk

Addresses for companies within The Random House Group Limited
can be found at: www.randomhouse.co.uk/offices.htm

The Random House Group Limited Reg. No. 954009

A CIP catalogue record for this book
is available from the British Library

ISBN 9780099472063

The Random House Group Limited supports The Forest Stewardship
Council (FSC), the leading international forest certification organisation.
All our titles that are printed on Greenpeace approved FSC certified paper
carry the FSC logo. Our paper procurement policy can be found at:
www.rbooks.co.uk/environment

Mixed Sources
Product group from well-managed
forests and other controlled sources
www.fsc.org   Cert no. TT-COC-2139
© 1996 Forest Stewardship Council

Typeset in Sabon by Palimpsest Book Production Ltd,
Grangemouth, Stirlingshire
Printed in the UK by CPI Bookmarque, Croydon, CR0 4TD

To Kristina

1

She felt a prick in her right foot, under her toes. She had been feeling her way forward, but the bottom was covered in seaweed here, a sort of long, thick grass that swayed with the current. It was brown and nasty. Like dead flowers.

Now she was standing on a small sandbank. She balanced on one leg and examined her right foot: she could see it was bleeding, but only a little. It wasn't the first time this summer. Par for the course.

She suddenly found herself thinking about a cramped classroom smelling of musty clothes . . . and musty thoughts. Rain against the windowpane. Questions on a sheet of paper and the scratching of pens, answers that would be forgotten as soon as the papers had been handed in. Now it was all over, though. She'd passed her final exams, three bloody big cheers. And now a summer that would never end. Neeeverend. She could hear the tune in her head.

The cut would be no more than a little scratch by tonight, and it wouldn't hurt at all; but she would still feel the heat on her skin, from the sun and the salt. From the shower. Before the evening got under way.

She swam, kicking with her legs, and water flowed all around her. A sailing boat chugged slowly into the bay on its engine. She could see the little ferries, three of them, from where she was swimming. All the people on their way down to the islands in the southern archipelago. She was drifting on her back. She couldn't feel the water any more, it was like floating on air. I can fly, she thought. I can do anything. Be whatever I like. I can be famous.

I can forget.

Summer, and then she'd be starting at the medical school – but that was a million years away, millions of drops of water tasting of salt and sand when she dived.

The water was green and a bit cloudy. She saw a shadow that might have been a fish.

She'd study for a year and then take a gap year, no matter what her father had to say. He'd comment that she was good at planning sabbaticals, but what about all the rest?

She didn't want to be at home.

She stayed under water for as long as she dared, then kicked off and tried to leap high above the surface. She swam back to the rocks – picking her way carefully through the seaweed – and heaved herself up onto one jutting out into the water.

The wound under her big toe was still bleeding. She clambered up to her blanket, pulled her towel from her bag, dried her hair and took a drink of water, then sat down on the blanket and blinked away some drops of salt water from her eyes. She took a breath, then another, a deep one, full of sun that almost scorched her lungs. The surface of the water was glittering like fish scales, as if tens of thousands of fish were wriggling away out there. She could hear faint sounds from boats heading in all directions. Some disappeared into the horizon, melted away. The sky was nearly white in the distance, but there was no sign of any cloud. She lay on her back. A drop of water ran down from her hair and over her cheek, and she could taste it on her lips. She'd already closed her eyes. Everything was red and yellow inside her head now. She could hear snatches of voices from people nearby, half words, a splinter of laughter that sparkled like the surface of the water in the sun.

She hadn't the strength to read. She didn't want to do anything at all, just lie there for as long as possible. Do nothing, just live for ever.

*

The sun was at eye level when she gathered her things together and scrambled over the hill and down through the little ravine to the cycle stands. She felt quite dizzy. Her shoulders were smarting, in spite of the cream. Her cheeks were burning, but not too much. It would have died down by evening, sort of sunk in. It would look good in the lights of the open-air café.

She was starting to forget.

She cycled past the marina, threading her way through the crowds of people flocking off the archipelago ferries towards the trams and buses. Everybody was going home at the same time, as if they all had the same habits. Maybe we do, she thought. That's the way it is in summer. Everything is simpler. Sunbathe, swim, shower, party. Swim, sunbathe, shower, party. Shower, sunbathe, swim, party. She stopped, parked her bike and stood in the ice-cream queue to buy a tub with two flavours: tutti-frutti and old-fashioned vanilla. The ice cream started to melt straight away, but it would have been worse if she'd had a cone. A woman next to her said it was 33 degrees. Thirty-three degrees at 6.00. 'We shouldn't complain,' said a man

3

to the woman's right. 'Oh, I don't know,' said the woman, who could have been anywhere between forty-five and sixty. 'The gardens could do with a bit of rain.'

Bugger your gardens, she thought as she rode off. Let this never end. The gardens will get their fill of rain come autumn.

There was a smell of hay coming from the field sloping down to the creek on the other side of the road. She passed through a cluster of houses, speeded up when she came to the cycle track alongside the tram lines, and was home within ten minutes. Her father was sitting on the verandah with a glass of what seemed to be whisky.

'Here comes a beetroot.'

She didn't answer.

'Still, better that than a leek.'

'A leek?'

'The white bits on a leek.'

'I'm going up to my room,' she said, walking up the steps. It was whisky. She recognised the heady smell.

'I'll be lighting the barbie in exactly ten minutes, Jeanette.'

'What are we having?'

'Skewered salmon, angler fish. And a few other things.'

'When are we eating?'

'Precisely forty-five minutes from now.'

Her father took a sip and turned away. The ice clinked. She liked wine, or a beer, but never whisky.

By the time Jeanette was doing her make-up, the sun had already sunk into her skin, its colour grown deeper.

4

The room was in shade: she had drawn the curtains and dimmed the light, but she was radiating a warm, dry, wholesome smell, from her skin. She stood in front of the mirror, wearing only her pants. Her breasts glowed as white as her teeth.

Now the room smelled of the after-sun gel she'd just applied. Her skin had already softened in the fresh water from the shower. A lovely term: fresh water.

Her father was shouting from the bottom of the garden and, at that very moment, she could smell the grilled fish and, at that very moment, she felt ravenously hungry. Ravenously. And thirsty.

Elin's teeth were gleaming on the other side of the table.

'What are you doing tomorrow?'

'Sunbathing and swimming.'

'Shall we have another one?'

'I don't think so. This one's gone to my head,' Jeanette said, indicating the beer glass on the table.

'You really do look brown,' Elin said.

'Thank you.'

'And your hair's turned white.'

'I don't know if I should thank you for that.'

'It's fabulous.'

'OK, thank you.'

'I think I'll have another beer,' Elin said. 'I'm permanently thirsty.' She stood up. 'I reckon I'd better go in and serve myself. The waitresses never get this far out.'

They were sitting in the far left-hand corner of the open-air café.

'Sure you won't have one as well?'

Jeanette nodded. Elin headed for the bar. Jeanette watched her threading her way through the tables, just as she'd threaded her own way through some jelly fish earlier that day, out at Saltholmen.

'Hang on,' she shouted. 'I will have just a little one.'

They stayed out for ages. The heat piled up between the buildings, having sunk slowly down to street level.

'It must still be as hot as ever,' Elin said. 'No sun, but just as hot.'

Jeanette nodded without replying.

'Evenings really are the best part of hot summers in Gothenburg.'

She nodded again.

'Cat got your tongue?' Elin said.

'It's just that I'm so incredibly tired.'

'But it's only just gone twelve.'

'I know. It must be the sun.'

'Some people have all the luck. I've been slaving away at a check-out all day.'

'It's your day off tomorrow.'

'That's precisely why we've got to have a little *paarty*.' She said it again: 'Paaarty.'

'I don't know, Elin.'

'For God's sake! When I said that about you having white hair, I didn't mean it literally. Having white hair doesn't mean you can act seventy-plus. My God! Now you're yawning again.'

'I know. I'm sorry.'

'What's it going to be, then?'

'Tonight? Or this morning, rather?'

'No, I mean one night in November next year, of course.'

'I don't know . . .'

'Am I going to have to go to the club on my own?'

'No,' she said, 'the gang's coming.'

There they were. Three boys and two girls, and it was perfect timing, because she didn't feel like partying the night away. It must be the sun. A massive overdose of sun. And now she wouldn't have to go just for Elin's sake.

'Now you don't need to come along just for my sake,' Elin said.

'What are you on about?' one of the boys asked.

'Time for bye-byes here,' said Elin, nodding at Jeanette and smiling.

'I'm really tired, that's all,' she said.

'Go home and get to bed then,' the boy said. 'Shall I ring for an ambulance?'

She stuck her tongue out. He laughed.

'I'm off.'

'Walking?'

'Yes, walking.'

'It's a long way. And the last tram's probably gone.'

'There's always the night bus. Or I might take a taxi for the last bit.'

'Get one now,' Elin said.

'Eh? You can't mean that . . . What do you mean, in fact?'

'You shouldn't walk through town on your own.'

She looked round.

'On my own? The place is full of people.' She looked round again. 'People of all ages, come to that.'

'You do as you like,' Elin said.

'Are we going, then?' asked one of the gang.

They stood up.

'Eleven tomorrow morning, OK?' Elin said.

'Can you manage to get up by then?'

'I can manage when there's some sunbathing in store.'

'You know where to find me,' she said, bade them good night and set off walking southwards.

'Rest in peace,' said one of the lads.

'That was a ridiculous silly thing to say,' Elin said.

Jeanette hesitated when she got to the taxi rank. She suddenly felt livelier, as if walking had triggered off some spare engine inside her or something. She paused. Looked at the park. There were as many people there as had been at the pavement café, maybe more. There were lights everywhere, the trees and bushes sparkled in bright colours that seemed to have been painted onto the leaves. There was a pleasantly cool breeze coming from that direction, she could feel it. It smelled good. And cool. She could take a short cut through the park to the street beyond. There were thousands of people around, everywhere. She could hear music coming from the café across the pond to the right. It was only a hundred metres away.

Something was tugging at her, from the park. She stood on the grass. It smelled even better from there. She could hear voices on all sides, just as by the water earlier. She closed her eyes and heard fragments of voices, splinters. It wasn't red and yellow inside her head now, more green, and perhaps just a touch of yellow. She opened her eyes again and set off across the lawn. People everywhere. Voices everywhere. She entered a group of trees and could see the street beyond them. Another twenty metres, perhaps.

She felt awake, wide awake, like in the morning after a good night's sleep and breakfast.

There was a rustling in the branches above her. The path was more like a grove. She could see street lamps

8

everywhere. It was already getting light. The sky was bluer now than it had been an hour ago. It was only just gone 1.00. There was a rustling, a swishing. Cars, laughter. She was already wondering when the first taxi would come rolling down the street.

A rustling to her right, a shadow in the corner of her eye, perhaps. She heard something, a bird. A laugh on the other side. A bush moved in a sudden gust of wind.

She was out in the street now. Cars passing by.

She walked along the pavement, then turned back into the park to cut off the last corner before emerging on the other side. There would be people absolutely everywhere and she wasn't scared and there was no reason to be, either. The very thought almost made her laugh. Just a few more steps to go.

2

She had gone numb, lapsed into unconsciousness, come back to life. Reached home. The sun was already hot, it felt like mid-morning. She'd walked down the hill hiding her face, so that nobody would see what had happened to her, what she had DONE. What somebody else had done to her.

The room looked the same as before, but nothing would ever be the same as before.

She ripped off her clothes, RIPPED off her clothes, and flung everything into the washing machine without looking and switched it on. The sound of the water was comforting.

She stood under the shower and washed herself UNDER her skin, or so it seemed. She stood there for a long time, rubbing her body and destroying all the evidence while the washing machine tossed her clothes backwards and forwards, dissolving the evidence, backwards and forwards. There was nothing left by the time Detective Inspectors Fredrik Halders and Aneta Djanali from the local CID arrived an hour later; nothing when the forensic officers from the police station in Ernst Fontells Plats eventually tried to find something among the threads and fibres.

*　*　*

The officer in charge had sent them out, Detective Chief Inspector Erik Winter, who suspected serial rape every time a rape was reported. He'd been right on two previous occasions.

Aneta Djanali eyed the park, Slottsskogen, as they drove past – the girl had told her mother and father it had happened in the park, they knew that. Djanali noticed the dog. Not something to play with. Nothing was to be played with. Three uniformed police officers were hovering around the car park. There were about ten cars there.

'Do you think they're checking the cars?' asked Halders, who was driving.

'Not just now, from the looks of it.'

'You get this big show every time.'

'Show?'

'They go mad. Twenty-five coppers with their hands in their pockets, and the bastard could have run off and left his car behind, that could be it there in the middle. That green Mantra. Or that black Volvo.'

'There are three of them, not twenty-five.'

Djanali saw one of the officers take a notebook out of his pocket and start writing down the registration numbers.

'They're starting now.'

The Bielkes' house was set back from the road, within a walled garden. The sea glistened only a few hundred metres away. Halders could smell the salt, see the water, hear the gulls, see the sails, a couple of ferries, a catamaran, the oil storage tanks, three cranes in the abandoned wharf on the other side of the estuary. A horizon line.

The house must have been worth ten million, but he

11

couldn't let that affect him. People had a right to more money than he had. It might be newly built. Inspired by Greek architecture. The thing looked like a whole Greek village.

He wiped the sweat from his brow, felt it on his back under his shirt. Aneta looked cool. Must be to do with genes or something. Black on the outside, cool on the inside.

'Right, then,' he said and rang the doorbell, which was a tiny button barely visible in the yellow-tinted plaster.

The door opened immediately, as if the man inside had been waiting for the bell. He was wearing shorts and a shirt, barefoot, sunburned, maybe fifty, glasses with thin frames, thinning hair longer at the back. Thin all over in fact, Halders thought. Red eyes. Scared eyes. Something had invaded his home.

Now reality was intruding for the second time: first a daughter who had been raped, then two plain-clothes police officers. The two always go together. Hadn't occurred to me before, Halders thought. We're the ones who do the chasing up, the good after the bad; but for him we're each as shitty as the other.

They introduced themselves.

Kurt Bielke ushered them in. 'Jeanette is in her room.'

'Yes.' Halders glanced up the stairs. 'It won't take long. Then she can go to East General.'

'East General?'

'The hospital. Women's clinic.'

'I know what it is,' said Bielke, stroking his high forehead. 'But . . . does she really have to go?' He turned to face Aneta Djanali. 'She says she doesn't want to.'

'It's important,' Djanali said. For numerous reasons, she thought to herself.

'Can we have a word with her now?' Halders asked.

12

'Yes . . . Yes, of course,' said Bielke, gesturing towards the stairs. Then he just stood there, as if frozen, until his head moved once again. He wasn't looking at them. 'It's up there.'

They went up the stairs and came to a closed door. Djanali could hear the sounds of summer outside. A sea bird laughed out loud, and the laughter was followed by more. The birds drifted off over the bay. A dog barked. A car tooted. A child shouted out in a shrill voice.

Bielke knocked on the door. There was no answer, and he knocked again.

'Jeanette?'

They could hear a voice from inside, but no words.

'Jeanette? The po . . . the police are here.'

Some word or other from inside again.

'Let's go in now,' Halders said.

'Shall I come as well?' Bielke asked.

'No,' said Halders, knocking on the door himself. He turned the handle, the door opened and they went in.

The girl was in her dressing gown, sitting on the bed. It was as dark as she could make it in the room, with the venetian blinds closed. The bright light of the sun was trying to break through. It's as though the girl is trying to hide from it on one corner of the bed, thought Djanali. She's clinging to the wall. She's called Jeanette, not 'she'. She's got a name, but suddenly it has no meaning for anybody else; maybe not even for her now she's the victim.

Now it's my turn to speak.

Djanali introduced herself and Halders, who nodded, said nothing, sat down on the desk chair and observed her, gave her a friendly nod.

Half of Jeanette's face was hidden under the towel

13

she'd wrapped round her head after her long shower. She was holding the collar of her dressing gown closed with a dainty hand. Djanali's eyes had grown used to the half-light in the room by now, and she contemplated the fragile skin on the girl's fingers. It seemed to be sodden.

She's been in the shower for hours. I'd have done the same.

Djanali asked a few brief questions, the simplest she could think of, to start off the first interview. The answers were even briefer, barely possible to comprehend. They had to move closer, but not too close. Jeanette spoke about the park. Yes, it had been late. No, early. Late and early. She'd been on her own. She'd walked there before. Lots of times, at night as well. Alone? Yes, alone at night as well.

This time she'd only just become alone. Or maybe it had been a few minutes. She'd been to two different places and she said where they were and Halders noted them down. She spoke about the others who'd been there with her, for a short time at least. They'd been to a graduation party, just a little one. A quarter of the class. It was nearly a month since they finished their exams.

Djanali could see Jeanette's white cap on the chest of drawers under the window. She could imagine her joy at passing her exams, and earning the right to wear her white cap. It seemed luminescent in the darkness.

A little graduation party. Djanali shifted her gaze from the white cap to Jeanette's face. Nineteen years old. She would like to have asked her about boyfriends, but knew it was better to wait. The important thing now was basic questions about what had happened; when, how, when, how, when, how. Ask, listen, look. She'd done this often enough to know that the most important thing as an interrogator was to pin down what she called the incident behind the incident. Not just to take an account at face value. The victim's account. No, to start thinking about the difficult questions: Is that really true? Is that really what happened?

She asked Jeanette Bielke to tell her what impression she'd got of her attacker.

Suddenly Jeanette said she wanted to go to the hospital, she wanted to go now. Djanali knew that would come, or maybe ought to have come before now.

'Soon. Just one more question. One second only.'

'But I want to go NOW.'

'Can you tell us anything about this man?'

'I can't remember.'

'Was he tall?'

'He was big. Strong. Or maybe I didn't . . . didn't dar . . . want . . . didn't dare to try and struggle. I did try at first . . . but then I couldn't any more.'

She'd started to cry. She pulled at the towel and rubbed it over her eyes and it came loose and fell down and her wet hair became visible, stuck to her head as if by glue.

'He . . . he'd tied me,' she said.

'Tied you?'

'Yes.'

'How?'

'Well, tied . . . he had a noose round my ne . . . round my neck. My arms . . . then . . .' She grasped hold of her throat.

Djanali could see it now, a red mark like a narrow line around her neck. Jesus Christ.

'It was like a dog lead,' Jeanette said. 'It didn't smell

15

of dog, but it was like a dog lead.' She was looking straight at Djanali now. 'I could see it shining. I think so.'

'Shining?'

'It was shining round the collar. I think so. As if there were studs in it, or something.'

She gave a shudder, cleared her throat, then shuddered again. Djanali looked at Halders, who nodded.

'Just one last question, Jeanette. Did he say anything?'

'I don't remember much. I fainted. I think he said . . . something.'

'What did he say?'

'I didn't hear what it was.'

'But you could hear words?'

'Yes.'

'You didn't hear what language?'

'It wasn't like a language.'

'What do you mean? Not like a language?'

'It was . . . just sounds . . . didn't mean anything. It was just something he . . . something I couldn't understand.'

Djanali nodded, waited. Jeanette looked at her.

'He did it three times, or whatever. Repeated it. Or maybe it was just once. Just when he was . . . when he . . .'

The gulls were laughing outside the window again: they'd come back from the sea. A car engine started. A child shouted again. Jeanette rubbed hard at her hair with the towel. It was hot and stuffy in the room.

Djanali knew Jeanette had said all she was capable of saying just now, and that it was high time they got her to the hospital.

She could see Halders getting to his feet. It had all gone as usual. Rape. Report. First interview.

16

Request for legal documentation. Car to the women's clinic.

This was real. Not just imagination.

*

Jeanette Bielke was being taken to the clinic: Aneta Djanali and Halders drove to the park where it had happened.

'What do you reckon about the description?'

Halders shrugged.

'Big. Strong. Dark coat. No special smell. Armed with some kind of noose. Made strange sounds. Or said something incomprehensible.'

'Could be any man in the street,' Halders said.

'Do you think she's reliable?'

'Yes.'

'I'd have liked to ask her more.'

'You got what information you could, for now.'

Djanali looked out at the summer. People weren't wearing much. Their faces were beaming, trying to outdo the sun. The sky was blue and cloudless. Everything was ice cream and lightweight clothing and an easy life. There was no headwind.

'Let's hope it isn't the beginning of something,' said Halders, looking at her. 'You know what I mean.'

'Don't say it.'

Halders thought about what Jeanette had said regarding the man's appearance, in so far as she could see anything. The rapist. They'd have to wait for the tests, but he was sure they were dealing with rape.

They could never be sure about appearances. Getting a description was the hardest thing. Never put your trust in a description, he'd said to anybody who cared to listen. None of it is necessarily related to the facts.

The same person could vary between five foot ten and six foot three in a witness's eyes and memory. Everything could vary.

The previous year they'd had a madman running round and knocking people down from behind, no obvious pattern, just that he knocked them down and stole their money. But he did have a habit of introducing himself from the side, that was the nearest to a pattern: some greeting or other to get his victim's attention, then wham.

The victims all agreed on one thing: he'd reminded them of the hunchback of Notre Dame – stocky, hunch-backed, bald, dragged one foot.

When they eventually caught up with him, in the act, he turned out to be six foot two with thick, curly hair and could have landed the job of Mr Handsome in any soap opera you care to name.

It all depended on so much. What they saw. How dark it was. Where the light came from. Fear and terror. Most of all the terror.

He turned into the park and stopped the car. The uniforms weren't there any more. The scene was roped off, two forensic officers were crawling on the ground. There was a bunch of kids hanging round the far barrier, whispering and watching. Some adults came past and stopped, then walked on.

'Found anything?' Halders shouted. The scene-of-crime boys looked up, then down again, without answering. Halders heard a short bark, and saw the dog and its handler.

'Found anything?' he said to the handler.

'Zack picked up something over there, but it melted away into the wind.'

'Or up a tree,' said Halders, looking up.

'Were you there when we caught that bastard the other year who tried to hide up a tree?' the dog handler asked.

'I heard about it.'

'Them trees are clean now, anyway.'

'How did he get away, then?'

'Ran, I suppose. Or drove. You'd better ask forensics. But I doubt there'll be any tracks. Everything's so bloody dry.'

Halders looked round. Djanali was watching the SOC team. The police dog was scrutinising first Halders, then the SOC team. Halders looked round again, walked a few paces.

'Have you been here before?' he asked the dog handler.

'How do you mean? For another crime?'

'I'm not talking about your private life, Sören. Have you ever been called out here after a rape?'

'To this park, you mean?'

'Yes. And to this very spot.'

Halders was standing just outside the police enclosure: it looked out of place, as if it had been made by the kids who were staying on to watch. The pond was to the right. It reflected pink from the flamingos standing on one leg by the water's edge.

The SOC team was crawling around in some shrubbery.

Next to it were two trees. Two metres or so to there. Maples? There was a passage between them, wide enough to get through. It was shady inside. A rock sticking out turned it into a hollow, almost a cave behind the trees. The forensic officers were moving around there now, on their way into the cave.

A perfect place to commit rape.

Good God! Halders thought. He could see it all now. It was HERE.

The tarmacked path was about ten metres away, but it might as well have been a hundred. A thousand. There was a minor road the other side of the car park. A hedge between the cars and the park itself. The lighting in the park was a joke. He'd walked there hundreds of times at night, and the lighting was more of a hindrance than a help. They hadn't improved it, in spite of what had happened here.

A perfect place. It was as if the shadow between the trees was lying in wait. He hadn't caught on at first.

'This spot?' asked the dog handler. He looked round. 'I don't think so.' He looked at Halders. 'What are you getting at?'

'It's happened before,' Halders said.

'I'm not with you.'

'This is where it was.' Halders looked at his colleague. 'Bloody hell, Sören, it's the very same spot. The same spot!'

'I don't get what you're on about.'

'Weren't you based in Gothenburg five years ago?'

'I came here four years ago.'

'But you've heard about the Beatrice Wägner case, surely?'

The dog handler looked at Halders.

'Beatrice? That girl who was murdered?'

'Five years ago. She was raped too. Raped and murdered.'

'I know about it . . . course I do. I read about it at the time. We'd —'

'It was here,' Halders said.

'Here?'

'This is where it happened,' Halders said to Sören and Djanali, who had just joined them. 'This is where Beatrice was found. This very spot. She was in that hollow,' he said, nodding towards where the SOC team was still combing the ground. 'Lying between the trees, she was. It's like a cave in there.'

Raped, and strangled, he thought.

He noticed the dog following his gaze towards the cave and then back again. It jerked at its lead, then was calm again.

3

Winter could feel the tiny hand gripping his finger. Elsa gurgled a greeting. He kissed her behind her ear, she laughed, he blew gently on her neck and she laughed again.

He still hadn't got used to that laugh and that gurgle; they could be floating around in the flat for ages. His daughter would soon be fifteen months old. Her sounds tore the silence from the walls like old wallpaper. Amazing that such a tiny body could make such a loud noise.

Angela came in from the kitchen and sat down in one of the armchairs, unbuttoned her checked blouse and looked at Winter and Elsa on the blanket on the floor.

'Breakfast,' she said.

Winter blew behind Elsa's ear.

'Time for breakfast,' Angela said.

Elsa laughed.

'She doesn't seem hungry,' Winter said, looking at Angela.

'Bring her here and you'll see. This is going to be the last time, though. I can't go on breastfeeding her any longer for God's sake.'

He carried the little girl over to Angela in the armchair. She seemed to barely weigh anything at all.

* * *

Winter saw the files lying on his desk when he entered his office. The sun had already warmed the room, and there was a smell of summer. Two more months, and then it would be some time before he saw this office again. A year. He was going to take a year's leave, and who would he be the next time he stepped into this gloomy office where nearly all thoughts were painful to think?

Would he ever come back at all?

Who would he be then?

He went to the washbasin and drank a glass of water. He felt thoroughly rested. At an early stage Elsa had decided to sleep from 8.00 at night till 8.00 in the morning. He and Angela were very lucky.

Sometimes Angela would cry, at night. Her memories would come flooding back, but more and more rarely now. He hadn't asked her what happened in that room in that flat the day before he got there. Not at first, not directly. She used to talk about it, night after night, in mangled sentences. Now it had more or less stopped. She slept soundly for hours on end.

It wasn't even eighteen months ago.

He sat down at his desk, opened the first of the files and took out the documents and photographs. He held up one of the pictures. The rock. The trees. The lawn and the path. It was all very familiar in a . . . depressing sort of way, like an illness that recurs after several years. A cancerous tumour that has been cut away, but continues to grow.

Still, Jeanette Bielke was alive, and they were waiting for her test results.

He stood up, with the photograph in his hand, and opened the window. The sun was on the other side of the city. He could smell the light, almost weightless scents of summer. He thought of Elsa. There was a knock at the door and he shouted, 'Come in.' Halders was in the doorway. Winter gestured towards the visitor's chair, but stayed by the window.

'It was completed intercourse,' Halders said. 'I've just had the report. Purely technical, that is. But it is rape.'

'What else does it say?'

'That the girl is probably telling the truth.'

'Probably?'

Halders shrugged. 'You know how it is.'

Winter didn't reply. Halders looked at the files on the desk.

'You sent down for them I see.'

'Yes.'

'Have you had time to read through them?'

'No. Only this photograph,' said Winter, holding it up.

Halders could see a picture of Beatrice Wägner on one of the newspaper cuttings by Winter's elbow.

'Is it a coincidence?' Halders said.

'The place? Well . . . it's not the first time somebody's been attacked in Slottsskogen Park.'

'But not at that particular spot.'

'Not far away.'

'Never at that particular spot,' Halders said. 'You know it. I know it.'

It's true, Winter thought. He knew that part of the park. Since Beatrice Wägner's murder he'd been back there regularly. Would stand there watching people milling around. Halders had done the same. They'd occasionally bumped into one another. You're not among the suspects, Halders had muttered on one occasion.

They were looking for a face, a movement. An action. A voice. An object. A belt. A noose. A dog lead.

24

They always return to the scene of the crime. Every policeman knew that. Every one. Somehow or other, at some time or other, they always go back. They go back after ten years, or five. To carry on. Or just to be there, to breathe, to remember.

Just being there was the thing. If he was there and the man who'd done the deeds came down the path at that moment, he, Winter, would know, *really* know, and so it wouldn't be a coincidence. It had nothing to do with luck. Nothing to do with chance. And at that very moment – when he was still holding the photograph in his hand and looking at Halders and the damp patch on his shirt under his left armpit – at that very moment he had the feeling that it really would happen. He would see the man and it would be as if a nightmare had turned into reality. It would happen.

'That bastard's back,' Halders said.

Winter didn't reply.

'Same modus operandi.' Halders ran his hand over his short-cropped hair. 'Same spot.'

'We'd better talk to the girl again.'

'She's going home this afternoon.'

'Then go and see her there. How were her parents?'

'Desperate.'

'Nothing funny?'

'Aneta had a look around, of course, when we went to talk to the girl.' Halders' left eye twitched slightly, as if he had a tic. 'No. The old man had the shakes – clearly hung over – something like this isn't exactly going to help him recover.'

Halders looked at Winter. 'He's back, Erik. How many did he manage last time? Three victims, one of which died?'

'Mmm.'

'Maybe we'd better talk to the other two girls again.'

'I've already done that. They don't remember any more now than they did back then.' Halders stood up.

'Fredrik?'

'Yes?'

'I feel just the same as you do about this. I can't forget Beatrice either.'

'No.'

'It's not just because it's on the unsolved list.'

'I understand.' Halders sat down again. 'It's the same with me.' He scratched his head. Winter could see a patch of damp under Halders' other armpit as well. 'You can feel it all over the station. Everybody's talking about it.'

'I'll have a look at the old pattern,' said Winter, gesturing towards the documents on his desk.

'There'll be another one,' Halders said. 'The same again.'

'Take it easy now.'

'Yes, yes, OK. One rape at a time.'

The sound of sirens drifted in from the east. Somebody was shouting underneath Winter's window. A car started. Halders ran his hand over his hair.

Winter suddenly made up his mind.

'Let's go there. Now.'

Everybody was wearing shorts or lightweight skirts. It was over 30 degrees. There seemed an unusually high number of people in town, he thought – they ought to be down by the water.

'It's sales time,' said Halders, pointing to the shopping centre. 'Summer Sale, where the prices are a dream and buying is one long party.'

Winter nodded.

'I ought to go myself,' Halders said.

'Oh yes?'

'It's nothing for you, I suppose, but things can seem a bit on the dear side when you're separated and have two children.' He turned to look at Winter. 'Maintenance, heavy stuff. Not that I'm complaining.'

'How old are your kids now?' Winter asked.

Halders looked surprised. 'Seven and eleven,' he said, after a moment's hesitation.

'A boy and a girl, is that right?' Winter was driving along the Avenue. He was the only one in the middle lane. All other traffic seemed to have disappeared. He blinked, and all the cars came back again. He blinked once more, and stopped at an amber light, after glancing in his rear-view mirror.

'Er . . . yes. It's the boy that's the youngest.'

'Are you sharing custody?' Winter asked.

Halders looked at him.

'They live with Margareta, but come to me every other weekend.' He looked away, towards the river, then back at Winter. 'Sometimes they stay a bit longer with me. Or maybe we go away somewhere. It depends.' Halders had gone into his shell. Winter cast him a sideways glance. 'I always try to think of something interesting.'

Winter stopped at an amber light again. A large family in Gothenburg for the day was crossing the road: map, wide eyes, comfortable shoes. A boy, maybe ten, and a girl, about seven, looked at them, then caught up with their parents who were preoccupied with a pushchair containing two small children.

'How's it going for you?' Halders asked. 'With the baby. Does she keep you up all night?'

'Not at all.'

'Hannes had colic,' Halders said. 'It was horrible. Four months of terror.'

'I've heard about it,' said Winter.

That sounded almost apologetic, Halders thought. As if he'd got away with things too lightly.

'That was the beginning of the end,' said Halders, as they arrived.

The place was just as sorry a sight as ever. There, five years ago, the SOC team had carefully collected leaves, grass, pieces of bark. Then as now. Winter was still waiting for his promotion back then, and impatient. Halders had been an Inspector too, but slightly less impatient, and still married. Home every day to a house full of life.

At least it isn't murder this time, Winter thought. Two women went past, pushing prams. The sun was hidden behind the trees. Voices of children swimming in the pond. A man was lying flat out on the grass, fifty metres from the scene of the crime. Winter watched the man stagger to his feet then stumble forward a few metres before sitting down again, producing a carrier bag and drinking in classic wino style, without taking the bottle out of the bag.

'And no witnesses,' Halders said.

Winter was observing the drunk.

'Have we thought about the homeless?' he said, mainly to himself.

'Then? There weren't any then,' Halders said.

'Now.'

'I've no idea,' Halders said.

'No doubt there are some sleeping rough around here.' Winter watched the man make another effort to move, and this time he managed a few paces more. 'Especially now, in summer.'

Halders followed his gaze and reached for his mobile phone.

Five minutes later a patrol car turned up and Halders pointed out the drunk, who was still attempting to walk the tightrope down the wide gravel path. They watched as the man was escorted to the car.

'Shall we hear what he's got to say right now?' Halders asked.

'It can wait,' said Winter. He walked over to the rock in the trees, entered through the passage. Same place, same cave.

*

He knew what it was even before he was even fully awake, and he reached for the telephone on the bedside table. It was all still part of his dream, a continuation of the night that one could touch, smell. It was as if he knew what the voice in the receiver was going to say.

He watched Angela as he listened. He could see the top of Elsa's little head snug in her cot.

'Yes, yes,' he said into the mouthpiece. 'Yes.'

He phoned Halders. 'I want you to come with me.'

'I'm as good as there,' said Halders.

Winter drove through the morning light. It had nuances of milk and spinach.

They met at the car park. Halders looked tense, a mirror image of himself. They could have made their way blindfolded to the scene of the incident. There was no other place.

It was lit up now, by a pale electric light that would soon be unnecessary. Forensic officers were crawling all over the place. More than ever. He could see more uniforms than ever. More onlookers than ever. People were still out and about and were loitering now on the edge of the park. Winter walked to the trees and the rock and the passage between and saw the girl's legs like two sticks and then he saw the rest of her body, all of it except her head, which was still in the shadows.

He could have stopped there and then, gone back to his gloomy office at the police station, opened the old files and read about what had happened five years ago. He knew that's how it was, and so it proved, later, when the post mortem was completed and he had all the facts currently available.

It was still early morning. He saw the doctor, a new one whose name he didn't know. He looked young. Came over to speak to Winter. Made a few comments that he took on board.

She had stopped breathing because somebody had tightened a noose around her neck. Other things had been done to her body, not yet clear what. Her purse was still in the handbag that Winter could see lying on the ground, not far from her hand.

Go on, stretch out your hand and grab the handbag, he thought. You can do it. You can still do it.

She was eighteen or nineteen or so. He could look if he wanted to, but he wasn't to touch anything yet. She-had-been-eighteen. That's what it was destined to be. I'll stop there. Eighteen was as far as she was going, nineteen maximum. No adult life, no family, no breast-feeding, no pram, no colic, no divorce.

Halders was standing beside him. He said something to one of the forensics officers in a low voice. A night-bird uttered a cry that reminded Winter of something. It wasn't the situation. That was familiar without the aid of sound effects.

Torches were shone into the hollow. He could see a face on the ground. Oddly enough it still seemed to be in the shadows.

He could hear a tune inside his head from the pavement café that same night. Had she walked past? Had she walked past that very place with her friends?

4

The girl's name was Angelika Hansson. She could be identified from documents in her handbag.

She had dark hair, and her clothes were in a mess. There had been leaves and strands of grass in her hair. She had been lying with her head on a sort of pillow of grass. It was almost as if somebody had made a pillow for her. This was the image he had in his head when he turned up at the post mortem. Pia Fröberg, the forensic pathologist, was busy with Angelika Hansson's body. He was pretty used to it by now. The body, under the spotlights. The doctor's white coat, picked out by the dazzling ceiling lights. Naked body parts. No sign of life.

How many times had he been in this situation? Not many, but more than enough even so.

He knew she'd been strangled. Some kind of strap round her neck that she hadn't been able to remove, that couldn't be untied. Pia confirmed this: it could be some kind of collar, a dog lead, a noose. It might well have been a rope. Not a bootlace.

It happened only a few hours before the alarm was raised. What had he being doing at that time? The thought came into his mind. What exactly *had* he been doing then? What had she been doing during the hour before it happened? What had Angelika Hansson been doing? She'd been drinking, perhaps too much. She might have been holding somebody's hand.

She was nineteen. He thought about what Halders had said regarding Jeanette Bielke. She too was nineteen; passed her final school exams just over a month ago. Halders said Jeanette Bielke had the white cap Swedish students wear at their graduation parties, singing songs about their happy schooldays. Used to be compulsory, but not any more. Had Angelika had a student cap? Had she known Jeanette? Did they have any mutual friends?

'She was pregnant,' said Pia Fröberg, walking over to him.

Winter nodded without answering.

'Did you hear what I said, Erik?'

He nodded again.

'I must say you get quieter and quieter by the year.'

By the month, he thought. Quieter by the month.

'How far gone?' he asked.

'I can't say for certain,' she said, 'but not many weeks.' She looked back at the girl's body. 'I wonder if she even knew herself.'

'But you're sure, about the pregnancy?'

'Of course.'

Winter took two steps towards the dead body. They knew nothing about her as yet, apart from what was in her handbag, and that was with Chief Inspector Beier in the forensic department.

He'd soon go round to her home. He had the address. Her parents were in another room only a few metres away, harshly lit. Two faces, pale with shock. He hadn't noticed a boyfriend with them, nobody who might be a boyfriend. Nobody with the parents, who could be

33

no more than a few years younger than he was himself. People had kids when they were twenty-two. Angelika Hansson would have been one of those. A pregnant daughter. Did they know?

'What?' The man's face had turned ashen. Lars-Olof Hansson, Angelika's father. His wife was standing next to him, the girl's mother, Ann. Eyes shrunken with sorrow and desperation. 'What the hell are you saying?'

Winter repeated what he had told them.

'She hasn't had a boyfriend for two years,' the father said. He turned to his wife. 'Have you heard anything about a boyfriend, Ann?'

She shook her head.

'It can't be true,' he said, turning back to Winter. 'It's not possible.'

'She's never . . . spoken to me about that,' the mother said. She looked at Winter. Her eyes had grown bigger. 'She would have said something about it.' She was looking at her husband now. 'We spoke about everything. We did, Lasse. You know we did.'

'Yes.'

'Absolutely everything,' she repeated.

She didn't know, thought Winter. I don't think she knew. He hadn't had all the details from Pia yet. There was somebody else who might not have known. It needn't be a boyfriend. A casual partner, maybe. How many of those had she had? He looked at her parents. He'd be forced to ask all those questions, at the worst possible time. But there again, the best, when everything was . . . fresh. He pictured the girl's body on the metal table in the neighbouring room.

'We need to know everything about her friends,' he

said. 'Everything you can remember, about all of them.'

'This business of her . . . pregnancy. Has that anything to do with the murder?' asked the father, fixing Winter with piercing eyes.

'I don't know,' he said.

'Then why the hell are you asking so much about it?'

'Lasse,' his wife said.

He turned to look at her.

'He's only doing his job,' she said, and Winter suddenly had the impression she looked stronger. 'We want to know, after all.'

I'm only doing my job, Winter thought.

*

Halders drove back to the Bielkes' house. He was on his own, and had phoned ahead. He parked the car and crunched over the gravel. Jeanette was on the verandah. Halders wondered what she was thinking about. She glanced up and saw him approaching. Looked as if she were about to throw up. Halders had reached her by then.

'Let's get out of here,' he said.

She didn't move.

'Would you like to nip out to Saltholmen?'

She shrugged. Irma Bielke came onto the verandah and looked at her daughter.

'We're going out for a little drive,' said Halders, but she didn't seem to hear him. They're all still in a state of shock, he thought. The idyll has been blown away and reality has taken its place, even in this posh neighbourhood.

Jeanette got into the car, which had warmed up in the sun. Halders started the engine. As he changed gear he accidentally brushed her left knee, and she jerked away. He pretended not to notice, headed down the drive and out into the road.

'Have you got a favourite spot out here?' he asked as they approached the rocks and jetties.

'Yes . . .'

'Shall we go and sit there?'

She shrugged.

There were cars everywhere. Halders parked illegally opposite the ice-cream stall and stuck his police pass on the windscreen. Lots of people were streaming past, either going down to the boats or coming back from them. A child was screaming, being dragged along by its parents. Two girls about the same age as Jeanette smiled, maybe at him, maybe at her.

'You'll have to show me the way,' he said. 'How about an ice cream, by the way?'

She shrugged.

'Every time you shrug I'll interpret it as a "yes",' Halders said.

She smiled.

'Old-fashioned vanilla,' she said. 'And tutti-frutti.'

The ice cream had started running down Halders' fingers as they walked to the rocks. He licked at his cornet as quickly as he could. She had taken a tub.

They climbed up to the top of the slope and down the other side. There was a clear view of the sea. Sails everywhere. The wind carried a strong smell of hot salt. There were fewer people on the rocks than he'd expected. Nobody was lying in her favourite spot.

'Here it is,' she said.

They sat down. She looked out over a narrow channel

leading to the harbour. A boy was diving on the other side.

'I was here the same day,' she said.

Halders nodded.

'It's unreal,' she said, looking at Halders. 'It's like . . . another time, sort of. A different country, or something.' She turned back to look at the water. 'It's as if it had never happened. Like a dream, you know?' She looked at Halders again.

What is dream and what is reality? he wondered.

'I couldn't tell you what's a dream and what's reality,' she said. 'I wish I knew what was what . . . which of the two what happened to me is . . . but that's not the way things are of course.' Halders noticed her benumbed expression, full of worry. There was something closed in that face of hers. She's been extinguished, he thought. Something has been extinguished. I could kill that bastard. I really could. No. That's not the answer. They wouldn't be able to rehabilitate him into society if I did that.

'So you don't know Angelika Hansson?'

'No, I've already told you.'

'Met her, maybe?'

She had seen photos of Angelika. Halders had one in his breast pocket, but he didn't get it out.

'She'd just passed her final exams as well,' he said.

'Are you saying that means we must know each other?'

'Don't you have a communal party?'

'Are you serious? Do you know how many people in Gothenburg finish school every year?'

'No.'

'Neither do I. But way too many for there to be just *one* party.' She was looking at Halders now. 'It's called a ball, incidentally. Graduation ball.'

37

Somebody dived into the water on the other side of the channel again. Several people tramped past on the rocks above them.

'What happened between you and your boyfriend?'

'That has nothing to do with this.'

'Tell me, even so.'

'What if I don't want to?'

Halders shrugged. It was his turn now.

He watched a boat moving along the channel, towards the sea. A man on board waved, but she didn't wave back.

'We finished, simple as that,' she said.

Halders noticed that the man on the boat was still waving, and waved back to put a stop to it.

'He didn't think so though, did he?' he asked.

'I'm not with you.'

'He wouldn't accept that it was all over, would he?'

'Who told you that?'

Halders didn't reply.

'Don't believe them,' she said.

'Believe who?'

'Mum and Dad, of course. They're the ones who told you, aren't they? They said there was a row, I suppose. That was it, wasn't it?'

Halders said nothing.

'They've never liked him,' she said.

'But it's all over now?'

'Yes.'

'Really?'

'It's finished, for Christ's sake. FOR CHRIST'S SAKE!' She looked him straight in the eye. 'Has it never happened to you?'

'Yes.'

'Have you had to explain how? And why and where? And to a detective?'

'No.'

'Well, then.'

'You know why I'm asking,' he said. He could feel the sun on his bald patch. He'd have to buy a cap, an ordinary cap. Not one of those bloody baseball caps. 'He turned up at your house a few times and wanted to come in, didn't he?'

'Maybe the odd time. The odd evening.'

'He was a bit . . . noisy. Wanted to come in and talk to you.'

'He was drunk,' she said.

'Why?'

'Oh, for God's sake!'

'Why?' Halders insisted.

She heaved a sigh.

'He was upset,' she said.

'Because it was over?'

She shrugged. A yes.

'But you wanted it to be over?'

She nodded.

There's something she doesn't want to tell me. Something important. What is it?

'And he couldn't understand that,' Halders said. 'That you wanted to finish.'

'Can't we stop talking about Mattias now? Why are we talking about him all the time?'

'Have you seen him . . . since?'

'Since I was raped?'

'Yes.'

'Say it then. Raped. RAPED!'

Halders could see a woman on the next rock stumble.

'Since you were raped,' Halders said.

'No, I haven't. Have you?'

'No.'

39

'You should do. I mean, you talk about him all the time.'

'I am going to meet Mattias. Tomorrow.'

'A waste of time,' she said. 'It wasn't him, if that's what you think.'

*

Winter read the files. Had it started again with Jeanette Bielke? Continued with Angelika Hansson? Would it keep on going?

He had the familiar feeling of impotence. Speculations about crimes that had been committed. About crimes waiting to be committed. Waiting to be committed.

But something was different. He thought the same person who had raped Jeanette Bielke had murdered Angelika Hansson. Sometimes it was more than just knowing.

Another crime was waiting to be committed, and on his desk in front of him was the result of what had happened so far. He'd dug out all the old material on Beatrice Wägner. The uncomfortable feeling of yet again coming up against an appalling crime. Like a meeting in the dark. The fresh memory of her father's voice; no more than a few months ago. They'd kept in touch over the years. Winter didn't know for whose sake.

As long as I keep talking to the family, the case hasn't been shelved. Now we have a new opportunity.

His mobile rang on his desk. He could see from the display that it was his mother, direct from Nueva Andalucía in the mountains beyond Marbella. A white house with three palm trees in the garden. Balcony, and sun and shadow. He'd been there two years ago, in the

40

last century, when his father had been buried under the Sierra Blanca.

'How are you surviving the heat?'

'How are you surviving yours?' Winter replied.

'They say on the telly here that it's hotter in Scandinavia than it is in the south of Spain,' she said.

'The flow of tourists will go into reverse, then,' he said. 'Spaniards will be coming here to get some sun.'

'I hope so.' He could hear a clinking of ice in the background, and glanced at his watch. Gone five. The Cocktail Hour. Happy Hour. Time for a very dry and very cold Martini. I wouldn't mind one myself.

'What are you up to?' he asked. 'Lotta said you were hoping we could come and visit in September.'

His sister had told him the previous day. A family get-together on the Costa del Sol.

'You really must come. I just have to cuddle Elsa. And all the rest of you, of course.'

'You only need to come home.'

'The children think it's so much fun to come here,' she said.

'What children? Apart from Elsa?'

'What do you mean? Lotta's, of course.'

'They're teenagers.'

'Don't be like that, Erik.'

He heard the clinking of ice again, and thought of water and a bath and a drink.

'How *is* Elsa?'

'She's talking, and getting into all kinds of mischief.'

'Does she talk much?'

'All day long.'

'That's fantastic. She'll go far.'

'Well, just at this minute she's not going anywhere at all.'

More clinking of ice. Coolness spread through his body. He needed a *drink*.

'Soon she'll be running all over the flat.'

Winter didn't respond.

'But you really must start thinking about a house now, Erik.'

'Mmm.'

'If only for Angela's sake. Surely you can understand that? She can't be lugging children and prams and God knows what else up and down all those stairs.'

'There's a lift.'

'You know what I mean.'

'There are two of us doing the lugging.'

'Erik.'

'We like living in the centre of town.'

'Angela as well? Really?'

He didn't answer. That wasn't a problem. The thoughts came flooding back. He had other problems.

The door opened. Halders walked in without knocking.

'I've got a visitor.' Winter said his goodbyes and hung up.

5

Halders' forehead was red where his hairline had once been. He shut the door and ran his hand over his bald patch.

'The heat out there's breaking all records,' he said, sitting down opposite Winter. His ears were also red. They stuck out prominently and gave his face a softness despite the hardness of his other features.

'Have you been sunbathing?'

'You could say that,' said Halders, scratching his forehead. 'With Jeanette Bielke. At her favourite spot among the rocks.' Halders looked at Winter and stroked his left ear. 'Although it doesn't seem to be her favourite any more.'

'Did she say anything?'

'We talked about her boyfriend.'

'And?'

'Or her ex-boyfriend. Though he doesn't seem to be able to grasp that. Mattias Berg. His name's Mattias Berg.'

'I know.'

'He doesn't want to let her go, but she's made up her mind to ditch him.'

'Not exactly unusual,' Winter said.

It's happened to me, Winter thought. A long, long

time ago. I once stood banging away on a door that refused to open. At the time it seemed a matter of life and death.

'No,' Halders said. 'Not unusual. But I want to have a word with the lad.'

'Of course,' said Winter, standing up and walking to the washbasin. He took a glass from a shelf and filled it with water. 'Would you like some?'

'Yes, please,' Halders said. He reached over the desk when Winter held the glass out for him. He could see the forensic report on Angelika Hansson.

'I've just received it,' Winter said.

Halders nodded and drank.

'It wasn't a consummated rape.'

'Just a murder.'

'He'd tried. Or so it would seem.'

'Couldn't get it up,' said Halders.

Winter shrugged.

'So we're waiting to hear from SKL.'

SKL, Winter thought. He'd waited for reports from the Swedish criminology lab in Linköping before. DNA analyses that had produced the goods: analyses that hadn't. It was always worth waiting. His work involved waiting, and the hard bit was finding new roads to go down while doing the waiting. Not being totally reliant on technical and chemical analyses to solve all the problems. He'd had technical solutions to riddles that explained how and who and where, but not why. He'd been left with the big *why*. As a memory impossible to forget.

'SKL can tell us if it's the same bastard,' Halders said. He took another gulp of water, spilling a little as he changed his position on the chair. 'Do you reckon it's the same guy? Who attacked both girls, I mean.'

'Yes.'

He hadn't intended replying at all, but the 'yes' slipped out, like a subconscious desire to have something to get straight to work on.

'And the next question: the same bastard as murdered Beatrice?'

'I don't know,' Winter said.

'I asked what you thought.'

'I can't answer that yet,' said Winter, picking up Pia Fröberg's report. 'What I can say is that Angelika Hansson was definitely pregnant. Probably seven weeks gone.'

'That sounds early,' Halders said. 'Seven weeks.'

'It is early. But she should have known herself by the fifth week.'

'Always assuming she suspected anything,' said Halders. He stood up, went to the washbasin and refilled his glass. Winter could see that the back of his neck was red too.

'I had a word with Pia,' Winter said. 'She says the girl hadn't had a period after the fifth week, so she must surely have suspected something.'

'Some people repress that kind of thing,' said Halders.

'Her parents didn't know, so neither did she – is that what you mean?'

'I don't know. But she hadn't said anything, that's for sure. If she did know, she kept it to herself.'

'Maybe not completely to herself,' said Winter.

'You mean the father of the child?'

'Exactly.'

The father, thought Halders. Probably some pale nineteen-year-old without a clue where his life is taking him. Unless he's something much worse, and the one we're looking for.

Winter thought about the father. They had so many people they could cross-question – friends, acquaintances, classmates. Family. Relatives. Witnesses. All kinds of witnesses. Taxi drivers who used to be good witnesses but were now useless because they'd seen nothing and heard nothing – because they shouldn't have been on that road that evening because they shouldn't have been driving at all because they were being employed illegally. And so on and so on.

'Perhaps he doesn't know,' Winter said. 'If she didn't know herself, then he can't know either. Or maybe she did know . . . had just found out, but kept it to herself and was intending to keep it that way. If you see what I mean.'

'Abortion,' Halders said.

Winter nodded.

'But in any case, he knows she's dead,' said Halders. 'That can't have been kept a secret. He can't have missed hearing about that.'

'Assuming he's in Sweden.'

'Well then he'll come to us when he gets back. If we don't get a name before then.' He looked at Winter. 'We need a name. We're going to get a name.'

'Yes.'

'If he doesn't come forward, he's in serious trouble.'

Maybe more trouble than we realise just now, Winter thought.

Halders' mobile rang in his breast pocket. Winter glanced at the clock: just after four in the afternoon. He suddenly had the feeling he wanted to get away from there, longed to be with Angela and Elsa, yearned for a hot bath and something to give him *hope*. He wanted to get away from all these hypotheses about death and lives cut short. Angelika Hansson's life was like the first chapter in a book, and her unborn child was . . .

'I'm having trouble hearing you,' said Halders in a loud voice, rising to his feet. His forehead was striped white when he frowned. 'Say it again, please.'

Winter could see Halders' expression change as he began to understand what the voice was telling him.

'Wh—' said Halders. 'What the hell . . . ?'

His face twitched as if he'd lost control of his muscles. It was unnerving. Winter could tell that something serious had happened. Something unconnected with the investigation.

'Yes . . . Yes of course,' said Halders. 'I'll go there straight away.' He hung up and looked at Winter with a new expression on his red face, which had turned pale. Almost grey.

'It's my ex-wife,' he said in a voice Winter had never heard before. Halders was still staring at him. 'My ex-wife. Mar– Margareta. She was run over and killed an hour ago. On the pavement.'

He ran his hand over his head, scratched the red patch on his brow again, it was as if the last time he did it had been in another age. Nothing would be the same again.

'On a bloody pavement. On a pavement outside a supermarket in Lunden.' He gestured towards the window. 'That's just down the road.' His face muscles were twitching again, out of control.

'What happened?' asked Winter. He had no idea what to say.

'Run over,' said Halders, still in the strange voice. 'Hit and run.' He stared past Winter into the beautiful afternoon light. 'Of course, it would be hit and run.'

'Is it . . . definite? That she's . . . dead?' Winter asked. 'Who phoned?'

'What?' said Halders. 'What did you say?'

'Where are we going?' said Winter, getting to his feet. Halders stood motionless. His face still twitching. He tried to say something, but no words came. Then he looked at Winter, his eyes became fixed.

'East General,' he said. 'I'm off now.'

'I'll drive,' said Winter.

'I can manage,' Halders said, but Winter was already halfway out of the door. They jumped into the lift and hurried into the car park. Halders sat beside Winter without a word, and they drove off in an easterly direction.

A cruel message, Winter thought. Couldn't they have said that she'd been badly hurt? Who was it that had given Halders the news?

He'd once heard a joke on this theme. He suddenly thought of it as the car was plunged into the shadows cast by the tall buildings on either side of the road.

The joke was about a man who is travelling abroad. He phones home and his brother says straight out: Your cat's dead. The man ringing from abroad tells him you shouldn't come out with such cruel news in such a direct manner. You could say the cat was on the roof . . . yes, that the fire brigade had arrived, and the police, and everybody did all they could to get the cat down and in the end they managed to capture it but it wriggled out of their grasp and jumped and landed awkwardly and they took it to the animal hospital and a team of vets operated throughout the night but in the end they had to concede that it was impossible to save the cat's life. That's the way you should tell somebody about a tragic event like this. Tone it down a bit. His brother

48

says he understands now, and they hang up. A few days later the man rings home again and his brother says a tragic event has just taken place. What? wonders the man. His brother says, Mum was on the roof . . .

Winter didn't laugh. Halders said nothing. They came to a roundabout and turned off for the hospital. Winter could feel the sweat gathering at the base of his spine. Traffic was dense, with holidaymakers returning after a day on the rocks on the big islands to the north, or by the lakes to the east.

'The children haven't been told yet,' Halders said.

Winter waited for him to elaborate as he drove into the hospital car park. The shadows were sharp and long.

'I have two children,' Halders said.

'I know.'

They'd talked about it, but Halders had forgotten.

'They're at their after-school club now. For God's sake!' Halders suddenly blurted out.

Winter parked. Halders was out of the car before it had even stopped moving, and started half-running towards one of the hospital buildings.

He was a stranger to Winter, and yet like a member of the family at the same time.

That's exactly what Winter thought as he watched Halders hurry over the tarmac through the sunlight, then into darkness as he came to the A & E entrance. Halders had become more distant, and yet more close, simultaneously. Winter had a new feeling of unreality, like entering into a dream. He could no longer see Halders, and didn't know what to do.

He'd been here only the other day, had accompanied the Hansson girl from Slottsskogen Park to her post mortem. Now he was here again.

* * *

49

Halders stood by the stretcher. Margareta's face was just as he remembered it, the last time he'd seen her.

Only three days ago. Sunday. He'd been to Burger King with Hannes and Magda, and Margareta had opened the door with a smile and he'd muttered something then left without even going in. Not this time. Not that they weren't on friendly terms. It was all so long ago. So long ago that he'd been an idiot. He was still an idiot, but back then he'd been one in a different way.

He couldn't see the rest of her body underneath all that white, and he didn't want to either. He thought about Hannes and Magda as he thought about Margareta. He thought about the dead girls too, and that was sufficient to make him start slumping towards the floor, lose his balance, recover it, hold on to the stretcher, bend down towards Margareta's face, cling on to the moment that he knew would be the last.

Now it's happened to me, he thought. Hit me with full force. This is no dipping into somebody else's misfortune. This is my very own.

He stroked Margareta's cheek.

There had been a first time.

Damn the thought. He'd been nineteen . . . no . . . yes, nineteen. He'd been like the girls he and Winter had been talking about only half an hour ago.

Then he was twenty-two, soon to be a fully qualified cop.

He stroked her cheek again.

The divorce hadn't meant anything. Not in that way. It didn't come between them in that way.

Somebody spoke. He wasn't listening, kneeled by the side of the stretcher, intended doing so for a long time.

He felt a hand on his shoulder and looked up to see Winter.

*

It was as light as day when Winter got home that evening. Light shone into the flat. There was a smell of food in the hall, but he wasn't hungry any more.

He'd phoned Angela some hours previously.

He went in to Elsa and wondered about waking her up, but contented himself with smelling her, and listening.

Angela was waiting in the kitchen with a glass of wine.

'I'll have a whisky,' said Winter and went over to the work surface, took one of the bottles and poured a few centimetres into a chubby glass. This wasn't the time for a delicate malt whisky glass.

'Oh dear.'

'You can have the rest if I can't manage to drink it all.'

'Just because I've finished breastfeeding doesn't mean I'm ready to become an alcoholic.'

'Cheers,' said Winter, taking a swig. Angela raised her wine glass.

'Are you hungry?'

Winter shook his head, felt the punch of the whisky reverberate through his body, sat down at the table and looked at Angela, who was a little flushed. It was hot in the kitchen.

'How's Fredrik?' she asked.

Winter absently waved his hand: Halders is still with us. He hasn't broken down altogether.

'What'll happen to the children?'

'What do you mean?'

51

'What I say. How are the children?'

'You said "what'll happen to the children". That's obvious, surely. They're with Halders.'

Angela said nothing.

'Don't you think he can handle it?'

'I didn't say that.'

'It sounded a bit like it.'

Angela didn't reply. Winter took another gulp.

'They're in the house at Lunden,' he said. 'Halders thought that was best. For the moment.'

'I agree.'

'He was resolute, I suppose you could say,' Winter said. 'When we left the hospital. Drove to their school.'

Angela took a sip of wine, thought about the children.

'It was horrific,' Winter said. 'An horrific experience. A teacher stayed with them in the school until we got there.' He took another slug of whisky. It didn't taste of anything any more, apart from alcohol. 'It had happened while they were still in class and so . . . well, they were still there.'

'Did you drive them home?'

'Yes.' Winter looked at the clock. 'It took a few hours.'

'Of course.' She stood up, went to the cooker and switched off the fan. There was a different kind of silence in the kitchen. Winter could hear sounds from the courtyard. Glasses. Voices. 'But they're not on their own there now, I take it?'

'Hanne's there,' Winter said. He'd phoned the police chaplain, Hanne Östergaard. She was good at talking to people. Consoling them, perhaps. He didn't know. Yes. Consolation. 'Halders didn't object when I suggested it.' He could hear the voices again, a bit louder,

52

but no words that could be made out. 'Hanne was going to phone for a psychologist, I think. They talked about it in any case.'

'Good.'

'And Aneta came.'

'Aneta? Aneta Djanali?'

'Yes.'

'Why?'

'Halders phoned her. She came straight over.'

'Do they work together a lot?'

'Nearly all the time.'

'Don't they have a bit of a strained relationship?'

'Where do you get that idea from?'

'Come on, Erik! We've spent a bit of time with them. You've said the odd thing . . .'

'Oh . . . that was just the kind of thing you say.' He raised his glass and saw to his surprise that it was empty. He stood up and went over to the bottle. 'He evidently needs her now.' He poured. Three-quarters of an inch. 'It's not good to be alone. With the children.'

'No relatives?'

'Not in Gothenburg, it seems.'

Angela looked out of the window when he sat back down. It was beginning to get dark out there, with yellow lines over the sky above the rooftops. She could hear voices and the clink of glasses from the courtyard.

'I haven't been able to stop thinking about the children,' she said, turning to face Winter again. 'Were they completely devastated?'

'No. Not superficially at least. Very quiet. The shock, I suppose.'

Somebody burst out laughing in the courtyard below, others joined in. He stood up and went to the window. Four storeys down, a group of friends was making the most of the summer's night. He closed the window, but stayed where he was.

What would happen now? He needed Halders, but he wouldn't dwell on that for a single minute if Halders decided to stay at home. It was up to him. Winter was not going to lean on him. We're people before anything else, after all.

He went back to Angela and his whisky.

6

It was hot in his office, suffocated by summer. No wind outside, nothing to suck into the room that would change the air clinging to everyone's skin.

Winter looked at the stack of files in front of him; papers, photographs. There were fresh print-outs made by Möllerström from the hard disks, but most of the stuff smelled of the past. Five years ago, another summer. Beatrice Wägner. The papers concerning her violent death had an odour of dust and dry darkness, gave a false impression of peace, so pervasive that it almost made him push aside these cold case notes and instead take up the newly begun file on Angelika Hansson.

Reports on murder collected for eternal reading, over and over again. No peace. He'd had a special file of press cuttings brought to his office. The newsprint felt as if it were a hundred years old when he touched it.

He stood up, went to the open window and lit a Corps. The cigarillo tasted pure and soft after leafing through the old documents. It was his third of the morning. He smoked more than twenty a day. Each one was going to be his last. No smoking at home any more, which was a good thing. Another good thing: Corps Diplomatique was a brand on its way out. His tobacconist had warned him. Every pack could be his last, but Winter was not in favour of hoarding. When Corps were no longer available, he'd stop smoking.

He inhaled, and watched the flow of traffic on the other side of the river. Tram, bus, car, tram again, pedestrians. All bathed in sunshine that cast no shadows now, as lunchtime approached.

When there are no Corps any more, I'll pack it in.

When there are no corpses any more, I'll pack it in. Ha!

He went back to his desk. He'd made up his mind to work his way through the files on the Beatrice Wägner case, from the very beginning. All the witness reports, all the summaries. If there was anything there that could be of use to the present investigation, he'd find it. Try to find it. No – find it.

Beatrice Wägner had lived with her parents in a detached house in Påvelund, a western suburb of Gothenburg. Just over a kilometre south of the house in Långedrag where Jeanette Bielke lived. And it couldn't be much more than two kilometres south from Påvelund to the house in Önnerud when Angelika Hansson had lived, Winter noted. Due south.

He stood up again, went over to the wall map of Gothenburg and traced with his finger a line running due north from the Hanssons' house through the Wägners' and ending up at Jeanette Bielke's home. A dead straight line. It was a peculiarity, but didn't necessarily mean anything. Probably didn't.

He kept looking at the map. Beatrice Wägner had attended the grammar school in Frölunda. Like Angelika and Jeanette, she'd passed her final exams. She'd stayed in Gothenburg when most of her friends had gone away on holiday. He recalled that she'd had some sort of summer job. Jeanette hadn't had a summer job. Angelika had worked in a warehouse.

Three girls, all of them nineteen years old. Just left school. Two of them this summer, and the third in summer five years ago. Three different schools. Jeanette had said she didn't know Angelika. Had she known Beatrice? He must ask her about that. It wasn't impossible, after all. They lived quite close to each other, in up-market suburbs next to the sea.

Had it always been the case? Had they attended the same primary school, perhaps? Junior school? Calm down, Erik. There's no time to find the answer to every question now.

Had Beatrice and Angelika known each other?

Three girls. One was still alive, the other two were dead.

He remained standing by the map. If he boiled down all his questions to just one, to The Question, would it be: did they all fall foul of the same murderer? The same bastard, as Halders had put it in this very office. Jeanette too?

Winter continued reading, smoking at his desk now. Followed Beatrice through her last hour, or hours. She'd been in the town centre with some friends. Had she been with them the entire time? That wasn't absolutely clear. They'd split up soon after one in the morning. Sunday morning. Five of them had gone off together and stopped off at a 7-Eleven five hundred yards from the park, and there, outside the shop, or inside it, something had happened to cause Beatrice to leave her friends.

Winter read through the witness reports. There was

a slight mist around the words, as if these young people had memories that weren't really functioning. Winter knew what the problem was, he'd seen it hundreds of times. They were simply drunk, or at least in various stages of inebriation, and now the alcohol had started to leave their bodies, but their senses were not properly sharp and such things can make a person irritable and nervous, and something like that had applied to the scene at the shop. Something had annoyed Beatrice and she'd left. Yes, they could recall that she'd been annoyed, but nobody could remember why. Perhaps she'd tried to light up a cigarette inside the 7-Eleven. Perhaps she just hated the whole world at that drunken moment. There had been alcohol in her blood, but not very much.

She'd walked towards the park. Her friends had seen her go. Let her go. She'll be back in a minute. But when they left the shop Beatrice hadn't come back. They'd called for her, walked in the direction of the park and called out again.

They'd turned back then. She'd turn up eventually. She'd be on the other side of the park by now. She'd have caught the night bus. She was already at Lina's, waiting for her. She'll be sitting there waiting for me, Lina had said, out there in the night, five years ago, and then the night bus came and . . . well, they'd all jumped aboard and looked out of the window as they passed by the park and there was no sign of Beatrice, which meant that she must be waiting for them at Lina's, didn't it?

Beatrice wasn't waiting for them. She was in among the trees all the time. Perhaps. She was definitely there at 11.45 on Sunday morning, behind the bushes in the shadow of the big rock: naked; murdered. The sun had been high in the sky, as high as it was now.

Her clothes were in a heap by her side. Winter read the list of clothes she'd been wearing that evening, the clothes the murderer had pulled off her. They were all in the inventory, but that wasn't what he was looking for. He was looking for what was missing. Sometimes something was missing that the victim had had, but the murderer had taken away with him.

In Beatrice's case, it was her belt.

Winter found it in the interrogation of her friends, and, later, in the interview with her parents. Beatrice had been wearing a leather belt that had not been found in the untidy pile of clothes next to her body. One of the detectives who had conducted the interviews had referred to it as a waistbelt. The word jumped off the page when Winter saw it. It seemed a wry comment on a waste of a life.

That could be what the murderer had strangled her with, wasted her life. They couldn't know for certain as they had never found the belt.

Winter turned to the newer case notes. Angelika Hansson's. He searched for the inventory of her clothes: T-shirt, shorts, socks, pants, bra, hairband, trainers – basketball type, Reebok. But no belt. Would she have worn a belt with her shorts?

Had anybody asked about her clothes? He couldn't see any reference to a belt. He read Pia Fröberg's report. Angelika could well have been strangled with a leather belt. He picked up the phone and dialled the direct number to Göran Beier on the SOC team. No reply. He phoned the main lab. Beier answered.

'Ah, Göran, it's Erik. I hope I can disturb you for a couple of minutes?'

'No problem.'

'I'm sitting here with the Wägner case notes. Beatrice.'

'OK.'

'Were you on duty then?'

'Beatrice Wägner? Let's see, that must be what . . . four years ago? Five?'

'Five years. Exactly five.'

'Whatever, it's not a case you forget.'

'No.'

'We did what we could.'

Winter thought he detected a hidden meaning in Beier's words.

'I haven't given up,' he said.

Beier made no reply.

'That's why I'm ringing,' Winter said. 'Maybe there's a connection.'

'Meaning?'

'Do you remember that Beatrice had a belt that she evidently always used to wear, and that it couldn't be found after the murder?'

'I do. One of her mates had made some comment about it the same night as she was murdered,' Beier said. 'I read that in the preliminary reports.' He paused. 'Now that I think about it, I seem to remember that it was you who signed it off. My memory's that good.'

'I have it in front of me now,' said Winter, picking up the document. He could see his own signature. Erik Winter, Detective Inspector.

'That was before the glory days of Chief Inspector,' said Beier. 'For both you and me.'

Winter didn't reply.

'I suppose it was Birgersson who was in charge of the investigation?'

'Yes.'

'I remember we had a chat about that belt,' Beier said.

'What conclusion did you draw?'

'Only that we thought the belt might have been used to choke her. But we never found it, of course.'

'And now it's Angelika Hansson we're dealing with,' said Winter.

'I heard from Halders that you thought there might be a link,' Beier said.

'There could well be.'

'Or not.'

'There could also be a belt,' Winter said.

There was a pause. 'I see what you mean,' Beier said, eventually.

'Is it possible to find out if Angelika Hansson generally wore a belt with those shorts she had on that night?'

'We've already established that,' said Beier.

'I beg your pardon?'

'Don't you read the reports? What's the point —'

'When did you send them?'

'Yesterday, I think. It sho . . . Hang on, somebody's telling me something here.' Winter could hear Beier talking to a colleague. Then he spoke in the phone again. 'I apologise, Erik. Pelle says he hasn't sent them off yet. He wanted to che—'

'OK, OK. But she did have a belt in fact?'

'There had at one time been a belt in the waistband, so the answer is yes. Of the shorts lying in the heap by her body. We can say that for sure. It's not complicated at all.'

'But I can't find any mention of a belt in the inventory of what was in that pile of clothes,' said Winter.

'No, because it wasn't there.'

'So he took it with him,' said Winter, mainly to himself.

Beier said nothing.

'Angelika Hansson could have been strangled with her own belt, then,' Winter said.

'That's a possibility.'

'Just like Beatrice Wägner.'

'I understand what you're getting at,' Beier said. 'But take it easy.'

'I am taking it easy.'

He took it easy for another hour while the sun outside crept slowly across a cloudless sky. The smoke lingered inside the room. He continued to trace the hours and the days after the murder of Beatrice Wägner.

Witnesses had seen cars leaving the scene. One car had seemed in a hurry to get away, according to one woman, but he knew that could be an impression she'd formed after the event, a dramatisation because she so badly wanted to help them with their investigation, although most such efforts had the opposite effect.

Then, as now, the season had been a problem, because fewer people than usual were at home during the summer. He had now started reading the cuttings from each case in parallel, and smiled at one sentence that jumped off the page, spoken by Sture Birgersson one summer's day almost exactly five years ago: 'The problem the police are up against in this murder investigation is the holiday period,' Birgersson had said.

Birgersson was Winter's superior at the CID. Winter had an appointment with him that afternoon.

A house-to-house operation around the park had

produced as little by way of results that summer as this, so far.

Winter paused at one detail from the night Beatrice Wägner had been murdered. Two witnesses had independently observed that a man and a boy had been packing a car for some time in the early hours of the morning. That had been outside one of the three-storey apartment blocks to the north-east of the park, a hundred metres away. The two witnesses had noticed the man and boy from different directions, but at more or less the same time. The man and the boy might have seen or heard something, but nobody knew as they had never made themselves known to the police. They had issued an appeal, but nobody had come forward. They had simply been unable to find a man and boy in the building matching the description they'd been given.

Just then, Winter's desk telephone rang. He answered and recognised Birgersson's voice.

'Could we meet a bit earlier than planned, Erik? I now find I have to attend a meeting at four.'

'OK.'

'Can you come up now?'

'Give me quarter of an hour. I want to ask you a few things, but I must do a bit of reading first.'

Birgersson stood by his window smoking as Winter asked his first question. Birgersson's scalp was visible through his close-cropped grey hair, lit up by the rays of the sun. The boss would be sixty next year. Winter would be forty-two. Birgersson was more of a father to him than a big brother.

'I don't know where it would have led us,' said Birgersson, flicking ash into the palm of his hand, 'but we really did try to trace that pair: father and son or whatever they were.' He looked at Winter. 'You were involved, of course.'

'Reading about it now, I recall getting very angry at the time.'

'I got a bit worked up about it as well.' The muscles in Birgersson's lean face twitched. 'But that was only natural. We didn't have much to go on, and so that detail seemed to be more important than it might really have been.'

'Do you often think about the Beatrice case?' asked Winter, from his chair by the desk in the middle of the room.

'Only every day.'

'It hasn't been like that for me. Not quite every day. Until now.'

'You're still a young man, Erik. I run the risk of retiring with that bloody case still unsolved, and I don't want to do that.' He pulled at the cigarette, but the smoke was invisible against the light from the window. 'I don't want to do that,' he said again, gazing out of the window, then looking back at Winter. 'I don't know if this is a sort of twisted wishful thinking, but I hope it is him who's come back. That this business has never ended.'

'That's why I'm scrutinising the Beatrice case notes,' said Winter.

'The belt,' Birgersson said. 'The belt is a key.'

'It could well be.'

'Did the Bielke girl have a belt?' Birgersson asked.

'That's one of the things I wanted to check before I came here,' said Winter. He lit another Corps, stood up and went to keep Birgersson company by the window. 'But she didn't have one. She doesn't wear one.'

'Maybe that's what saved her,' said Birgersson. He looked Winter in the eye. 'What do you think, Erik? Maybe she wasn't as interesting as a victim when there was no belt for her to be strangled with. No belt to take home, as a trophy.'

7

She felt a prick in her right foot, under her toes. She'd been feeling her way forward, but the bottom was covered in seaweed here, a sort of long, thick grass that swayed with the current. It was brown and nasty. Like dead flowers.

Now she was standing on a small sandbank. She balanced on one leg and examined her right foot: she could see it was bleeding, but only a little. It wasn't the first time this summer. Par for the course.

She heard shouts from the rocks. Leapt into the water, which was warmer than ever, like a second skin, soft, like a caress.

'Anne!'

They were shouting again. Somebody held up a bottle, but all she could see was a silhouette against the sun, which was on its way down. Could be Andy. As far as he was concerned the party had begun the minute they got here, or even in the car, still in town.

'Anne! Paaarty!'

She could see him now, wine bottle in hand, a grin on his face. Party. Why not yet another party? She deserved that. Three years of school at Burgården. Who wouldn't be worth a few parties after that?

There was something else that made her deserving of it. She didn't want to think about it now.

'Anne!'

She clambered over the rocks, hung onto a projecting stone, and felt the sting in her foot again.

She had reached the top, checked her foot. Half a metre of seaweed had wrapped itself around her shin. She pulled it off. The seaweed felt slippery.

'Here comes the little mermaid,' said Andy.

'Give me a drink.'

'Have you ever seen an evening as beautiful as this?'

'A drink. Now!'

*

Fredrik Halders was sitting on a sofa he didn't recall seeing the last time he'd been there. He looked around him like a stranger. The house was more foreign to him than ever.

He'd begun to feel unreal in the house immediately afterwards. Immediately after the divorce. He'd seemed to be wandering around in a dream. Everything was familiar, but he no longer recognised it. Couldn't touch anything. He was an outsider. That's how it had seemed. He'd been standing outside his own life. That's how it had felt. The divorce had made him stand outside his own life, and things hadn't improved much since.

Maybe that was why he'd been so angry those past few years. In a rage. He'd woken up in a rage and gone to bed in a rage and been in even more of a rage in between. Just living had been a pain, you might say.

But that had been nothing. Nothing at all compared to this.

Hannes and Magda were asleep. Magda had sobbed herself to sleep. Hannes had stared at the wall. He'd tried to talk to them about . . . about . . . What had he tried to talk to them about? He'd forgotten.

67

It was past midnight. The patio door was open, letting in scents from the garden he didn't remember. He could see Aneta Djanali's face in the doorway, which was lit up by the lamp on a shelf to the left.

'Don't you want to come outside?'

He shook his head.

'It's lovely out here.'

'I'll fetch a beer,' he said, getting up and going to the kitchen.

'It'll start getting light soon,' Djanali said when he'd come out and sat down on the bench next to the house.

He took a swig and looked up at the sky. It was already light enough for him. If he could stop the passage of time, now would be the moment. Let there be darkness. Forever darkness, and rest. No children to wake up in the morning and remember. With the whole of their lives ahead of them. Sometimes I feel like a motherless child, he suddenly thought. Then he thought of Margareta.

He took another swig and looked directly over the patio at his colleague. And friend.

'Shouldn't you go home now, Aneta?' He could make out her silhouette, but no more. At any other time he'd have joked about it, as he usually did; her black skin was not much of a contrast to the night. Not now.

'I don't mind staying.'

'I'll manage.'

'I know that.'

'So, why not go home and rest? You're on duty tomorrow morning, aren't you?'

He couldn't see if she'd nodded.

'Will you have to get up early?' he asked.

'Yes. But I've never needed much sleep.'

'Me neither.' He emptied the bottle and put it down

on the table. 'In that case, we can sit here a bit longer.'

'Yes.'

She saw that he'd put a hand over his face. She heard a muffled sound. She went to sit on the bench beside him, and put her arm round him, or as far round as she could. He was ever so slightly shaking.

'I need to work.'

They were still sitting on the bench. It was morning now, a few minutes past three. The light had come back. The shadows in Halders' face were like bays of the sea, formed in the last few hours. Djanali could hear the shrieks of seagulls. A car passed by on the road behind the hedge. Some small birds flew up out of a bush, perhaps disturbed by the car. She didn't feel tired. That would come later, that afternoon, in the car patrolling up and down in the heat.

'Do you understand what I mean?' Halders turned to look at her. A blood vessel had burst in his left eye. 'It's not because I want . . . to get away. Not in that sense.' He rubbed his face, under the base of his nose. 'But I think it's best . . . for everybody . . . if I go to work.'

'If you feel up to it, OK.'

'Why shouldn't I feel up to it?'

She shrugged.

'Do you think I don't understand myself?'

'No.'

'Do you think I'm not taking the children into consideration?'

'Certainly not.'

Halders stroked his face again. He could hear the rasping from his stubble, which now seemed longer and thicker than his crew-cut hair.

'We must get back to normal just as soon as possible,' he said, looking as if he were seeking support in the far distance. 'The important thing is that we all try to get back to normal as soon as we possibly can.'

But first have a breakdown, thought Aneta Djanali. It's imminent.

*

Winter was still searching through the two sets of case notes, one thick, the other thin.

He'd asked Bergenhem to read them as well. Lars Bergenhem was a young and talented detective who'd just come back to work after being off sick with severe headaches and listlessness, but Winter knew what was really wrong. Even police officers were affected by depression at times.

I sometimes wonder if I am at risk myself. It could be the heat, or this case that is so difficult to wash off with a dip in the sea after work.

*

They drove to the park. The air conditioning was on in Winter's Mercedes. The streets were almost deserted.

'I sometimes come here,' Winter said when they'd walked to the spot. The trees were still. You could hardly see the rock. The area was still cordoned off. Anybody who didn't look closely might think there was some new gardening project under way, thought Bergenhem. There is a new project, but not of that sort.

He could see children swimming in the pond. The flamingos were standing on one leg, studying the splashing.

'I've come here several times over the past few years,' Winter said. He looked around. 'Do you understand what I mean?'

'Yes.'

'What do I mean?'

'They always return to the scene of the crime.'

Winter nodded and watched two young girls walk past, glancing at him and Bergenhem as they stood in front of the cordon.

'He's been here at least as many times as I have,' said Winter. 'That's the way it goes. He's been here all right.'

'Maybe at the same time,' Bergenhem said.

'No.' Winter looked at his colleague. 'I would have known.'

All we can do is keep at it, he thought. That's the way it goes.

He'd been here spring, summer, autumn and winter after the murder of Beatrice Wägner. Not every day, of course, but he made it his business to pass here at weekends and in the evening, sometimes at night.

Late one evening he'd seen a shadowy figure standing by the rock and had gone to investigate, his heart beating a bit faster, and found himself face to face with Birgersson when the shadow turned round.

And he knew that Halders sometimes came here too.

He didn't think they'd scared anybody off. They didn't walk into the park hip-swinging with guns drawn, silhouetted against the sunset.

'The girl's our best bet,' Bergenhem said. 'Jeanette. The one who got away.'

'Maybe that was the intention,' said Winter.

'What do you mean? That she got away?'

Winter shrugged. 'Could be.'

'If it *is* him, she's seen him, touched him. Heard him.'

'Yes.'

'Those sounds. Some sort of mantra.'

'Hmm.'

'She said he repeated something she couldn't understand. The same thing. She thought he'd said the same thing maybe three times.'

'Yes.'

'While he was raping her.'

'Yes,' said Winter, watching the two girls who'd passed a couple of minutes before walking back again, each holding an ice-cream cornet. They looked curiously at the cordon. 'While he was raping her.'

'Maybe there's more,' Bergenhem said.

Winter looked at the girls. An ice cream was just the thing. In weather like this what you needed was ice cream and a cold drink.

'Maybe she'll remember a lot more now,' said Bergenhem.

'I'm seeing her tomorrow,' said Winter. 'Ten o'clock.'

Bergenhem went up to the trees and peered inside. When he spoke again his voice was muffled by the enclosed space.

'How far do you think he had to drag them?' Bergenhem said.

'Ten metres,' Winter said.

'Were there drag marks after Beatrice Wägner as well?'

'Yes.'

'What about Jeanette? Was she also dragged in there?'

'We'll talk about that tomorrow. So far all she's said is that she can't remember. She fainted.'

Winter looked over his shoulder, and saw the girls had left.

'How about an ice cream?'

Bergenhem emerged from the copse.

'OK.'

They walked round the pond to the ice-cream stall.

The noise from the children swimming was not as loud here. A couple about the same age as Winter whizzed past on rollerblades. A man was selling balloons in the middle of the lawn. Three people were queuing up at the stall.

'This is on me,' said Winter.

They walked back with their cornets. The ice cream started to melt.

'We should have had a tub instead,' said Bergenhem.

They sat down on the grass. It smelled dry and brittle. There were patches of yellow in the light green.

'Why did he try to strangle Jeanette?' said Winter after a while.

'What do you mean?' Bergenhem asked.

'She wasn't wearing a belt that he could use . . . as he did with the other two, Beatrice and Angelika, but even so he'd had something with him . . . a dog lead, perhaps. He had it with him but he didn't strangle her with it. He didn't kill her.'

'You're assuming the rapist also killed Beatrice and Angelika.'

'Yes. I am. For the moment, at least.' Winter could feel the cold ice cream on his fingers. It felt good.

'The same person,' said Bergenhem. 'Five years on.'

'Yes.'

'Did Angelika have a belt?'

'According to Beier she'd been wearing a belt with her shorts. I checked with her parents later, and that was correct.'

'But now it's gone.'

'Yes.'

'Just as with Beatrice Wägner.'

'Precisely.'

* * *

Anne had one last swim. Andy too. The rest of the crowd sang a song for sunset, or maybe it was about the sunset. She felt a bit dizzy after the two glasses of wine, and it was as if she became sharp and focused again thanks to the water, which felt cooler now than it had done an hour ago, or maybe it was two.

The whole crowd would go out tonight, and she was looking forward to it. It hadn't always been like that. Several times she'd stayed at home. She wasn't sure her mum approved. She'd said it was nice to have her at home in the evening, but she wasn't sure she'd really meant it. But now that she'd finished school it was as if Mum wanted her to be out having fun as much as possible. As if this were the last summer. The last summer. Wasn't there a film called that?

Several times she'd gone straight home from *there*. Two more times, and then she could stop.

She should never have done it. If anybody had asked her, she wouldn't have been able to explain why.

But it didn't matter.

She dried herself quickly – it felt almost chilly now that the sun was merely red.

There was no wind as they travelled back home, but even so, there seemed to be a sort of chill over the fields.

Back in town it still felt hot in among all the buildings. Like going inside a house after cycling home through the fields by the sea. They stopped in the Avenue, locked their bikes and sat at one of the pavement cafés. Same as usual.

'A large beer for everybody,' said Andy when the waitress appeared.

'We really ought to go home and take a shower first,' she said. 'It feels better sitting here, though.' Their beers arrived. There were five of them round the table. 'It's like finishing work for the day.'

'It's hard work, lying flat out by the sea all day long,' said Andy, taking a swig of his beer. 'But this way you get a double whammy.' He smiled, a very white smile. 'We relax with a beer, then you go home and have a shower and freshen up, and then we meet here again.'

Somebody laughed.

Her mobile phone rang. It was her mother. Yes. She'd be home shortly. In half an hour. Yes. Going out tonight. She rolled her eyes so the rest could see. Andy gestured to the waitress, who was teetering past with a tray full of beer for another table. Andy would probably stay there all evening. He didn't need to freshen up. He never looked as if he were in need of freshening up.

'That was Mum,' she said, putting her phone back in her handbag.

'Really?'

'I live on my own now, but she always feels the need to keep an eye on me.' She eyed Andy's beer. 'I suppose you'll be staying here?' she said.

'*Skål*,' Andy said.

'Right, I'll be off now.'

'You've turned your phone off, I hope?'

'What do you mean?'

'No more unwanted interruptions, if you don't mind.' Andy took a drink and smiled, white, white.

No more unwanted interruptions. A few days ago she and Andy had been having a cuddle and might have gone further than that, but she, or maybe he, must have knocked the speed dial on her phone and as they lay there suddenly they heard a voice and . . . well, it had connected to her mum's answering machine.

Not nice.

'Thanks for reminding me! I hope that never happens again,' Anne said.

She emptied her own glass, waved, went to her bike, unlocked it and set out along the Avenue. There were more and more people, processing up and down in droves. It seemed to have grown warmer again. She was longing for a shower.

Her mobile rang, the display said 'incoming call'. But nobody spoke when she answered. She hung up, and put the phone back into her bag.

She turned into the cycle lane heading west. It seemed to be a bit cooler once she'd left the Avenue. The smell of food wafted out of the Grand Hotel.

8

Winter gave shaving a miss. He put on a short-sleeved shirt and a pair of linen trousers. Angela and Elsa were both asleep when he left at 6.30. It was cool on the stairs. There was still a smell of paint after the renovations in early summer. He missed the ancient smell from the walls and the shiny wood in the banisters. They had always been there, ever since he moved into the flat ten years ago. Now it was like starting all over again. Which it was, in fact. Which means that the renovations and the new smell did fit in, he thought as he emerged through the front door and into the balmy morning.

The Public Works Office was busy cleaning up Vasagatan, the brushes under the strange-looking contraptions scraping against the road surface and water trickling away towards the east, the same direction as he was walking. The Avenue was empty, completely empty. He could hear a tram, but couldn't see it.

There was no wind over Heden. The big thermometer on the wall of the building opposite said 24. It was 6.50 a.m. and already 24 degrees. These were tropical conditions. It had been over twenty all night. When the mean temperature over twenty-four hours exceeds 20 degrees, that's tropical.

He took the lift up to his office, which was unlocked. Inside he noted the same smell as always. Nothing new there. He'd left the window ajar all night, but it hadn't made any difference.

The papers were still on his desk. His reading glasses on top. He had one pair here and another pair at home. He was starting to have problems with his long-range vision too. Before long he'd be groping his way along walls, being guided. Pushed in a wheelchair. He was forty-one after all.

*

A male witness had said that he'd heard a scream from the park. It had been about 2 a.m., maybe closer to 1.30. Half an hour to an hour after Beatrice had disappeared into the trees. The man lived nearby and was on his way home from a private party. He'd been drinking, but felt 'clear in the head' as he put it, and one of the interviewers had noted that his account seemed reliable.

He'd gone into the park to investigate and passed about fifteen metres from the place where Beatrice's body had been found, but he'd neither seen nor heard anything else. He'd thought he'd heard noises before then, as if somebody was being chased. Yes, chased. A scream, or maybe two. But then nothing more.

Winter remembered the witness. He hadn't interviewed him himself, but he'd met him briefly a few days later. He recalled that the man had still seemed jumpy, or perhaps he was always like that. Jumpy.

He'd run away from the park after investigating that scream and raced to the nearest residential building, and on the pavement outside it he'd stopped a couple 'aged about thirty-five' who had both been 'dressed in white', and had told them what he'd heard. The couple had just walked through the park and the woman thought she might have seen somebody. She'd told the jumpy witness.

She thought she might have seen somebody.

The police had never spoken to her, nor to her companion. Winter remembered how they'd tried to trace that couple 'dressed in white'. Urged them to contact the police.

It was exactly like that business with the man and the boy packing their car in the middle of the night. It was as if they didn't exist. Perhaps the couple ought not to have been together at that time and in that place. Such facts tend to prevent witnesses from coming forward. Private problems. What is a murder compared to such considerations? An illicit affair. The sentence passed by society on illicit affairs is far too harsh, Winter thought. Possible unfaithfulness gets in the way of the police doing their job. Can you pass laws about morals? Something to tone down the condemnation would help, bearing in mind all the investigations that come up against a brick wall because of it.

But the man and the boy . . . Five years on, and still not a word from them, even though neither of them could very well have forgotten packing a car in the middle of the night near a park in the centre of Gothenburg.

There was something else as well.

He took off his glasses and rubbed his nose. He looked at his watch: 8.00. In two hours' time he would be seeing Jeanette Bielke at her home. He'd asked her where she'd prefer to talk, and she'd said at home.

He went to the coffee room and made himself a cup. He was the only one there. They'd cancelled today's meeting. He'd have to sum up tomorrow, but everybody knew what they had to do today.

When he got back from his discussion with Jeanette, he would be expecting to know the outcome of the checks on known felons, potential suspects. They were likely to have drawn a blank, but even that was an outcome of sorts. Elimination. This or that person couldn't have done it. Not this time. A convicted rapist had a solid alibi for that particular night. This particular murderer had been in jail. That one had been in bed asleep, with cast-iron proof. The ruthless GBH merchant had been busy beating up somebody else at that moment, but at the other end of town, or the other end of the country. Or somewhere abroad.

And so on and so on.

The tarmac outside looked white in the glow of morning. It was probably 30 degrees by now. Just like Marbella. He thought about his father, buried in a pretty little churchyard on the mountainside overlooking the sea at Puerto Banús, and the house in Nueva Andalucía where his mother had decided to stay put.

Winter had been present when his father died. Had attended the funeral, spent the night in the garden with the three palm trees and eventually managed to think about nothing at all.

He returned to his office. The sun seeped in through the venetian blinds, creating patterns on the brick walls of the corridors.

Back in his office, he stood in front of the window, smoking. It was his first of the day, after nearly two hours of work, and that was a step forward. Tomorrow he'd work for an extra quarter of an hour before his first Corps.

He sat down again and put on his glasses.

There was another thing. A woman in her twenties had been attacked and raped by a 'slim' and 'quite tall' man three days after the murder of Beatrice. There were similarities – but then, there always were in rape cases. This woman said she thought the man had been talking to himself when he attacked her, 'mumbling', as she described it in the report Winter was holding in his hand.

The house was overlooked by trees that could be a hundred years old. The house itself might also be a hundred years old, Winter thought. A well-preserved centenarian. Old money. Like so much around here, the oldest part of Långedrag. He had grown up only a mile or so closer to town, cycled along these streets occasionally. *Welcome to Pleasantville.*

Two boys came towards him on skateboards. They were good. He stood to one side then continued over the street and up the drive to the house. A man was sitting on the verandah and stood up when he saw Winter coming up the steps. They shook hands. Jeanette's father. Winter hadn't met him before. Nor had he met Jeanette, it had been Halders. But Halders had different problems today.

'Is this really necessary?' Kurt Bielke asked. He was rather shorter than Winter, but didn't look up when he spoke to him. His tone was not aggressive, more of a troubled sigh.

That was a good question. How many times could one come back to the victim without it getting her back up? That would do more harm than good.

'If you push them too hard you'll get all you want

out of them in the end, but is what you get the truth?' Halders had said two days ago when they were sitting in Winter's office. A good point. You can overdo questioning.

'We need to talk a bit more to Jeanette.'

'We?' said Bielke. 'I can only see one of you.'

'I.'

'What do you need to talk about? She's told you a hundred times now what she's been through.'

Winter made no reply. He wondered whether there was any point explaining about all the little details that could slowly find their way into a victim's consciousness, bits of an experience that build up to form something more substantial. Sometimes everything could come out at once. At 2 a.m. in a lonely place, like a sword in the soul. If Jeanette remembered now it would make things easier for her later.

'Things sometimes become clearer after a while,' said Winter. 'After a few days.'

'What kind of things?' Bielke was gazing into the distance behind Winter. He still didn't sound aggressive. His face was tense, stiff, as if moulded out of aluminium. 'Exactly what happened second by second during the rape? How he pulled the noose round her neck or what?'

Winter said nothing.

'What good will it do her to remember all the details?'

'I don't know,' said Winter.

'Why are you here, then?'

'There's been a murder,' said Winter.

Bielke looked at him. He'd moved closer. Winter thought he could smell spirits, but it might have been shaving lotion. Shaving lotion was alcohol after all.

Bielke wiped his brow. Winter could see the sweat at his hairline. He was feeling the heat himself, now that they'd been standing still for a while on the verandah under a canopy that seemed to raise the temperature, if anything. The verandah must be like a sauna during the afternoon.

'My God, yes,' mumbled Bielke. 'I should have realised.' He wiped his brow again. 'You think it might be the same . . . criminal?'

'It could be the same person,' Winter said. 'We have no proof, but it's a possibility.'

'You call it a possibility?'

'I'm sorry?'

'I wouldn't have used that word,' said Bielke.

He blinked repeatedly. Winter suddenly had the feeling that Bielke was thinking about something quite different. He seemed lost in memories.

'Can I see Jeanette now?' asked Winter, taking a step to one side.

'She's up in her room.' Her father backed away, as if the path was now clear to walk on. Cleared of mines. 'She didn't want to come down.'

Winter entered the house with Bielke behind him. Bielke pointed up a staircase to the left of the door. Winter could hear the sound of chinking glass and china coming from somewhere inside the house. He saw nobody else as he went up the stairs. The house reminded him of a palace.

Jeanette's door was open. Winter could see the corner of a bed, and a window in the shade of one of the big trees. The uncomfortable feeling he'd had in the car on the way here had grown stronger after the conversation with the girl's father. It crept all over him, inside all his professional thinking. Angela would say that was no bad thing. That it had to be that way, or it was not good, not good at all.

'Come in,' she said when he knocked on the door frame. He still couldn't see her. 'Come on in.'

She was sitting in an armchair. There was a sofa and a table, and a bit further away a desk, next to a door that he could see led into an en-suite bathroom. Old money, or new, or a combination of both.

She was brushing her dark brown hair. A face without make-up, as far as he could see. Jeans, T-shirt, no socks. A fine gold chain round her neck. She continued brushing her hair with long strokes and her face distorted slightly with each one: her eyes narrowed, giving her an almost oriental look.

She gestured towards the sofa. Winter sat down and introduced himself.

'It was a different one before,' said Jeanette.

Winter nodded.

'Is that a sort of tactic?' she asked.

'What do you mean?'

'You send different people to take care of the . . . talking. Interrogation, or whatever you call it.'

'Sometimes,' said Winter. 'But not on this occasion.'

'What do you mean by that?'

Winter didn't reply.

'I liked the one who was here before,' said Jeanette, putting down her brush. 'Fredrik . . . Inspector Halders.' She looked at Winter. 'Isn't that good? In which case it's a rotten tactic to change that, don't you think?'

OK, thought Winter. I'll tell her. And he explained what had happened to Halders' ex-wife.

'I won't ask anything else,' she said.

'Is it OK if *I* do?' Winter leaned forward on the

84

sofa. She nodded. A bird flew against the window then flew off without her seeming to notice the dull thump on the pane. 'Is there anything that's . . . come to mind since you last spoke to Fredrik? Anything at all?'

She shrugged.

'Such as what?' she asked.

'Anything at all. From that evening. That night.'

'I prefer not to think about it. I told that to . . . Fredrik as well.' She started brushing again, and her face changed. 'All I can think about is, am I going to get Aids or something.' She was brushing even more vigorously, and looked at Winter through eyes that were mere slits now. 'Or HIV, rather. I don't know the exact terminology.'

Winter didn't know what to say. He considered getting up and smoking a Corps by the window.

'Do you mind if I stand by the window and smoke?'

'Course not,' she said, and there might even have been the trace of a smile when she added: 'But look out for Dad. Don't let him see you.' She looked away. 'He sees everything. He knows everything.'

'What do you mean?'

'Oh, nothing. But look out.'

'Look down, you mean,' said Winter, standing up and taking the slim white packet from his left breast pocket and removing the cellophane from a cigarillo.

'What did you say?'

'I have to look down from here, to make sure your dad doesn't look up to me.'

'Ha, ha.'

Winter opened the window and lit his cigarillo. The lawn looked about as big as a football pitch between the branches of the trees. He could hear the clink of ice cubes in a glass from down below, and faint voices that he couldn't quite catch. Something was poured into a glass. Half past ten, not time for a lunchtime drink yet. But it was holiday time. He blew smoke out of the window and turned back into the room.

Perhaps their daughter *had* been infected with HIV.

'What I meant a minute ago when I said I'm not sure about the terminology was that I was supposed to be starting my medical studies this autumn,' she said, 'but I shan't bother now.'

'Why not?'

'Ha, ha again.'

Winter took a drag at his cigarillo and blew the smoke out through the window. He heard a woman saying something in what sounded like an agitated voice and Kurt Bielke came into view as he strode across the lawn and then along a path to a black car standing in the drive. He started the engine and drove away towards the centre of town. Winter remained standing with his back to the room. He heard a lawn-mower, saw a cascade of water coming from a sprinkler, saw the two boys coming back on their skateboards, saw a woman with a pram. Everything was normal out there in paradise.

'Do you dream about what happened in the park?' Winter asked after half a minute, turning to face the room.

'Yes.'

'What do you dream?'

'That I'm running. Always the same. Running, and I can hear steps coming after me.'

'What happens next?'

'I'm not really sure . . . it's mainly that . . . running . . . chasing.'

'You never see anybody?'

'No.'

'No face?'

'Afraid not.' She paused in her brushing and looked at Winter. 'That would be great, wouldn't it? If I saw a face in my dreams that I'd never seen in reality, and it turned out to be him. That it was that particular face.' She put the brush on the table again. 'Would that suffice as proof?'

'Not on its own.'

'Pity.'

'But you haven't seen a face?'

'Not then, and not now. In my dreams.'

'Do you get dragged?'

'What do you mean, dragged?'

'Does anybody drag you in those dreams? Pull you, try to carry you off?' Winter took another puff. 'Drag you.'

'No.'

'What happened in . . . reality?'

'I've already answered that. I don't know. I fainted.' She seemed to be thinking about what she'd said. 'I must have done.'

'But when you came round you were in a different place from where you'd been walking? Where you remembered that you'd been walking before you were attacked.'

'Yes, it must have been.'

'When did you come round?'

She brushed and brushed. Winter could see the suffering in those narrow eyes. It was as if she were trying to brush the demons out of her head with vigorous movements flattening her hair against her scalp.

'Sometimes I'm sorry I came round at all,' she said.

Winter heard the noise of a car behind him and saw

87

Bielke park in the middle of the drive and walk briskly into the house. He could hear voices, but no words.

'Please pass on my greetings to him . . . the other detective. Fredrik.'

'Of course.'

'Is he at work?'

'Not at the moment.'

'Surely he won't be able to work again after what's happened? Not for a very long time?'

Winter looked at her. If you can live, you can work. He thought of what she'd said about coming round, not coming round.

He heard the sounds of glass and china again from the verandah. Whatever had been said down there hadn't prevented them from having lunch.

'Excuse me,' said Jeanette, going into the bathroom and closing the door behind her.

Winter looked around. The room was tidy, almost neurotically so. Everything was neat; in piles, rows. He went to the bookcase. The books were arranged in alphabetical order, by author name.

'Neat and tidy, eh?'

He turned round.

'Since . . . it happened I've done nothing but tidy up in here,' she said, nodding in the direction of the books. 'Now I'm wondering whether to arrange them by subjects instead.'

'There are a lot of books,' Winter said.

'But not so many subjects.'

'Mostly fiction, I see.'

'What do you read?'

Winter felt like laughing. Did so. 'I read fewer and

fewer real books. Literature. But I'm going to change that. I'll be taking quite a long time off soon. At the moment I read mainly reports connected with preliminary investigations. Witness interviews, stuff like that.'

'Exciting.'

'It can be very exciting,' said Winter. 'And I'm not kidding. But first you have to learn how to interpret the language. Different police officers have different languages. When they write their reports. Sometimes it's a bit like trying to crack a code.'

'What's so exciting about it?'

'When you come across something that's linked to something you've read somewhere else. And when you eventually see something that you've stared at a hundred times before without actually seeing it. It was there all the time, but you hadn't noticed it.'

'What do you mean?'

'You haven't realised the significance. Or you may have interpreted it wrongly. But then the penny drops.' Winter thought about lighting another Corps. But he didn't. He sat down in her armchair.

'I've stolen most of the books in there,' she said.

Winter said nothing, but stood up, walked to the window and lit another cigarillo after all. There was a middle-of-the-day stillness out there now. Everything he'd heard before was silent.

'Did you hear what I said? Stolen!'

'I heard.'

'Aren't you going to do anything about it?'

'I don't believe you.'

'Really?'

'Tell me about the sounds he made.'

'Eh?'

'You said before that he'd made sounds you couldn't understand. Talk about it.'

'I have talked about it, it was exactly as you said. Just a noise. That's what I heard.'

'Have you thought any more about it?'

She shrugged.

'Could you make out any words?'

'No.'

Winter thought for a moment. 'Can you try to show me what it sounded like?'

'Show you what it sounded like? Are you all there?'

'It might be important.'

'So what?'

'What's happened to you could happen to somebody else.' He looked at her. 'Has happened to somebody else.'

'I know.'

Winter nodded. 'Good.'

'It's a bit much, though, asking me to . . . to imitate that bastard.'

'Think about it.'

'For Christ's sake, that's exactly what I don't want to do.'

'OK, I understand.'

'It must be difficult.'

'What do you mean?'

'Being forced to ask all these questions when you know the person you're asking wants to be left alone. *Ought* to be left alone.'

'It is difficult, yes.'

'There you are, you see.'

'I can't avoid it. I'm not here for fun.'

'But you chose to do your job.'

'Yes.'

'Why?'

'Let me think about it,' said Winter with a smile.

'Only until next time,' she said. He couldn't see if she was smiling as well. He could feel a breath of wind through the window. He noticed a cloud in the west. Suddenly it was there.

9

Halders walked through the house. Everything seemed strange now that he no longer lived there. They'd moved in together, then he'd moved out. Margareta had stayed on with the children, and he'd taken a flat in the centre of town. It wasn't cheap, but it was the best solution. The house was still there for the children. And anyway, she earned more than he did.

Had earned more.

Hannes and Magda had stayed at home yesterday, but they were back at school today. He was back in the living room. He'd made the tour. Most of the furniture was from then. Most of it was still there. She wasn't there, but everything else was. Margareta hadn't been seeing anybody else as far as he knew, but he didn't know everything.

He'd asked the children about school, if they'd prefer to stay at home for a few days. Magda had said no at first, and Hannes hadn't replied.

'Can we still live here?' Hannes asked from his bed when Halders went into his room.

Halders sat down on the edge of the bed.

'Can we still live in the house? I want to stay here.'

'If you want to live here, that's where we'll live.'

'Will you live here as well, Dad?'

The boy's question made him feel very cold. It was a horrific question. He suddenly thought about how exposed children are, how vulnerable. In the boy's mind it wasn't patently obvious that Dad would live with them. Come back to them . . . full time.

He felt so tremendously sad as he sat there. Endlessly sorrowful.

'Of course we'll live together, Hannes.'

'Magda as well?'

'Magda as well.'

'Shall we live here, then?'

Halders thought about his flat. His shitty little flat. Now it was gone, almost. He no longer owned this house, but it must be possible to solve that problem.

'I reckon that's what we'll do.'

'Do I have to go to school?'

'No. Like I said before.'

'What's Magda going to do? Is she going to school?'

'If she wants to. She decided in the end she did want to.'

The boy sat up. There were posters on the wall over his bed, some heavy metal bands whose name Halders vaguely recognised.

'Won't they have started the first lesson after lunch?'

'Not yet.'

'Then I can go.'

Halders drove the children to school, then went back to the house and did his tour again.

He phoned Winter.

'Did you see her?' he asked.

'Yes.'

'How did it go?'

'How are you feeling, Fredrik?'

'You're answering a question with a question.'

'I wanted to know how it's going for you.'

'Great.'

'Stop it, for Christ's sake.'

'OK, not great. But in the circumstances . . .'

'What are you doing?'

'Walking round the house. Round and round. It looks as though I'll be moving back here. The kids want to stay.'

'Walk round as many times as you like.' Winter could hear Halders breathing. 'Jeanette Bielke asked me to send her regards.'

'I'm coming in,' said Halders.

'Take a few days off.'

'No.'

'Well, I can't force you.'

'If I collapse at least it will be while I'm on the front line.'

'I'll pretend I didn't hear that,' said Winter.

'I've got something else you maybe *would* like to hear,' said Halders. 'Something occurred to me in connection with the murder of Angelika Hansson. Something we haven't talked about.'

'Can't we discuss it now? Over the phone?'

'I'm coming in. It can wait for an hour.'

'It will have to be this afternoon. I'm seeing the Wägners in half an hour.'

'Did they ask for the meeting?'

'No, I did.'

*

She had cycled home and hung up her damp swimming costume on the line behind the house. Or in front of it,

94

if you go in through the kitchen door. As she had done.

It was quiet indoors. She had the evening to herself if she wanted to stay here. She could wander around with a beer or a glass of wine and smell the scents wafting in through the open windows when night fell. There was so much greenery outside that it was a joy to wander round the house, experiencing it.

She took a shower. The answering machine was blinking when she went back to her bedroom. She listened to the message, and immediately returned the call.

'I was in the shower.'

'Hmm.'

'Did you ring earlier? Somebody called my mobile and didn't say anything.'

'No.'

'So . . . what's happening?'

'Can you come here tonight?'

'I don't know . . . I haven't got the strength.'

'Do you really mean that?'

'It's true. I feel really lazy.'

'You can be lazy here as well. Relatively lazy.'

'It's on the other side of town.'

'Take a taxi.'

'Too expensive.'

'I'll pay.'

'No.'

'I will, I promise.'

'I didn't mean it like that. I feel like staying in tonight. Taking it easy.'

'OK.'

'You won't be angry?'

'You'll regret it.'

'Are you angry?'

'Yes.'

'Really?'

'No.'

'We could meet tomorrow maybe?'

'I can't, sorry.'

'Oh.'

'I'll call you.'

10

It was raining when Winter left the police station. It was still hot but the atmosphere was close and he could feel sweat spring up on his brow, as well as rain in his hair. The grass next to the car park had turned greener after just a few minutes, and the air was heavy with the smell of it. This was the first rain for over a month.

Suddenly the sounds coming from the traffic on all sides were different. The swish of tyres on wet tarmac. A softer sound.

The colours were clearer than when he'd last driven through the centre of town. Not many people were wearing rain gear. Three young men naked from the waist up danced over the Allé when he stopped at a red light. One of them gave Winter a thumbs up. He nodded through the windscreen of his Mercedes.

He drove through the tunnel then turned off and continued along minor roads until he pulled up outside the house. The rain had stopped by the time he got out of the car. There was no wind. His back felt sweaty despite the air conditioning.

The house looked as melancholy as it always did. It was more than two years since he was last here. They'd kept in touch. Birgersson as well, but the fact was that Winter had felt a . . . stronger need to stay in contact with Beatrice's parents. Maybe a duty, in addition to his professional reasons. Their daughter's murderer was still out there somewhere. They were prisoners of that crime for the rest of their lives, bound by the memory and the sorrow. Shut up for ever inside the brick-built house that was so heavy and dark in the mist; the windows were black, the door closed, but it opened as Winter walked along the short path from the gate. Bengt Wägner came out, closing the door behind him, and shook hands with Winter.

'Lisen won't come out,' Wägner said. 'She's lying down. It all came back to her.'

'I'm sorry.'

'It's not your fault. It's no use trying to pretend it hasn't happened,' said Wägner. He took a few steps on the lawn that had stopped growing in the heatwave. 'It's best if Lisen confronts her grief. Otherwise it'll be worse. And worse still next time.' He looked at Winter. 'So, it's happened again.'

'A girl called Angelika Hansson.'

'In the same place.'

'Yes.'

'Exactly the same place?'

'It seems so.'

'And another girl has been attacked too, is that right?'

'Yes.'

'Also raped?'

Winter nodded again.

'No doubt there's more than one rapist running loose in town?'

'Depending on how you count them, there are several,' Winter said.

'But there's one who's special,' said Wägner.

'It's a hypothesis.'

'Does it make sense to work on that basis?'

'I think so.'

'What good does it do us?' Wägner gave a snort, almost like a dry little laugh. 'What do *we* get out of it?'

Winter lit a Corps, exhaled and watched the smoke mix with the air that was growing clearer now that the last of the dampness from the sky was sinking into the grass at their feet.

'If we can find a link it could help us. It could be of enormous help to us.'

'How? What link could there be?'

Winter took another drag on his cigarillo. He'd offered one to Wägner who'd accepted it, and now lit up.

'Angelika Hansson's murderer could be the same one as murdered Beatrice. Neither you nor I can stop thinking about the fact that he's still on the loose. It's devastating for you, I know, but I can't forget it either.'

'But what kind of a link do you expect to find by going through all that bloody shit yet again?' said Wägner, puffing at the cigarillo and studying the smoke as it rapidly became invisible.

'If there's something in common we'll find it,' said Winter. 'That's what's going to help us.'

'But what could it be? That *really* means something?'

'It could be anything at all.'

'You've read all the documents and reports and all the rest of it several times, Erik. Over and over again. Surely there can't be anything you've missed?'

'I haven't had anything to compare it with.'

'No, I can see that. But there must be lots of things that can be . . . well, in common, without it meaning anything at all. Obviously there are three girls about the same age. Maybe with the same interests, for all I know. The same hobbies, perhaps. The same favourite parts of town. Maybe . . . maybe they used to go to the same places. You said all three had only just left school. Good God, there's loads of things they have in common. There must be. How will you know what's important and what isn't when you read it and compare?'

'I can only hope that I see it.'

'Hope? Is that the best we can wish for?'

Winter gave a little smile and took another puff.

'Pretty strong, these things,' said Wägner, looking at the long, thin cigarillo in his hand. 'I was going to buy a packet a few months ago, but they didn't have any.'

'I'm the only one smoking them,' said Winter. 'And when they don't make them any more, I shall give up.'

'But you won't give up on . . . Beatrice.'

'Never.'

'Will you . . . we . . . will we find that bastard?'

'Yes.'

'Now you're hoping again.'

'No. By the end of this summer we'll have got him.'

'It could be a long summer,' said Wägner, looking up at the sky.

*

Winter phoned from Wägner's lawn. Halders answered after four rings. Winter drove back eastwards and found the house in Lunden, following the instructions Halders had given him. Halders' car was parked outside. Winter pulled up behind it.

'I could have come down to the station,' said Halders, who was waiting at the gate.

'I was out anyway.'

'It's a great job, lots of freedom, eh?'

'Have you got anything to drink?'

'Will low-alcohol beer do?'

Winter said it would and followed Halders into the house.

'I hadn't been here for four years or thereabouts.'

'Not at all?'

'Only to the gate.' Halders took a can out of the fridge. 'Here you go.'

Winter opened the can and drank.

'I can get you a glass.'

Winter shook his head and took another gulp. It was light in the kitchen. There were no piles of unwashed crockery on the draining board. No crumbs on the work surfaces. Hanging on the wall over the kitchen table was a framed poster from the sixties advertising a toothpaste that no longer existed. Next to the telephone in front of Winter was a tear-off wall calendar, and he noticed that the date was old. Nobody had torn off the pages from day to day. Winter knew what date it showed without needing to work it out.

'There's something fishy about her dad,' said Halders. 'Jeanette's dad.'

'What do you mean?'

'Or between the pair of them. There's something odd there.'

'Can you be a bit more concrete?'

'There are several details on which their versions of events don't agree. The night she came home. After it had happened.'

Winter had noticed the discrepancies. It wasn't uncommon. It needn't necessarily mean that one of them was lying, not consciously at least.

'I wonder which of them's lying,' Halders said. 'I think it's her, and he knows but doesn't want to say anything.'

'It happens.'

'We've got to be tougher on them.'

'On him, in that case.' Winter emptied the can. 'Jeanette needs to do a bit of thinking. Get us off her back for a while.'

'I wonder what time she got home?' Halders said. 'I don't think it was when she says.' He went to the fridge and got a beer for himself. 'But then why doesn't he say anything about it? I don't think he was asleep.'

They had a witness who'd seen Jeanette coming home around three hours later than she'd said.

'She's the key,' Halders said. He looked at Winter, came closer to him. 'Jeanette Bielke is the key here. She went somewhere that night but doesn't want to say where.'

The key, thought Winter. One of the keys.

'Her old man might know.'

'We'll question him again.'

'*I'll* question him.'

Winter could see how tense Halders' face was. Not just the usual Old Bill pessimism. The question was, how would it affect Halders' work? How would Halders react in a critical situation? It could end up in tragedy if he made a bad decision then.

Should he take Halders off the case? What would be the right thing to do? Would it sort itself out?

'There's another thing I've been wandering around thinking about,' said Halders, sitting down at the kitchen table. 'Sit down.' Winter did as he was bidden. 'Why haven't we found the bloke who put a bun in Angelika's oven?'

'I can't tell you why, Fredrik.'

'It was a so-called rhetorical question.'

'There's nobody in her circle of friends who knows,' said Winter. 'Of those we've talked to so far. Nobody who wants to say anything, at least.'

'That's bloody odd.'

'She may have kept it secret. From everybody.'

'Even from herself?'

'She may not have known,' Winter said. 'Or may have suppressed the thought that she was pregnant.'

'Which amounts to the same thing,' said Halders. 'But he does exist. The father.'

'One of her friends knows,' Winter said.

'She must have had a number-one boyfriend?'

'Not according to her parents.'

'They know nothing about that kind of thing,' said Halders. 'Parents haven't a clue about what their former little children get up to.' He looked at Winter. 'Am I right or am I right?'

'You are right in that parents might not always be completely reliable witnesses.'

'We've got to find this guy,' Halders said, pulling a face. 'He would have been a parent as well.'

They had to find him. Winter felt the full burden of the case as he drove back to the police station. They had put a lot of resources into finding Angelika's boyfriend, but they had failed.

Maybe they'd solve the problem when they found the father of the child that would never be born. Maybe he murdered Angelika. Maybe it was as simple as that.

The man who murdered Beatrice was somebody else.

And the one who raped Jeanette somebody else again.

No.

He'd parked the car and was inside his office within five minutes. There were a few raindrops still on the ledge under the window he'd left open.

The phone rang.

'We've got a new witness,' Bergenhem said.

'Oh?'

'It's . . . er, the murder of Angelika Hansson, that is. A young man who says he heard some strange noises as he walked past the park that night.'

'Does the time fit?'

'Yes.'

'What did he hear?'

'A hissing noise, he says. A repeated hissing.'

'What did he do?'

'Kept on going. Speeded up, in fact.'

'No more curious than that?'

'He thought it was a badger, and was scared.'

Winter could understand that. He'd once been chased by a badger.

'But now he doesn't think it was a badger any more?'

'He's seen the news,' said Bergenhem.

'And it was at the very spot?'

'It seems so.'

*

That evening they went to the park. Angela was licking away at an ice cream, Winter was in charge of the pushchair and Elsa was asleep, although she woke up when they were overtaken by a group of youngsters on rollerblades.

'It was about time anyway,' said Angela, and picked Elsa up as she reached out for the ice cream. 'No need to arrest them.'

'She wants an ice cream.'

'I haven't got any cash on me.'

'It's a good job there's somebody here who has,' said Winter, carrying Elsa to the kiosk only to find it had just closed. The youth in charge of it was just about to get on his bike and ride off, and Winter wondered whether he should order him to open up again. Elsa realised she wasn't going to get an ice cream, and was not pleased.

'She needs something to capture her attention,' said Angela when they came back.

'It was closed, though,' Winter said.

'Think of something else, then.'

He carried Elsa to the pond and dipped her feet into the water: the tears turned to laughter. He dipped them in again and mumbled into her ear, then looked over the water. It was all so familiar. He could see the little open area in front of the circle of bushes, and the trees, and the rock glinting in the last rays of the sun.

He could see a shadow to the left, just where the police cordon blocked off the black opening. The shadow was motionless. Winter didn't move either until he felt Elsa squirming in his hands. He didn't take his eyes off the shadow, which had the shape of a person, even more so now as the sinking sun beamed further in like a searchlight. The shadow moved.

Winter heard Angela say something just behind him, lifted Elsa out of the water and dumped her in Angela's arms without a word, heard the child's disappointed cries as he sprinted behind the hedge to the left of the pond, came to the pathway on the other side of the bushes and could see the opening and the cleft that was no longer lit up by the sun and he pushed his way past a young couple and darted through the shrubbery and saw the trees and all the rest of the nasty but familiar sights and his pulse was racing as he felt for his gun that was in a cupboard a long way away.

11

There was nobody there by the time Winter arrived. He could see the opening between the trees, and the rock, and twigs and bushes at the sides, and patches of dusky sky – but no shadow.

The grotto was empty.

The grass outside was bone dry again. There was no point in searching for footprints. But he ought to summon somebody who could search for any new objects that might have appeared there. You never knew. You just never knew.

He circled round the clearing, then hurried onto the path behind and followed it for fifty metres. He went back again, and there was Angela with Elsa in her pushchair, and she was staring wide-eyed at him as he ducked underneath a sapling.

'If you're going to play hide-and-seek with us, the least you can do is to tell us before you run off,' Angela said. 'Or maybe you want to hide and then go seeking yourself?'

He brushed a few pine needles off his shoulders and reached for the packet of cigarillos that was no longer in his big, wide breast pocket.

'Now's the time to give up,' said Angela, who had seen what happened.

Winter contemplated the packet on the ground, and bent down. Several of the cigarillos had fallen out and were lying in a semicircle. He walked over to it, picked up the packet and then the cigarillos one by one – then he noticed a button lying next to the last but one. Just a button, white or bony white, a shirt button.

They would have found it if it had been there when they first cordoned the place off after the murder of Angelika. And after the rape of Jeanette.

Since then, anybody at all could have walked past and lost a button.

'Have you got a tissue?' he asked, turning to Angela. He was still squatting.

Angela produced a Kleenex out of her handbag. Winter took it and wrapped it round the button.

'What is it?'

'A button.'

'You don't say.'

'A shirt button,' said Winter. 'I think.'

'Oh yes? Well, now we've seen how you go about your business,' said Angela, turning to Elsa. 'This is how detectives work, Elsa. Look and learn.'

'Do you want Elsa to grow up to be an investigator?' said Winter, crouching down again, this time by the pushchair. Elsa made a sound. 'She said detective,' Winter said.

'No. She said *perspective*.' Angela looked at him with a smile. 'I think she means that you've got to put your job in perspective.' She looked towards the bushes. 'Is this the way it's got to be when we go for a walk in the evening?'

'I thought I saw somebody,' said Winter.

'Oh for God's sake!'

'It's more complicated than you might think.'

'You can say that again.'

'There was somebody standing there. It wasn't just your ordinary . . . passer-by.'

'Don't forget the button, Erik.' She'd seen his eyes glaze over. It had turned cold in among the trees. Elsa was trying to clamber out of the pushchair. He helped her. 'Sorry, Erik. I know it's important . . . and serious. Awful. But I couldn't resist teasing you a bit.'

'That's OK.'

He picked Elsa up. They went back to the pond.

'Do you think that . . . that he's returning to the scene of the crime?'

'Yes.'

'You think that's what always happens.'

'That's my experience. Others think the same.'

'And the shadow that you saw could . . . have been him?'

Winter shrugged. 'The moment I saw him I had the distinct feeling that it was . . . important. Important for the case.' He turned to look at her with Elsa on his shoulder. 'I don't know any more, for fuck's sake.'

'Fuck,' Elsa said. It was one of the first words she had pronounced correctly.

*

'What's a private life? You tell me,' Halders said to Aneta Djanali in the passenger seat beside him. They were parked outside the Hanssons' house. Djanali could smell the salt of the sea through the open window.

'When does a life stop being private?' asked Halders, turning to look at her. 'I can't keep my various lives apart any longer.'

'No.'

'I've become the philosopher now as well.' He gave

a laugh. 'Private philosopher.' He laughed again, shorter, drier. 'Amateur philosopher.'

He ought to be at home, Djanali thought. Why doesn't Winter take him off the case? Or Birgersson? It would cause less of an upset if Birgersson did it.

'I know you reckon I ought to be taking time out at home just now,' Halders said. 'That's what you're thinking.'

'Correct.'

'I know you mean well, but you're wrong.' He opened the car door. 'There are lots of ways of dealing with sorrow.' He put a foot into the road. 'If I find the kids don't want to go to school any more, or develop other problems, I'll run a mile from all this. But only then.' He was outside in the street now, and bent down towards Djanali. 'Are you coming, or aren't you?'

*

Lars-Olof and Ann Hansson were sitting at opposite ends of the sofa. Djanali and Halders were facing them, in armchairs. She looks shattered, thought Aneta when Angelika's mother turned to stare out of the window, seemingly to study the various shades of green out there.

Lars-Olof Hansson stared down at the table.

Behind the couple was a sort of bookcase and a recently taken photo of Angelika. Her student cap was brilliant white, contrasting with her black skin. She's even blacker than I am, Djanali thought.

Lars-Olof Hansson had noticed what Djanali was looking at, and turned to face her.

'That was taken just five or six weeks ago.'

Djanali nodded.

'That's about the age she was when we adopted her,' said her father. 'Five or six weeks.'

110

'Shut up!' shouted his wife leaving the room in a huff.

He's so full of sadness, Halders thought. There are so many ways of dealing with sorrow.

When he spoke again his voice sounded hollow. He looked at Djanali. 'Were you born here?'

'I was, actually,' Djanali said. 'In East General Hospital. But my parents are from Africa.'

'Where exactly?'

'Upper Volta. That's what it was called when they came here. It's called Burkino Faso now.'

'Hmm.' Hansson was staring down at the table, then looked up at her. 'Have you ever been there?'

'Yes.'

'What was that like?'

'Well . . . I'd expected to feel more than I did,' Djanali said. This interview is turning out a bit different from what I'd expected. But what the hell? 'I'm glad I went, though.'

'Angelika wanted to travel as well,' said Lars-Olof Hansson, just as his wife re-entered the room.

'That's enough, Lasse.' She gave him a look like nothing Djanali had ever seen. He suddenly looked completely helpless. Like a drowning man, she thought.

'To Uganda,' he said. And that was all he was capable of saying about Angelika Hansson's origin, or Aneta Djanali's.

'We have a few problems working out how Angelika was making her way home that night,' Halders said.

'What do you expect me to do about that?' Lars-Olof Hansson was standing now, leaning against the wall by the verandah door. 'I've told you everything. Everything I know.'

'Why was she on her own in the middle of Gothenburg for several hours?'

'You are the ones who should be telling me that.'

'Nobody we've spoken to was with her for nearly four hours that night. Or evening.'

'I've told you everything I know,' said Lars-Olof Hansson.

'But what was she doing?' asked Halders.

'I don't know, I've told you already.'

'Might she have had a job?'

'What do you mean, a job?'

'A job. A summer job.' Halders persisted.

'She'd have told us if she had.'

'Did she ever go out on the town by herself?'

'Would it be so bizarre if she did?'

'Did she?'

'I didn't follow her.'

Halders waited. He could see there was more to come.

'She thought a lot about . . . about her origins,' he said. 'She became a bit . . . confused, I suppose you might say.' He looked at his wife, but she didn't respond. 'It seemed to get worse. Yes. I suppose she might have gone off and thought a lot about that. I don't know.'

'Was she depressed?'

'I don't know.' He thought about it. 'I haven't a bloody clue.'

'What about boyfriends?' Djanali asked. Ann Hansson looked up. Djanali turned to face her. 'You must have thought about that these last few days.'

The woman nodded. Her face lost all vestige of character, just like that of her husband a few minutes before. Precisely the same kind of helplessness.

Djanali waited. She wanted to be able to offer her leads, prompt her. But she didn't have any.

'There weren't any boyfriends,' Ann Hansson said. 'Not that we knew about, at least.'

'Did you talk about it?' Djanali asked.

'Talk? Me and . . . Lasse?'

'You and Angelika.'

'Well . . . what can I say . . . ? Of course we talked about it. But she hadn't had a . . . steady relationship,' said Ann Hansson, beginning to weep, silently, for the first time since they'd visited her. 'This business of the . . . preg–, pregnancy – it's absolutely incomprehensible. It's like . . . like a nightmare inside a nightmare.'

'This is no nightmare,' said her husband. 'This is reality.' He looked at his wife. 'Come on, we've got to face up to it.'

*

Bergenhem was in Winter's office. It was 10.30 in the morning. The air conditioning was clattering away. Bergenhem was tanned after many hours spent on the sun-drenched cliffs to the north-west of Gothenburg. He looks stronger than he's done for ages, Winter thought. Calmer.

'I suspect she did have a boyfriend,' Bergenhem said. 'I spoke to a mate of hers, Cecilia, who just got back from Paris yesterday, and she reckoned she'd seen Angelika with a bloke. Several times.' Bergenhem consulted his notebook, then looked up. 'Twice, in fact. You've got the report, written up immediately after the interview.'

'Just one bloke, then.'

'Yep. She'd seen Angelika and this guy twice: once at a café where they'd arranged to meet, and once when she passed them in a tram.' Bergenhem looked up. 'That time at the café the young man was on his way out, and she just said hi to him.'

'She's only seen him those two times?'

'Yes.'

'Never on his own? Or with anybody else?'

'It seems not.'

'What had Angelika said about him?'

'They never discussed it.'

'Hmm.'

'She'd asked, of course, but Angelika had kept schtum.'

'In what way? Did she laugh it off? Or look worried or frightened or annoyed or disappointed – or what?'

'I don't know,' Bergenhem said.

'Find out.'

'Yes. Of course.'

'And this friend of hers – she didn't recognise the guy at all?'

'No.'

'Are you planning to question her again?'

'Later this morning. I just wanted to have a word with you first.'

'OK. Bertil and you can talk to her.'

Bergenhem nodded.

'I want this guy tracked down, and soon,' Winter said. 'He's out there somewhere.'

But they couldn't find him. They had several conversations with the girl but got no further, and it looked as if the only chance they had of finding the missing boy was if Angelika's friend Cecilia happened to see him again in town.

She had given them a description of him.

Another day passed. They had hoped to make a public appeal. But the information was so vague. They didn't have a face yet.

'If he's in the country he'd have been in touch by now,' Bertil Ringmar said at the morning meeting.

Winter's right-hand man, older than he was, was sitting on a chair at the edge of the group. There'll be fewer and fewer of us for every week that passes, Winter thought, for every week with nothing to show, but we won't know for certain until we can come up with something resembling a key to it all.

'Have we covered everybody she knew?' Bergenhem asked.

'We've interviewed everybody we know about, yes,' said Ringmar. 'Those that are at home, that is, and we're pretty sure we've seen the whole lot. We're not so sure about those who are abroad.'

'It might just have been a casual acquaintance,' said Djanali. 'It might not even have been the same boy on both occasions. Cecilia might have been mistaken.'

'Why didn't Angelika say anything about it?' Bergenhem asked.

*

The phone rang after she'd dozed off. She answered sleepily.

'Yes . . . Hello?'

'I hope I didn't wake you up?'

'Well, you did.' Anne sat up. It was almost dark outside, which meant it must be the middle of the night. There was a smell of flowers and seaweed through the half-open window.

'Sorry about that.'

'What do you want?'

115

'Can you work tomorrow? Just one more time.'

'I've told you that I don't want to.'

'Anne.'

'No.'

'OK, OK.'

'Don't phone here any more.'

'I might.'

She felt afraid now. It was in her voice. She knew that he knew.

'You don't need to be scared of anything,' he said. 'But I want you to come here tomorrow.'

'I don't want to work. And I'm not scared. What should I be scared of?'

'Just come here. We have to talk.'

'There's no point. I've told you.'

'Hmm.'

'A thousand times.'

'See you, then.'

He hung up.

12

Hannes was waiting in his teacher's office. Halders hugged him. The teacher was standing next to them. She removed her hand from Hannes' shoulder after a while.

'Magda wants to stay until the end of lessons,' the boy said. 'I asked her.'

Halders hugged his son even tighter.

'Can we go now, Dad?'

They drove home through the rain. It had started raining during the afternoon.

'I hope you aren't angry with me, Dad.'

'Why should I be angry?'

'Because you had to leave work and collect me before lessons were finished.'

'If you don't want to be there, you don't have to be there,' said Halders, giving his son's shoulder a squeeze with his right hand. 'And I don't need to be at work either.'

The boy seemed satisfied with that reply, and said nothing for the rest of the drive home. Halders parked the car, and they went in. He'd moved some of his things there from his flat. He wasn't at all sure where his home was now, apart from with his children.

'I'm tired,' Hannes said.

'Go and lie down for a bit. I'll be here in the living room.'

'Do you get more tired when you're sad, Dad?'

'Yes.' The thought had never occurred to him before, but now he knew it was true. He knew now. He was bloody well certain of it. 'Let's both have a lie-down before we go to collect Magda.'

*

'I don't know exactly what she was doing every second of the night,' said Kurt Bielke. 'I've never kept that sort of track of her.'

There's something fishy about her dad, Halders had said. Jeanette's dad. Or between them. Something funny going on there. Can you be a bit more concrete? Winter had asked. There are several details on which their versions of events don't agree, Halders had replied. The night when she came home. After it happened.

'But you're sure that she was back home before three?'

'Round about then. I've said that lots of times now.'

'Not two hours later?'

'No. Who says that?'

'We have witnesses who saw Jeanette come home.'

'Really? They must have seen wrongly.'

They were sitting in the living room. It was very light, despite the heavy rain outside.

'You've spoken to my wife as well. Jeanette got home about three, and I can't understand why the hell you are trying to suggest otherwise.' He glared at Winter. 'She's told you that herself, hasn't she? Why on earth would she lie? It's absolutely ridiculous.'

'Tell me again about the telephone call you had that evening,' said Winter.

118

Kurt Bielke sighed loudly.

'Inspector Winter, I'm doing my best to be patient. But you must forgive me if I start to get a bit impatient. Or become reluctant to answer your questions. We're a family that's been dealt a heavy blow . . . Jeanette has had a shattering blow . . . And you come here and start quibbling with me about my statement.'

'We are investigating a serious crime,' said Winter.

'You almost make it sound as though I'm guilty,' said Bielke.

'Why do you say that?'

'I beg your pardon?'

'Why do you say it sounds as if you are guilty?'

'Because that's the way it does sound, almost.'

'Tell me about that telephone call.'

'She phoned at about eleven to ask whether anybody had called her,' Bielke said.

'Anybody in particular?'

'No, just anybody.'

'And had anybody?'

'No.'

'She'd borrowed a friend's mobile,' Winter said.

'That's what you tell me.'

'You couldn't hear the difference?'

'No. But I do remember that there was a different sort of background noise,' Bielke said.

'She said she was outdoors.'

'Yes.'

'Anything to confirm that?'

'The call only lasted a few seconds.'

Her own mobile was being repaired. Winter had had that confirmed.

'It's not clear who lent her a mobile,' Winter said.

'Does it matter?'

'We're not clear about where Jeanette was for a few hours that night,' said Winter. 'Maybe even longer.'

'You'll have to ask her. Again. I don't like it, but if you have to, you have to.'

'I'm asking you, now.'

'Wrong person.'

Winter noticed that the man had changed during the course of the conversation. Or the interrogation. And he noted how much Bielke had changed since they'd met for the first time. He'd become . . . more aggressive. That could be due to Winter, or to Halders. Or it could be due to something entirely different.

'Don't you want to know?' Winter asked.

'What do you think?'

Winter didn't reply. He'd heard something from upstairs, footsteps. Soft footsteps, even a stumble. Perhaps she'd been listening, but he ought to have noticed in that case. At that point Jeanette came into the room from the kitchen. It had been somebody else upstairs. Irma Bielke wasn't at home, according to what Bielke had said when Winter arrived.

It was raining outside. Harder now. The garden was a mass of wet greenery. The temperature had fallen, but it was still warm. The sound of waves breaking against the rocks could be heard from the west.

Winter drove southwards. He'd have to change his passenger-side windscreen wiper. His vision to the right was blurred and greasy, like looking at houses and trees through a thin layer of jelly.

He had to wait at a crossroads where a section of road was being filled with tarmac. His thoughts were faster than the efforts of the workmen.

The girls had been to the same place. Beatrice and Angelika. That's where they'd been found, where they'd been murdered. Or within a few metres of there. And that's where Jeanette had been attacked. She'd said it was there. And why doubt her?

What did it mean? What was the significance of the location?

He'd been delving backwards into the case . . . to Beatrice . . . but had somebody else been doing the same thing? Was there a copycat? He hated the word. But it was no secret what had happened to Beatrice. Nor where it had happened. Was that knowledge being exploited by somebody? Was he approaching the case from the wrong point of view? Should he be looking forwards instead of backwards?

One of the workmen waved him on, past the vehicle that looked like a field kitchen for an army battalion, or something out of a Mad Max film. The hot tarmac was simmering in the rain, giving off steam. It smelled like an infantry attack coming through the car windows.

They had traced the three girls' last hours in as much detail as they could. He was including Jeanette in this aspect of the investigation. There was another peculiarity. She was still alive, but what had happened to her that evening before the crime was hardest of all to work out. There were fewer witnesses. Several couldn't remember.

He'd spent ages poring over the map, trying to work out if they'd followed the same route to the park, to the rock, the opening, the bushes. Maybe there was a common route, or something that amounted to the same thing. If you added up all the evidence from friends about where they'd been and what they'd done and what they were going to do that night, there was something like a route that Beatrice, Angelika and Jeanette might have taken before they came up against the rapist. It started to the north of the city centre, and everybody knew where it ended.

North of the city centre. What had they been doing there? It must have been near the river, the old harbour, or around the Opera House. Or on the other bank, perhaps? Winter had read the case notes backwards and forwards and over and over again, but hadn't found a place mentioned where they might all have started off on the same journey. Was it all a coincidence? He didn't know, but he would keep at it. He would force his way into the reality of the map, into the very spot.

He'd been looking for some connection between the cases, and here one was – extremely vague at the moment, but even so. What else was there for him to do?

Winter turned left. Angelika Hansson's father was at the door waiting for him, just like last time.

'Leave me on my own in here for a while,' said Winter, and Lars-Olof Hansson closed the door on him. Winter started looking round Angelika's room. He needed to start from the beginning all over again. He opened the left-hand door of the wardrobe.

13

There was nothing in the wardrobe he hadn't seen before. Nobody had moved the clothes since he and Bergenhem had been there on their first search and removed jumpers and trousers, a job he wouldn't wish on his worst enemy. He had an inbuilt reluctance to touch dead people's clothes. He wasn't cut out to be a forensic officer. Those clothes would never be worn again. He'd seen it before: they'd lie there for years on their shelves and in their drawers, just as all the furniture would stay exactly where it had been, the papers would still be on the desk, the books on their shelves, the few ornaments would be untouched.

They were all concrete memories now, memories they didn't want in that house, but they didn't have the strength to obliterate them. Or the will. Or both, he thought as he closed the wardrobe door.

What am I looking for? If he knew, he wouldn't be here, intruding on the despairing parents in the next room. If he knew, he'd already have found it, taken it away to be examined under a brighter light.

A secret.

The thought had been in the back of his mind since he'd spoken to Jeanette's father that first time. There was a secret. Either the father or the daughter was hiding something. Maybe both of them. Something they hadn't said. It wasn't something he could point to like a physical piece of evidence, but it had to do with the crime committed on the daughter, the rape. He couldn't pin it down, not yet. But he could sense it. And Halders could sense it. He needed Halders. This was a case for Halders as well, a complicated case that required a sort of thinking that aimed straight for the target, without too many sidetracks.

And here he was now, in this room that would only ever allow in a mixture of half-light and half-darkness through the closed venetian blinds.

He sat down at the desk and looked at a photo of Angelika on a jetty by the sea. A young black body and a smile as big as the horizon, and just as white.

These confounded photographs that took no account of the future. He had already stared at a thousand pictures similar to this one, like a clairvoyant predicting a tragedy that is going to happen. Everything in photographs like these acquires a significance different from what one sees on the surface, it seemed to him. When I look at this picture, it's as if I'm coming to that jetty from the future, with a death announcement.

Angelika's father had no secret of that kind. Winter could hear him clearing his throat somewhere in the house. Her father – an adoptive father but her father even so – had been genuinely ignorant about his daughter's pregnancy and possible boyfriends.

But did Angelika have a secret? Who was it she had come up against in the night? Just like Beatrice she'd split off from her friends and been alone. Or had she met the man who'd made her pregnant some eight weeks earlier?

What had she done then? She had almost finished

her twelve years of schooling and was on her way out into the big wide world. Did she bump into a rapist and murderer who lay in wait for his victims in the summer night? A coincidence. Bad luck, to put it mildly. Or was there a motive behind it? Was it a planned crime?

The location could have been carefully selected . . . in either case. By the madman. Or by the murderer who was waiting for somebody in particular, only for her.

But then this wasn't about Beatrice Wägner, or Jeanette Bielke. Or was it, in fact?

Perhaps the three girls had something in common that had led to their attacks, perhaps it wasn't just a case of being in the wrong place at the wrong time. Had they *done* something that . . . linked them? Could that be it? For God's sake, I must concentrate on *this* particular murder. It's possible to find common denominators in everything.

Winter sat with his head in his hands, thinking, then stood up and opened one of the desk drawers. He needed a cigarillo, but controlled his craving. It had got stronger since he'd become a father. He had thought it would grow weaker, or maybe disappear altogether; but it had become worse. He was smoking more than ever. That meant it was time to stop. Angela's discreet hints had slowly developed into something else. Not nagging. Never that. But maybe . . . irritation. It wasn't just the doctor in her. It was healthy common sense. Healthy.

He stood up, walked through the house and as soon as he was outside he lit a Corps.

When he came back he searched the room methodically. He spent some time studying the photograph again, her skin against the water. He opened the desk drawer and took out the eight bundles of photographs he'd just been through. He started once again, sorted them into small piles, re-sorted them. Angelika in various locations, mostly outdoors. Smiling, not smiling. He put the outdoor pictures together, the indoor ones together. Summer snaps. Winter snaps. The bright colours of autumn leaves. Angelika in a snowdrift, black, black, white, white. Angelika on a hillside in spring with wood anemones gleaming white. Angelika with her mother and father, on the same hillside: her parents so pale after the winter they looked almost ill.

There were no dates on the photos, but they all seemed to have been taken during the last year. It was a guess, but became more than that when he checked the dates on the envelopes. There were nearly 300 pictures. It was like an open diary of her last year. Summer, autumn, winter, spring, summer again. Her last summer, or half summer, he thought, and turned to a series of photographs taken at her graduation party. Flowers, balloons, all the traditional things, a one-year-old Angelika enlarged eighteen times on a poster hanging above their heads.

There were a lot of people standing around, in a wide semicircle, a lot of faces. Winter recognised her parents, but nobody else. Angelika was wearing her white cap and laughing at the camera.

That was six weeks ago.

Winter continued sorting the photos into different piles. Why am I doing this? Is it a sort of private therapy because this case is so bloody distressing? A sort of patience game? Patience. It was all a matter of patience.

The birds were singing outside the window. After a break, the rain was now pattering against the panes once again. Winter had been sitting with a photograph of Angelika in some kind of room with an exposed brick wall behind her. The brick was . . . well, brick coloured. She was looking straight at the camera, but not smiling. Her face was actually expressionless, it seemed to him. There were a glass and some bottles on a table in front of her. A few empty plates with what could be some food leftovers. There was a shadow of something in the top left-hand corner of the picture. A lamp shade, perhaps, or something hanging on the wall.

It was definitely indoors, the light was coming from all directions and he could see no suggestion of daylight. Maybe there was a faint, shadowy outline of the photographer.

He put the picture down and picked up another one with Angelika in half-profile at the same table in front of the same wall, but with no shadow in the top left-hand corner. It was taken from a different angle.

A restaurant perhaps, Winter thought. A pub.

The photos had been in the same envelope as the winter pictures. Maybe they had been taken around the same time. He hadn't found any negatives with them.

Perhaps it was a place she often went to. Maybe one of her regular haunts. Did they have any information about the places she used to go to in her free time? Yes. There were some. Was this brick wall in any of them?

There were no other photographs of places of entertainment or restaurants or pubs among the 300 pictures Winter had sifted through and laid out in about a dozen piles on the table. Not ones taken indoors. There were a few of pavement cafés. There was a waiter pulling a face in one of them.

He stood up, left the room and went to look for Lars-Olof Hansson, who was sitting by himself in the dining room, watching the rain trickle down the windowpane.

'There's something I'd like you to take a look at,' said Winter. 'If you've got a minute.'

'Only one,' said Hansson. 'I'm waiting for the rain to run down this windowpane.' He pointed. 'It can't make up its mind.'

Winter nodded, as if he understood.

'What is it?' Hansson asked.

'Some photos,' said Winter. 'I'd like you to have a look at them.' He gestured towards the hall. 'In Angelika's room.'

'I'm not going in there.' Hansson tore his eyes away from the windowpane. There was a smell of both heat and dampness in the room, like the air outside. The wind was making the trees sway. It was like dusk both inside the room and in the garden the other side of the glass, which was streaked with rain. 'I never go in there since it happened.'

'I'll bring them here,' said Winter, going out and returning with the photographs. He handed them to Hansson. The man looked at them, but didn't seem to take them in.

'What's this?' he asked.

'I don't really know,' said Winter. 'Some kind of a pub. A restaurant, maybe. Don't you recognise it?'

'Recognise what?' asked Hansson, looking at Winter.

'The place. The wall in the background. Or anything else. Angelika's sitting there after all, and I wondered if you knew where it is.'

Hansson took another look at the photo he was holding in his hand.

'No,' he said. 'I've never been there.'

'Angelika was there,' said Winter. 'There were a

128

few pictures in her desk drawer taken there.'

'I've no idea where it is,' said Hansson. 'And . . . does it make the slightest difference?'

'I don't know,' said Winter.

'I mean, she used to go to several different places, the way young people do. I never kept a check on them.' He looked at the picture again. 'Why should it be important to know where that bloody brick wall is?'

'It depends on who else was there,' Winter said.

'Angelika was obviously there,' said Hansson. 'Maybe she was on her own.'

'Somebody must have been holding the camera,' said Winter.

'Timer,' said Hansson, producing a series of cough-like chuckles. It sounded like an explosion in the enclosed room. 'Sorry,' he said when he finished.

'She was there not long ago,' Winter said.

Hansson seemed too tired and far too desperate to ask how Winter could know that.

'Other people might have seen her,' said Winter. And seen other people as well, he thought.

He had another idea. He went back to Angelika's room and fetched the pictures of the graduation party, handing them to Hansson who reached out a hand in a way that seemed almost apathetic.

'It's her graduation party,' Hansson said.

Winter nodded. 'Could you help me by identifying the people in the picture?'

Hansson studied the photograph.

'Even the ones with their backs to the camera?'

'If you can.'

Hansson pointed at the photograph.

'That fatty over there on the left,' he looked up at Winter, 'that's Uncle Bengt. My brother, that is. He's looking the other way and chewing at a turkey leg or something.' He held up his hand to his mouth. 'Compulsive eater.'

'Who else do you recognise?' Winter asked.

Hansson named them one after the other, sticking his index finger into their faces.

When he'd finished, there were still four left.

'Never seen them before,' he said.

'Are you sure?'

'Why the hell shouldn't I be?'

Winter looked at their faces. Three men and a woman. Two of the men looked about forty. One was dark and the other blond, with a beard and glasses. There was something vaguely familiar about him. The third was a boy of around Angelika's age. The woman looked around forty too, maybe a bit younger. She was on the outside, as if about to step out of the picture. She was looking away, in another direction. One of the men was standing next to the boy. The man looked like the boy, or maybe it was the other way round. Southern European appearance, dark and yet pale, pale faces. The man with glasses and a beard was holding a balloon and laughing just as Angelika was laughing. Winter tried to think where he might have seen him before. He didn't recognise the face. Maybe it was his bearing, leaning forward slightly.

'Never seen them before,' Hansson repeated.

Winter felt his flesh creep. Something was happening just now, just there. Something happening. He looked at the four people with the unknown faces. It was as if the others standing round the girl were known to him, now that Hansson had identified them. But these four were strangers. They could have been sent from some unknown place. Something was happening.

'Isn't that a bit odd?' he asked.

Hansson shrugged. 'There were quite a lot of people at the school hall, you can see that yourself.' He pointed at one of the pictures. 'I expect these people I don't know got in this photo by mistake.'

'Is that likely?' Winter nodded towards the picture. 'They look as though they're . . . part of it. As if they know Angelika.'

'Well I don't know them in any case.'

'You didn't speak to them?'

'I've just said I don't know who they are, for Christ's sake.'

'OK.'

Neither of them spoke. Winter could no longer hear any rain pattering against the windows. He could hear a car driving past, the sound of the tyres on wet tarmac.

'What the hell were they doing there?' said Hansson suddenly, looking again at the photo. 'I hadn't invited them.' He looked at Winter again. His expression had changed. 'I didn't notice them at the time. I suppose I ought to have done?'

'There were lots of people there, as you said yourself.'

'They can't have been there,' said Hansson.

'What do you mean?'

'They turned up . . . afterwards.' He looked at the photo again, then up at Winter, who could smell his sweat and the odour of fear and despair. 'Don't you understand? They turned up later! They'd been sent to that bloody party but nobody could see them!' He stared into Winter's eyes like a blind man. 'Nobody saw them. Angelika didn't either. But they came with a message. A message from Hell!'

131

He continued staring right through Winter's head like a blind man.

'And now they've gone back!' he shouted.

He needs counselling, thought Winter. Or he may be right, but in a way I don't understand.

Hansson's expression changed again. He shook his head and stared at the photograph in his hand. 'You'll never find this gang,' he said.

'Do you think they belong together, then? Like a . . . gang?'

'It doesn't matter,' said Hansson. 'They don't exist.'

14

Halders had chosen to play Led Zeppelin at the funeral, towards the end. Aneta Djanali recognised the tune, of course. It was something new for Winter, who was sitting in the third row with Angela and Elsa. The music sounded big in the little church.

Hanne Östergaard conducted the service. She had been working part-time as a vicar for the police for several years. Somebody to talk to after disturbing experiences.

I must admit that she's been a rock since Margareta died, Halders thought.

'Led Zep was her favourite band,' Halders had told Djanali an hour before the funeral. 'She has memories associated with that tune, as do I.' Then he'd said: 'That's something we share. Memories.' He'd looked at her. 'Do you think it's inappropriate? The choice of music?'

'No. People often choose their own music at funerals nowadays.'

'I haven't been to one for ages.'

'Led Zeppelin is good,' she said.

'It's only a song, after all.'

* * *

Halders stood beside his children as the soil was scattered over the coffin. No cremation. It was raining, but would probably ease off during the day.

He spoke to people afterwards, but didn't register what they said. The children stayed close to him.

'Is Mummy in heaven now?' Magda asked.

'Yes,' he said.

Magda looked up and the clouds seemed to part in all directions. There was blue in the middle.

'Look, a hole!' she shouted, pointing upwards. 'Mummy can pass through that hole!'

He tried to look at the sky, but all he could see through the tears was a blur.

'Can you see the hole in the sky, Hannes?' Magda turned to look at her brother.

'There isn't a hole,' he said. 'It's just space.' He looked down at the ground, which was wet.

'Oh yes there is,' she said, taking down her hand and grasping tightly hold of her father's hand. 'Oh yes there is.'

*

They were driving to the rocks south of Gothenburg. It was twice as hot now, after the rainy days. Angela was driving. Elsa was in the child seat in the front. Winter was in the back, looking out over the fields glistening in the sunshine. He asked Angela to switch off the air conditioning and wound down the window so that he could appreciate the smells.

They parked the car. He carried Elsa on his shoulders as they walked over the paddock. They paused to look at a foal, resting in the grass. The mother was standing by its side, nuzzling her offspring.

There was nobody else in their little inlet. Winter

changed rapidly, walked down to the water's edge with Elsa, and kept dipping her into the sea. Angela took over, and he swam out. It was calm. He lay on his back and watched Angela and Elsa on their blanket on the rocks.

The oppressive feeling he'd experienced earlier sunk down through his body and under the surface of the water. There was not much of it left when he turned over and swam even further out. He lay on his back again, and gazed at his family, who had become smaller.

Halders had looked as if he were sinking after the funeral. Winter didn't know when he'd come back to work. Tomorrow, or never. Impossible to say.

During the funeral Winter had felt like stone. It had been hard to raise his heavy body from the pew. Earlier memories came back to him, from recently, when Angela had been so close . . . when Elsa . . . when what was Elsa . . . when he'd stood outside that door as if frozen fast to the floor, as heavy as stone. He'd felt his own life falling, faster and faster, down into the bottomless depths.

He closed his eyes and felt the sun on his face. A boat passed by, a hundred yards out into the creek, but he kept his eyes closed. Gulls cried. A voice came floating over the water. There was a smell of petrol, wafted towards him from the boat by the slight breeze.

'You almost turned into a dinghy out there,' said Angela when he walked up, wetter than he'd ever been. 'Firmly moored.'

'I didn't know I was that good at floating.'

'I know the reason,' she said, poking him in the stomach, which was just a little bit rounded. *He* couldn't see any sign of a pot belly when he looked down. Elsa poked him as well, several times. She almost hurt him.

'All that needs is just one fifteen-k jog,' he said. 'Come to think of it, I could run back home.' He had his trainers in the car boot. It was rather more than fifteen kilometres to the centre of town. Perhaps too much more? No.

'Do you dare to eat that?' she said, nodding in the direction of the baguette with chicken salad he had just picked up.

'Yes,' he said, and Angela suddenly burst into tears. She wiped her eyes. Winter put down his sandwich and leaned over the blanket to hug her. Then Elsa started crying. He included her in his embrace as well.

Elsa built a hut between them and crept out. Angela wiped her face again and gazed out into the bay where boats of various sizes were sailing.

'I was so sad when I saw Fredrik and the children,' she said.

'Yes. I took it pretty hard as well.'

'I hope it turns out all right.'

'He's going to try to keep going.' Winter fumbled for his packet of cigarillos. 'He doesn't want to take time off. Not much, at least.'

'I hope it turns out all right,' Angela said again.

They drove home as dusk started to fall, when the red of the traffic lights mixed with the red glow of the sunset. No running home this time. Elsa was asleep in her seat. Her head was on one side, and a stream of dribble hung down from her mouth and onto her jumper. Angela drove fast and well, better than he did. He relaxed into his seat. His body was warm from the sun and salt, dry, his skin stiff in a pleasant way.

It was quiet in Vasastan, but not deserted. There were lots of people sitting at the pavement cafés.

Angela parked in the basement garage. Elsa was still asleep when they put her into her pushchair.

'Let's have a beer,' Winter said.

They sat in the nearest pavement café with an empty table and ordered two glasses of draught beer. There was a smell of cooking, and of heat from the day wafting along between the high stone buildings.

'Are you hungry?' he asked.

Angela shook her head.

'Well I am,' he said and ordered a grilled salmon steak. Angela changed her mind. The food was served, they ate, and Elsa slept in her pushchair next to the table. There were several parents there with children asleep in their prams. Three teenage girls walked past and started laughing when one of them said something into her mobile; Winter thought of his three girls, at that very moment, and for the first time that's exactly how he thought of them, *his three girls*, and he pushed his plate away and ordered another beer when the waiter came by; he glanced at Angela, but she didn't want any more.

'I'm driving out to Påvelund tomorrow morning,' he said. 'To the Wägners'.'

She didn't react, adjusted something next to Elsa's face. Several more teenage girls walked past.

By 10.00 the next morning he was with Bengt and Lisen Wägner. It was Saturday.

'I apologise.'

'For God's sake, don't do that,' said Bengt Wägner. 'You can come and live here if that's what it takes to find out what happened to Beatrice.'

'Who,' said Lisen Wägner. '*Who* happened to Beatrice.'

'Yes,' said the man, looking at his wife. '*Who* did it.'

They ushered him into her room. The morning sun was filtering through the venetian blinds. There was no need to turn on the light.

'I want to look at all the photos you have of Beatrice,' Winter said. He saw Lisen Wägner give a start, a slight but nevertheless obvious reaction. 'I'm sorry, I didn't put that very well. I mean the ones taken during that last year.' Oh, God. The woman looked even more worried. How should he word it, in order not to put his foot in it? Whatever he said turned out to be wrong.

'Why?' Bengt Wägner asked.

'I don't really know.' He turned to look at the man. 'I'm looking for something. So that I can compare. A particular place.'

'You looked at everything when . . . when it happened,' said Lisen Wägner. 'You took nearly everything away and went through it. All the photos as well.'

'I know.'

'Why didn't you find anything then?'

Winter stretched out his arms.

'If you didn't know what it was then . . . why do you think you know now?'

Winter told them as much as he could.

'An exposed brick wall?' Bengt Wägner said. 'I can't think where that might be, but that doesn't mean Beatrice never went there, of course.'

'I didn't see all the photographs,' said Winter. 'And I don't remember anything like that either. But things can take on a greater significance in the light of new events.'

'Here's a boxful anyway,' said Lisen Wägner, who'd fetched the photos from the dressing room at the other end of Beatrice's bedroom.

* * *

138

Winter sorted through the photos in the same way as he'd done in Angelika Hansson's room. Spring, summer, autumn, winter. Outside, inside.

Lisen Wägner came in with coffee and a warm Danish pastry smelling of vanilla. Winter adjusted the blinds as the sun moved, and it grew darker in the room. He could see Bengt Wägner through the window.

Eventually he'd picked out five pictures in which Beatrice was sitting in something that could have been a restaurant or a pub, whether outside or inside. There was no sign of an exposed brick wall, nothing that resembled the backdrop in Angelika's pictures. One of her parents was in three of the photos, and both of them in one of the others.

He looked out of the window and saw Bengt Wägner still hovering around the flower beds with his secateurs. Winter went out and showed Wägner the photographs. He recognised the location immediately. She often went there.

'Are there any more photos?' Winter asked.

'I have no idea.'

'Is it possible that she might have kept any photos somewhere else?'

Wägner seemed to be thinking that over. He put his secateurs down on the lawn. Lisen came out to join them, and Winter put the same question to her.

'As a bookmark,' she said.

'Yes, of course,' said her husband.

'She sometimes used a photograph as a bookmark,' said Lisen Wägner. 'That was something she'd done ever since she was a little girl.'

What books? Winter thought. There were about four or five shelves of books in her room, and maybe thirty more in the living room.

Winter went back to Beatrice's room and started going through the books one by one. After half an hour Bengt Wägner came and asked if Winter would like to stay for lunch. He said he would.

He had a metre of books to go when he got back to work. He opened every one, but found nothing.

'There are some in the attic as well,' said Bengt Wägner. 'Children's books. A box full of them.'

'Could you fetch them, please?'

Wägner disappeared, then came back with an oblong box. Winter looked through the books; stories about young boys and girls. There was also a series of books with green covers for young adults. In the third book from the top was an envelope glued to the inside of the front cover. He looked at Bengt Wägner, who shook his head.

'Never seen it before.'

'When did this go up into the loft?'

'I don't know.'

'Who took it up?'

'Beatrice.'

'When?'

'A long time ago, Erik.' Wägner looked out of the window at the shadows under the trees. 'It's a long time since she died.' He turned back to look at Winter. 'It might have been that same . . . summer. After she left school.' He looked back at the shadows outside. 'As if something had come to an end. She'd kept masses of stuff from the time when she was . . . growing up. And then that was all . . . in the past.' The sun was shining in from the left and reflected in Wägner's eyes, full of tears. 'Time for something new,' he said, still gazing out of the window.

Winter carefully cut open the envelope. Without touching it with his fingers, he tipped the contents into the plastic bag he'd put on the desk.

There were two photographs.

Winter recognised the location immediately. Beatrice was sitting at a table with plates and glasses in front of an exposed brick wall. There was a shadow up to the left. It was the same place, the same camera angle. A different young woman, though.

'Don't show this to Lisen,' Bengt Wägner said.

'Have you ever seen this photo before?'

'No. And promise you won't show it to Lisen,' he said again.

'I might have to.'

'OK. But wait a bit.'

'Do you recognise where this might have been taken?'

'No.'

'Not even somewhere that could be a little bit similar? Vaguely familiar?'

'That wall is pretty distinctive. I'd have remembered if I'd ever been there. Wherever it is.'

'Angelika Hansson, the most recent victim, had been there as well.'

'Really?'

'I have a photograph. Same camera angle. Same lighting. Same wall.'

'Let me have a look.'

Winter produced the photographs of Angelika. There was no doubt. No doubt at all.

'Good Lord,' said Wägner. 'What does this mean?'

'I don't know yet.'

'You'll have to find this place.'

'Yes.'

'I hope it's here in Gothenburg.' Wägner looked at

Winter. 'I mean, she did go on a few package holidays with friends.'

'I know.'

'Maybe the other girl did as well. Angelika.'

'Yes.'

'So it might be there,' said Wägner. 'Cyprus, or Rhodes.'

'We'll see.'

'Why had she hidden the envelope?'

'Is that how you see it? That it was hidden?'

'That's what it looks like, yes.'

'But she hadn't thrown the pictures away.'

'Why should she want to do that?' Wägner said.

'I don't know either.'

'Can there really be a link between this and . . . the girls, I mean. . . with . . . their deaths?'

'That's what I'm trying to find out,' said Winter. 'Or trying to exclude.'

'So you'll be looking for this place?' said Wägner.

'And the photographer,' said Winter.

'I don't think they knew each other,' said Wägner. 'Beatrice and . . . Angela.'

'Angelika.'

'I don't think they knew each other. Beatrice would have mentioned her.' He looked at the photograph of Angelika sitting in front of the brick wall. 'I'd have recognised her if I'd seen her before. There aren't very many black girls in Påvelund.' He looked again at the picture of Beatrice. 'It seems to be a nice place. She looks like she's having fun, at least.'

'Do you think you can say when this picture was taken?'

'Not off the top of my head.'

'Roughly.'

142

'She looks just like she did . . . towards the end.'
Wägner turned to face Winter with a pained expression
on his face. His voice sounded thick. 'Did you hear what
I just said, Inspector? *She looks just like she did.* It's a
good job Lisen isn't here.'

Winter said nothing. Wägner's voice returned to
normal.

'It could have been newly taken, if you see what I
mean.' He looked at Winter again. 'I think we'd better
talk to Lisen after all. She's better than I am at . . .
details.'

15

'I recognise the dress,' Lisen Wägner said. Her face was heavy with sorrow as she studied the photographs. 'She bought it a few weeks before . . . it happened.'

'Are you sure about that?' her husband asked.

'Yes.'

'Two weeks before?' asked Winter.

'About that.' She seemed to feel the doubt coming from both men. 'I can't forget it.' She looked at her husband. 'I've thought about it a lot. About that dress.' She looked at Winter. 'As if it were the last. Her last.'

'It's several years ago,' said Bengt Wägner.

'That makes no difference.'

'In that case she must have collected the pho—'

Winter was interrupted by Lisen Wägner: 'Just before she was murdered.'

Winter gazed at the window, avoided her eye. He didn't want to use that word in there.

'There's a date on the back,' said Bengt Wägner. He sounded surprised as he eyed the white surface.

Winter had seen the date. Beatrice had collected the photographs the week before she died. If her mother remembered correctly, then, these photos can't have been taken more than a few days beforehand. But she must have had a full roll. There must be more pictures from that roll.

'Where do you usually have your films developed?' he asked.

'The photo shop at Mariaplan.'

'Beatrice as well?'

'I suppose so,' Bengt Wägner said.

Lisen Wägner had sat down. Her tan was fading. Winter could see the daughter's features in the mother's face.

Winter looked at the photograph in his hand. Beatrice had been in a room where there was an exposed brick wall and tables and crockery. Probably a bar, or a restaurant.

She had been there a few days before she was murdered. She had saved the occasion as a secret souvenir. Why?

Angelika Hansson had also been there. It must be the same place. When had Angelika been there? There was no date on her photograph. It must have been developed in another shop. Winter pictures. Not . . . hidden away. But it was the same background, the same place. He had found a link.

*

Winter sat in his office. It was still Saturday, still hot. Bergenhem was sitting opposite him, browner than before. Looking even stronger.

'So, she saw Angelika with a young man several times,' said Winter as he read the document. 'Cecilia, her friend.'

'Twice,' said Bergenhem. 'Once at a café and once from a tram.'

'And he still hasn't contacted the police,' muttered Winter to himself.

'No. She's been shown a few pictures but that hasn't

helped.' Bergenhem started rolling up his shirtsleeves. 'I expect the lad must be abroad.' He'd finished with his sleeves. 'Otherwise he'd have seen our appeals.'

Perhaps he's dead, Winter thought. He knew Halders had wondered the same thing.

They needed a name and a face. Cecilia had tried to describe him. He was roughly the same age as Angelika. 'He looked sort of pale. Dark, but pale. Kind of Southern-European looking.' Winter picked up the photographs from the graduation party he'd found at the Hanssons'.

There had been four people whom Lars-Olof Hansson didn't recognise. Three were men and one was a woman. Though one of the three men looked more Angelika's age.

He looked sort of pale.

Winter had felt his flesh creep when he first set eyes on the figure in the picture, and he felt it again now.

Something was happening.

He showed Bergenhem the photograph.

'I'll phone her straight away,' Bergenhem said, and did so.

'That's him,' said Cecilia. She was wearing a thin blouse and khaki shorts, and had brought the sweet scent of sun cream with her into Winter's office from the rocks she'd left when Bergenhem called her on her mobile. Her hair was stiff from the salt water and the wind. 'That's him,' she said again.

'Take your time,' said Winter.

'I don't need to.'

'There's no rush.'

'I've seen enough. There's no doubt. One hundred

per cent certain.' She studied the photograph, the location, the balloons, as if she were looking for her own face. 'I was there myself, but I'm not in this picture.'

'You didn't see him at the party?'

'No.' She looked at the picture again. 'He looks a bit like that older bloke.' She looked at Winter. 'They could be father and son.' She turned to the photo again. 'I ought to have recognised him.'

Winter said nothing.

'Do you know *him* then?' asked Bergenhem. 'The one who might be his father, the older man? Or anybody else in the picture?'

'Er . . . I don't know.' She was still looking. 'I really don't know. Some faces are pretty familiar . . . and I've known some of them for ages. But I don't remember those two.'

'What about her?' asked Winter, pointing to the woman on the edge of the frame, as if about to leave it.

'No.'

'This fair-haired man, then? With the beard.'

'No, 'fraid not.'

They were strangers to Cecilia, just as they had been to Angelika's father.

They turned up afterwards, Lars-Olof Hansson had said. *Don't you understand? They turned up later! Nobody saw them . . . But they came with a message. A message from Hell!*

Good God.

'But I do recognise the boy,' Cecilia said.

'It was him both times? At the café and when you were on the tram?'

'Yes. Definitely him.'

'And you spoke to him?'

147

'We only said hi.'

'Nothing else?'

'No.' She looked again at the photo. 'This is awful,' she said. 'He was at the party.' She nodded at the photo. 'Why didn't I see him?'

'What did Angelika say about him?'

'I've already said to him over there that she didn't want to talk about it,' she said, indicating Bergenhem.

'She must have said something.'

'Only that she had no desire to talk about it.' She turned to Winter again. 'But I still don't understand why I didn't see him there, at the party.'

'But you'd seen them together before the party,' Winter said.

'Yes . . . at least, I think so.'

'You said a moment ago that you ought to have recognised him at the party. In that case you must have seen him beforehand, surely?'

'Yes . . . that's true.'

'Tell us again when it might have been. At the café and from the tram.'

She thought again. Yes. It must have been beforehand. In the spring. Late spring, May. May both times. That was what she'd told him over there.

Winter thought. He tried to picture this girl at the graduation party. What might she have done there? Apart from watching and celebrating with her friends?

'Have you any pictures of your own from that day?' he asked, nodding at the photo.

'Er . . . yes, I do actually.'

'Can you fetch them?'

'What, now?'

'Yes.'

'I don't know . . .'

'You'll be taken home by car to get them.' Winter had stood up. 'We'd really appreciate it.'

An hour later Cecilia was back with a brightly coloured envelope. He noticed she'd got changed and done something to her hair.

Winter took out the photos taken at the graduation party and laid them on his desk, which was only just big enough.

It was the same occasion. Possibly also the same time. But a different angle. Whereas Lars-Olof Hansson had taken his pictures from straight in front of his daughter, Cecilia had taken them from the side. From Lars-Olof Hansson's left.

There were several people in the way.

He couldn't see the boy, nor the man who might have been the boy's father. Nor could he see the man with the beard and glasses.

But he could see the woman. The woman who was on her way out of the picture. Winter produced Hansson's photo and looked at the woman standing on the left of the frame, then at Cecilia's picture, and there she was, taken from in front. As if she'd left one photograph and walked into the other.

He showed Cecilia. 'There's the woman, in your picture.'

'God, you're right. I don't remember her. Not taking a picture of her.' She looked at Angelika's pictures, and then at her own. Winter and Bergenhem waited. She looked up. 'But . . . shouldn't we be able to see at least a little bit of . . . the others, in my photos as well?'

'If the pictures were taken at the same time,' Winter said.

'But she's in the shot. So it must be the same time. The same minute, surely?'

Winter said nothing.

'This is spooky,' said Cecilia. 'It's like . . . ghosts.'

They turned up later!

'But the boy's real,' said Winter. 'You've seen him in town twice, with Angelika.'

'But not here. Why didn't I notice him here?'

Winter didn't reply, nor did Bergenhem. There was no answer they could give at the moment. Winter felt his flesh creep again.

'There's something else I want to show you,' he said.

Cecilia looked hard at the brick wall.

'No, I don't recognise the place.'

'Take your time.'

'That wall is quite unusual. I think I'd have noticed if it was in a bar I'd been to.'

'But you recognise her?'

'Are you kidding? That's Angelika.'

'Do you recognise anything she's wearing?'

Cecilia studied the picture of her friend.

'Those are winter clothes,' she said. 'I mean, she's wearing the kind of clothes you wear indoors in winter.'

Winter nodded.

'I think I bought her that cardigan last year.'

'When exactly?'

'Last winter.'

'When, exactly?'

'I think it was after New Year. Yes. After New Year.'

'This year, in other words?'

'Eh? Yes, it must have been, then.'

Bergenhem was making notes.

'How often did you go out together?' Winter asked. 'You and Angelika?'

'Quite a lot.'

'What does that mean? In terms of frequency?'

'I don't kn . . . Why are you asking me that?'

'How close were you?'

She paused to think before answering. She looked again at the picture of Angelika at the table in front of the brick wall.

'Angelika was a bit . . . private that way. She never said very much about what she got up to . . . on her own.'

Winter waited.

'Like with that guy. She just refused to talk about it.'

'What about this place?' Winter gestured towards the photo she was still holding.

'I don't know.' She looked at Winter. 'I mean, if she went somewhere when I wasn't with her she's hardly likely to come and describe the decor to me afterwards! It doesn't have to be a secret just because she didn't tell me about it.'

'Who said anything about it being a secret?'

'It seems like that. Like all this is about secrets.'

'But isn't it normal to chat to one another about places you've been to?'

'I suppose so . . . Yes.'

'Why didn't she say anything about this place, then?'

'Well, she might have done,' said Cecilia. 'That's what I mean. She wouldn't necessarily say there was a brick wall there though, or anything like that.' She looked at the picture again. 'Who knows, I might have been there myself. Maybe in a different room.'

'Would you be able to make a list of all the places

in Gothenburg you and Angelika went to, and others that you knew about?'

'All you need to do is read the Gothenburg Entertainment Guide.'

'Did you go out that much?'

'No, no. But all the places we went to would be in there.'

'So you should be able to point them out for us now then.'

Bergenhem had left. Winter reached for his packet of Corps on the shelf next to the washbasin, and found that it was empty. He needed a smoke. An excellent excuse to leave, buy some more, and then go home before Elsa went to bed.

It was a pleasant evening. He walked by the water. There wasn't much traffic near the railway station. A lot of people were sitting outside Eggers. A group with suitcases came out of the hotel and walked towards the station. Winter thought he could see the envy in their eyes as they glanced furtively at the pavement café. Travelling on a night like this when they could be sitting out there. He waved to some colleagues who were getting into a police van outside Femman. They drove off, with a flash of the headlights.

Gone. He had some of the photographs in his inside pocket, and pictured them in his mind's eye, saw the faces of the four people that nobody had recognised, who were there but not there. Gone. Apart from the woman. She had been there in both versions.

The boy had been there, at least in Angelika's pictures. They'd made an appeal for him to come forward immediately after they'd first spoken to Cecilia. But now they had a picture of him, his face would soon be displayed everywhere. Bergenhem had gone to take care of that.

Winter walked across Brunnsparken and came to his tobacconist's in the arcade.

'I'm sorry,' the woman in the shop said. 'I did warn you, but I didn't know myself that the time had come.'

'The time had come?'

'They're not importing Corps any more. We can't get them at all.'

'What!' Winter felt his mouth go dry. A tingling in his chin. He swallowed. He felt bad. 'You can't get them at all?'

'I was just about to put aside the last packet yesterday but a customer came in and, as I had it in my hand, I couldn't very well claim I hadn't any and hide it under the counter for you.'

'I suppose not.'

'Well, I couldn't, could I?'

'No, of course not,' said Winter. 'Thanks for the thought anyway.'

'You could take it up with Swedish Match.'

Winter tried to smile.

'I phoned around the other tobacconists in town, but nobody has any left,' she said. 'Haven't had any for ages, they said. We were the only ones still selling them, and you were the only customer who still asked for them. Apart from that man yesterday.'

Another victim, Winter thought. He felt he'd been taken by surprise, more than that. Mustn't panic.

He'd been thinking about giving up. This was his opportunity. Divine intervention. A favour. Fate had done him a favour. The tobacco distributor. Everybody was working together to safeguard his health. His family needed him, his child needed him. Now was the moment to choose a life free of poison.

He suddenly felt desperate for a smoke, absolutely bloody desperate.

'There are other brands, you know, Inspector,' said the woman, turning to the well-stocked shelves behind her.

'I've been smoking Corps for fifteen years,' said Winter. 'No other brand.' He hoped he didn't sound as if he were about to burst into tears.

'But there are others.'

'Not for me,' said Winter, and bade her farewell. Now he needed to concentrate on getting home in one piece and discussing what to do next with Angela. She was a doctor. He needed some of those nicotine patches. Nicotine gum. Morphine.

The sun was behind a cloud. It was shining from a clear sky for everybody else, but everything was black for him.

There were other things. Corps weren't everything. He could give up. He was weak, but other weak people had managed to give up.

As he walked across the market square he felt a pain in his chest. He had just lost a friend.

16

Anne arrived at the club three minutes after midnight. She recognised a few faces in the bar, all of them looking somewhere else – possibly towards the brick wall in the other room. You could see it from one side of the bar counter.

The music surged through the room, like hawking, she thought, something nasty forcing its way up through your throat. Not something to lie back and enjoy, but the punters who come here didn't think like that. Their faces were white and green and violet in the glow from the ceiling lights.

He came out of the office near the bar.

'We wondered where you'd got to,' he said.

'I'm here now.'

'You haven't really got fed up, have you?'

'Yes.'

She waited before saying it. Waited. Said it.

'Why don't you say anything about Angelika?'

'What do you mean?'

'You haven't said a word about Angelika since . . . it happened.'

'What am I supposed to say?'

'Surely it would be natural to say something?'

'I let other people do the talking.'

'But this is your place, isn't it?'

'What are you getting at, Anne?'

'Don't you understand?'

'I assume you know I had nothing to do with it.'

'If you had I wouldn't be here now. If I thought you had.'

'But that doesn't mean that I don't care.'

'Mourn?'

'Yes. Mourn. Of course. She was one of us.'

'One of us?'

'You're on. Go.'

She could see that the door next to the stage was ajar. The stage, oh yes. He nodded in that direction. She turned round. One of the faces at the bar seemed familiar.

'Oh no. Not him again.'

'Does it matter?'

'All you think about is your regular "customers", or whatever I'm supposed to call them.'

'Well. He's been coming here for a long time.'

'You're not the one performing in there. You don't know what it feels like.'

'You don't need to be afraid you know.'

'It's easy for you to say that. But anyway, that's not it.'

'What is it, then?'

'I can't explain it.'

'Just close your eyes.'

She might have laughed as she walked towards the door. The face seemed to move from the bar, big and white and horrible. She entered the dressing room before the face came too near. She got herself ready and went out into the cage, closed her eyes and moved in time with the music from the loudspeaker. It was a different tune now.

*

It was raining. Ringmar had shut the window, but after five minutes it was too hot. He opened it again, and there was soon a little pool on the floor under the window. Winter could feel a bit of a breeze. Nice. He was chewing some awful-tasting nicotine gum. His headache had started half an hour after breakfast, exactly as Angela had predicted.

'How long do I have to put up with this?' he'd asked over coffee at breakfast.

'Until you've driven the devil out of your body.'

'He's been in there for a long time.'

'You'll make it, Erik.'

'There are other brands.'

'This is your opportunity. Destiny has finally given you a chance,' she'd said.

'Swedish Match, more like,' he'd replied.

He put another lump of chewing gum in his mouth, chewed, then spat it out again. Images were flitting through his mind. Another investigation, another set of pictures being circulated around the team. Pictures of dead bodies, body parts. Children. Children's drawings. Houses. Cars. Trees. Rocks. Sea. Forest clearings. Several bodies. Dead faces: swollen, shot away, mashed. Year after year. No end to it.

Brick walls. Graduation parties. Living faces that would be dead within a few weeks. They had some sort of key, but what was it? A skeleton key that didn't fit any lock. This had happened, but why and how and when and who and . . . ?

'Unlicensed clubs,' said Halders. He was back at

work, three days after the funeral. He looked leaner, thinner. No badinage, no jokes. A new man. No oral wrestling with Aneta Djanali who was sitting a couple of chairs away. Winter wondered if she might miss that. Maybe they'd all miss the old Halders? He would never return.

'This reeks of unlicensed clubs,' said Halders, looking at the slide currently on the screen. Möllerström had drawn the blinds and started the projector. First Beatrice. Then Angelika. The same wall.

'We'll have to check everything,' said Ringmar.

'There are people who keep an eye on restaurants,' said Bergenhem. 'Check up on pubs and bars. Health and Safety folk. And the Fire Brigade, I assume.'

'Yep,' said Winter. 'Follow that up. Bring in the uniforms as well.'

'Of course.'

'Report back with this location.'

'I'll find it.'

'Unlicensed clubs are springing up like mushrooms wherever you look, all the time,' said Halders. 'You cut one out, and two new ones grow to replace it.'

'Not this one,' said Winter. 'Always assuming it is an unlicensed club.' He turned to look at the slide, with Beatrice and the wall behind her. 'This picture was taken at least five years ago. It seems to be the same place.'

'The wall in the background looks the same,' Halders said. 'But we don't know that for sure. It could be a different one, couldn't it?' He looked round.

'I'll find it,' said Bergenhem, turning to look at Halders.

* * *

They were in Winter's office. Winter was pacing back and forth between the window and his desk. Ringmar was just sitting there.

'You seem to be a bit on edge,' he said.

'Can you see any cigarillos in here?'

'I can't, to be honest.'

'There's your explanation.'

'Have you tried patches?'

Winter pulled up his shirt and displayed his stomach.

'Chewing gum?'

Winter opened his mouth.

'Exercise?'

'No time.'

'Work?'

'Yes.' He sat down. 'Who was pointing that camera?'

'Do you think it's the same person? The same photographer?' Ringmar asked.

'We don't get that kind of luck.'

'I take it that it was her own camera? Beatrice's. I assume the pictures were taken with her camera?'

'We're checking with a photography specialist. They might even be able to tell us the make of camera.'

'Sounds difficult.'

'And then?'

'Who was pointing it,' Ringmar said.

'Perhaps they were just taking pictures of each other,' said Winter.

'Everybody says they didn't know each other.'

'But they might have done.'

He'd shown the photo of Beatrice to Cecilia, Angelika's friend. She hadn't recognised her. Never seen her before.

'I don't claim to be an expert, but these pictures give the impression of having been taken by an amateur,' said Ringmar.

They looked at each other. They knew there was no camera at Angelika's place. She'd had one, but they hadn't found it. They didn't know which lab had developed the pictures.

Beatrice's camera was still at her parents' house. In all probability the pictures they'd found there had been taken with that camera. They had the pictures and they had the camera.

But who had taken the picture of Beatrice? Who had pointed her camera? Who had taken the picture of Angelika? Who had pointed the camera? What camera was it that time?

*

Halders and Djanali went to see the Bielkes again. The father looked disapproving, but let them in. Jeanette came downstairs and they went out into the garden. Halders was in his shirtsleeves, Djanali was wearing a thin blouse. Jeanette looked as if she were freezing.

She examined the photographs Djanali handed her. The wall behind Angelika, the same wall behind Beatrice.

'I recognise the black girl, but she's been in all the papers,' she said. '*Is* in, come to that. They're still writing quite a lot about it.'

Halders nodded.

'Why are you showing me these?'

'Because you might be able to help us find that club they're at, or whatever it is.' Halders took back one of the pictures. 'We don't go out clubbing every night.'

'Really? I thought you knew all about the clubs and pubs in Gothenburg.'

'Not this one. We're looking, but we haven't found it yet.'

'Keep looking,' she said.

'That wall's quite an unusual feature.'

'Never seen it before.'

'Have you ever been to an unlicensed club, Jeanette?'

'Eh?' She looked at Djanali, who had asked the question. 'What did you say?'

'An unlicensed club. There are lots of them in Gothenburg. Have you ever been to one?'

'No.'

'But you've heard about places like that?'

'Yes.'

'From whom?'

'How do you mean?'

'How have you heard about them?'

'I can read. They write about such places.'

'Do you know anybody who's been to one?' Djanali asked.

'No.'

'Do you know anybody who's spoken about them?'

'No.'

'You've only read about them.'

'Yes.'

'Do you know any names?' asked Halders.

'How would I know that?'

'The night you were attacked. You hadn't been to one of those places?'

'What is all this?' she said. 'How long are you going to keep on at me?'

'I'll be absolutely honest with you, Jeanette.' Halders gave her as stern a look as he could manage. 'Spell it out. The fact is that when somebody's been through something as awful as you have . . . they're frightened

161

of appearing in a bad light. After what happened. Some don't want to say they'd been drinking. Or gone off with somebody they shouldn't have gone with. Or been somewhere they shouldn't have been.'

'Such as an illegal club.'

'Yes.'

'But that doesn't apply to me. I wasn't there.'

Jeanette caught sight of a sparrow hopping over the lawn. The sun hit the sparrow and made it look like a little flame. It flew up and disappeared.

*

'Where is that bloody boy?' said Ringmar.

'Or his dad,' said Winter. 'If that *is* his father in the photo from the graduation party.'

'There's been a country-wide appeal,' said Ringmar. 'Somebody ought to have turned up by now.'

*

Anne did what she was required to do to the music, then returned to the dressing room. When she came out she noticed that face in the bar. It was looking at her with eyes she couldn't and didn't want to see. There was something insane about those eyes.

There were signs of light in the sky when she left the building, like thin fingers of cloud pointing in the direction she was going. She walked down the steps that smelled just as awful as they always did. There weren't many people in the street. The glow from the street lights blended with the night.

As she crossed the road she turned round and saw the man with the face coming down the steps. She speeded up and looked round again. He was no longer there.

Her mobile rang in her handbag.

'Where are you?'

'On my way,' she said. 'That was the last time.'

17

Anne ordered a beer. There were hanging baskets with flowers all round the pavement café. It was still hot, almost stifling. A black cloud loomed in the east. The birds were flying low.

'False alarm,' said Andy, following her gaze. 'It's not going to rain.'

'Not that I want it to,' she said.

'I wouldn't mind a drop. The crops could do with a soaking, as the farmers say.'

'Really?'

'Oh yes, they're always saying that.'

'It must be ten years since you last crossed the city boundary, Andy. Here comes my beer.'

Andy raised his glass.

'I've been longing for this,' she said.

'Was it so awful?'

'One more week, and then I'm packing it in.'

'You said when you phoned that this was your last show.'

'I'm packing it in next week.'

'Why haven't you stopped already?'

'You know why.'

'Money isn't everything,' he said, taking another drink. He looked up and saw that the swallows were flying higher now. The black cloud on the eastern horizon was sinking down.

'I needed some at the time.'

'Money tends to create a need for more,' he said.

'It's not all that much.'

'Enough.'

'It's not the way you think,' she said. 'I don't *need* the money any more. Not in that way. Not because of that.'

'And then, I suppose earning it isn't as easy as you thought.'

'No.'

'Did you really think it would be?'

She shrugged. 'I can close my eyes.'

'Not all the time. You have to look sometimes or you'll lose your balance.'

'He was there again last night,' she said after a short pause.

'Relax.'

'He has this . . . look.'

'Don't they all?'

'He's so bloody scary, Andy.'

'Aren't they all?'

She took another sip of beer and waited for a group to edge their way past to the big table behind them.

'He frightens me.'

'That's no doubt a good thing.'

'It's as if he . . . knows something. As if he wants to say something.'

'What?'

'He smiles sometimes, as if he knows something. As if he knows that I know.'

'Know? Know what?'

He looked at her and waited. The newly arrived

group started singing. One of them looked proud, perhaps slightly embarrassed.

'Andy, I haven't said anything about this.'

'About what? Now you've lost me completely.'

'The girl that was murdered. Raped and murdered. Angelika. Angelika Hansson.'

'I know about that. You can't miss it the moment you pick up a newspaper.'

'I knew her . . . From the club,' Anne said.

'From the club? Was she a dancer?'

'No. She worked behind the bar.'

'When . . . when it happened? I mean, was she working there when it happened? That same night?'

'I think so. I saw her the day before.'

'And?'

'What do you mean?'

'What conclusion have you drawn from that?'

'I'd rather not.'

'That there's a link between the club and what happened to her?'

'I don't want to think like that.'

'Why should it be linked to the club?'

'It's just what I think.'

'It has nothing to do with the club,' Andy said. 'Why should it have? It's a coincidence.'

'Yes,' she said, and in her mind's eye she saw that face. That smile.

*

'Do you feel sorry for me?' Halders asked.

'What sort of a question is that?' Djanali said.

'You're answering a question with another question.'

'It's hard to talk about things such as people needing pity.'

'I don't need pity,' said Halders. 'Not like that. It's a catastrophe but it's twice as bad for the kids. Twenty times as bad. A thousand times.'

'It affects all of you,' Djanali said.

'It's worse for them.'

They were sitting on the patio outside the house where Halders' children had always lived, and would continue to live if he had anything to do with it, and he intended making sure he did.

Hannes and Magda were asleep. He'd just been with them. Hannes had mumbled something in his sleep. Then Magda had said something as well. It was as if the children were talking to each other.

Djanali stood up.

'Time I was off home.'

He nodded.

'Will you be all right?'

He nodded again.

'Are you sure?'

'I'll be all right.' Halders looked up at the sky that was growing dark in the east. An aeroplane on its way into the distance winked down at them. 'Tomorrow is another day, and all that stuff.'

'What are you going to do tomorrow?'

'Talk to the girl's boyfriend. Jeanette's.'

'Mattias. The one that was being awkward.'

'Yes. I wonder why.'

'Is it so odd? She wanted to finish with him.'

'It's not that. I've spoken to him. It was something else. There was something he wanted her to do but he wouldn't tell me what. Wouldn't tell us. Something he'd said to her.'

Djanali waited, standing there. A car passed by on the road behind the hedge. There was a crunching of gravel.

167

'There's something going on there . . . he was upset, but not just because she'd finished with him.' Halders looked at Djanali. 'Do you understand? It's something you sense.'

'Yes.'

Halders stood up.

'I'll go with you to the car.'

He bent down as she settled behind the wheel.

'Thank you for coming.'

'Go to bed now, Fredrik.'

He held her hand, let go as the car moved off.

*

Winter was in Beier's room. He could hear noises all around from the forensic officers: test shooting, vacuum cleaners, the sound of running water, the sound of clothes being removed from plastic bags, the rustling of paper, the sound of flash-guns.

Beier had just phoned.

'The boys in Linköping have done as much as they can.'

'Same attacker?'

'We don't think so, but it's not possible to be a hundred per cent sure.'

It had taken them two weeks to carry out the DNA analysis. Or rather, the pathologists concerned had decided it would take them two weeks. Not top priority, but not far off.

'Unfortunately, with the Bielke girl, they say there's not enough to go on.'

'Jeanette,' said Winter. 'What did they actually have?'

'Nothing, really.' Beier took a sip of the coffee he'd offered Winter as soon as he arrived. 'She had washed and scrubbed exceedingly efficiently.' He put his cup down and wiped his hand over his mouth. 'And Angelika wasn't raped. There was no trace of anything of the sort.'

'So, not the same bastard,' said Winter. 'Beatrice Wägner five years ago and Angelika Hansson now. Five years in between. Same place. Same . . . weapon.' He leaned forward. 'You can't say anything more about the belts? Nothing more concrete?'

'No. They were strangled, but I can't say precisely what was used.'

'Even so, this is a breakthrough of sorts,' said Winter. 'If you look at it that way. We eliminate possibilities and block out a few questions.'

'Yes.'

'The next step is the cameras.'

'I checked as soon as you mentioned it. You're right.'

It was not possible to say what camera had taken the picture of Angelika, not on the basis of the print, and a print was all they had. But there was a small dot on the photograph and Winter had noticed it and Beier's men had studied it more closely and it was probably due to damage on the lens.

'I compared it with other pictures that may have been taken with Angelika's camera, but there were no signs of that spot on them.'

'I'm with you.'

'We know that her camera is gone, but we can assume that it wasn't the one that took the picture in the bar, or wherever it is.'

'So now we know that.'

'We've checked the other girl's, Jeanette's, and there's no sign of damage on her camera lens either.'

Winter nodded.

'So somewhere out there is a camera that took the

picture of Angelika, and it has a damaged lens,' Winter said.

'Find that, and you may have found the murderer,' Beier said.

Neither man spoke. Winter could feel the sun on the back of his neck from the window behind him. He was no longer hungry.

'That button, by the way: it's a standard one you'll find on any shirt you buy from a chain,' Beier said.

The button Winter had found in the park was on Beier's desk with all the other things.

'I don't buy my shirts from a chain,' Winter said.

'I didn't mean you personally.'

'Ah.'

'I meant people who don't only buy designer shirts from Baldessarini.'

Beier himself was wearing a suit from Oskar Jakobson, white shirt and tie.

'It would have been easier if it had been a Baldessarini button,' said Winter.

'These are just some of the things we found at the scene,' said Beier, pointing at the objects spread out on his desk. 'How much of this belonged to the killer?'

'You tell me.'

'Nothing, so far as we know.'

'Hmm.'

'If I can get a decent set of fingerprints, I might be able to help.'

'You'll have to keep on looking.'

'We are looking, and looking.'

'One other thing,' said Winter. 'What do you say about the unidentified party guests?'

'I can't explain it,' said Beier. 'They are on the picture taken at the graduation party. The one Angelika

Hansson's father took. They were there. He might not be able to recognise them, but they were recorded on the film. So they were there.'

'Yes, that's the assumption we've generally worked on,' said Winter. 'Living people standing in front of a camera normally end up in the photograph.'

'Which they did,' said Beier.

'But not in Cecilia's photo of the same scene,' said Winter. 'A different angle but more or less the same scene.'

'One explanation is obvious,' Beier said. 'When Cecilia took her picture the other three had moved.'

'That had occurred to me,' said Winter.

'I hoped it might have,' said Beier with a smile.

'But when you compare the two photographs it's hard not to believe that they were taken at more or less the same moment.'

'A lot can happen in a second.'

'I suppose so.'

'How's the hunt for the bar going?' Beier asked.

'No nibbles yet.'

'It's bound to be an illicit joint.'

'No doubt.'

'Don't you know about them all?'

'We don't know what they all look like inside,' Winter said.

Beier stood up, went over to the window and pulled up the blinds. The room turned white.

'You ought to be worried about how difficult it is to find out exactly what those girls were doing the hour or so before they were attacked.'

'I am worried,' said Winter. 'I think they were at that bar or pub or whatever it is. They were there and they left and somebody else was there and went with them.

Or followed them.' He looked at Beier, who was a silhouette: black against white. 'When we find the place I'll be less worried.'

'Or more,' Beier said.

18

A male witness had said he'd heard screams coming from the park. It had been about 2 a.m., or closer to 2.30. Half an hour to an hour after Beatrice had last been seen, entering the park.

Winter read through the Wägner case notes, the same thing over and over again. Winter read the witness's account but nothing emerged from it, he could see no subtext; he read it all again and tried to find the secret hidden underneath, but couldn't see it.

Something had happened, though.

Beatrice's final hours. He'd started interviewing some of the old witnesses again, her old friends. It was so long ago. They tried to remember, just as he was doing now. They'd grown older, would be twenty-five soon. He'd spoken to four who'd been part of the group that last night. Two of them had kids now. Finished studying. A new life. One could still have passed for nineteen. One might pass for thirty. Where would Beatrice have been on that scale? What would she have looked like? I miss her, one of the women had said. I really miss her.

Winter compared what they'd said now with what they'd said before.

There was one thing that didn't match, not quite.

A blurred memory, perhaps, ravaged by time. But perhaps not.

That last night? Surely there's nothing else to add? He'd looked hard at Winter. Klas, an old friend of Beatrice. Finished his studies. Does he realise he's a survivor? Does he think about it? Winter had felt for his packet of cigarillos in his breast pocket, a reflex action. He'd felt reflex pain when he groped after the packet: a tumour attached to his chest that had been cut away. He'd been having a sore throat. Felt worse since he'd stopped smoking. A cold spreading all over his body, waiting. Set free when the nicotine no longer protected him. Who had protected Beatrice? That last night. There was something that didn't add up. Klas remembered it all differently now. Or they'd asked the questions differently then. Beatrice hadn't been with the rest of the gang for the whole of the evening. Yes, they'd met up. But . . . sort of, afterwards. Most of them had been for a meal, but she'd turned up later and then she left again and it had been a few hours before the rest of them went their different ways home.

Hang on. Winter thought back to what it said in the case notes. Hadn't they asked what had happened the *whole* of the evening?

'Were you not all together for the whole evening?'

'Not as I recall, no.'

'What was she doing when she was not with you, then?'

'Her own thing, I suppose.'

'What was her own thing?'

'I dunno.'

'Oh, come on!'

'I don't know.'

'What's the matter with you? Can't you see this is important?'

'Calm down, Inspector.'

'What was her own thing?'

'There was some place she used to go to, I think.'

'What place?'

'Somebody said something about her going to some place or other. A club. Surely I said that when . . . when it happened. When she was murdered.'

'No.'

'I suppose I didn't know for sure. She'd never said anything about it to me personally.'

'And?'

'I wasn't sure, as I said. I probably didn't say anything because I didn't know for sure.'

Winter looked hard at him.

'Who did know?'

'Nobody.'

'But somebody said something.'

'I don't know who it was. That's the truth. The truth!'

'You deserve a good beating.'

Winter had blurted that out because he felt completely . . . unprotected and on edge. The nicotine which used to act as an inner protection, a barrier, had gone. There were other brands. A good man doesn't become less good because he changes his habits.

Klas had stared at him.

'You what?'

'I'm sorry. But this is something you ought to have said earlier.'

'But it's only a little thing. And anyway, it's your job to . . . map out what she did.'

* * *

That's the problem. There are gaps. Winter returned to the text in front of him. The male witness. But before starting to read again he stood up and paced up and down the room for a bit, trying to subdue his craving for the poison. He switched on the kettle, made himself a cup of coffee, then sat down again.

The witness had heard screams. Winter read through the text for the tenth time. He'd been scared and rushed to get help. He'd met a couple aged about thirty-five, wearing white clothes. The couple had just walked through the park and the woman thought she had maybe seen somebody. According to the witness.

The police had never talked to that couple because they'd not come forward.

He thought about that again. Why had they not come forward?

A man and a boy had been packing a car next to the park that night, perhaps at the very time that it happened. They had never been tracked down. Why had they not come forward?

*

Winter drove to Lunden with his window down. He passed Halders' house, but that wasn't where he was going. Halders wasn't there. Halders was taking things a day at a time, an hour at a time. There was a hedge outside the house, about one and a half metres high. Winter could hear a dog barking.

He turned right about three streets after Halders' house and stopped outside another house with another hedge. There was a brand-new BMW parked in the street outside. The car gleamed in the sun. Winter could feel the sweat under his shirt collar and down his back. He went in through the open gate and turned left, continued down a sloping path made out of flagstones, round the house and into the back garden where the man he always referred to as the gangster was reclining on a lounger with a beer in his hand. The sun glittered on the surface of the swimming pool. The gangster watched him approach.

'You're wearing too many clothes,' he said, raising his beer by way of greeting.

'I'm at work.'

'I'm on holiday myself.'

'On holiday from what?'

'Sit down, Erik.'

Winter sat on the chair next to him.

'Would you like a beer?'

'Yes.'

Benny Vennerhag got up and disappeared into the house through the patio door and returned with a bottle of beer that felt cold in Winter's hand as he accepted it.

Vennerhag sat down again. Swimming trunks didn't suit him. He was an old acquaintance, if you could call it that. He'd been married to Winter's sister Lotta at one time. For a very short time.

What the hell had she seen in him?

'I heard about your murders.'

'They're not mine,' said Winter, taking a swig of beer.

'Not mine either. But I told you that when you phoned.'

'What about the other thing?'

'Illegal clubs? Not my field.'

'Isn't it strange how nothing I ever ask you about is your field, Benny?'

'What's strange about that?'

'How do you make ends meet when nothing is your field?'

'That's a business secret.'

'We know quite a bit about your secrets, Benny.'

'And nevertheless, here I am in my cozzie taking it easy,' said Vennerhag, gesturing towards the pool and the mosaic tiles and the fresh green lawn.

Winter took off his shirt and trousers.

'Here we go again,' said Vennerhag as Winter dived into the pool. It wasn't the first time he'd been swimming there.

Vennerhag stood up when Winter surfaced, walked to the side of the pool and handed over the bottle of beer. Water ran down Winter's face from his hair, which was plastered flat against his scalp.

'Illegal clubs are sensitive things,' Vennerhag said.

'What do you mean?'

'I'm not the type to spill the beans about that kind of thing. I think it's a legitimate activity that satisfies the needs of nice ordinary people.'

'Codswallop.'

'It would do you good to go to one of those places now and again, Erik.'

'What would do me good just now is a Corps,' said Winter, squinting up at the sun.

'Shall I get you one from your shirt pocket?'

'There aren't any there. I've given up.'

'That was rash of you.'

'They don't import them any more,' Winter said.

'There are other brands.'

'So I'm told.'

'Think about what your job entails.' Vennerhag made as if to protect himself. 'You don't want to be turning violent again and trying to strangle somebody or anything like that.'

It wouldn't have been the first time.

Winter heaved himself up onto the side of the pool.

'A place that was in business five years ago.'

'Hmm.'

'At least five years ago.'

'Why an illegal club? Have you checked out the rest of the pleasure places in town? The legal ones?'

'We are doing.'

'Have you brought the photos you were going on about?'

'Yes.'

'Can I see them?'

'All in good time.'

'Oh yes?'

'What have you got to say, Benny?'

'About unlicensed clubs five years ago?'

'That are still in business.'

'I don't think there are any.'

'Think? Or know?'

'Think. I think,' Vennerhag said, with a little laugh. He turned to look at Winter. 'I know what this is all about. I'm keen to help.'

'Good for you, Benny.'

'Murder isn't my field, you know.'

'I know.'

'Nor is rape.'

'Glad to hear it.'

'If we can put that bastard behind bars I'll be the first to start clapping.'

'We'll be the ones to put him behind bars. You're not involved in that.'

'I did say we.'

'I'll go and get the pictures,' said Winter.

*   *   *

'Nice wall,' said Vennerhag.

Winter nodded.

'The girls look nice. This is terrible.' He looked at Winter. 'Fucking terrible.'

Winter nodded again.

'I've never seen this place before,' said Vennerhag. 'It's unusual to have exposed brickwork like that indoors.'

'Find out what your business contacts have to say.'

'I'll need these photos for that.'

'You have them in your hand.'

'Are these my copies, then?'

'Yes.'

'Is that allowed?'

'Who cares?'

'OK,' said Vennerhag, putting the photographs down on the grass.

'How long will you need?' Winter asked.

'No idea. But if this place *is* in town, somebody ought to recognise it.'

'Good.'

'That wall is quite eye-catching.'

Winter nodded.

Vennerhag stood up and went back to his lounger. Winter went back to his chair as well, draining the last of his beer on the way.

'Another?'

Winter shook his head.

'A cigarillo?' asked Vennerhag, lighting a Mercator and grinning through the smoke.

Winter shook his head. Then leaned forward, took hold of the packet in Vennerhag's hand and picked up the lighter from the ground next to Vennerhag's big, pale left foot.

'You're shaking,' said Vennerhag as Winter lit the cigarillo.

He inhaled and savoured it.

'You're just as bad as us others,' said Vennerhag.

'You mean we. Not us.'

'Oh, it's we now, is it? It was different a minute ago.'

Winter said nothing, simply inhaled and made the most of the effects of the poison. Just this one, to remind me of how awful it is to be addicted.

Vennerhag watched him.

'Have the activities of unlicensed clubs changed over the last few years?' Winter asked after a while.

'Dunno. Not my field, like I said.'

Winter took another puff, and watched the smoke climb up towards the blue sky. Not a cloud in sight, not a single one. The sun was more white than yellow. Later it would turn orange, and the sky as well. That meant that the sun would rise again tomorrow and the sky would be blue again and there wouldn't be a cloud in sight.

'What do you mean by that, anyway?' said Vennerhag, turning to look at Winter again.

'Just something that crossed my mind. If they've taken over from the sex clubs, for instance.'

'Well, that's even further from my—'

'Not your field. Yes, I know.'

'Could be, though.'

'Hmm.'

Vennerhag puffed at his Mercator.

'Now that you mention it, it occurs to me there might well have been a few places with . . . er . . . that sort of menu over the last few years.'

'Menu? You mean sex?'

'I mean adult entertainment.'

'I see.'

'A few places, mebbe. I'll have to check.'

'I'll phone you this afternoon.'

'Tonight. Make it tonight.'

Vennerhag reached for the photographs again and took another look, one at a time.

'So, you reckon this is some little club, operating on the sly, is that it?'

'I reckon that's it, yes.'

'In that case, what were these little girls doing there?'

'Working.'

'Working? You've got a worse imagination than me, Erik.'

'Imagination's not your field, Benny.'

'You're a pessimistic bastard.' He looked back at the photographs, then at Winter. 'As for me, I think the best of everybody.'

'Maybe those girls did as well,' said Winter, nodding at the photographs in Vennerhag's right hand.

'And that's why they were working at an illegal club with extra-illegal activities in the form of . . . extra services.'

'I don't know.'

'You're on the wrong track.'

'Then help me to get back onto the right one,' said Winter, standing up and putting his shirt back on.

19

Halders met the boy at a location chosen by the boy himself. There was a splash of sun across the rocks. The sails out there where white. The sea beyond the harbour sunk down into blackness. Halders felt as if he were operating on automatic pilot. He'd hugged his children when they went to school, and waved to them from the car. Magda had played hopscotch, just the once, then disappeared into the school building.

Mattias squinted up at the sun. Halders aped him.

'Day after day,' he said.

Mattias watched a yacht heading for the open sea, and turned to Halders.

'A record summer,' he said. 'A fantastic summer.'

Halders raised the peak of his cap a whisker and scratched his forehead, which was roasting despite the protection.

'What are you making of all this?' Halders asked.

'The summer, you mean? I'm working, but I told you that.'

'Apart from that.'

'Nothing.'

'But it's a fantastic summer.'

'Not as far as I'm concerned.'

'Fed up?'

'Eh?'

'Are you feeling depressed, Mattias?'

'What are you on about?'

'You seem depressed.'

'You don't seem all that cheerful yourself.'

'That's true.'

'Are you?'

'No.'

'Well then.'

'Have you spoken to her again?' Halders asked.

'Not since the last time,' said Mattias, and seemed to be smiling at his answer.

'You know what I'm getting at.'

'Not since the rape,' Mattias said. 'Not with him there.'

'Him? Who are you talking about?'

'You mean you don't know?'

'Tell me. Who?'

'Her father,' Mattias said, gazing out at the horizon where several ships were falling over the edge.

'I gather you don't like him.'

The boy mumbled something, and stared out to sea. His nose was peeling. His hair is like straw, Halders thought. There was a time one summer when my hair was like that. He ran his hand over what remained of his close-cropped hair. He could see Jeanette Bielke's father in his mind's eye. Kurt Bielke. A comfortable chair on the verandah. Jeanette was never there. Jeanette was usually in her room, occasionally in the garden. Never on the verandah.

'I didn't hear what you said.'

'It's true that I don't like him,' Mattias said.

'Why not?'

'Ask Jeanette.'

'I'm asking you.'

The boy shrugged.

'I'm asking you,' Halders said again.

'Does it matter?'

'Yes.'

'So you think he's a bucket of shit too, eh?'

'Tell me why you think he's a bucket of shit.'

'I don't just think.'

'Tell me, Mattias.'

'Ask Jeanette. Again.'

'Why do you keep saying that I should ask Jeanette?'

'Don't you see?'

'What are you trying to tell me, Mattias?'

The boy didn't reply. The sea looked even blacker. Halders closed his eyes.

'You were furious the last time you spoke to Jeanette,' he said.

'You don't say.'

'She'd finished with you.'

'So what?'

'So, you were furious with her because she'd dumped you.'

'You don't say.'

Halders grabbed the boy by his shirt collar.

'Don't try that crap with me, young man.'

'For Christ's sake . . .'

'I'll throw you into the sea, you little shit, if you don't help us with this case.'

'Help you how?'

Halders grabbed his collar more tightly. The boy could see the fury in his eyes.

'Jesus Christ, you're out of your mi—'

Halders tightened his grip even more, then suddenly let go and walked away.

* * *

Benny Vennerhag phoned that night. Elsa was asleep. Winter was out on the balcony. Angela watched him with a smile that could have been a bit on the sarcastic side. Winter was savouring the scent of tropical fruit and leather from the cigar he had in his hand, a Corona he'd bought along with several others on his way home an hour ago.

He came in from the balcony.

'I have a few names,' Vennerhag said.

'Let's hear them.'

Vennerhag named a couple of clubs.

'We've already been to those,' said Winter. 'There's no wall in either of them like the one in the photos.'

'That's the best I can do at the moment.'

'Well, thanks for nothing, in that case.'

'There's no need to be like that.'

'I thought you were more abreast of things than this, Benny.'

'Allow me to say the same about you.'

'I'm looking forward to our next little chat,' Winter said.

Vennerhag hung up without further comment. Angela shouted from the kitchen. He took a beer from the fridge: 'I think I'll shackle myself to the computer for a while.'

'I thought we could sit on the balcony for a few minutes,' she said.

'OK.'

The park was deserted. The sky was vast. The traffic down below seemed like sparks in all the blue. Sounds floated in on the wind. Winter lit his cigar again.

'So, you had no will-power?'

'I'm afraid not.'

'You don't seem unduly put out.'

'I've realised that I can't concentrate without nicotine.'

'So you feel better already.'

'Yes. Ideas are flowing.'

'You're imagining it.'

Winter inhaled again. The smoke drifted away.

'Could be. But I can't afford to risk it. This case. The girls.' He took another drag. 'There's somebody out there.' He gestured with the cigar. 'Down there.'

'There's always somebody out there,' Angela said. 'Always will be.'

'And I'll always be here,' he said with a smile. 'The story of my life. Somebody out there, and me in here.' He contemplated his cigar. 'And then I'll be on my way to get him.' He looked at her. 'A bit melodramatic, don't you think?'

'Before I met you I didn't used to think the police analysed themselves like that,' Angela said, taking a sip of beer. 'That they tried to . . . define their role.'

'Do you mean to say that you actually considered the way police officers' minds work before you met me?'

'No.' She took another sip. 'I suppose I thought they didn't think at all.'

'And then the penny dropped.'

'And then I found that my suspicions were confirmed!'

'And how did that feel?'

'Frightening.'

'Well, now you know.'

She nodded.

'That's why this is necessary,' he said, holding up his cigar. 'Something to help us summon up the little concentration we're still capable of calling on.'

*　*　*

'I nearly threw a young man into the sea today,' Halders said.

They were sitting on the patio. Hannes and Magda had gone in.

'But you didn't,' Djanali said.

'No.'

'Just as well.'

Halders chuckled.

'I made a mess of it, no matter how you look at it.'

'Hmm.'

'He was going to say something important. About Jeanette's father. But he didn't.'

'What do you think he was going to say?'

'Would you like a glass of juice?'

'Answer the question, Fredrik.'

'I'll answer the next time I've talked to him.'

'What did he have to say about her finishing with him?'

'That's not what we're after any more.'

They went inside. Halders poured out some juice. They could hear the kids talking in the background. Hannes had a pal in his room. A computer game. Laughter. The sound of shooting from a computer. A single shot to start with, then a series of salvoes. Halders looked at Djanali, who was listening to the war.

'Better that they do all the shooting now, before they grow up,' Halders said.

She smiled.

The gun battle petered out, and was replaced by a car chase.

Aneta Djanali left, and Halders poured himself a beer. Magda came in with a grazed knee from the flags in the garden. Somebody started shooting again in the computer game Hannes was playing with his friend. Bang, bang. Halders cleaned up his daughter's knee, but didn't apply a plaster. He just sat at the kitchen table, took a swig of beer now and again, and thought of nothing in particular.

20

Birgersson summoned Winter. When Winter entered his office, the Super, unusually, didn't have a cigarette in his hand.

'Yep,' Birgersson said. 'I've packed it in.' He looked almost as if he were apologising. 'My lungs have had enough. They really have.'

'I've started,' Winter said. 'Again.'

'I didn't even know you'd stopped,' said Birgersson, taking a deep drag on his white nicotine inhaler. He took it out of his mouth and looked hard at it. 'A ridiculous thing.' He looked at Winter. 'What's going on?' He indicated the chair in front of his desk. 'Take a seat.' Winter sat down, crossing his legs. 'The young guy's background?'

'We haven't a clue.'

'Is he a ghost?'

Winter didn't respond.

'Recently come down to earth?'

'I don't know, Sture.'

'There's got to be an explanation.'

'Yes.'

'An illegal immigrant?'

'Why isn't he hiding away, in that case?'

'But surely he is? Pretty well, come to that.'

'He met the girl. Angelika. Quite above board, it seems.'

'Love is all you need,' Birgersson said.

'No,' Winter said. 'There is a limit. And that's where it's at.'

'If you say so.'

'I take it you've seen how this case has been developing?'

Birgersson nodded, and sucked at his ridiculous gimmick.

'It's developing outwards, and collapsing inwards. The more that happens, the less we know,' Winter said.

'The opposite would have been preferable.'

Winter smiled. Birgersson fiddled with his dummy. The sun shone in through the venetian blinds, as usual. They were sitting there, as usual, talking over the latest tragedy. Everything was just as exciting as usual.

How was it going to turn out? Would the streets come up with a solution? Would all the threads come together in the end? Where do they start? Have I got them in my hand? Winter looked again at the ridiculous empty holder Birgersson had in his mouth, flicking up and down like the back end of a wagtail. Ridiculous. He could have been somewhere else. Sunbathing on the rocks. Elsa and him. Five metres out. She's gasping for breath. They go for a drink. Sand in their sandwiches. Somebody kicking a ball. Living is easy. Not like this: nasty and sweaty and life-threatening. Dead kids, hardly out of the nest. Nobody could care less about them apart from us, and we're paid for trying to sort things out.

Pack it in.

But that's not the only reason why.

'How's Halders?' Birgersson asked.

191

'Screwed up, I think.'

'As usual, you mean?'

Winter didn't answer.

'Can he go on working? Really?'

'Yes.'

'Talk to people?'

'Better than ever, it seems. He can't let go of the Bielke family.'

'Should we?'

'Maybe, for the time being. We have another murder on our hands,' Winter said.

'And the whole population will be back at work in a few days.'

'Meaning what?'

'Everything will be starting up again.'

'I'm impressed by your philosophical perspective,' Winter said.

Birgersson took out his dummy cigarette and put it on his desk.

'That club, or whatever it is. For crying out loud, we ought to have pinned it down by now.'

'If it exists at all.'

'If it exists? What the hell do you mean?'

It's not so easy, working with folk who are de-toxing, Winter thought.

'Take Bergenhem off the case and put somebody else onto it,' Birgersson said.

'No. Not yet.'

'Is it you or me who's in charge here, Erik?'

'Me.'

*

Bergenhem was sitting in the bar. His tenth in two days. Other officers were in other bars. Everybody had been informed, questioned: the fire brigade, the health authorities, publicans, trade unions, the general public. Known drinkers, known eaters. The in-crowd. Whores. Pimps. Rude boys. The ones who've survived at least, thought Bergenhem as he showed the photograph to the restaurant owner sitting on the chair beside him. He looked hard at the photograph. Nobody had recognised the location so far.

'You reckon it's here in Gothenburg?' asked the man, studying the table and the wall, the cutlery and the glasses, and the girl sitting there. Beatrice. And later Angelika. Bergenhem didn't mention that there was a five-year gap between the pictures.

'We don't know.'

'So what you're saying is it could be anywhere at all, anywhere in the world?'

'Yes.'

'It seems familiar,' the man said. His name was Peter Nordin.

Bergenhem waited. There were no other customers in the bar. The barman started brewing some coffee, then busied himself putting bottles of beer in the refrigerator behind the bar.

'Yes. I recognise it. There used to be a little cellar bar in Nordstan. It had an exposed brick wall just like that, with tables in front of it.' He looked again at the photograph. 'You see that shadow on the wall, on the edge there? Looking like a bunch of grapes, or something of the sort? Well, it *was* a bunch of grapes. There were several porcelain bunches of grapes hanging from the ceiling there.' He looked at Bergenhem and burst out laughing. 'Awful!' He laughed again. 'Just like the name they gave the place. Towards the end, at least. Barock. Spelled with a

c. k. Have you heard that name before? Barock?'

'Did you go there?' Bergenhem asked.

'One of the few who did. Near the end.'

'You mean it wasn't very popular?'

'Well, yes: but not with the general public, if you take my meaning.' He looked again at the photograph. 'It was an interesting place. The people who ran it kept changing the decor. They used to hang various tapestries over the walls. That kind of thing. The place looks bigger in this picture than it really was. Even though this is only a little corner. It was really a sort of side room, a kind of offshoot of the bar itself. Mainly for . . . well, for the staff, I suppose. Although there was a bar in there too.'

'Where is it?'

'Well . . . these pictures must be old ones. The place was demolished quite a few years ago. The whole building, and quite a bit more of old Nordstan. I reckon that building was one of the last to go.'

'You're quite certain that the place has been demolished?'

'Why would I lie about a thing like that? The place was demolished at least three years ago. Absolute minimum.'

'I'm not suggesting you're telling lies.' Bergenhem was looking at the photograph of Angelika. 'But the fact is that this photograph was only taken last winter.'

Nordin examined it again.

'Hmm. I suppose it must be somewhere else, then. But in that case it's a pretty good replica.' He pointed at the shadow once again, then looked at Bergenhem. 'Just look at that. Bunches of grapes.'

* * *

Winter and Bergenhem were at the old address. New buildings on all sides: office blocks in red brick, newly designed cobbled streets to encourage the traffic of newly designed shoes. Where the club used to be was now a travel agent's. The air was warm. Winter wondered if it shouldn't be cooler, given all the shadows.

'Do you reckon we should start digging?' Bergenhem asked. 'Expose the basements?'

Winter tried to smile.

'The adventure continues,' said Bergenhem.

A woman emerged from the travel agent's. The window was full of photographs of beaches and palm trees. They ought to be showing pictures of snow, Winter thought. He could feel the sweat running down his back.

Bergenhem had been efficient in following up the information he'd received. The old building had been demolished four years ago. There could well have been a club in the basement, but it hadn't yet been possible to establish that for sure. If there had been one, though, it had clearly been unlicensed. There was no above-board club registered there when the building was felled. Those were Ringmar's words: 'The building was felled.'

'Well, where does our Angelika fit into all this?' asked Winter, watching a man emerging from the front door next to the travel agent's. He looked pale, not in the least cheerful. No doubt he'd taken his holiday in May, when the rainfall was the worst this century. Now he's busy writing reports. Just like me.

'We've got to track down the owners,' said Bergenhem. 'I reckon they'll be at it again, somewhere else.'

'Or buried under here.'

'Ha, ha.'

'Get after them,' said Winter. 'You'll have three men to help you.'

'OK.'

'I'll have a word with somebody I know.'

Winter met Vennerhag in the café on the corner. He was wearing shorts, as was Winter.

'Is that really allowed when you're on duty?'

'Were you ever at Barock, Benny?' Winter asked, gesturing at the travel agent's some fifty metres away. 'That was the name of the place. Or at least, one of its names.'

'No.'

'Don't lie to me, Benny.'

'If I'd been there I'd have recognised the place from the pictures you showed me the last time we had a chat. You've got to trust me.'

Winter made no comment.

'I'm your friend.'

Winter swigged his Zingo from the bottle.

'Now that we think we know where, we want to know who.' Winter drank again and looked at Vennerhag over the neck of the bottle. 'That's where my friends come in.'

'Thank you.'

'You don't even recognise the name?'

'No. But that's not so odd, Erik. There were clubs . . . and clubs. Were. Some . . . well, I know about them, and others are simply not of much interest, purely from a financial point of view. Not for me, at least.'

'You and your, er, colleagues,' Winter said.

'OK, OK. But I don't know anything about Barock, or whatever you said it was called. I knew there was a place here, but it was called something else. I can't remember what.'

'What do you think the people who ran this place are doing now?'

'You want me to guess?'

'Yes, have a guess.'

'I've no idea, honest. Now that I know where it was and what it might have been called, maybe I can get somewhere.'

'Thanks for agreeing to help.'

'Christ, Erik, I hope you're on the right track. That this place really is important for your . . . your preliminary investigation. Trying to find answers.'

'In which case you've got something useful to do with your time, Benny.'

*

Halders sat in Winter's office. Winter was standing in the window, smoking. There was a slight evening breeze now. Halders ran his hand over his hair. He was looking cheerful. He was there, which must mean somebody else was looking after his children.

'Aneta's with the kids tonight,' Halders said.

'Good.'

'She's sacrificing her free time.'

Winter said nothing.

Halders stood up. 'Jeanette's old man used to have some kind of restaurant business.'

'So you said.'

'I've tried to check him out, and it seems he was mixed up in that kind of thing.'

'But legitimate, presumably?'

'What is legitimate when it comes to restaurants and pubs in Sweden?' said Halders.

'Don't let the occasions when you've had to put up with poor service influence you,' Winter said.

'He's evidently used to running that kind of place,' said Halders. 'Sort of on the side. He's never mentioned it, though.'

'We haven't asked.'

'We will do now.'

'Wait a bit.'

'Why?'

'Just hold back for a while.'

'Why?'

'I don't want to be pulling at too many strings at the same time, that's why.' Winter took a puff at his cigarillo. Just this one, then that's it. Not for at least an hour. 'We've got a fresh murder and an old one, neither of them solved, and I've been thinking as you have that Jeanette Bielke fits into the pattern somehow, but I can't quite see how at the moment, and we have other leads that we need to pursue which are more pressing. By all means poke into Kurt Bielke's business interests, but hang on a bit before you talk to him.'

Halders said nothing.

'OK?'

'They took the wall with them,' said Halders.

'If it actually was a wall.'

'Stage scenery?'

'Something of the sort.'

'Unless the ghosts are at it again,' said Halders. 'Do you believe in ghosts, Erik?'

'People come and go in real life as well. Things exist, and then they disappear. Places vanish. But they exist even so.'

'Where are they, then?'

'Somewhere. We're going to find them.'

Anne was on her way through the night, or was it the early morning? It depended where you drew the line. There were still a lot of people around in the centre of town. Somebody shouted, but not to her. Andy wasn't there, she'd left the other place without telling him. She hesitated halfway up the steps to the outside part of the restaurant.

'It's full,' said the doorman. His face was red after standing in the sun for so long, and it looked even redder in the neon lights. He looked like an idiot with his bleached hair standing up on end. Like somebody in a cartoon who's just seen something horrific.

Me, perhaps.

'I'm not going in anyway,' she said, turning back.

There was a smell of cooking and alcohol all the way down the Avenue. Sun cream, after-sun, all the other nasty stuff.

She waited for a tram to rattle past, then jumped on her bike and pedalled away down the Allé. There was a slight breeze, and it felt like taking a lukewarm bath.

I'll have a bath when I get home. Light a candle in the bathroom and watch it burn down.

There weren't many cars about. One was behind her. Overtook her and stopped at the traffic lights. She ignored the red light, turned left and headed for home.

21

She pedalled slowly through the night. Gothenburg was under siege this summer, with roadworks everywhere, cables coming up and going down, drums of hot tarmac. Nobody around at this time. Everything quiet. A faint buzz from cars on the other side of the buildings. People were asleep behind black windows. Some people had to work through the worst of the summer heat, and get up early in the morning, she thought.

The park was lit up to the left and right. It was dark in the centre. The cycle track went through the middle, but she knew. She wasn't stupid. There was another path that was a bit longer but a bit lighter. There was traffic on the other side of the pond. A few cars out late, taxi cabs with their roof signs lit up.

There was a smell of petrol. Somebody had just driven along here. Unless the smell came from the road on the left. There was a car parked under a tree, in the shadows. The streetlights were few and far between, producing a dirty yellow glow, maybe more of a white, but it didn't extend very far and wasn't much use and she speeded up but suddenly her foot slipped off one of the pedals and she veered to the left and the handlebars twisted out of control and her heart jumped almost into her mouth and then she twisted back again and nearly regained her balance and she wobbled into the light of the next lamp that was just as dim as all the rest. Then she felt a prod in her side and she'd seen the shadow the moment before, and she felt scared now and then another prod and she fell off her bike and her terror was like an ice-cold block of stone inside her and her heart went bang, bang, bang.

*

Three hours earlier: Winter had been trying to contact Hans Bülow and Bülow had phoned and left a message and Winter called him as he walked over the football pitches at Heden. A ball came bouncing towards him and he kicked it back and play was able to restart in one of the matches. A pity he couldn't join them, it would be nice to work up a sweat that warm evening.

It was late. The digital clock on the building behind him had just changed to 22-something. But they'd still be working at the newspaper offices, preparing for the next morning's edition.

'GT, Bülow.'

'Winter here.'

'You were supposed to phone ages ago.'

'Didn't have time.'

'If you want help, you have to put yourself out a bit as well,' said the reporter.

Winter paused as he came to Södra vägen. A car full of teenagers sailed past. Eddie Cochran's voice at an aggressive volume, girls in sweaters, there are always girls in sweaters in cars full of teenagers.

'Hang on a minute.'

He crossed over the street and came to the pavement-café section of Kometen. A table was just becoming available as a party of four prepared to leave. Their bill was on the table.

'If you can manage to drag yourself away from your desk, you'll find me at Kometen.'

'I'll be there in ten minutes.'

Winter ordered a beer. Bülow arrived and followed suit.

'Have you always been a crime reporter?' Winter asked as Bülow took a swig of his beer.

'Ever since I learned to write.'

'I'm thinking of giving you a piece of highly sensitive information.'

'About time, too.'

'It won't be the first time,' Winter said.

Bülow took another drink, puffed at his cigarette, waited. He'd leaned his bicycle against the wooden fence.

'A boy might have been murdered.'

Bülow put down his glass.

'Who? When?'

Winter didn't answer.

'For God's sake, Erik.'

'Nobody knows.'

'You shouldn't say things like that.'

'Highly sensitive, as I said.'

'No.'

'You mean you don't want it?'

'You've just given it to me, for Christ's sake! Jesus . . . you think I'd keep quiet about a murder. Another one?!'

'Keep your voice down, if you don't mind.'

Bülow looked round. Nobody seemed to be listening. Some new customers had just arrived at the next table and were in the process of ordering, all talking at once, blah, blah blah blah.

'Let's have the details, please.'

'We can find him. This is my own suspicion, if you see what I mean. We're in a situation where we need to make

202

a breakthrough.' Winter looked Bülow in the eye. 'I need to smoke somebody out. I want you to write something.'

*

Cut cut cut. Rip rip rip. It was deafening inside her head. She could feel breathing against her cheek, a smell she'd never come across before, sweat, smell, cut, cut, her heart was leaping like a wild beast inside her chest, cut, breathing, a voice saying something right next to her but also far away, rip, rip.

She was lying on the ground, could see her bike beside her, the wheel still turning round and round, a noise that could be from the wheel or . . . something pulled at her, she was lifted up and dragged along and there was nobody else there and why didn't somebody come and oh God and who and where is th– and she tried to put her hand into her handbag that seemed to be open and she didn't know why and she tried to reach her mobile and even if she couldn't phone she could smash it into the head of . . . and she was LIFTED up and her face was scratched by the bushes and she tried to scream and felt the hand pressing against her mouth before she could open it.

She felt a blow to her head. Breathing again, close to her again. Somebody saying something. Breathing, like a voice. A voice. A voice now, yes. A chant, words, words, the same words, words, sounds, can't hear what, oh God.

Another blow. Red, white, red in her mind.

*

'An illegal immigrant,' Bülow said.

'No.'

'You don't think so?'

'No, something else,' Winter said.

'You can't find him?'

'Something has to turn up soon.'

'So you want me to write as if he were dead?'

'As if he might be.'

'Are you planning on dictating the article?'

Winter didn't answer that. All the tables were full now. Everybody on all sides was pretty drunk.

'Have you paid?' he asked.

'Am I supposed to pay for this?'

Winter stood up. 'Let's go home,' he said.

Bülow pushed his bike. Three men were fighting at the hot-dog stall. Vague punches making holes in the air smelling of grilled sausages. One of the men had blood on his forehead. Another started vomiting, the sick shooting out of his mouth like a lance. The third burst out laughing, like a loony.

Winter and Bülow made a detour to get round them.

'They're getting in training for the Gothenburg street party,' Winter said.

'Huh. A damp squib.'

Vasaplatsen was deserted. A tram approached from Landala. There was the sound of music from one of the cafés at the corner of the square.

'So, we have a deal?' Winter said.

Bülow laughed.

'You can count on me, one hundred per cent.'

'Good night.'

Winter opened the front door of his building.

'Greetings to your family,' said the reporter, but the door had already closed.

*

The phone rang. Four times. The answering machine was triggered. The message echoed in the silent room. Nobody was listening.

Her voice: 'I can't take your call just now, but . . .'
Then the message.

Breathing, panting, like a wild beast, her voice, perhaps a prayer, now . . . a noise like something from the pews of a four-square gospel church, speaking in tongues, chanting, chanting, a hoarse voice from another world, no, from here, from there, NnnnnnnaaAAAAieieRRRRAaaaaaiiiiyyyyyiyyiyi!!

NNNAAAIEEEIEIIE!!!

*

They were asleep when he got home, both of them. He took off his sandals and tiptoed into the kitchen, closing the door behind him. It creaked.

He put the coffee on.

'So, no sleep tonight either,' said Angela, who had been woken up. She sat down at the table and yawned, hair spilling over her eyes.

'Not like you,' he said. 'You're asleep now, here. Sitting.'

'Can't you ever go to bed? You have to be wide awake tomorrow morning, surely?'

'I am wide awake.'

'I said tomorrow morning.'

'I've got to think.'

'Best done when you're awake.'

'I AM awake. I just said so.'

'No need to shout.'

'I wasn't shouting.'

'Oh . . .'

'I WASN'T shouting.'

'Elsa's asleep. Or was.'

'There wasn't a sound from here until you appeared.'

'Ha, ha.'

'If you just leave me in peace for an hour or so, it'll be all quiet on the western front, and I'll go to bed. OK?'

Angela said nothing.

'OK?'

She stood up, hid her face. He could hear a sob.

'But . . .'

She strode out and closed the door behind her. It creaked.

Winter put down his cup and considered banging his head against the fridge door, just once. The kitchen window was open, and a few people were sitting out in the courtyard, four storeys below. He could hear every word they said. Maybe he ought to stick his head out of the window and inform them that his family needed to get some sleep? SHUT UP.

He was out on the balcony, with a cigarillo. There was a smell of smoke, but a different kind of smoke, and from another direction. Something was on fire.

The trams had stopped.

Angela came out.

'I'm sorry,' he said.

'You have us as well.'

'I know I can be a fool. I fail—'

'That's not what I mean. We can be a support as well.' She seemed translucent in the light from the street-lamps down below and the sky up above. 'You don't have to see us as something that gets in the way.'

'I've never done that.'

'I never say anything about your work, do I?'

'Of course not.'

'Well, don't let it eat you up.'

'I try not to, Angela.'

'Perhaps you ought to talk to somebody.'

'About what? Who to?'

'A lot has happened lately.'

Shouldn't she be the one? he thought. Who needs to talk? Something happened to her that was beyond comprehension. He could look at as many dead bodies as anybody was prepared to put before him. But he couldn't get anywhere near understanding *that*. She needed to talk. To somebody else. What I want, my dear idiot, is silence.

'Are you thinking about your dad?'

'Dunno. No.'

'Things are pretty good between us. Isn't that right, Erik?'

'That's not the problem. I'm just tired.'

She nodded and said good night and went back inside. He'd be able to explain things better tomorrow. He put down his cigarillo and watched it glowing. There was still a smell of smoke from elsewhere. The phone rang inside the flat. He heard Angela answer.

22

Winter could see the faint glow on the other side of the park as he drove down the hill. The light was like a pale mist under a clearer, purer sky. The forerunner of a new day. It would be hot again. It was already 22 degrees, even though it was strictly speaking still night-time.

The girl would never experience the new day. Winter had seen strangled corpses before. She was naked from the waist down. His colleagues were rooting around the scene. The pathologist was bent over the girl like an angel of death. It wasn't Pia Fröberg. Winter remembered that she was on holiday. This was a man, and he looked big and clumsy in his shorts and baseball cap. Or was he made to look that way because the girl lying in front of him was so small and slim?

Like a dead sparrow by the roadside.

Winter walked back. Her bicycle was lying in the middle of the cycle track. The handlebars were pointing inwards. It looked almost as if one of the wheels was still spinning. A uniformed policeman was standing beside the bicycle, and a patrol car was parked behind him. The lights were spinning round on the car roof. The girl's face was lit up, plunged into darkness, lit up. Winter preferred the darkness.

He approached the police officer, whom he didn't recognise. A young lad. Only a couple of years older than the girl, at most. Hardly a policeman. A police boy.

'I hear you were first on the scene.'

'Yes, it was us who . . . found her.'

Winter nodded.

'What's your name?'

'Peter. Peter Larsson.'

'How did you find her?'

'The bike,' said the young constable. 'We were driving past, and noticed it.'

'Do you drive past here every night, Peter?'

'More or less.'

Winter sized up the road as far as the bend. After the bend the road continued round a pond. On the other side of the pond was a little clump of trees and beyond that another pond and on the other side of that pond some bushes, a few trees, a big rock. A murder scene twice over.

Not a third time on this occasion. But not far off: four hundred metres, as the crow flies. He thought about the girl. A dead sparrow.

'You didn't see anybody else?'

'Not a soul.'

'How did you find the girl?'

'We saw the bike, as I said, and stopped. I got out to investigate. It was obvious somebody had been walking at the side of the road. I didn't have to look very hard to find her. I mean, you've seen for yourself.'

'Yes.'

'We've all got our eyes peeled as well, after what's happened recently.'

'Well done, Peter.'

The constable looked at Winter, then into the bushes and trees.

'Is it the same old story?'

'What do you mean?'

'Has he been at it again?'

'No idea,' said Winter, going back to take another look at the girl.

'Do you reckon it's rape?' asked Ringmar, who'd arrived only minutes after Winter.

The pathologist shrugged.

'He asked you a question,' Winter said.

'Probably,' said the man, rising to his feet. The peak of his cap was pointing to the sky. That doesn't fit in here, Winter thought. Doesn't fit in anywhere, come to that. The doctor looked at Winter. 'OK, I know what you're getting at. Could be. I'll be as quick as I can.'

'We'll have to bring in the coroner's office in Linköping as well,' Ringmar said. 'Where's Beier, by the way?'

'In New York.'

'New York?!'

'A conference. Didn't you know?'

'New York,' said Ringmar again. 'It must be even hotter there than here.'

'I'll get her out of here now,' the pathologist said.

'She's called Anne Nöjd,' Winter said. 'She has a name.'

Her handbag had still been lying there. She had a name and an address. She lived on the west side. Winter had an uncomfortable feeling as he drove through the tunnel and out onto the motorway. All the victims lived on the west side.

It seemed lighter there, even if the sun was rising behind them. There was a smell of the sea through the wide-open window. They were driving along narrow streets through old coastal communities.

He felt like he was in Lilliput. There was a number over the verandah.

'That must be it,' Ringmar said.

There was a hedge all the way round. Boats were anchored only fifty metres away. The smell of the sea was even stronger now. Winter listened to the sound of the waves. He knew there were rocks just behind the promontory that lots of young people used as a base for swimming. If he went out onto it he'd be able to see the rocks. Jeanette had gone swimming there. And Beatrice, in another age, the previous century. Angelika too. Had Anne Nöjd sunbathed and swum there as well? Was that significant?

The house was in darkness.

She was twenty. This was evidently where she'd lived. That was all he knew. The house looked smaller as they drew closer to it. It ought to be the other way round. Winter bent down and peered through the window. He could make out dark silhouettes of objects. Ringmar knocked on the door. And again, harder this time. No response.

Ringmar produced a bunch of keys that they had taken earlier from the girl's handbag. There were four keys. Two seemed similar and looked like they might fit the lock. The second one opened it. Ringmar shouted into the house. He shouted again and looked at Winter. Winter nodded. He could hear the first seagull of the morning as they entered the house.

It was lighter inside than they'd expected, from what they'd seen through the window. They were in a hall, then turned left into a kitchen that couldn't be any bigger than six metres square. There was a newspaper on the table, and a cup beside it. There was a half-full glass of wine, glistening in the morning sunlight that was growing stronger by the minute now. Winter bent over the table and watched the sea shifting in the sunlight, changing in swell and colour.

It must be great sitting here, watching the morning reflected in the water.

Ringmar shouted from another room. Winter went back into the hall and then into a room off to the left that wasn't much more than a cupboard with a little table and a chair. The next room was a bedroom with a bed, a bedside table and a chair. The floor was wood, pine, polished. There was a smell of flowers. Ringmar spoke again. Winter continued into the living room. That was the whole of the house. The living room was a maximum of eight metres square and the windows looked out onto the road where he could see the tyres of his own car. There was a wood-framed sofa and an attractive-looking carpet in colours he couldn't yet make out. In another hour, perhaps, but not yet. There were pictures of various sizes hanging on the walls. In the dawn light the pictures looked like holes. Ringmar was standing by a table and on the table was a telephone with an answering machine. The red light was blinking. Ringmar looked at Winter, eyebrows raised. The light blinked.

They hadn't found a mobile phone in the girl's handbag. Winter was sure that Anne Nöjd must have had a mobile. All young people had a mobile. Everybody did, come to that. They would have to search around the place where the body had been found. They'd also have to check if she'd had a contract.

The light was blinking. A gull called outside the window. Winter nodded and Ringmar pressed gingerly on the button with his gloved finger. A shrill peep. Static. A voice.

'Andy here. I got held up. You know how it is. Phone me when you get home. *Ciao*, baby.'

The static again. Peep.

Nothing.

Something.

Ringmar leaned forward to hear better. Winter took a step closer.

They could hear her voice now. A scream. Another one. A . . . grunting, or . . . a weird noise, a scratching, like something brushing against branches, bushes . . .

'What the hell . . . ?' Ringmar said.

'Shush,' Winter said. 'It's her.'

Ringmar's face was stony. His eyes flitted from Winter to the answering machine, from the answering machine to Winter.

'How on earth . . . ?'

Winter held up his hand. He could feel it shaking.

We're listening to a murder.

NNNAAAAIEIERRYYYY!!!

Words they couldn't quite make out. Sounds. Was this what Jeanette had meant when she talked about the noise her attacker made?

He stared at the answering machine as if it were alive, a black beast, potentially lethal.

They listened to the screams, the yells, the grunts, the roars, the repeated words naaieieier . . . quietly the first two times, then louder, NNAAAIEIERRYYY!

Sudden silence. Winter checked his watch. Not many minutes had passed but . . . the message should have been cut off earlier. They waited but there was nothing else. There was a series of clicks from the answering machine and the tape rewound to the beginning. Ringmar pressed play again.

'Andy here . . .'

They listened once more. Ringmar made notes.

Silence.

'We need to find this Andy,' Winter said.

A gull screamed again. The sun had climbed over the hill to the west now, tumbled down the other side and scrambled as far as the house. The answering machine was suddenly lit up by the sunlight.

*

Halders put on another record. Twenty more minutes and it would be light. Aneta Djanali could smell the whisky on his breath when he came back and sat on the sofa beside her.

The music started. Some tentative piano chords. Then Bob Dylan's voice singing 'Blind Willie McTell'.

Halders sang along for a few lines then mumbled something.

'What did you say, Fredrik?'

'No one can sing the blues like Bob Dylan.'

She didn't answer.

Halders started singing again.

'Maybe you should go to bed now, Fredrik.'

He leaned forward, picked up his glass and drank.

'Am I behaving myself, do you reckon?'

'You look tired.'

'Tired? Huh!'

'Don't drink any more now.'

'That's up to me. Maybe I need it.'

'Tell me that tomorrow.'

'Tomorrow? You mean you're staying?'

She stood up, went to the kitchen and came back with a glass of water. There were streaks of the new day in the sky through the patio door.

Dylan and Halders continued their rendition.

'You have to take the children to school tomorrow.'

'No need to remind me of that.'

'We're on duty at eight.'

'I said you didn't need to remind me about . . . about . . .'

The music stopped, Halders stood up and put the track on again. Then he turned to Aneta.

He sang: 'There's no one that sings the blues like Blind Fredrik McTell.'

Then he fell over the end of the sofa and ended up with his head almost on the floor.

'Fredrik!'

Djanali rushed over to him and bent down. Halders' eyes were still open.

'Fredrik?'

He mumbled something and shook his head. He scrambled to his feet.

'I'm . . . I'm not all that drunk.'

He started crying. Aneta Djanali hugged him. She felt his shoulders shaking. His neck was as tense as a steel cable. He wrenched himself free, stood up, then sat down again.

'This is all going to pot, Aneta.'

She sat down as well.

'Have you really allowed yourself to grieve, Fredrik?'

He stared at her like a man who didn't know what she was talking about. Or didn't want to know, it seemed to her.

'This is all about you, Fredrik. Only you. And your children. You can't imagine. It's dangerous. You've just got to be yourself, and let yourself feel what you feel. Really feel. Do you follow me? Feel . . . and let it show.'

*   *   *

215

Forensics had the answering machine. Winter had a copy on tape. He listened to the beginning. Who was Andy? They could find out what number he'd called from, but a mobile was . . . mobile. It moved with whoever was using it. He could have made the call from anywhere.

Anne Nöjd had evidently lived alone. The SOC team was over there now. The forensic boys were crawling over wherever you looked. They'd found some names: parents, or other relatives. Winter had made a few unpleasant telephone calls. Her mother. That was just a couple of minutes ago.

Now his own mobile rang. It was nearly 5 a.m.

'I was wondering,' Angela said.

'I haven't had time to ring.'

'Come home when you can and I'll make *caffelatte*. Give me an hour and I'll go to the baker's and get some poppy-seed rolls to have with it.'

'I'll try to get back for then. And stay for a while at least.'

His desk phone rang. He said goodbye to Angela, then took the other call. It was one of the forensic officers from the house at Långedrag.

'We have a young man here called Andy who was looking for the girl.'

'Where is he?'

'He's here, standing beside me now.'

'Let me speak to him.'

Winter heard a different voice. It sounded young, scared. 'What's going on?'

Winter said who he was.

'Can you come and see me now, right away?'

'What's happened to . . . to Anne?'

'If you get yourself into the car that's waiting where

216

you are and come over here to me now, I'll fill you in on everything.'

'What's happened to Anne?!'

Winter hesitated.

'She was murdered last night. That's why it's so incredibly important that you get yourself here as quickly as possible, Andy. We need your help.'

He heard a yell, or a scream. Static. It sounded as if the mobile had been thrown high into the air.

'Hello? Hello?'

Winter heard the forensic officer's voice again. 'We'll bring him in.'

23

Winter waited in his office, which was illuminated by the grey light of dawn. The greyness was in tune with his mood. A strange feeling as it was blended with the excitement he felt at what was coming next. Something was happening. He had a feeling of anticipation that was cold and, in its way . . . undignified. It was like travelling through a barren landscape without hope, but feeling something reminiscent of hope even so.

There was a scent of newly woken heat from outside. Birds were singing again. The street on the other side of the river was being cleaned by a sweeper-lorry. He could hear the enormous brushes from where he was sitting.

The door was open, and in came a young man aged about twenty-five, accompanied by one of the forensic officers, who greeted Winter and then left. Andy looked as if his face had collapsed. His face *had* collapsed. Winter gestured towards the chair.

'What . . . what's happened?'

Winter told him as much as he knew. But first he asked the young man's name.

'Andy.'

'Your surname as well.'

'Grebbe. Andy Grebbe.'

Andy sat down. The T-shirt he was wearing was torn in the left sleeve. His hair was cropped short but looked unkempt even so. There was a black ring under his left eye but not under his right. Winter could smell stale booze from the other side of his desk. Andy was sober enough now, but very tired. Nervous.

'When did you last speak to Anne?'

'Er . . . that would be tonight . . . no, I mean yesterday. Last night.'

'When?'

'What do you mean? I said—'

'What time?'

'Er . . . about eight, I think. Eight, or thereabouts.'

'Where?'

'Where? It wasn't anywhere . . . if you see what I mean. The telephone. I phoned her from home.'

'And she answered?'

'Ans– of course she answered. I told you, I spoke to her.'

Winter nodded.

'Then I phoned again later on, but she was out.'

Winter nodded again.

'I left a message on her answerphone. It must still be there.' He looked at Winter. A look that was white and red and black and tired and maybe hounded. 'If you play back her messages it must be there.'

'We have done,' Winter said. He tried to hold Andy's eye. Was it now something would happen? Would he break down?

'OK. So you've heard it.'

'Yes. What time did you phone?'

'Er . . . after two. Half past two or so.'

'Where from?'

'From a place in Vasastan.'

He said the name of the bar. Winter knew the one.

'Why did you phone?' he asked.

'Is this a cross-examination?'

'I'm just asking a few questions.'

'Do I need a lawyer?'

'Do you think you do?'

'No.'

'Why did you phone?'

'Well . . . we were supposed to have met up earlier but I couldn't make it and then she didn't turn up at the bar and so I phoned and asked her to give me a ring when she got home.'

'Where were you going to meet?'

'At the bar.'

'I meant the first time.'

'At a café.'

Andy said the name before Winter had time to ask.

'But you didn't go?'

'Yes, I did, but it was too late. She wasn't there.'

'Had she been there?'

Andy didn't answer.

'Had she been there?' Winter asked again.

'I don't know. I looked inside but she wasn't there and there was nobody I knew to ask.'

'What did you do then?'

'Wandered around town for a bit and then went to the bar.'

'And she didn't get in touch?'

'No.'

'Where was she?'

Andy didn't answer. He took a drink of the water Winter had given him. His thoughts suddenly seemed to be miles away, in another world.

'Where was Anne last night?' Winter asked again.

'I don't know,' said Andy, looking at something next to Winter. The greyness in the office had blended with the sharper light of morning, and it seemed to Winter that two lights mingling in that way caused confusion. It wasn't at all clear where they should go when they met in the middle of the room. The new light fell over Andy's face. Winter wondered why he was lying.

*

Halders wondered why she was lying. They were sitting in the garden. Her father was on the verandah. He's casting his shadow over her, Halders thought. He's thirty metres away, but his shadow is falling over her. It looks as if she's freezing cold, but it's 30 degrees.

'Don't you want us to put that bastard behind bars?' Halders asked.

'Of course,' said Jeanette.

'You don't seem all that interested.'

'I've told you all I know. All I . . . experienced. How I experienced it.'

'What have you got to say about last night's murder?' Halders asked. Her expression didn't change. It was as if she hadn't heard.

'I know no more than anybody else,' she said before Halders had time to repeat the question.

'And you didn't know this girl either? Anne Nöjd?'

Jeanette Bielke shook her head.

'Never seen her?' asked Halders, showing her again a picture they'd found in the girl's house.

'I don't know.'

'What about the house?'

She shrugged again.

'It's not far from here,' Halders said.

'All those little houses look the same,' she said.

221

Halders nodded.

'They shoot up like mushrooms.'

Kurt Bielke had come down from the verandah and approached the table where they were sitting, underneath the maple that formed a sort of green roof.

'I think Jeanette needs to be left in peace now,' he said.

Halders made no comment. Bielke looked at his daughter.

'You can go up to your room now, Jeanette.'

She didn't look at her father. She started to get up. It's like slow motion, Halders thought.

'I haven't finished,' he said. 'We have some more to discuss.'

'You always do.'

Jeanette looked at Halders. He nodded to her, and she stood up.

'Goodbye, then, Jeanette,' he said, stretching out his hand. Hers was cold as he shook it. She left.

'How is she?' Halders asked. He had turned to face Bielke.

'How do you think she is?'

'What's going to happen about her studies this autumn? University?'

'We'll have to see.'

'What about the business?'

Bielke had been on the point of walking away, but stopped in his tracks and turned back to face Halders. 'I don't follow.'

'Your businesses. You are co-owner of several places of entertainment, aren't you?'

'Am I?'

'It's not a secret, is it?'

'Isn't it?'

'So it is a secret, is that it?'

'There are some questions you can't answer with a simple "yes" or "no",' Bielke said. 'Such as: "Have you stopped beating your wife?" or the one Mr Police Constable just asked.'

'*Have* you been beating your wife?' Halders asked.

Bielke took a step forward.

'Or your daughter?'

'What is this?'

Halders took a step back and turned away. He'd gone too far. That's the way I am. Maybe it was the right thing to do. Maybe I'd been intending to do that all the time, but didn't realise.

'Bye, then,' he said over his shoulder.

'I'll be phoning your fucking boss,' Bielke said. He followed Halders out. Halders got into his car, which was parked in the shade of an oak tree. Bielke stood on the other side of the fence.

'Winter,' said Halders, before closing the door. 'DCI Winter is my superior officer.'

Halders drove south. There were patches on the road that might have been water, but it was a mirage. Caused by the sun. He squinted and lowered the visor whenever the sun attacked the car.

The buildings in Frölunda were shimmering in the heat. He parked in the vast car park, half of which had been dug up. The other half was being excavated as tarmac was being laid in the first half. Halders could smell the pungent fumes, made more acrid by the hot wind. The labourers were in shorts, gloves, tough boots. Their skin was the colour of the tarmac. This is what real workers ought to look like, thought Halders.

The square was full of people. Some had no doubt just come back from holiday, but hardly as many as this, he thought as he bought a pear from a wrinkled old man from Syrabia or some such place. There weren't all that many people hereabouts who could retreat to their summer place for the hols, or even go abroad. To Syrabia or wherever. The shrivelled old man had seen more of the world than most of these Swedish plebs who shuffled around all hunched up, glancing around furtively, with fat backsides and cheap clothes. For fuck's sake, Halders thought. What's the point? This country's kaputski.

Mattias was waiting outside the sports centre, at the bottom of the steps. The local drunks were staggering around on the other side. A woman sat with her head in her hands. A man – really more of a boy – was swigging from a bottle of whisky that an older mate was trying to reach out for from his lost world. As Halders walked past he could smell the stench of piss and stale spirits. At least it's nice and warm for them, he thought.

'Have you been waiting long?' he asked Mattias.

'Well, sort of.'

'Let's go, then.'

'What's wrong with here?'

'The stench,' said Halders, walking up the steps. 'The stench from the dregs of society.'

Mattias followed him, caught up.

'Why don't you kill 'em all off?' he asked, looking at Halders. Mattias was tall, taller than Halders. He seemed pretty heavy.

'We don't have the resources.'

'You could make a start. Who would select the victims?'

'Me,' said Halders as they sat down in the café in front of the big, red building.

224

'Nobody would want to use the indoor pool on a scorching day like this,' said Mattias.

'It can be pretty good to take a sauna on a day like today, though,' Halders said.

'Really?'

'Yes, really. I used to work for the UN around the Middle East, and we used to take saunas in places like Nicosia when the temperature outside was forty-five. It felt good afterwards. Cool.'

'If you say so.'

'And what do you say, Mattias?'

'What about?'

'About Jeanette.'

'Like I said when you phoned, I'm squeezed-out, for God's sake. There's nothing more to say.'

'I spoke to her today.'

'Oh yeah?'

'Not long ago. And to him.'

'Her old man?'

'Yes.'

Mattias looked up at the sky. It was motionless as there were no clouds. A girl came to take their order. Halders asked for coffee and Mattias for an ice cream.

'You're right,' said Halders.

'What about?'

'About him. Kurt Bielke.'

'Right? What do you mean right? I don't remember saying anything about him.'

'There's something funny about him. Know what I mean?'

The boy said nothing. Their order came. The ice cream had already started to melt. Mattias eyed it without touching it.

'Take him as well,' he said.

'What do you mean?'

'When you're selecting the ones to kill off.'

*

The holiday period is always a problem for the police investigating a murder.

Winter was reading the file on Beatrice Wägner. Newspaper cuttings now.

'The house-to-house operation hasn't produced much information. Most people aren't even at home,' says Superintendent Sture Birgersson.

Police working on witness statements today.

It should say *the* police *are* working on witness statements, thought Winter. These headline writers mangle the language. The police are working on witness statements today. Five years later. The old ones, and the new ones. And *the* police *are* still wondering about the missing witnesses.

The phone rang. Winter's mother, her first call for a few days. There was a rustling on the line from the Costa del Sol.

'I heard on the news that it's still warmer in Scandinavia than it is in Spain.'

'You should congratulate us,' he said.

'Just you wait and see, if it goes on like that. It'll be unbearable. You're talking to somebody who knows.'

'Is that why you're still there in the south of Spain?'

'I'm coming in August, you know that. Then it's absolutely impossible to live down here. Impossible.'

'You'll be welcome.'

'Have you thought about a house yet, Erik?'

'No.'

'But Angela said that—'

'Angela said what?'

He could hear the sharpness in his voice.

'What's the matter, Erik?'

'What do you mean? What did Angela say?'

'She just said that you might be looking for something in the autumn. Maybe.'

'Really?'

'What's the matter, Erik?'

'Nothing. It's hot, that's all. Hot, and there's a lot to do.'

'I know.'

'Oh, do you?'

He could hear the rustling on the line again, the fragmentary chatter from a hundred thousand voices all over Europe.

'Erik?'

'Yes, I'm still here.'

'Is everything all right with you? With you and Angela?'

24

It was silent. Winter braced himself to listen to a murder. He'd brought a new Metheny with him the day before yesterday, but he still hadn't played it. It was on the pile on the shelf above the Panasonic, to the left of the window.

He put the tape recorder on the table. The birds had stopped singing outside. He switched on the message from Anne Nöjd's answering machine.

Screams and . . . and that other voice, like something from hell. Like something totally unhuman, he thought. Would they be able to separate the voices? Put them side by side and then listen?

There was a message there, unintentional. There's a message in everything.

Jeanette had talked about something her attacker had said. Three times perhaps, the same thing. She hadn't seen his face, but heard his voice. The sound. Assuming it was the same attacker.

Were there any words there? Real, actual words? Would it be possible to separate everything and hear the words, if there were any? Or parts of sentences. Filter the sounds. It should be possible. There were technicians in the building, only fifty metres away, and if they couldn't do it there were always the sound technicians at Swedish Radio.

There was a knock on the door and Ringmar came in. He was not alone. She looked scared.

*

Jeanette listened to the recorded message. Winter had tried to prepare her for it as far as possible. It wasn't possible.

'I don't want to,' she said after three seconds.

'It hasn't even started yet.'

'I know what it is, though.'

'You kno—'

'CAN'T YOU LEAVE ME ALONE?' she shouted. She got to her feet.

Winter stood up. Jeanette suddenly toppled over backwards and hit the floor hard. Winter rushed round the table. She lay with her eyes closed. He bent down, and she opened them.

'I broke my fall with my hand,' she said, wiggling her wrist. She looked at Winter. 'OK, put the tape back on.'

'You don't have to.'

'That's why I'm here, isn't it?'

Winter looked at her eyes. He didn't recognise her. She was there but not there.

She took a seat, looked at the tape recorder, then at Winter. He started the tape.

She listened: Nnaaaaieieieierryyy . . .

Winter stopped the tape.

'I don't recognise it at all,' she said in a voice that sounded rehearsed, as if it too was recorded on tape. She looked at Winter.

'It's horrible. Is it really genuine?'

*

Bergenhem and Möllerström were looking into who had owned the place. It was taking time. Barock hadn't been registered in the usual way. Some of their colleagues knew of it, of course, but it wasn't at all clear who had owned it. There had been registered owners. Several names and faces, but they'd had no luck yet. They would eventually, but it was painstaking work, took days and involved many interviews.

*

'There are a lot of names,' said Möllerström.

But there was one particular name that stood out. It was linked to a dance restaurant – the kind with live music and old-fashioned ballroom dancing – south of the river. The name was one of the most familiar in the Gothenburg restaurant world, had been for ages. One of several, and they'd worked their way down the list and come to the name and they would ask the person in question before they went back to the list. Bergenhem had no great hopes.

'What is a dance restaurant nowadays?' asked Möllerström.

'A place where people eat and dance,' Bergenhem said.

'Isn't that something from another age?'

'Eating and dancing?'

Möllerström grinned.

'Proper dancing. Makes me think of the Royal Hotel back home.'

'We'll soon find out,' said Bergenhem.

They drove through the hordes of tourists. Many of them looked tired and lost as they passed in front of the car. Visitors from faraway towns. Möllerström thought again of the Royal Hotel in the town where he had grown up.

The oil storage tanks were gleaming on the other side of the river. The place they were looking for was in one of the sand-coloured-brick buildings in one of the dockland streets.

Inside it smelled of dust and stale smoke, and the premises looked like a dance restaurant: a large dance floor in a semicircle around a stage, beyond it chairs and tables in another semicircle, and furthest back, a horseshoe-shaped bar. The tables had white cloths and on every one was a flower in a bud vase.

There was nobody behind the bar. There were musical instruments on the stage. A woman was pushing a grey rag on a stick over the floor. She dipped the rag in a bucket of water. A few rays of sun came in through one of the windows and lit up her face as if she'd been on the stage ten metres away, starting to sing the first love song of the evening. She turned her head away from the sunlight and stared down at the floor, which was black-and-white checked. It was dark in the big room, but as light as it would ever be. A beam of sun suddenly fell on a saxophone in its stand on the stage, and it glistened like gold.

'Dance restaurant,' said Möllerström.

A door opened to the left of the bar, a man came out and walked over to them. He stretched out his hand and introduced himself. He was tall, taller than either Bergenhem or Möllerström, bald head and trimmed sideburns. He was wearing a white T-shirt under a dark jacket, and smart black trousers. There was something familiar about him. Bergenhem shook hands and introduced himself and Möllerström.

'Pleased to meet you,' said Johan Samic.

Bergenhem explained why they were there.

'You've come to the right place,' Samic said.

Bergenhem waited. Möllerström looked surprised.

'We had that place in its final years,' said Samic. 'That's not exactly a secret.'

'We haven't said anything about it being a secret.'

'Barock was a decent club,' said Samic.

What the hell does he mean by that? wondered Bergenhem.

'We turned it into a respectable place.'

'Wasn't it respectable before?'

Samic smiled.

'Can we take a look around?' Bergenhem asked.

'No.'

'No?'

'I don't like any old Tom, Dick or Harry wandering in before we're open and looking around,' said Samic.

'We're investigating some serious crimes,' said Möllerström.

'I know, but what's that got to do with my restaurant?'

'We've just explained.'

'Exactly. So what are you doing here?'

'We've got a few more questions to ask you,' Bergenhem said.

'Well?'

'Maybe we'll ask them round at our place.'

'Round at your place?'

'At the police station.'

'Very funny.'

'OK, let's go. Are you ready?'

'What the—'

'You can't refuse to come, Samic. I'm sure you know that.'

'OK . . . for God's sake, it's just that I have a lot to do right now, but do wander around and poke your noses in wherever you like.' He looked round. 'The toilets are over there.' He pointed with his thumb. 'You have my permission to visit the ladies' as well.'

'Arrogant bastard,' said Möllerström as they drove past more groups of tourists. Or maybe it's the same people going round and round in circles all day, he thought.

'He seemed familiar,' Bergenhem said.

'The type, you mean?'

'More than that. The man himself.'

'You didn't show him the pictures of the girls. Nor the wall.'

'No.'

'Why not?'

'It wasn't the right time.' Bergenhem turned to face Möllerström, who was driving. 'He'd have sworn blind he didn't recognise any of them no matter what.'

'You reckon?'

'There was something familiar . . .' Bergenhem breathed in the wind that was blowing into his face. It wasn't pleasant, but it wasn't unpleasant either. 'I'll have to have another look at Winter's photos.'

*

Richard Yngvesson listened to what Winter was saying. The technician was sitting at his computer, which was connected to a mixer board and other equipment that Winter didn't know the name of, nor what it did.

'You don't need to go to Swedish Radio,' Yngvesson said. 'A pity you found it necessary to mention them.'

'Sorry about that.'

'I didn't know you lot were so ignorant.'

'Come on, Richard. Is it possible to get anything from that tape?'

'What do you want?'

'Anything at all that makes sense. A sentence or a word. A voice that sounds natural. Anything other than that row, whatever it is.'

'The problem is that there's no stereo tracks for me to work on,' Yngvesson said. 'The answering machine's only mono, so everything's in the middle.' He turned to face Winter, who'd sat down beside him. 'Do you follow me? There's just one signal for everything.'

'I've got a vague idea about what mono is,' said Winter.

Yngvesson pressed a few buttons, changed a few connections and put the cassette into something that looked nothing like a tape recorder. The sound started.

The technician listened intently.

'What we need to do is to try to filter this sound image,' he said. 'Give it a good wash.'

'Is that possible?'

'Of course.'

'Good.'

'Don't expect too much. The main thing is cutting out the bass so that it isn't so deep, and increasing the descant in the middle register.'

'When can you start?'

Yngvesson looked at a list on the notice board next to his computer.

'In a week.'

'The hell you can.'

'You're not the only person we're dealing with here, Winter. You seem to think that as soon as you come storming in, we can drop everything else.' He looked almost angry. 'There are other things going on here, you know.'

'Which murders are you referring to?'

'There are—'

'Give me the cassette.'

'Eh?'

'I'm taking it to somebody at Swedish Radio.'

'Hang on a minute—'

'I can't make head nor tale of people sometimes,' Winter said. 'Here I am working on a complicated case, to say the least, with young girls being raped and murdered while Gothenburg basks in the summer sun, and you sit here rabbiting on about something that is evidently more important.'

'Are you giving a speech?' asked Yngvesson. 'Tell me when you've finished so that I can start work.'

'On what?'

'On your murder,' said Yngvesson, turning to one of the computer screens and gaping at Winter as if in a mirror.

'Plural,' said Winter. 'It's several murders.'

Yngvesson listened to the cassette again.

'Three minutes,' he said.

'Yes.'

'It took her three minutes to die.'

'Unusually long for an answering machine.'

Yngvesson shrugged.

'When do you think you can come up with a result?'

'I'd rather not talk about results.' Yngvesson did something with his keyboard. 'Give me three days.'

'Three days?'

'Back off now, Winter. You should really be waiting for a week, possibly two, and you've got it down to three days. OK?'

'OK.'

'Three minutes, three days,' said Yngvesson. 'But be prepared for it to take longer.'

'What are you going to do?'

'I'll put it into the computer and let a few programs get to work on the sound image. There's software that can clean up the sound and analyse it. If there's some kind of background noise, for instance, a constant hum or something, such as an air-conditioning fan, I can remove those frequencies.'

'Hmm.'

'It's not something you can rush. I have to work on the sound a little bit at a time. Do you understand?'

'I understand.'

'What I've heard so far is partly treacle, what we call treacly sound that's muffled and vague. I'll try to raise the descant and see if I can winkle out what I assume you're interested in.'

'I'm interested in everything,' Winter said.

'The voice,' said Yngvesson. 'Aren't you trying to hear words? Or at the very least a voice? Bits of words, or whatever else we can produce?'

'Of course.'

'There are voices here, but it's not possible to hear anything intelligible apart from the girl's cries for help now and again. You could say most of it's a sort of whisper. And then there's the other stuff . . . the grunting or whatever you might call it.'

'That's it,' said Winter. 'That's the stuff I'm mainly interested in.'

'All right. I'll concentrate on the middle register, do a bit of work on the compression. Amplify the faint bits. Try to dampen the loud ones.'

Winter made no comment. Yngvesson listened to the tape again.

'Right, let's see if we can manage to dig out a few bits of words. It sounds as though the mobile was inside something. Presumably it was in her handbag, is that right?'

'I've no idea. We haven't found the phone.'

'That makes it more difficult. If it was in her handbag, that is. It also sounds as if they were at varying distances from the microphone.'

Winter could picture the scene. The handbag, the ground, the man, the girl, the struggle, the blows, the hands, the dog lead. Death. The lead? Why had he thought of the 'dog lead'? He hadn't thought of 'the belt'. He could see a dog lead round the girl's neck. What was the difference between a lead and a belt?

'There's something positive here as well,' said Yngvesson. 'She had a hands-free set.'

'You reckon?'

'She must have had. It sounds as if the microphone was outside the handbag. At the end here at least. The sound is clearer, if you can call it that. The mike has picked up clearer sound.'

'We didn't find anything to support that. No earphones.'

He wondered where they might be now. Would anybody use that mobile phone again?

He played Brecker at top volume and watched the clouds disperse, maybe for good. The music had chased them away.

He phoned Angela.

'The sun's coming out. Look.'

'Is that why you rang?'

'Isn't that a good enough reason?'

'Here's Elsa.'

He spoke to his daughter. Angela returned to the phone.

'We've been invited to a party on Saturday, by the way.'

'Where?'

'At Agneta and Pelle's.'

'Ah. A beach party, I suppose?'

'You can make it?'

'Saturday? I certainly hope so.'

25

Bergenhem was reporting on the visit.

'Samic?' Winter said.

'Does the name mean anything to you?' asked Bergenhem.

'No.'

'He's been around quite a while.'

'I'll check up on him.'

'We don't have anything on him. I ran a few searches.'

Winter lit a cigarillo. He didn't have the strength to go to the window. Bergenhem had changed into shorts in his office.

'I've just had another look at those graduation party photos,' Bergenhem said, taking out his copies, leaning over the desk and pointing. 'Look at this.'

Winter looked at the dark-haired man standing next to the boy.

'That could be Samic,' said Bergenhem.

'It could be anybody at all.'

'Yes . . .'

'You have to be certain.'

'I'm not.'

'What are the similarities?'

'Something about his face. There again, this bloke has hair whereas Samic is going bald.'

'Wig?'

'Or a toupee.' He looked at Winter. 'Surely that can be established?'

'How?'

'Aren't there any experts who can tell us if hair is real or false?'

'By looking at a photograph?'

'There are experts at everything,' said Bergenhem.

Apart from finding murderers before panic breaks out among the general public, Winter thought. He also thought about the reporter Hans Bülow. Winter had read the article that morning. Seen the picture of the boy in the photographs; the one who might be the father of Angelika's child. Nobody had phoned in as yet.

'I'll go there,' said Winter.

'To Samic's place?'

Winter nodded. He studied the photograph again.

He had it in his inside pocket when he shook hands with Johan Samic half an hour later. A waiter was lifting chairs off the tables. There was a clinking noise from the bar where the barman was preparing ice and cutting up lemons.

'So, the boss has come in person,' Samic said.

'Do you recognise this girl?' asked Winter, showing him the photograph of Angelika sitting in front of that wall. Samic looked at it without Winter being able to notice any change in his expression.

'Who is she?'

'I asked you if you recognised her.'

'No.'

'Has she been here?'

'No.' Samic smiled. 'She's too young.'

'What do you think about the setting?'

'Ugly.'

'More specific,' said Winter.

'A bodega on the Costa del Sol if you ask me,' Samic said.

'Or a dodgy bar in Gothenburg.'

'Could be.'

'Do you recognise any of it?' Winter said.

'Not a thing.'

'You don't know where it is?'

'I don't see how I can express myself more clearly.'

'Barock.'

'Barock? That old dump?'

'Yes.'

'I went to Barock hundreds of times. This wasn't taken there.'

'No? Weren't you a part-owner for a while?'

'Yes.' He looked at Winter. 'What is this?'

'Questions.'

'Yes, yes. But Barock . . . huh! What next?'

'Another question. Where *could* this picture have been taken?' Winter asked.

Samic looked briefly at the photograph again.

'I haven't the slightest idea.'

'What I need is help,' Winter said. 'This isn't an interrogation.'

'You're turning it into one,' Samic said. 'It's becoming an interrogation.'

We'll meet again soon, Winter thought on his way out.

Samic could have been wearing a toupee at that graduation party earlier in the summer, but then, it might not be him in the picture at all. It was impossible to decide if he was the man in the photograph.

You could have fried eggs on the pavements.

Winter was hungry and went to a Vietnamese restaurant. He ordered the day's special, one of the five to choose from, all of which seemed to be the same. He picked rice with minced meat, and found a table outside under the parasols. The trams seemed to be struggling to force their way through the heat. There wasn't a cloud in the sky. Aeroplanes were criss-crossing it. There was a smell of petrol and tarmac and maybe also a whiff of the river, which was not far away. People were wearing as little as possible. He was in shorts and a khaki shirt Angela had bought for him the previous week.

He hadn't thought about Angela for two hours. He'd thought about Elsa, but not Angela.

The food arrived and he started eating, although he wasn't as hungry now. Everything tasted of glutamate and he slid the half-full plate to one side, drank his mineral water, lit a cigarillo and looked up to glimpse Samic's profile as he drove past in a Mercedes the same colour as Winter's, which was parked outside the department store over the road.

Benny Vennerhag must have quite a bit to say about Samic. Is he going somewhere as a result of our little chat?

A woman went past with two dogs, each on its own lead. She was wearing too many, too expensive clothes. One of the dogs squatted down and deposited a pile on the pavement while the woman looked round, waiting impatiently, then walked off, leaving the muck behind her. Winter considered shouting her back and giving her a good telling-off – why not? But in fact he stayed where he was and watched the dogs strut off with their mistress.

They thought it was a dog lead. So did he. The mur-

242

derer had tightened a lead round his victims' necks. Or a belt. Or a lead.

Did he have a dog? No. No dog. Just a lead that he always carried around with him. Maybe hanging loose when he walked through the park . . . like a dog owner who'd just let his dog run off for a while and was strolling along nonchalantly after it and was just about to call it back again. A lead hanging loose. Over his arm, perhaps.

Back. Went back. Again. Wandered around with the lead. Or took it out when he was *close*, when he was as close as he could get. He had to be close. Back again.

His mobile rang in the breast pocket of his khaki shirt.

'Where are you?' Angela asked when he answered.

'In town, eating a pretty awful lunch.'

'You could have come home.'

'No time, Angela. I've been sitting here for too long already.'

'Can we go swimming this evening?'

'Of course. Six o'clock. Be ready.'

'Six down in the street?'

'Have everything packed and ready. Don't forget my swimming trunks. And the sardine sandwiches.'

He hung up, but his phone rang again immediately.

'Somebody's phoned in and claims to recognise the boy from Angelika's photo,' Bergenhem said.

'Only one?'

'Only one who seems reliable.'

'Where?'

'Frölunda. The high-rise buildings behind the square.'

'Do you have the address?'

Bergenhem read it out, Winter paid his bill and drove off westwards.

The big digital thermometer displayed in the square showed 34 degrees. The high-rise buildings lining the car park were colourless, seemed to be hovering in air that was layers of glass.

Bergenhem was standing by the newspaper kiosk. They walked over to the high-rise buildings. Clumps of people were sitting in the shade. Winter could smell the whiff of cooking. A lot of people here were immigrants, from the south. They'd be down by the sea tonight, staying much longer than the Swedes who would all leave by seven. Apart from Winter and Angela and Elsa. The smell of grilled meat. Enormous families, all ages, football, shouts, laughter, life.

They passed the Arts Centre. Buildings became less frequent, lower. Bergenhem consulted a scrap of paper, pointed to a block of flats, went in and rang the bell of an apartment on the second floor. A man in a string vest and Bermuda shorts opened the door. He was chewing on something.

Bergenhem introduced himself and Winter.

'I think he lives over the road,' said the man, still chewing. 'Lots of bloody foreigners live round here.' He finished chewing and swallowed. 'Far too many.' He eyed Winter, who was behind Bergenhem. 'What's he done?'

'Where exactly?'

'You what?'

'Can you show us exactly where he lives, please?'

'Yeah, OK. Hang on, I'll just get my sandals.'

They walked across the courtyard. 'Number eighteen,' said the man. Two small children were playing on the swings in the sunshine. On the bench next to the swings was a woman dressed in black.

'Like I said, darkies wherever you look,' said the man, indicating the children on the swing.

'Shut your trap,' said Winter.

'Eh . . . ?' said the man, stopping dead in his tracks. The children put their feet down and stopped the swings and stared at the men in front of them. 'You don't talk like that around . . .' the man started to say.

Winter was striding towards number eighteen. Bergenhem followed him. The man turned to face him, and then Winter.

'I'll phone your boss,' shouted the man in the string vest.

They went inside and rang all the doorbells. About half of the occupants answered, but nobody recognised the boy's face. Bergenhem showed them the photo. Nobody had read the local newspaper.

At four flats there was no answer.

'Hmm,' said Bergenhem.

'The housing association that owns the flats,' Winter said.

'We've already talked to them.'

'Check again.'

They went back. Winter could see the sweat on Bergenhem's back through his shirt. They passed the tallest of the buildings.

'This is where Mattias lives,' said Bergenhem. 'Jeanette Bielke's ex-boyfriend.'

'Hmm.'

'That building.'

'I know.'

'Have you been to his flat?'

'Not yet.'

Winter's mobile rang.

'It wasn't consummated rape,' said the male doctor who was standing in for Pia Fröberg. 'Anne Nöjd.'

'I read you,' Winter said.

245

'Have you heard from the coroner's office?'

'Not yet, I'm afraid.'

There was a short pause. Winter could hear paper rustling.

'A belt or other thin . . . object,' said the pathologist.

'Such as a dog lead? Could she have been strangled with a dog lead?'

'Yes. That's one possibility.'

'Can you be more precise?'

'Not just yet.'

*

They were by the sea at 6.20. Some Swedes were on their way home to their barbecues. The new Swedes were carrying *their* barbecues down to the shore.

'We'll bring a throwaway barbie with us tomorrow,' Angela said. 'You can get them from filling stations.' She was undressing Elsa. 'I can't resist the wonderful smell of their grub any longer.' She was watching two women dressed in black who were starting to cook dinner on the beach.

'I'm all for that,' said Winter, lifting up Elsa who screamed and giggled as he swung her up and down and carried her to the water's edge, which was receding as dusk approached.

Elsa was sitting on his shoulders when they waded in. He squatted down and let her feel the lukewarm water. There were too many jellyfish, but the water was ideal. He lifted Elsa up, held her round her hips and spun round and round. Light dazzled. The horizon disappeared. He stopped, feeling how dizzy he was. When it settled down he realised there was something nagging in his mind. He searched for what it was as Elsa wriggled in his arms.

It was something he'd heard and seen, just as bright and dazzling as when he'd been spinning round. One second, two. He'd seen it. Seen it.

He heard voices and looked down. Two teenaged girls asking if they could hold Elsa.

'Ask her,' he said.

She said they could.

*

Everything was darker as they drove home. He picked Elsa up – she was in too deep a slumber to wake.

Angela served white wine. They sat in the kitchen, listening to the evening.

'You need a holiday,' she said.

'Two weeks to go.'

'Can you really go on leave if you haven't solved this case? Cases.'

'Yes.'

'Really?'

'It could be just as well. For the sake of the investigation.'

'I don't believe that for a minute.'

'Would you believe it, gone already.' He gazed at his empty glass.

'I'll get the bottle.'

She filled him up, and he took another sip.

'A penny for your thoughts, Erik.'

'Right now?'

'When else?'

'What a marvellous evening it is.'

'One in a thousand.' She looked at him. 'You were thinking about something else as well, weren't you?'

'Yes.'

'You didn't look pleased.'

He took another sip and put down his glass.

'I was thinking about the murders, of course. The girls.' He turned to face her. 'You can't just switch off, can you?'

'No. I don't think so.'

'They're wrong, the ones who say that you can,' he said. 'OK, you can switch off for a while, do something else. But then it comes back.'

She nodded.

'Tonight two teenaged girls wanted to hold Elsa. That's when it came back. Lots of images.'

'You looked unusually far away when you emerged from the water.'

'Something had struck me.'

'May I ask what?'

'I can't quite put my finger on it. It struck me that I knew something . . . new. I think. Something important.'

26

Winter phoned Halders. He'd just got up and was sitting on the balcony. Invisible birds were singing from a sky where two jets had painted a cross.

'I'll see what I can do,' Halders said.

'How are things?'

'It's hot already.'

'How's it going?'

'I said I'll see what I can do, didn't I?'

'OK, OK.'

Halders looked up and saw a new cross. The old one had already melted into the sky.

'As you can hear, there's still a bit of the grumpy old Halders left,' he said.

'There's hope yet, then.'

'I'll be coming in shortly,' Halders said.

'We'll try to find the flat where our missing boy lives in the meantime.'

'You'll have to do that at least.' Halders paused. 'I'll pay a call there later.'

He took the road alongside the river. The white pleasure boats twinkled on the water like sparklers. The tarmac felt soft under the tyres. It smelled like a different country. Julie Miller was singing 'Out in the Rain' on Halders' CD player. Halders turned up the volume and sang his way through his journey westwards as the sun punched at the roof of his car.

As he turned off the roundabout the silencer on his exhaust suddenly gave way. People turned their heads to stare at him.

The high-rise buildings in Frölunda swayed like drunks in the thin air. He parked outside one of them, diagonally opposite McDonald's.

The lift didn't work. He took the stairs up to the sixth floor. There was graffiti all over the walls, letters on cracked concrete. Stains everywhere, like black blood. A smell of piss and cooking had solidified in the stairwell between floors. Children screamed through closed doors, grown-ups shouted in a thousand different languages. He passed a man in a turban, a woman behind a veil, a man in a vest who passed by hugging the wall. He could see the madness in the man's eyes.

A door opened on the fifth floor and a young woman emerged with a double pushchair containing two small children who looked up at him in silence. The woman pressed the lift button. 'It's not working,' Halders said. She pressed again. 'I have to go and buy food,' she said.

Halders went up one more floor and rang the bell. Mattias answered after the third ring.

'I wasn't posh enough for them,' he said when they were on the sofa under a big window.

Halders nodded.

'Can you understand that?'

'I've even been through it myself.'

'You mean it's happened to you as well?'

Halders nodded again. He could see the sky and a reproduction of a painting of a field full of sunflowers next to the window. 'You were there yesterday, weren't you?' he said. 'Or outside the house, at least.'

'Who told you that?'

Halders didn't answer.

'That bastard of an old man, wasn't it?'

Halders shrugged.

'Jeanette hasn't said anything, has she?'

'Why don't you let her go, Mattias?'

'What do you mean, let her go?'

'You know full well what I mean.'

'I did that ages ago. Let . . . everything go.'

'Really?'

'Then you lot come nosing around all the time.'

'That's because something else has happened.'

'Yes, I read about it. But I don't under—'

He stopped when Halders held the picture of the boy in front of his nose. It was an enlargement of the graduation party photo.

'Do you recognise him?' Halders asked.

'No,' said Matthias after a short pause. 'Who is he?'

'You mean you haven't read about it?'

'No. Read? Read what?'

'This is a witness we'd like to get in touch with, but he's disappeared.'

'You don't say.'

'We've been told that he lives here.'

'Here?' said Mattias, looking round as if expecting to see the boy enter the room.

'In this area.'

'It's a pretty big area. A hundred thousand. A hundred thousand idiots.'

Halders spelled out the address.

'But that's the other side of the Arts Centre, surely?'

A woman had answered the door on the top floor, the fourth.

'He lives on the next floor down, I think,' she'd said when she'd looked at the photograph Winter had showed her. It was the same as the one Halders had just shown Mattias at the other side of the Arts Centre.

'Do you recognise this face?'

'Yes . . . I think so. At least, I've passed somebody on the stairs who looks like him.'

They went down the stairs.

'I've seen him going in there.' There were three doors on this landing. She pointed at the middle one. 'That one.'

The name plate said Svensson.

Winter pressed the bell, but couldn't hear it ring. Nobody answered. He knocked, twice. The woman was still standing beside him.

'Thank you very much,' he said, turning towards her.

She looked disappointed.

'We might get in touch with you again if we need any more help,' Winter said.

'Well . . . OK, if you do . . .' she said, going back up the stairs and looking behind her.

Winter knocked on the door yet again, but nobody answered.

*

'Have you checked up on her old man yet?' Mattias asked.

'What do you mean?'

'Have you spoken to Jeanette about it?'

'Have you?'

'Don't need to.'

Halders made no comment.

'Why don't you nail him?' Mattias said.

'Tell me how we can do that.'

'Follow him.'

'You mean keep a watch on him and see what he gets up to?'

*

Winter was waiting outside. He thought he saw the man who hated darkies walk past and gape at him from the other side of the playground. It was too hot for children to be playing there. Every window in sight was open. Winter felt very thirsty and checked his watch.

Halders approached from the other side of the playground. He handed over a Coke with ice.

'McDonald's,' he said, taking a drink from his own.

'You've saved my life,' said Winter, half-emptying it in one go.

'Don't exaggerate,' said Halders, looking up at the building. 'Did you find it?'

'A woman thinks she's seen him going into one of the flats on the third floor.'

'Thinks?'

Winter shrugged.

'Is that enough for us to be able to go in on?' Halders asked. 'You're in charge of this jamboree.'

Winter took another drink.

'Yes,' he said.

'I like it,' said Halders. 'Have you contacted the owner of the premises?'

'Here he comes now,' said Winter, indicating the man walking towards them.

The flat smelled stuffy. If only we could measure the age of air, lots of things would be very different, Winter thought: nobody's been here since 18 June. That's when the windows were closed.

'Cosy,' said Halders when they'd finished going through the flat in their protective overshoes.

There was an unmade-up bed in one of the two rooms, the smaller one. A lonely-looking little table and a sort of armchair in the bigger room. In the kitchen were a larger table and two wooden chairs. That was all. No decorations, no flowers, no pictures, nothing to suggest any character. No curtains, just venetian blinds, closed.

There was nothing at all in the bathroom. No toothpaste, no toothbrush, no bottle of shampoo.

'You can't take it with you when you go,' said Halders, looking round again. His voice echoed round the bare rooms. Winter could see the beads of sweat on his brow.

'We'd better start looking for Mr Svensson,' Winter said.

Halders laughed ironically. 'I know a sixth-hand flat when I see one.'

'Even so, there must be a first-hand contract,' said Winter. 'The start of the chain.'

On the way out Winter went up to the next floor and knocked on the helpful woman's door. She seemed pleasantly surprised when she answered.

He showed her another photograph. She nodded, several times.

'I'm quite sure,' she said.

'The girl has been here,' said Winter as they walked

through the playground to the car. 'Angelika Hansson. The neighbour saw her with our man.'

'An observant neighbour.'

'Indeed.'

'Some people see more than you would expect them to,' said Halders.

'I reckon she's reliable.'

'So the girl has been here.'

They had come to Winter's car. The paintwork was hotter than hell.

'He was in the photograph taken at her graduation party. They knew each other.'

'But her parents didn't recognise him.'

'There can be lots of explanations for that.'

'At this stage? When we're looking for whoever killed their daughter?'

'Strange things happen to people,' said Winter, touching the paintwork again. 'How much is it possible to explain? Explain properly?'

'Let's get out of here,' said Halders. 'I'm coming with you. I'll get my car later.'

They drove through the tunnel, past Långedrag. There was a lot of traffic heading for the seaside.

'I'm selling my flat,' Halders said. 'It's going to be the house for me from now on.'

Winter's mobile rang in its holder on the dashboard. He listened, said 'thank you' and hung up.

'There is a Svensson on the lease, but he doesn't actually live there.'

'Where does he live, then? Actually.'

'Watch this space,' said Winter. 'Sara's looking for the next link in the chain.'

'Who might lead us to the third?'

'We might come across a name we recognise.'

They came to the roundabout next to the park.

'Let's take a look,' said Halders.

Winter parked a hundred metres away. They walked over the grass. There was a slight whiff of damp from the pond. Lots of people were standing in it, up to their thighs in water. Others were in the shade of the trees. No cooler, but at least they were protected from the sun. A little queue of parents with children snaked back from the ice-cream van.

The police tape had been taken down. It seems so long ago, Winter thought. Another age.

'You can almost see as far as the place where the Nöjd girl was killed,' said Halders.

Winter looked. It was hidden by trees, but that was the place all right. You could walk over the grass to it, if you wanted to.

'Nothing new from the boffins playing with the tape?' Halders asked.

Winter shook his head, and looked at the hollow, the clump of trees and bushes. It looked cold, it was so dark in there. Another world.

'One of these days we'll see him come over the grass and stand in front of that bloody rock,' Halders said.

Winter said nothing.

'Then he'll take out the lead and look for the dog he doesn't have.'

Winter closed his eyes. Halders didn't speak. Winter could hear faint sounds from the pond, as if somebody was treading water. A faint noise, but a sign of life. He opened his eyes again and looked at the hollow and the surrounding trees. It was a dead spot, would always be dead. Grass ought not to grow there. No leaves on the trees. Nothing but rocks, darkness. He could hear the voice on the answerphone in his mind, the grunting, drowning out the faint sounds of life coming from all around him. It would be there to the very end.

27

Winter drove towards the town centre. The exhaust fumes that had built up in the tunnel irritated his nose. Halders started coughing.

Halders had taken his CD with him and put it into Winter's player.

'Modern country,' Halders said. 'Julie Miller.'

'Sad stuff,' said Winter. '"Out in the Rain", isn't it?'

'Cools you down,' said Halders.

They circled yet another roundabout.

What did the boy who'd disappeared know? Did he know anything about why and how? Who was he? Had *he* been strangled, the same as Angelika Hansson and Anne Nöjd? And Beatrice Wägner. Don't forget Beatrice.

Don't forget Jeanette Bielke either. Nor her father. Nor her mother.

'What impression have you got of Jeanette's mother?' Winter asked.

'Not much,' Halders said after yet another coughing fit. 'She's a sort of shadow.' He cleared his throat, opened the window and spat into the slipstream. 'She's kept out of the way whenever I've been there.'

They stopped at a red light outside the Opera House. Sails were slack on boats in the marina. Bronzed bodies in bathing costumes sat in the pavement cafés.

Everything was blue, white, yellow, brown, brick red.

'There's an awful lot of innuendo in this case,' Winter said.

'You can say that again,' said Halders.

'It's time we dug more deeply into that.'

'Unless it's just sidetracks.'

'Sidetracks are there to be followed until you come to the cul-de-sac.'

Halders didn't respond. He was watching two families crossing the street in front of them. Two men about thirty, each pushing a pram. 'You can say that about most things in this life,' he said when they moved off again.

'What, exactly?'

'Well . . . most things are really sidetracks that are there for you to follow, and they nearly always lead to a cul-de-sac.'

Winter didn't respond. The death of Margareta hadn't changed Halders' philosophy of life.

At the same time, it summed up their work. Sidetracks. Cul-de-sacs. Sidetracks. Cul-de-sacs. In the end there would be no more cul-de-sacs left, but if they worked hard and had a bit of luck there would be one last track and they'd follow it and this one wouldn't lead to a cul-de-sac. That was where they were heading, all the time. That was their job. Follow tracks as far as hell, where they might find some answers. Not answers to everything. You never find that, he thought. Seldom explanations. There aren't so many explanations for people's secrets. Who has ever had life explained to him? There is no ultimate summary of life. Life simply comes to an end, just like that, much too early for some; it simply stopped, like a sun suddenly falling out of the heavens.

*   *   *

Yngvesson was working in his sound studio when Winter arrived. The studio was a little room inside another little room. There was a jagged line dancing on one of the computer screens, like a heartbeat.

'Not pleasant listening,' said Yngvesson, turning to face Winter.

'What can you hear?'

'Well, the particular sound made by a noose being tightened around somebody's neck, for one thing.'

'What did she say before that happened?'

Yngvesson swung round to face the control console, which, like the room itself, was surprisingly small.

'It's mainly a struggle. Moaning. No specific cries for help.'

'A struggle? Is there any doubt in the attacker's mind about how it'll end, do you think?'

'What do you think yourself, from what you've heard so far?'

'No.'

'No,' repeated Yngvesson. 'But in cases of rape there's often a moment when the victim sees an opportunity of escaping. Of breaking free. Lots of victims have talked about that, afterwards. It's as if there's a sort of . . . gap in the struggle, or the assault, when the attacker hesitates, or seems to hesitate.'

'Apologises?'

'No. That comes later,' said Yngvesson. 'If at all.'

'What do you hear in this case?'

'I don't hear any doubt,' Yngvesson said. 'No doubt at all.'

It was silent in the studio. Winter could hear nothing from the world outside.

'I'm wondering if she knew him,' Winter said.

'How do you mean?'

'If there's any way you can hear that she recognised him. Knew him.'

'That I can't say,' said Yngvesson. 'Not yet at least.' He looked at Winter again. 'You'll have to rely on your detective work for that. And the clever way in which you phrase the questions you put to those who knew her.'

'Yes, OK.'

'What I can tell you, though, is that he says something to her,' Yngvesson said.

'Can you work out what he says?'

'If I can filter it out from the sound image when it's at its clearest.'

'When's that?'

'When they're close to her bag. That's when the sound is best.'

'So he definitely says something to her?'

'Or to himself. Do you want to hear?'

Winter nodded and sat down on the chair next to the biggest computer.

The voice came over the loudspeaker. This isn't black metal, Winter thought. This is the real thing.

NNAAAAIEIEIEYRRRRYY!

RREIEIYYYY!!

Winter looked at Yngvesson. His profile was sharp, calm, professional. God only knows what he was thinking.

'He might be saying her name,' said Yngvesson without turning his head. 'She was called Anne. AAAIEIEIE . . . that could be her name.'

Winter listened.

'Can you make it any clearer?'

'I'm trying, I'm trying. Not yet. I need to do some more work on the high register, try to lower it. There's a lot of background stuff that needs washing out as well.'

'Such as?'

'Various hums and buzzes. The wind, presumably. Traffic noise.'

'Traffic noise?'

'Yes, traffic noise. A car goes past. About thirty metres away, perhaps fifty.'

'It's several hundred metres to the main road.'

'Not on this tape. I think it's a car, and it's close by, as I said.'

'It's possible to drive a car along the cycle track there.'

'There you are, then.'

'So a car might have driven past while it was happening?'

'It seems so.'

'They ought to have seen the bike lying on the ground,' said Winter.

'People pay no attention to such things,' said Yngvesson.

'Somebody in the car ought to have seen something of what was happening,' Winter said.

'In that case you'd better start looking for another witness.'

'Can you tell what make of car it is?'

'Of course,' said Yngvesson dryly. 'Hang on a minute and the computer will tell you its registration number as well.'

Yngvesson played the sequence one more time.

'There.' He rewound, then played it again. 'There. That's a sentence of some kind. Or a sequence of words, at least. Not just a mad burbling.'

Winter could hear the burbling. It sounded worse every time he heard it. Like watching a snuff movie.

People being killed for real. A snuff tape. A real murder.

'I'll crack this, by God I will,' said Yngvesson.

'Can you tell if he's young or old?' Winter asked.

'One thing at a time.'

'But will it be possible?'

The technician shrugged, barely visibly, once again absorbed in his work.

*

Ringmar went to fetch some coffee. He muttered something as he headed for the half-open door.

'Come on, it's your turn,' Winter shouted after him.

Ringmar came back, but had forgotten the milk. He had to go back again. Winter was at the window, smoking. Mercator weren't as good as Corps. You could import Corps yourself from Belgium. Maybe ask one of the thousands at EU headquarters who commute between Sweden and Brussels.

A canoe passed by on the river. Winter watched the ripples from the paddle – the only movement out there this afternoon. No cars, no trams, no aeroplanes, no pedestrians; no sound, no wind, no smell, nothing except the man paddling eastwards with the sun like a spear in his back as rays found their way through the buildings at Drottningtorget.

'OK?' said Ringmar from behind him, putting the cup of coffee on Winter's desk.

'What do you say to putting a tail on Mr Samic, the club and restaurant king?' asked Winter without turning round. He took a last drag on his cigarillo before stubbing it in the ashtray on the window ledge.

'Why not?' said Ringmar. 'If we're clever with it.'

'I was thinking of Sara,' Winter said.

Sara Helander. One of the new detectives, already an

inspector and on her way to higher things. Relatively unknown about town. Good-looking, without being stunning. Nobody ought to look too stunning in this job, Winter thought. Except me. But that's in the past now.

He glanced down at his khaki shirt, shorts and bare feet in deck shoes.

'Have you spoken to her?' Ringmar asked.

'Yes,' said Winter, turning to face him. 'She knows as much as the rest of us, and is keen to do it.'

'When?'

'As from now.' Winter checked his watch. 'Exactly now.'

'Then why bother to ask me?'

Winter shrugged.

Ringmar drank his coffee.

'Is she on her own?'

'So far. Then we'll have to see.'

'Put somebody else on it, Erik.'

'I don't have anybody else just now.'

'Find somebody else.'

'OK, OK.'

'Which car are you giving her?'

'Yours,' said Winter.

Ringmar choked and spat out half a mouthful of coffee over Winter's desk, thankfully missing all the papers.

*

The shadows were long and stretched when he drove to the Bielkes'. The old houses were in the dark behind neatly trimmed hedges that held at bay the light trying to force its way into the gardens.

The big verandah was deserted. Winter parked close by it. The gravel crunched under his feet as he walked from the car to the steps.

Irma Bielke emerged from a door on the right before Winter got as far as the verandah. Just for a second he thought she looked very much like the girl in the photograph from Angelika's party. The same age. He looked again, but the similarity had gone.

She was fifty, but looked younger. He'd have thought she was about his age.

He hadn't phoned in advance, just gone there.

'Jeanette's not at home,' she said. 'Nor is Kurt.'

'I've come for a chat with you, as it happens,' Winter said.

'With me? What about?'

'Can we sit down for a few minutes?'

'I'm on my way out.'

On her way to the verandah, Winter thought. What she was wearing was equally suitable for lounging around at home, or for going out – the same as everybody else: shirt or blouse, shorts and bare feet in comfortable shoes.

A candle was burning in the room behind her. Winter could see it through the door. It was on a little table near the window.

'Are you allowed to just drop in on people like this?' she asked.

'Can we sit down for a few minutes?' Winter asked again.

'There's nothing else to be said,' she replied. 'Not to Jeanette, not to Kurt, and most of all not to me.'

'I'm not going to lay down the law,' said Winter. 'I just want to ask a few questions.'

'Are you suggesting there are any questions left to ask?' she said.

'It won't take long.'

She gestured towards the cane furniture further back on the verandah.

'Please spare me all the crap about this being for Jeanette's sake,' she said. There was a sudden trace of steel in her voice. 'Going on about how the rapists, or whatever euphemism you might use, will be arrested more quickly, the sooner we help you by answering all the questions that come raining in from all sides.'

Winter said nothing. He sat down. She remained standing, leaning against the wall. Her eyes were dead. Winter stood up, remained standing. There was a smell of trees and dry grass. The candle seemed brighter now.

'How is she?'

'How do you think?'

OK, Winter thought. Let's stop beating about the bush.

'She won't be going to university,' said Irma Bielke.

'Really?'

'The application had been sent, and she'd been accepted; but she's decided to turn it down.'

'What's she going to do instead?'

'Nothing, as far as I know.'

'Go in for something else?'

'I said nothing.'

She sat down and looked at him.

'Aren't you going to ask me how I feel?'

'How do you feel?'

She looked at the room where the candle was burning.

'It wasn't the end of the world. There are worse things to worry about.' She looked up at Winter as he sat down. 'Aren't you going to ask me about what worse things?'

'What worse things?'

'HIV, for instance,' she said. 'We got the test results this morning.'

Winter waited.

'Negative,' she said. 'Thank God. I've never known it so positive to have a negative response.' Winter thought she gave a curt laugh. 'You've chosen a good time to visit. We're happy again.'

She moved into half shadow. Winter wondered what to say next.

'Where is Jeanette this evening?'

'She's gone swimming with a friend,' she said. 'It's the first time . . . since it happened.'

'What about your husband?'

'Kurt? Why do you ask?'

Winter said nothing.

'Why do you ask?' she said again.

Here we go, Winter thought. The candle had gone out. There was a smell of sea, all the stronger now.

She was looking past him, at something in the garden. Winter could hear the wind, sounding like something moving through the treetops. Her face was expressionless. 'I don't know where he is.' She seemed to give a laugh, or it might have been something else. 'I seldom do.'

'Is he with Jeanette?'

'I don't think so.'

She stood up.

'Is that all, then?'

'Not really.'

'I have no wish to talk to you any more.'

'When did you last hear from Mattias?'

She stopped in her tracks. Like freezing a video frame, Winter thought, but more sharply focused.

'I beg your pardon?'

'Mattias. He's evidently found it difficult to stay away from here.'

'Are you referring to Jeanette's former boyfriend?'

'Are there several Mattiases?'

'Not that I know of.'

'I'm referring to the boyfriend,' Winter said.

'I've forgotten what you asked.'

'When did you last hear from him?'

'I . . . I don't know.'

'What happened between them?'

'Why is that important?' She seemed surprised, her face had surprise written all over it. 'Why does that matter? Now?'

'Don't you realise?' he asked.

'No.'

'Have you never thought about it?'

She thought, thought.

'Mattias? No. That's not possible.'

Winter said nothing. She looked at him, straight at him.

'Surely you can't think that? That Mattias . . . that he might have done something to Jeanette?'

No, Winter thought. Not him. But he didn't answer her question. Instead he commented on the sound of a car in the street.

'Is that your husband coming home?'

'It's his car,' she said, going past him again.

A car door opened and closed. Footsteps on the gravel, on the steps, a voice.

'What's he doing here again?'

Winter turned round. Kurt Bielke was standing at the top of the steps. He was wearing a white shirt, grey trousers and black loafers. There was sweat on his face. He came closer. Winter could smell the spirits on his breath. Bielke must realise he could smell it. He didn't care.

'There's no time to turn before you or some other

pi– CID character appears,' he said. He took a step forward, swayed for a tenth of a second, took another step, looked at his wife.

'What's he said?'

She didn't answer.

Bielke looked at Winter.

'What has she said?'

'Where's Jeanette?' Winter said.

Bielke turned to his wife. 'Can you fetch a beer?' She looked at Winter. 'I mean *one* beer,' said Bielke, nodding at Winter. 'The inspector can't have one. He's just leaving, and you shouldn't drink and drive.'

Calm down, Winter thought. This is an important moment. It's telling me something. It's saying something about Bielke and his wife. Perhaps about Jeanette as well.

Irma Bielke hadn't moved.

'Am I going to have to go myself?' said Bielke. He smiled and turned towards Winter. Bielke had switched on an outside light on the verandah. His face was white in the glare. He nodded at Winter, raised his eyebrows and laughed, as if at a joke somebody had told him in his head.

28

Sara Helander was out walking through the warm evening. Two couples were sitting on the steps down to the canal, snuggled up close. The moon was reflected in the water, a band of gold. The outlines of surrounding buildings stood out sharply against the sky, like charcoal drawings. Scents wafted past her as she crossed over one of the harbour streets. A taxi glided slowly southwards, its sign leaving a streak of light behind it. A lot of people were sitting at pavement cafés. She could hear the sound of glasses and crockery and voices combining to form that special mixed language common to all pavement cafés in all countries all round the world.

Cars came and went outside the entrance to the dance restaurant. It also had a pavement section, but nobody danced there. There wasn't an empty table. She sat down at the bar and ordered mineral water with lime.

'May I treat you to that?' asked the man on the next chair. Her water was on the bar.

She declined with a smile and took a sip. Then another: she realised she was thirsty after driving into town and walking from the multi-storey car park.

The man looked at her. He was about her own age, thirty or so. Quite good-looking. But she wasn't here for pleasure.

'Don't drink too quickly,' he said. 'It'll hit you after-wards.'

'It's mineral water,' she said.

'It's the ice you have to look out for – the cold upset-ting your stomach.'

'That's why I haven't got any.'

'It shouldn't be too warm either,' he said with a smile.

'It makes no difference what I say, is that it?'

'No.'

'If you'll excu—'

'OK, OK, I'll keep quiet.' He smiled a third time, got the barman's attention and ordered another beer. He looked at her glass and she shook her head. 'Sure?'

'I thought you were going to keep quiet.' She took a drink. 'All right, another mineral water with lime. Cold but no ice.'

'Shaken or stirred?' the man asked. The barman was waiting with an amused smile.

Sara Helander looked towards the entrance. Johan Samic was there, talking to a couple that had just come in. She was exchanging pleasantries with the man at the bar, but wasn't neglecting her work. Maybe it wasn't a bad idea to look as if she had company.

Samic contemplated his customers. People were queuing up on the pavement outside. It was 10.55. A quartet started playing inside the restaurant. A proper old-fashioned smoochy number. The last thing I'm going to do is dance to that! she thought.

The man's beer arrived. The music suddenly grew louder.

'Do you dance?' he asked.

'No, I sit on chairs.'

He took a sip of beer. Perhaps he looked slightly embar-rassed. You don't have to be so damned bitchy, Sara.

'It's not exactly my kind of music,' she said.

'Not mine either.' He took another drink. 'I prefer rock.'

She nodded.

'Oh, I've forgotten your drink,' he said, picking up her glass which she hadn't yet touched. He held it up. 'Shaken or stirred?'

'Shaken,' she said, as she watched Samic walk to the doorway where he stood with his hands behind his back. The man next to her gave her glass a little shake and put it down again.

'Maybe I ought to introduce myself,' he said, holding out his hand. 'Martin Petrén.' She shook it, automatically and somewhat diffidently as Samic was walking among the tables, perhaps on his way out.

'What's your name, then?'

'Pardon . . . what?'

Samic had turned and was on his way in again.

'I've just introduced myself.'

'Er . . . yes, of course . . . S . . . Susanne Hellberg.'

'Cheers, Susanne.'

He raised his glass, and she thought she'd better do the same. He was pleasant and not unattractive. Maybe some time when she wasn't on duty—

'Well, look who it isn't!'

She felt a hand on her shoulder, lost her hold on her glass, which was halfway to her mouth. A hand shot out and grabbed it before it smashed onto the bar or the floor.

She hadn't seen Bergenhem arrive. That was skilfully done.

'Nice to see you,' he said, still holding the glass. 'This is a pleasant surprise.' He wasn't smiling.

The man who'd introduced himself as Martin Petrén

had put down his glass and was getting to his feet.

'Aren't you going to pay?' Bergenhem asked.

'Wh . . . what?'

'Hold on to this but for God's sake don't drink it,' said Bergenhem to Sara Helander, giving her the glass and leaning over the man who was about the same age as him. Everybody was thirty this enchanting evening.

'I saw what you did,' said Bergenhem quietly. 'I'm a police officer. I have my ID, you can be sure of that. I promise to show it to you later. We can leave here quietly and calmly and discuss this somewhere else. Maybe I'm making a mistake, but nobody is taking any chances. Nobody.'

The man looked round.

'I don't know what you're on about,' he whispered.

'There's a tablet dissolved in that glass. I watched you drop it in. You might have more tablets in your pocket, or you might not. Shall we go?'

The man didn't move. Bergenhem bent further down over him, spoke even more softly. 'Shall we go?'

'Now look. What the he—'

'I'm going to stand up now, and you're going to do the same.'

Sara Helander watched the men stand up. She hadn't heard everything Bergenhem had said, but she got the gist.

'Pay for both,' said Bergenhem. 'Come to your car then, but take your time.' He looked at the glass she was still holding in her hand. 'Bring the glass with you. Don't drink out of it.'

'I get it,' she said softly. 'Am I an idiot or am I an idiot?'

'Let's go, mate,' and they walked away, walked, like two friends, one with his arm round the other. Or two good-looking poofs, Sara thought as she paid and asked if she could take the glass with her if she paid for it. She wanted to go down to the canal to drink her water. The barman shrugged and refused payment for the glass, she'd 'already paid for it, really'.

Bergenhem was waiting in the car park. It wasn't far.

'Who is he?' she asked.

'Give me the glass,' said Bergenhem. He put it in a special holder and covered it.

'Where is the swine?'

'The uniforms took him straight in.'

'Good Lord, are you sure about this, Lars?'

'Yes. But not of what it is. Hardly vitamins, in any case.'

'GHB?'

'Probably. Or Rohypnol . . . we'll have to see.'

'I'm not even fit to go round doling out parking tickets,' she said.

'Now *that's* a dangerous job.'

'You know what I'm saying, Lars. I've made an absolute mess of this job. I'm a triple idiot.'

'On the contrary,' said Bergenhem. 'Between us, we've copped one of the dregs of society in the act of spreading his poison. We lured the swine into a trap and caught him red-handed.'

She looked at Bergenhem.

'Is that what you're going to put in your report?'

'Of course.'

'You're an angel, Lars.'

'You can buy me a drink sometime.'

'Whenever you like.'

'Be careful about accepting drinks yourself, though.'

274

'I shall nev—'

'We'd better be getting on with the job,' said Bergenhem, tapping the glass. 'I'll have to take this shit in.'

'Do you really think I can go back there?'

'Nobody saw anything unusual.'

'Are you absolutely sure?'

'We're professionals, aren't we?'

'Well, you are at least.'

'I said we. Get yourself back there.'

It was the same barman.

'How was the moonlight?'

'Beautiful.'

'Another glass of mineral water?'

'Yes, please.'

'Anything to eat?'

'Not at the moment.'

Half an hour passed. More and more people arrived. Sara Helander stayed in the crowded bar, turning down offers of drinks. A new barman appeared. He didn't have time to favour his regulars.

She moved a bit to one side and caught sight of Samic again. He was wearing a smart, light-coloured summer jacket that he didn't have on before. He walked through the tables and out into the street. If he took a taxi that would be fine. They weren't planning to follow him by car tonight.

Samic walked northwards towards the water, on his own. Sara could hardly see him among the crowds of people flocking back and forth between the river and the town centre. He crossed over the main road and turned right towards the marina. Lights from the Opera

House glistened in the water. The pavement café that formed a semicircle round the building was packed.

Then she saw Samic on the other side of the basin. He was standing still and appeared to be thinking. Behind him was a café closing for the night. It was 1.30. Suddenly there was a woman in front of Samic, talking to him. Sara couldn't make out her face at this distance. After five minutes they started walking towards the far end of the quay. Sara walked quickly round the basin, keeping her eye on the pair. It was easier now as places were closing and there were fewer people around.

She saw Samic and the woman turn the corner. They were twenty metres away. She paused and thought. There was nobody between her and the corner. She took a few more paces. The sound of music drifted from one of the cafés. She didn't hear the engine but saw the boat emerge from behind the corner and set off northwards along the river. Quite a large motor boat that could be beige or light blue or yellow, but just now looked orange and black in the glow from the street lights. Samic was at the wheel. He didn't look back. The woman was standing beside him, hair fluttering in the breeze.

*

When Lars-Olof and Ann Hansson came home early next morning, having spent the night with friends in the archipelago, they could see that something was wrong. As they stood in the hall, they noticed that it still smelled of night, a cool scent.

The window of Angelika's room was broken and standing half-open. Paper and books and smashed ornaments were scattered over the floor. The desk drawers were wide open. Angelika's clothes were in a mess in the wardrobe, and its door was ajar. Her bed was in disarray. The uncovered mattress was lying sideways.

Ann Hansson fainted. Her husband phoned Winter.

Winter and Ringmar stood in Angelika's room. Winter noticed that the fresh flowers, formerly in a vase on the bureau, were now spread out in a semicircle.

'Somebody was looking for something,' Ringmar said.

'Can you guess what?'

'Photographs.'

Winter agreed.

'Didn't bother to tidy up afterwards.'

'He knows what we're looking for,' Winter said.

'Could be an ordinary burglar.'

'There's a television set here,' said Winter, pointing. 'And a telephone on the bedside table over there.' He gestured towards the bureau. 'I'll bet her jewellery is still in the top drawer.'

29

Winter tried to read something in Andy's face. It was a map showing different directions.

'On which side of the river?' Winter asked.

'I'm not with you.'

'There's a bar there, isn't there? That Anne went to sometimes?'

Andy's face indicated that he thought it was nothing to do with Winter, that it was irrelevant.

'It's very important,' Winter said.

'Eh?'

'Can't you get it into your head that this bar is relevant to her death?'

You little shit-heap.

Ringmar could see what Winter was thinking. His face was a map now too.

Winter put the photographs on the table. Andy took his time.

'I don't recognise either of them,' he said.

'They're both dead,' said Winter.

Andy was silent.

'In the same way as Anne.'

'I don't recognise them even so,' Andy said.

'Is there anything else you recognise, then?'

Andy turned to look Winter in the eye.

'What do you mean?'

'The place. The surroundings.'

'No.'

'Take as much time as you need.'

'I don't recognise it.'

Winter didn't speak, just sat. He could hear faint noises of summer. They were in an interrogation room containing nothing of all the things outside. There were no colours in there. Sounds were muffled, filtered through the air conditioning, flattened to a buzz that could be anything.

Winter felt for the packet of cigarillos in his breast pocket. He could see the sweat on Andy's brow despite the low temperature in the room.

Perhaps it would happen now.

'I don't recognise it,' Andy repeated.

Then he said it.

'I've never been there.'

Winter was holding the packet halfway out of his pocket.

'I beg your pardon?'

'I've never been there.'

'Where?'

'There,' said Andy, waving his hand at the photographs on the desk.

'Where is it, Andy?'

'Where . . . where they used to go.'

'They?'

'Yes, they. There are several of them, aren't there?'

Winter waited. A car set off on an emergency callout, he could hear it. A voice shouted, more loudly than usual. Or maybe it was at normal volume in the thin air.

'You know where it is, Andy.'

No response.

'Where is it, Andy?'

He looked at Winter. His face changed, then changed again.

'What does it matter?'

'Have you still not got it into your head?'

'I'm just thinking of . . . of her.'

Winter nodded.

'Do you understand?'

'You can help her now.'

'It was so . . . innocent.'

'What was innocent, Andy? What?'

'The . . . the dancing.'

'The dancing,' Winter repeated, as if he'd been waiting to hear those words all afternoon. As if everything had been leading up to those words: the dancing.

A dance for a murderer?

'Tell me about the dancing,' Winter said.

'It was just an extra job on the side.'

'Tell us about the extra job on the side.'

'I don't know exactly what it is.'

'Just tell us about the dancing, then.'

'A bit of strip,' Andy said. 'It was . . . nothing much.'

'A bit of strip? Striptease?'

Andy nodded.

'She was a stripper. Is that what you're saying?'

'Yes . . . that's what she told me anyway.'

Winter held his eye. Why hadn't Andy said anything right at the start? From the first minute he knew what had happened to Anne. Dancing naked wasn't the end of the world, not even to old men like . . . like him, like Winter, an old man of forty-one, knocking forty-two. It wasn't the most desirable summer job, but it didn't mean eternal damnation.

But had it meant eternal death for Anne? And for the others? Had the other girls also had summer jobs as strippers?

Winter wasn't shocked to hear that young girls of about twenty earned extra cash at strip clubs. It wasn't exactly news. It was rather an increasingly wearisome fact. He felt more angry about the unknown prostitution young girls could be led into. Not so much in the clubs, they had a pretty good check on those. But over the net. The Internet, which was supposed to spread happiness and socially useful information to mankind.

At the very start of the case he'd ordered a check on the dodgy places they knew about in the seamier parts of town and by the railway line running east. They reckoned they knew more or less all there was to know about them. And the girls who worked there. Some had only just started secondary school.

Winter looked at the photographs of Angelika and Beatrice. Had they been there? Had they wiggled and waggled to kitschy disco music beside that brick wall?

He thought, then something dawned on him. Something quite different. It wasn't a club, not a restaurant, not a strip joint, not a bar.

It was a home. Somebody's private house.

If so, that would mean they'd have to start searching in a new way. A new way that wasn't possible. It could be anywhere. Any house. Any dirty old man at all.

'You said before that you didn't know exactly where it was,' Winter said.

'Yes.'

'But roughly?'

'I know which part of town.'

It was an entirely different part from what Winter had expected. Not at all where he'd tried to find a common . . . starting point. Where the trails started. A different part of town altogether. Over the river and in among the houses. Over the hill, through the viaducts, under the motorways. A far larger area than the one he'd expected. If Andy was right, that is. He'd already decided to hold Andy for six more hours. He didn't think he'd be contacting the prosecutor after that, nor even during it. But what he thought now was of no significance.

'Did you never go with Anne?' Winter asked.

'No.'

'Why not?'

'She didn't want me to.'

'And that was enough?'

He nodded. 'And it wasn't all that often anyway.'

'What wasn't all that often?'

'Her doing it. Dancing.'

'Was that all she did? Dance?'

'What . . . what are you implying by that?'

'I'm just wondering why it's taken you so long to tell me this, Andy.'

'It hasn't.'

'Maybe you know more than you've told us so far?'

'What? What else am I supposed to know?'

Winter said nothing.

'I don't know any more,' Andy said.

'About the other girls.'

'I've never seen them before.'

'About where this . . . establishment is.'

'I don't know, I've told you.'

'Why didn't she say where it was?'

'Why should she?'

'Was she never scared?'

'Eh?'

'Was she never scared, Andy?'

*

'Let's forget Samic for the time being,' Ringmar said. 'In any case, I don't think he'll lead us to where we want to get.'

'I suppose you're right,' said Winter. 'Will you speak to Sara?'

'I already have. Provisionally. She didn't seem best pleased.'

'Let her continue for another night, then.'

'Is that an order?'

'No.'

'What would Birgersson say?'

'No, probably.'

'Well, then.'

'What she does in her spare time has nothing to do with us,' Winter said.

'So you are prepared to exploit your staff until they drop, are you, Erik?'

'Of course.'

Ringmar rubbed his brow. He had only a light tan, suggesting that he'd been hard at work, mainly indoors, crouching over databases and print-outs.

'Mind you, Samic deserves being shadowed by everybody there is, and charged, and sentenced.' Ringmar scratched his stubble that was two days old by now, and would probably still be there when he went on leave two days from now. 'He's a nasty piece of work.'

'Meaning what? Do you reckon we should jail people for not being nice?'

Ringmar scratched his stubble again. Rehearsing for his holidays. No doubt it would start pouring down the moment he set foot outside the police station. That would be OK. The farmers could do with a drop of damp.

'The way things are now, Kurt Bielke would be a better bet.'

'Why's that?' Winter had a good idea why, but he wanted to hear Ringmar's view. 'What's he done?'

'Nothing.'

'Why are you linking the rape of his daughter with this business?'

'Reasonable suspicion.'

'Proof?'

'Zilch.'

'Evidence?'

'Zilch.'

'That sounds like a pretty convincing starting point.'

'Might he have raped his own daughter, Erik?'

Winter lit another cigarillo, the eighteenth today. The smell from the cigarillo mixed pleasantly with the evening air. The sounds coming through the open window were pleasant. The lights were pleasant, soft in the blue dusk. He could see two couples walking over the river and they looked pleasant. The river was flowing: pleasantly.

But Bertil Ringmar's question was far from pleasant. His own thoughts five minutes previously had not been pleasant. Nothing they'd been talking about had been pleasant, nothing they were working on was pleasant. If there was a polar opposite to the concept of 'pleasant', they'd found it in their everyday work.

'There's a lot of tension in that family, but that might be fairly normal,' Winter said.

'Normal for whom?'

'Normal for them.'

'Or it might blow up,' said Ringmar. 'Explode.'

'And the results, if it does?' Winter wondered.

Ringmar didn't answer.

'Should we maybe bring Bielke in and have a chat with him?' Winter said.

'Better to see what he's up to.'

'Why not do both?'

'Or neither,' said Ringmar.

Winter gestured to the heap of paper on his desk. He yawned, tried to keep his face straight, could feel the tension in his jaw, a warning of cramp.

'I'll try to read through this little lot again tonight,' he said. 'Then we'll see. We can discuss it tomorrow.'

'Will you be staying here?' Ringmar asked.

'Yes, what do you mean?'

'Well . . .'

'Instead of doing it at home, is that it?'

Ringmar sort of nodded.

'It's quieter here,' Winter said.

'For whom, Erik?'

Winter sat down, picked up a piece of paper with his left hand and looked up at Ringmar, who was still there.

'I thought you were on your way home, Bertil?'

*

Sara Helander was on her way home. Drop Samic? Oh no, not after last night. The date-rape swine was under arrest, would be charged within four days.

She'd gone home, still thinking that she was an idiot, and thought about Samic. But perhaps even more about the woman standing beside him in the boat, looking expensive. Hair flying, and the half profile making it impossible to make out her features.

There was something there. Something to do with Samic. She'd find out what it was. She was no fool. Nor was she foolhardy. But she . . . needed something, needed to do something. Not some dashing heroic deed, that wouldn't be professional. But something . . . clever. Leading to a breakthrough.

It was nearly 9.00. The sky was a concert of shades. The sun was on its way to the other side of the world. Down Under. Her sister had been in Sydney. Waded through the junkies crawling around King's Cross. Hmm. It had been uplifting as well. Sunny, beautiful, like here. Distances that seemed bigger the further away you got from the cities. The red earth. The dead heart. She'd received a postcard from Alice Springs labelled 'A Town Like Alice', but hadn't got the point until she showed it to Aneta who explained about the book. Oh, I see.

She went to the harbour known as Lilla Bommen. There were hundreds of people there now, in the boats, on the quay, in the pavement cafés, in front of the ice-cream stall. The Opera House was basking in the final rays of the sun that pierced the abandoned cranes on the other side of the river.

She turned the corner. Not so many people. More boats lined up, all of them motor boats as far as she could see. A few sails in the distance. It was just as hot here. A couple were sitting on a bench, looking at the water. People coming and going. Engines spluttering over the water. Pennants fluttering half-heartedly in the warm breeze: Swedish blue and yellow, Norwegian, Danish, one German. Something blue with a red, white and blue cross pattern in the top corner – wasn't that

Australian? Had some tough customer sailed all the way from Down Under?

She strolled along the quay, as if winding down after work. Which was what she was in fact doing, in a way. No. That wasn't true, no way. She looked for the motor boat she'd seen Samic steering, and hesitated between two, or three. Was it that one, or that, or that?

She remembered a badge to the left of the name on the stern, some kind of decoration. There was a light above it, helping her to see it. It was like a flower, in a dark colour.

One of the boats had a lily next to its name, *Nasadika*. It had a motor at the back and a ship's wheel. She knew nothing at all about boats. It looked expensive, but so did they all.

There was a Swedish flag at the stern. She stood on the quay, looking down at the boat.

'Can I help you?'

She turned round and hoped the person who'd spoken to her hadn't noticed her start.

'Er . . . I'm . . . I'm sorry,' she said, trying to adjust her feet and ensure that she didn't topple over backwards into the water.

The woman seemed to be smiling. Her face was tanned, but not too much. Blonde hair. Perhaps it could fly in the slipstream. It might be the woman from last night.

'You're sort of standing in the way of the steps,' the woman said.

'Oh . . . I'm sorry.' She moved along a few paces.

'Thank you,' said the woman.

'I'm looking for a boat belonging to a friend of mine,' said Sara Helander. 'I'd just established that it's not round here.' She pointed towards the guest marina. 'I think I'd better start looking over there instead.'

The woman nodded and climbed nimbly down onto the deck. She might be forty, or she might be fifty-five. No younger, maybe older. She looked fit. Sara Helander got a good look at her now, her face. Her face in profile. She recognised it from the picture taken at the graduation party that Winter had shown her. She had a handsome nose that somebody ought to have remembered. They'd asked around.

I recognise her, Helander thought. I recognise her now.

Was it tension or excitement she was feeling?

*

The beach party had been changed to the evening. Winter felt as if Christmas had come early as he cycled southwards with Elsa in the child seat. Angela was pedalling away ten metres ahead of them. He was thinking mainly about wind and sun as they rode round the bay and parked alongside thirty more bikes, then clambered down to the beach.

Somebody had started the barbecues, and one of the men handed Winter a beer. Anders Liljeberg, the first time he'd seen him for months. He hadn't seen several of the people milling around since the early summer, and he was glad to be here now. He drank his beer and settled down on the sands. Angela took Elsa to the water's edge. He leaned back and let all the voices buzz over him. He could smell the barbies. He could smell the sand. He raised himself on an elbow and finished off the beer. Angela and Elsa were splashing about in the water. Liljeberg had donned his grass skirt. It looked dark brown through Winter's sunglasses. Liljeberg started dancing his version of the samba, and others joined in. Winter stood up and took off his shirt. Somebody passed him another beer. The music was Caribbean, and the evening was just as hot as the music.

30

The music flowed over them. From where she was lying she could see the contours of the buildings opposite, the outline of the rooftops. Something round that might be a tree. The music was soft: an acoustic guitar, viola, cello, a piano.

'It's beautiful,' she said.

'A map of the world,' he said.

'Hmm?'

'That's what the CD's called. *A Map of the World*. Pat Metheny. Film music, I think.'

'I haven't seen it in your collection before,' she said.

'I bought it today. This is the first time I've listened to it.'

'What do you think?'

'It's good. Not something I'd have discovered myself, but Winter had recommended it.'

Aneta Djanali didn't answer. She moved slightly to the right, a bit closer to Halders who was lying still on his back in bed.

The children were asleep, had been for hours. He'd slept, twenty minutes maybe. It seemed like it at least. She hadn't slept.

How had they got into this position?

Why not?

They still had their clothes on. It wasn't . . . like that. Not yet, at least, she thought as a new track started, just the guitar now.

What would she have done if Fredrik had unfastened the top button of her blouse?

He would never do that. She wasn't even completely sure that he would want to. But maybe he would. Maybe he'd been on the point of doing it. Should she do it? Or should they continue being almost like brother and sister? With the difference that grown-up brothers and sisters didn't go around together all day *and* all evening *and* half the night, as they were doing now.

Did he love his wife? He did in the beginning. He must have done. Then they'd lost each other.

She raised her right wrist and checked the fluorescent hands of her watch: 2 a.m. It was starting to be morning out there. She moved her head slightly to see better. The night was weak now, the light stronger. It was taking over. It had been the other way round for some hours and Fredrik had quoted Dylan Thomas, as he had done another evening, possibly wrongly, possibly correctly: *Do not step gently into the good night.* 'It's the only bit of the poem I know,' he'd said, 'but I remember it from the sleeve of a record Chris Hillman made a few years ago.'

He was wheezing beside her now, the man who got his literary education from the sleeves of country records.

He had loved his wife and perhaps still did, when he was on his own; but that was not something he'd spoken about. There were the children to consider. He'd talked about the children, then. Sometimes a lot, sometimes not so much. It was the children he cared most about now. The children were here, in their rooms on the other side of the hall. He kept going in to see them, when it was time for bed, and when they were asleep.

She'd sometimes thought that was all that mattered for Fredrik Halders. He didn't show it, didn't speak about it. He was one of those men who long for company but are scared of actual contact. Who hide behind words that are hard and slippery and sure and empty.

Who can do away with themselves, she now thought as the first signs of the sun appeared over the rooftops. Who suddenly want to leave, fast, right now, want to run away, as quickly as they can.

*

Winter had driven westwards in the light of morning. Bengt and Lisen had had coffee waiting for him, which he'd drunk in the kitchen. There was a smell of freshly baked buns, and he accepted one from a tray, still warm. 'When Beatrice . . . left us, I spent hours baking,' said Lisen Wägner, 'baked and baked away like a madwoman. Fruit cake in the middle of the night, croissants, bread rolls. I threw the lot away: while it was still hot I threw it all away,' she said, looking at the baking tray.

Winter chewed the bun.

How the hell was he going to put this?

Was Beatrice a stripper in her spare time, as far as you know? Was that the in thing among high-school girls five years ago?

He'd seen the looks on their faces and it was obvious they didn't know, hadn't known.

Had he and his colleagues checked thoroughly enough with the other relatives? They hadn't paid house calls on everybody associated with Beatrice and her family. At that time they hadn't had the photograph of Beatrice, sitting in the same place as Angelika five years later.

He'd finished chewing, swallowed and took out the photograph again.

'We can't find this place,' he said. 'We've searched the whole of Gothenburg.'

'Then it can't be here,' Bengt Wägner said.

'I think it is,' Winter replied. He mentioned Angelika's name again and produced the photograph of her as well.

'Hmm, I suppose that makes it more likely,' Wägner said.

'It might be in a private house,' said Winter.

'Whose?' asked Lisen Wägner.

'I don't suppose it could be somebody you know?'

'Eh? Who on earth would that be?' she wondered.

'For God's sake,' her husband exclaimed. 'What sort of an answer is that?'

She had turned away to look at the table with the tray of buns cooling down. He had looked at Winter.

'If we'd recognised it we'd have said so straight away, of course. It doesn't matter whether it's in somebody's house, or where it is.'

'No.'

'Can I keep this photograph?'

'Of course.'

'You never know.'

Winter handed over the copy. He'd intended doing that anyway.

He'd been to see Lars-Olof and Ann Hansson late last night. That conversation had been a replica of this one.

*

Sara Helander was sitting at the big table in the conference room. She was tanned, browner than he was.

'And then came the river bus, just in time,' she said.

'I ran to catch it and it set off and I had them in view the entire journey.'

'Well done, Sara.'

'Their boat was moored ten metres from the river-bus stop, and when I got off I saw them leaving their boat.'

Winter waited. Halders waited, Ringmar and Bergenhem waited, Aneta Djanali, Möllerström, everybody.

Helander had told them about the woman; the pictures from Angelika's graduation party had done the rounds again. It's her all right, Helander had said. It's her.

'And so I followed them,' she said. 'It wasn't very far. There were quite a lot of people going to and from the jetty and the river-bus stop, so it was no problem.'

'There should never be any problem,' said Halders.

'Then it was a bit more difficult . . . but naturally no problem then either,' said Helander, glancing towards Halders. 'And then . . . well, they went into a house on the other side of the road and I carried on walking past it.' She looked round. 'A pretty big house, timber built.'

'Did they both go in?'

'Yes.'

'Could Samic be the Southern-European looking man on the party picture here?'

'Could be,' said Ringmar. 'With a good toupee, it could be him. But we haven't been able to check all that thoroughly.'

'Our toupee experts have said that it isn't a toupee,' said Halders with a sort of smile.

I wonder what Fredrik would look like in a toupee, Djanali thought briefly. Bloody awful. A man in a toupee's nothing to go for. Nor a man with a comb-over.

Samic hadn't been wearing a toupee on the boat or in the restaurant. Why should he be wearing one at that party, she wondered, assuming it was him? And if he had been there – why?

'We'd better take a look at that mansion,' Winter said.

'I'll go,' said Halders. He looked at the others.

'He'll be suspicious if he sees you, won't he?' said Bergenhem.

'He won't see me.'

'Oh no?'

'That's where my new toupee comes in handy.'

Somebody chortled, but soon stopped.

'Shouldn't there be several of us?' Helander asked.

Winter thought about it. Caution. Yes. Either they marched in and brought Samic to the station for questioning – six hours minimum, because that is what the investigation needed – or they waited. They were looking for an unknown address and they had an unknown name and there might be a connection. Possibly. That's the way they worked. It was no coincidence that Helander had seen Samic and followed him. If the river bus hadn't turned up they'd have found the house even so, but it would have taken them longer.

Samic was lying, but lots of other people were as well.

He wanted to know what was inside the house before they reacted.

'You and Fredrik,' he told Sara Helander.

'When?'

'Tonight.'

'What should we d—'

'That's enough now, Sara,' said Halders, getting to his feet. 'Let's do a bit of thinking for ourselves, OK?'

Yngvesson phoned as Winter was on his way to his office. The ringtone echoed round the empty corridor.

'I might have something for you,' the technician said.

Winter was there within five minutes.

'Listen to this,' said Yngvesson.

He started the tape. Winter listened: there was less to listen to now. Yngvesson had filtered the sound image, taken away as much as he could of what he called 'the porridge'. Winter was reminded of the noise on the beach the previous evening, fragments of other voices.

He looked at the tape. Where he had heard a park before, he now seemed to be hearing a room, a barren room.

He heard the girl, Anne. 'Oh, oh, oh, no . . . no, no, no NOOOOO, NOOOOOOOO,' a scream, something from inside her throat, choking noises when . . . something was squeezed round her neck.

A mumbling now, like a prayer, like a devilish bloody prayer, a sort of mantra, loud, louder than when there had been other noises there, noises that came from that park and the traffic round about it. These sounds were different, they didn't belong, sounds that ought to be eradicated, Winter thought, nobody should be forced to listen to this.

But he was here. The girl was there. He couldn't switch anything off.

'Here it comes,' said Yngvesson.

Winter listened. At first to what he'd heard before, but clearer, the same . . . cries but as if they'd been trumpeted through a horn and down a long tunnel, straight at him, nnaaaaeieieierr, naaieieierrayy . . . NAEEEIEIEE . . . NEEEER . . . NEEVVAAIYGGEE . . . NEVER . . . NEVERAGI!! NEVERAGI!!!

Yngvesson switched off.

'Neveragi?' said Winter.

'Never again.'

'Yes.'

'I don't think I can get any closer than that.'

'Never again,' Winter said.

Yngvesson turned back to his computer. It was humming away merrily, totally unaware of how clever it was. It must be pretty good, being a computer at times, Winter thought. Efficient, and always merry and carefree.

'It can't be her, I suppose?' Winter said.

'What do you mean?'

'She can't be the one speaking?'

'No.'

'Never again,' said Winter. 'Our murderer says "Never again".'

'That was the last murder. For the time being, at least.'

'That's not what it's about.'

'I daren't speculate.'

'He's not saying it to himself,' said Winter. 'He's . . . showing her that it will never happen again.'

'What won't ever happen again?' Yngvesson swung round in his chair to face Winter. 'It won't happen again? Never again?'

'What she's done. He's punishing her for what she's done.'

'For what she's done . . . to him?'

Winter thought. He would listen to the tape again

in a moment, he was thinking and preparing himself.

'Yes. Either directly or . . . indirectly.'

'Indirectly? For what she's done to others?'

Winter suddenly felt depressed, infinitely depressed. He wanted to sink down into the ocean and never rise up again. The sun could rise, but not him.

'I don't know, Yngvesson. It's going round and round. I must sit down while it spins.' He sat on the other chair. 'What did we say? Indirect? She's done something he's punishing her for.'

'Hmm.'

'For God's sake, Yngvesson; I don't know what to say about this. We'll have to see later if anything I do say is relevant.'

'But this isn't . . . personal, is it? Not in that way? He didn't know her, did he?'

'He knew her, or didn't know her. I don't know.'

'It does make a bit of difference, surely?'

*

Sara Helander and Halders were sitting in his car about seventy-five metres from the house that Samic and the woman had disappeared into.

The house was timber built, as tall as a block of flats, Halders thought. Four or five storeys and no doubt a huge basement stretching under the whole thing.

It was one of four similar houses, in a row. They blocked out the sun, but only to a degree. Some rays were shining directly into their faces. Sara Helander was squinting with one hand over her eyes. Halders was wearing sunglasses.

'Perhaps we should have parked behind the house,' she said.

'No.'

'No, you're right. This side is where the traffic is.'

There wasn't much traffic, but a few cars passed at regular intervals, on the way to the ferries and the new blocks of flats that were only a few metres from the water's edge.

There was a car parked on the drive. The garage was out of keeping with the house. Seemed to have been built in a different century. Maybe even two centuries between them. Halders kept his eyes on the house, on all the windows that were almost invisible against the light.

It was darker now. Helander had brought something to eat and drink. No sun in their eyes now. Nobody had entered or left the house. Halders was tucking into a sandwich that might have been egg and mayonnaise, or ham and cucumber, he couldn't taste anything. He checked his watch. Almost midnight.

Two cars drove slowly by, but continued past the house. Then they came back from the other direction, despite the fact that it was a one-way street.

'Down,' said Halders, and they both ducked out of sight. The headlights on the first of the cars were shining directly at them. They heard voices, but no words. Car doors were opened and closed carefully. The engines were still running. Then the cars set off again, their lights just a few centimetres over the two police officers' heads.

'Exciting, eh?' Halders muttered.

'Somebody went in.'

They waited, then cautiously sat up again. Everything was as before, except that there was now a light on in a ground-floor window.

'Were there lights in many of the rooms when you were here last night?' Halders asked.

'No.'

'More than this?'

'Yes.'

'Hmm.'

'Do you think it was Samic who just went in?'

'Doesn't he come by boat and Shanks's pony?'

She didn't answer. They sat quiet for some minutes.

It was getting darker all the time. It was a little darker now than it had been at the same time last night. Just as warm, but darker. The darkness for a new season was moving in. 'Do not step gently into the good night,' thought Halders.

'Here comes another car,' Helander said.

It was approaching from behind them.

'Keep sitting up,' said Halders. He ducked down just a little bit.

The car stopped outside the house. The door opened. A woman emerged.

'Is that her?' asked Halders, speaking mainly to himself.

'No.'

The woman seemed young. She went into the house. No more lights were switched on. The car left.

They waited. Halders drank some coffee, which steamed shyly as he poured it out from his Thermos.

'Somebody's coming,' Helander said. 'On Shanks's pony.'

Somebody emerged from the shadows below them, from the river. He climbed up the steps to the street. The steps were almost directly opposite the house. It was a man, and he looked round before crossing the empty street that was now lit up by the moon and the stars and the street lights, or was it the sky? He was wearing a light-coloured suit and his hair was the same colour as the street lights. He wasn't a young man. He turned right and seemed to be looking straight at them, as they sat hidden in the darkness of their car.

'He can't see us,' said Halders. 'Sit still.' He'd placed a piece of paper over the steaming cups.

The man turned towards the house and went in.

'Kurt Bielke,' said Halders softly.

31

It was quiet again in the street. The man had disappeared into the remarkable house. Helander had never seen Kurt Bielke before.

Night was starting to turn into day. She could see the lights from the night's last ferry from Denmark on its way to the dock on the other side of the river.

Halders got out of the car.

'What are you going to do?' she whispered.

'Take a look at this place.'

'Isn't that a bit risky?'

'We'll soon find out.'

'Shall I phone for backup?'

'Good God no. I'm only going to take a little look.'

'Don't do anything silly, Fredrik. I'll check on you every twenty minutes.' The mobile phone would vibrate in Halders' pocket, but there would be no sound.

'I'll phone you,' said Halders. 'But if you do ring and I can't answer, I'll switch off to signal that all's OK.'

'Twenty minutes.'

He didn't reply, but left without a word. She never saw him cross the street, but shortly afterwards thought she might have seen a shadowy figure in the garden behind the house.

*

Halders stood under one of three trees ten metres from the house. There was a light in two of the windows, but he couldn't see anybody. There was no sound coming from inside.

Now what?

There was no door leading down to the basement. That would have been too easy.

The two windows on the left were dark. He moved swiftly over the lawn. Both windows were the old-fashioned sash type and appeared to be closed, but the left-hand one didn't close quite flush. Halders guessed there would be a catch that he couldn't see and he took a thin chopstick that he'd taken from Ming's that same afternoon from his inside pocket. He inserted it into the narrow crack, located the catch and unfastened it. It wasn't easy as the window was almost two metres from the ground.

He opened the window and put the chopstick back in his pocket.

He looked round. There was a water butt at the gable end a few metres to the left. He went up to it to test how heavy it was, and found it was quite light as there had been no more than one or two short thundery showers for ages. It wasn't difficult to carry it to the window.

He climbed onto it and peered in: furniture outlined in the murky darkness, a door looking greyish-white at the back of the room. Nothing animate in there.

Halders clambered through the window, and looked back but saw nobody racing up with a machine gun. Nobody came barging in through the door.

303

He could hear the usual sounds of night from outside.

Now what?

He went to the door and listened. No footsteps. A mumbling sound coming from somewhere, music perhaps. He could see there was no light on the other side of the door, so he opened it.

He found himself in a hall, empty. There were a couple more doors. A Chinese box, he thought. Go in through one door and you find another one. Go in through that, go in through the next one. You always go in, but never out.

There was a light behind the door to the right, at the end of the hall, but a weaker light under the door to the left. As if it were coming from further away. He walked quickly and quietly to this one and took hold of the handle. He opened the door carefully and saw a staircase leading down to the light.

Sara Helander expected Halders to come back at any moment. The idiot. I was supposed to be playing the heroic part in this drama. I found the house. It should be me creeping around inside.

She knew that she would never do that.

A car approached from behind and passed. She'd heard something but not seen it until it drove past and parked outside the house. It had been moving slowly with no lights on. A shiver ran down her spine. Had they seen her sitting in the car?

Nobody got out. She ducked down, but was able to see the silhouette of somebody in the driving seat. Their arm was bent. Whoever it was might be on the phone. Maybe talking about the occupied car not far away.

This is dangerous, she thought. More dangerous than we anticipated. I'll phone as soon as I can. More than twenty minutes has passed.

Halders went down the stairs. He *crept* down. It felt as if he were acting in a film. Normally he never crept. When had he last crept? When he reached the fourth step he suddenly thought about his children. He could see Margareta. The whole of my life is passing before my eyes. Does that mean I'm dying? Huh. We're all dying. Nobody lives for ever. Am I scared? No. I have my SigSauer in its holster and I'm strong. It's definitely stupid of me, coming in here. There's a woman I think I'm in love with.

He was at the bottom. This was the basement. There was another door in the Chinese box, and it wasn't closed. Ten metres to go. He could walk that without casting a shadow. There was music. He could see a shadow himself. The music was some awful disco rubbish from the lunatic seventies. He went closer and the music came closer. He saw that the door led into another hall, or a narrow corridor. Somebody was moving in there. Halders took out his gun, which was cold and comradely in his hand. What am I getting into? he thought. He could hear a voice, a woman's voice, and then a man's voice, shouting, or bellowing, no, something different, sobbing now, Good God, the voice was rising and falling, the awful music bounced down the brick-lined corridor, which felt narrower and narrower the further he passed along it. He could see the woman gyrating to the music; she was wearing a G-string, nothing else: she was chewing gum, thinking about something else, and Halders was closer, there was a pane of glass between her and the man who was on all fours in front of her and baying to the moon, wearing no clothes but a dog lead round his neck. Kurt Bielke was staring at everything and nothing without seeing, it was him, and Halders saw his body starting to twitch, like a religious fanatic in a state of ecstasy at some cult meeting, a cult meeting, Halders repeated to himself. I'll shoot that filthy bastard right between the eyes, he thought. Bielke swayed backwards and forwards and Halders had seen all he needed to see for the time being, thank you very much, and took a step backwards, then another, and felt the blow, actually felt it, *saw* it with the eyes in the back of his head, as if it were coming at him in slow motion, as if it were all over before it actually smashed into his skull.

*

A dog started barking on the other side of the street but stopped abruptly, as if it had been beaten. Winter got out of the car and crossed the street in his shirt and shorts. The shirt felt tight round the collar. He'd spoken to Angela on the phone, and she'd sounded . . . flat. Tomorrow they'd try to get down to the beach, in the evening. He'd have to get some sleep first, but he didn't know when. 'It's too hot in the flat,' she'd said. What she'd actually said was that houses are cooler. Still, before long all this heat would be over and they wouldn't have another summer like it until the next millennium and by then they'd all be very, very old in their flats or houses.

The front door was open, as were all the windows Winter could see. Benny Vennerhag was outside at the back, as always. The pool shone: black water. Vennerhag turned to face him.

'Have a midnight dip.'

Why not?

Afterwards he dried himself on the bath towel Vennerhag had brought him, and pulled on his shorts without underpants, which he'd wrapped inside his shirt: he didn't intend wearing that again tonight.

'Would you like to borrow a shirt?'

Winter shook his head.

'Enjoy that?'

Winter nodded.

'How about a beer?'

'Yes, please.'

Vennerhag stood up with difficulty, swayed unsteadily and disappeared into the house. He came back with two beers and sat down again, heavily.

'Are you drunk?'

'A bit.' Vennerhag opened the bottles and handed one to Winter. 'An intimate little dinner here at home with lots of decent drinks.'

'Nothing to eat?'

'Cotriade.' Vennerhag saluted with the beer bottle. 'What do you say to that, you snobby bastard? You thought I gobbled egg 'n' bacon morning, noon and night, didn't you, eh?'

'I never said any such thing.'

Vennerhag took another drink, yawned and looked at Winter over the bottle neck.

'Couldn't this have waited until tomorrow?'

A telephone rang inside the house, possibly several as the sound was so clear. Winter looked at Vennerhag's mobile on the plastic table under the parasol, but it was switched off. No compromising conversations in front of the Chief Inspector.

'I have to ask for your help in finding out more about

the boy,' said Winter. 'Have you any good contacts among the new Swedes?'

'New Swedes? I like that expression.'

'What do you prefer, niggers?'

'No, no, I'm just as politically correct as the next man.'

'This has nothing to do with that. Politically correct is a negative term used by cowardly types who try to hide their own sloppiness by accusing others of being politically incorrect.'

'Of course, of course.'

'Can you do this or can't you?'

'The answer's obvious, isn't it?'

The telephone rang again, ring after ring after ring. Vennerhag didn't stand up, looked at the silent mobile but didn't touch it. The phone continued ringing away in the house, making a racket like a car alarm. Vennerhag had renounced answering machines at an early stage, which according to him meant he had a better chance of living longer.

'Aren't you going to answer, Benny?'

'Not at this time of night. Only fools call now.'

'The fools seem keen to talk to you.'

'I'm also being polite to you as my guest. By not answering.'

Winter bowed.

'Are you dry now?'

'That was also considerate. What you really mean is: piss off.'

'In my own way, yes.'

The telephone rang again. Vennerhag looked at Winter, at his mobile. The foolish calls are piling up, Winter thought, getting to his feet.

'I'd better give you an opportunity,' he said.

'I shan't answer later either,' said Vennerhag.

'I admire you.'

Winter walked through the house, which was silent now. He noticed the smell of high-class cooking that persists in a house for hours.

Had Benny kidnapped a cook?

As he drove off, he heard the telephone ringing yet again, through Vennerhag's open door and windows.

*

Vennerhag stayed by the pool. He thought he could still hear Winter's car sweeping down the hills. He drank the rest of his beer and reached for his mobile. There were four messages and he listened to all of them: they were all from the same caller and all said the same thing. He suddenly felt sick.

The telephones in the house started ringing again. He stood up, swayed unsteadily, went inside and picked up the nearest receiver.

'Why aren't you answering?'

'I've just listened to your messages. What's happened?'

'Father-in-law's disappeared.'

The man was using the prearranged code. Vennerhag had always thought it was silly, but it was necessary. His house wasn't bugged, and he couldn't believe his phones were tapped, not by the police at least, but it was dead easy to trace old calls nowadays. Not to mention mobiles.

'I had a visit from a good friend of mine. He's just left,' said Vennerhag.

'What about Father-in-law?'

'I'll come now. At Mum's place?'

'Yes.'

'I'll be there as quick as I can,' said Vennerhag, and Johan Samic heard a 'pang!' as Vennerhag slammed down the receiver.

*

Sara Helander waited. Two cars came and went. One stopped outside a house further down the road. She rang Halders' mobile but there was no reply. Nobody switched it off.

She checked her watch. He'd been gone for a long time. Fredrik was an idiot, but not that much of an idiot.

She waited. An estate car drove past and went round the corner, but she thought she could still hear it through the open window.

It was hot in the car. It wasn't much cooler outside. She thought she could make out a long shadow at the back of the house. The trees were grey and black. Was that something moving there? A seagull cried. It would soon be a new day. Soon she wouldn't be able to see lights in the windows.

How many times have I sat in a car like this so far? she wondered. Stake-outs. But this is different, and we must get out of here. It'll soon be daylight.

There were vibrations over her right breast. At last.

'How's it going?' asked Winter.

'Oh, I thought it was Fredrik.'

'Isn't he there?'

'He . . . went a bit nearer to the house to . . . check.'

'Check what?'

She didn't answer. She didn't know what to say.

'When was that?' Winter asked. His voice sounded tired, like a rasp from his vocal cords.

'When he left?' She spoke softly. A young woman

310

came out of the house and got into a car that had driven up. It did a U-turn. She ducked down.

'Sara?'

'I just ducked down a bit. Er . . . it was nearly an hour ago.'

'An hour?!'

'Fredrik knows what he's doing. And it's less than an hour in fact.'

'How long, then?'

'An hour.'

'And he hasn't phoned?'

'No. I've phoned him several times but there's been no answer.'

'I'm coming there,' said Winter.

'It's starting to get light.'

'Yes, of course it is.'

'So I don't know if—'

'Bollocks to the light,' said Winter. 'I'll see you there. Stay in the car, but you don't need to hide. Check to see if anybody comes or goes.'

'I've been doing that the whole time.'

'I'll park in front of the house,' Winter said. 'Then you can get out.'

32

She saw Winter pull up outside the house. He got out of the car and waited for her to join him.

'We saw Bielke go in,' she said, 'Kurt Bielke.'

'Yes.'

'You don't seem surprised?'

'Let's ring the bell.'

They went up the steps. Seagulls were crying on all sides, laughing at them as Winter pressed the bell-push in the middle of the door.

'Fredrik recognised him,' said Sara Helander.

'Was he sure?'

'Yes.'

Winter rang again but still nobody answered. He knocked hard with his fist but there was no sign of any response. It would soon be fully daylight. The outline of furniture could be seen through the window to the right of the door.

'Come on, we'll go round.'

There was no door at the back. A window was open with a water butt underneath it.

'That's where he got in,' said Winter.

Winter looked down at the lawn and saw a few drops of dew on his deck shoes. He looked closer at the grass that hadn't needed cutting for weeks. There were tyre marks.

'Did you see a car here during the night?'

'I think so,' she said. 'A big shadow.' She looked back at the road. 'An estate car went past shortly before you arrived. Maybe a Volvo. I think it turned off into the neighbouring plot.'

She pointed. It was only partly built on, and it would be possible to drive over it, hidden by the house they were standing behind.

Winter approached the window and climbed onto the water butt. It was harder to keep his balance than he'd expected. The damp grass under the window had been flattened in places.

'Hello?' he shouted. The window was not secured, and he could open it with his elbow. 'Hello?'

*

Vennerhag collected Samic under the viaduct and drove west.

'Whatever's gone on, it's nothing to do with me,' was the first thing Vennerhag said.

Samic told him what had happened.

'It's got nothing to do with me,' Vennerhag repeated.

'You're as much in the shit as I am,' said Samic.

'I was part owner once upon a time last century, and that's all.'

The sun announced its arrival behind them. There were the beginnings of a glow on the horizon. They were alone on the road.

'Where are we going?' Samic asked.

'As far away from Gothenburg as possible,' Vennerhag said.

'You stink of booze.'

'Can you see the fuzz anywhere?'

'No.'

'Then shut up.'

'What are we going to do?'

'Nothing.'

'That won't be good enough,' said Samic.

'They don't know anything. There's nothing left in the place, is there?'

'I certainly hope not,' said Samic.

'And I don't want to know any more than is absolutely necessary.'

'Do you have conflicting loyalties?'

Vennerhag didn't answer, just kept on driving towards the sun.

'Are we on our way to the islands?' asked Samic.

'As far as you're concerned, it doesn't matter where you hide away.'

'Won't it seem suspicious?'

Vennerhag laughed out loud but there was no humour in the eyes that examined Samic in the rear-view mirror.

'Here comes the bridge,' Samic said.

They drove over it and Vennerhag turned briefly to look at the calm surface of the sea stretching away as far as the eye could see.

'We'll have to hide the boat,' said Samic.

'It's already been moved.'

'Not to here, surely?'

'Just shut up,' said Vennerhag, leaving the bridge and continuing in silence. He turned off after two miles and drove where the forest was thickest.

*

Winter clambered through the window. Sara Helander was standing outside. She heard a car on the road.

'If that's Lars and Bertil, tell them I'll try to open the front door as soon as I can find my way there,' said Winter.

314

'What if you run into trouble?'

'I won't,' Winter said.

A feeling in the pit of his stomach warned him to be cautious, or perhaps he was worrying about what might have happened to Halders. Halders had not been in touch. He'd gone in but hadn't come out, as far as Sara had been able to see.

The door was open, the hall empty and dark, there was no light anywhere apart from some pale daylight under the door at the other end. He went to the door and opened it: it led into a large room, and he could see the street through the windows. There was a hammering on the door. He went to unfasten the lock. Ringmar, Bergenhem and Sara Helander were standing outside.

'It's all quiet in here,' said Winter.

'Shall we take a storey each?' Bergenhem said.

They did so and Winter retraced his steps, and tried another door.

The staircase was steep. It was as dark as night. He switched on his torch and shone it down. The stairs led to a narrow corridor that led in turn to an empty room. He could see a curtain and a pane of glass. There was a CD player. The torch beam bored its way into the wall and shadows darted around the room, which smelled of stale sweat. Or something even worse, he thought. Fear.

He found a light switch. He pressed himself against the wall and switched on the light, which was white and dazzling for a second.

*

Vennerhag drove back with the sun in his face. The weather forecast on the radio said it was going to get even hotter, which sounded impossible.

He'd turned off the air conditioning so that he could feel the morning breeze through the open window. It smelled of things he recognised but had forgotten the name of. He was thinking about a lot of things. He felt calm, but the situation was complicated.

Ha, ha.

He hadn't asked for it. Things had grown worse and worse, but that wasn't his fault, not in that way, unless silence in itself was wrong. Well, yes, of course it is. You don't keep quiet about things like *that*. Even if it's got nothing to do with you.

He drove down the last of the hills towards the centre of town. He tried to think what he should do with her. With *her*. He hadn't had any help from Samic. Samic was dangerous for everybody, worse than *he* was. They could have him.

Better to wait and see what happens. Must think. Sleep.

*

Winter stood in front of the glass panel and understood. They'd find similar set-ups elsewhere in the house.

It was here. There was an answer. The girls had been here, they must have been here and done whatever they did. Danced.

Beier's forensic technicians would have plenty to occupy them here.

The house was deserted. Why? Because of Halders? Yes. Halders had appeared and that was why they'd all disappeared. 'All'. Who was all?

Where was Halders?

Winter looked round. The dust would have stories to tell for forensics: marks, stains, prints, fibres.

He went back up the stairs and into the big room, which was also a hall with a staircase leading up to other floors.

Ringmar appeared at the top of the stairs.

'Come up here, Erik.'

Ringmar waited for him at the top. A new hall, morning light coming through the door to another room.

It was a bar, and the trappings were familiar. The wall seemed to be built of real brick, but when Winter touched them he could feel the plastic. There was a table and some chairs, and peculiar decorations on the walls.

'Just like in the photographs,' said Ringmar.

'We've Sara to thank for this,' said Winter.

She had come into the room and heard what he said.

'Don't thank me until we've heard from Halders,' she said. 'I ought to have stopped him.'

'Stop Halders?' said Ringmar.

Bergenhem appeared in the doorway. 'I've been all round the place and it seems deserted, to say the least,' he said.

'OK, let's go and pick up Bielke,' said Winter.

They rang the doorbell and Bielke's wife answered, wearing a white dressing gown. Her expression was sleepy.

Bielke didn't say a word in the back seat of Winter's car. A patrol car was behind them. Bielke turned round once.

'Now you've overstepped the mark,' he said when they were in the interrogation room with no windows.

Winter was accompanied by Ringmar. 'This is an abuse of power.'

'We want to ask you a few questions,' Winter said.

Bielke didn't seem to be listening.

'We have some new information.'

'I'm saying nothing without a solicitor present,' said Bielke, whose face looked angular in the bright fluorescent light. His tan was criss-crossed by white diagonal lines.

'OK. We'll pause until he gets here,' Winter said.

Bielke's solicitor looked as if he'd seen it all before. It was 8.00 in the morning, but he was dressed as if for dinner. Perhaps he wondered about the weariness in the eyes of the two detectives.

Nevertheless, Winter detected uncertainty in the young man, in his movements, his eyes.

Winter started the interrogation again: 'I'd like to have some details about your movements last night,' he said.

Bielke waited.

Winter specified the times.

'It's impossible to ask—' the solicitor began.

'If you're going to keep interrupting you'll be out of that door,' Winter snapped.

'Wh . . . what?'

'You are interfering with the interrogation. You may ask questions if you want when I give you permission to do so, but you will do that when I've finished or you will be out.'

The solicitor looked at Ringmar, who nodded with a friendly smile.

'Is it legal to proceed like this?' asked Bielke,

looking first at Winter and then at his solicitor.

Winter asked another question.

*

Bielke was resting. His solicitor had left, but promised to come back.

'You need to get a bit of sleep, Erik,' Ringmar said.

'You're right.'

'Go home.'

'I'll sleep here. Two hours.'

'Three,' said Ringmar. 'We'll keep him for another six.'

'I want him put on remand,' Winter said.

'Molina will no doubt want more on him than we've got,' said Ringmar. 'And that's an understatement.'

Mr Prosecutor Molina always wants more than we've got, thought Winter.

'Send Bergenhem and a few of the boys round to his house.'

'It'll be your decision.'

'It is my decision. I've just made it.'

'What are they supposed to be looking for?'

'Angelika's camera,' Winter said.

'What?'

'The dog lead, the belt, cameras. Anything we need to nail that bastard.'

'I think he's sick,' said Ringmar.

'*That's* an understatement.' Winter looked at Ringmar. 'One hour from now Cohen will sit down with him and his solicitor, if he dares to come back.'

'Right.'

Cohen was an experienced interrogator whom Winter always relied on when he couldn't ask the questions in person.

'We have to press him for more information about Fredrik,' Winter said. 'I briefed Cohen about that.'

'I don't think Bielke knows what's happened,' said Ringmar. 'I don't think he saw Fredrik in there.'

'Fredrik may have seen him.'

33

It was Aneta Djanali who collected Hannes and Magda from school. Margareta's mother would arrive later in the afternoon and stay with her grandchildren, who were parentless for the time being. Djanali thought about that word: parentless.

'How long do you think it will take?' Grandma had asked when they made contact, with traces of hope in her voice.

How should she reply to that?

Djanali felt dizzy as the children came towards her, as if everything was happening somewhere else, as if she were seeing everything through a filter. As if a train were moving through the landscape, and she was sitting in it, looking out.

'Where's Daddy?' asked Hannes.

How should she reply to that?

'He's . . . on a mission,' she said.

'When's he coming back, then?'

'We're not sure. That's why I'm here to fetch you and Magda.'

The boy and his sister seemed satisfied with that. They all clambered into the patrol car. I don't want to drive them myself, Djanali had told Winter.

They got out when the car pulled up outside Halders'

house. She went in with the children and checked the time. Their grandma would arrive in two hours.

'Are you hungry?' she asked them.

*

She took some hamburgers and rolls from the freezer and Hannes showed her where the ketchup was kept, pointing with a tiny index finger. On the next shelf down was an onion and a head of lettuce starting to turn brown at the edges.

She fried the grey meat until it turned brown, and prepared the hamburgers. No onion for Magda.

'Are you from Africat?' the boy asked, speaking with his mouth full.

'Africa,' said his sister, looking somewhat embarrassed. 'It's called Africa.'

'My mum and dad come from a country in Africa called Burkina Faso,' Djanali said. 'It used to be called Upper Volta.'

'It's on top of Lower Volta!' said Hannes, giggling.

His sister gave him a nudge. Djanali felt the nudge herself. Fredrik, Fredrik, please come in through that door and say something idiotic about Ouagadougou. Anything at all, at any time. We'll get married a second later. Buy a house in a mixed-race area. Live here. Move to Upper Volta. Commute to Ouagadougou. Come in through that door. Phone me on your mobile, you big darling idiot.

'What's it like?' Hannes asked.

'In Burkina Faso? There's a lot of sand.' She looked at her untouched hamburger that was starting to go dry on her plate. 'I've only been there once, ten years ago.'

'Why not more often?'

'Well . . . I was born here. Here in Gothenburg. I'm Swedish.'

'Are there any lions?' asked Hannes.

'Not so many. There are more camels than lions.'

'Is it a desert?'

'Quite a lot of it is desert.'

'Have you heard about the aeroplane that crashed in the desert?' Hannes asked.

'It's a joke,' said Magda.

'No,' said Djanali, turning to Hannes.

'Well, the captain sent all the passengers out looking for food,' said the boy with a grin the width of his face. 'They'd all survived the crash, of course. He sent them all out, and they came back saying that they had good news and bad news.' He looked at her. 'Are you with me?'

'I'm with you.'

'"OK," said the captain, "let's hear the bad news first." "There's nothing to eat but camel shit," the passengers told him. "What about the good news, then?" the captain said. And the passengers told him: "There's lots of it!"'

She laughed.

'Dad told us that one,' said Magda.

The children went off to do their own thing. She washed up, and the sun was in her eyes so she pulled down the blind. In the living room she could hear the faint hum from Hannes' computer, the metallic ghostly voice from some game or other.

She turned to the collection of CDs. Hmm, Fredrik certainly had good taste, she thought, then adjusted that to: *has* good taste. HAS. American singer-songwriters, with a few dashes of alternative country.

She sat down with lots of covers in her hand. Outside,

the garden was dormant in the afternoon heat. The birds were asleep in the trees. Maybe the children were mercifully asleep as well? The computer in Hannes' room had gone quiet.

She played Buddy Miller – maybe Fredrik would hear it and come bounding in through the verandah door: Who the hell is playing my record, the bastard?

*

Winter had dozed on and off for an hour and a half, dreamed violent dreams that he'd forgotten when he woke up but which pounded away at his brain like a fever.

Fredrik Halders' face was the first thing he saw even before he'd opened his eyes. When he did, the wall in front of him was empty and piss-yellow.

He sat up, rubbed his face hard and checked the time. He reached out for the telephone on the narrow table in the overnight room and rang home.

Angela sounded worried.

'What's happening to you, Erik?'

'Don't worry about me. Fredrik's the one in trouble.'

'No news?'

'No. Is Elsa there?'

'She's having her afternoon nap.'

'Like me.'

'When are you coming home?'

When this is all over, he thought. It could go quickly now.

'We have a witness we need to talk to a bit more.'

'I've no idea,' said Bielke. His face was still austere, carved up by white lines. He hadn't slept. Winter had prevented him from smoking. His solicitor was present, listening and making notes. There would be complaints. Let 'em come. Winter read a few lines on the documents in front of him. 'I'm telling you yet again that I haven't seen that police officer,' Bielke said.

'He was in the same building as you, at the same time.'

'That's impossible, as I was at home in bed then. How could he be?'

'One of our police officers saw you go in through the door of the house in question.'

'That's a lie because I've never been there. I don't even know where it is, and I still won't know no matter how long you go on asking me about it.'

'Why are you telling lies?' Winter asked.

'Why are *you* telling lies?' Bielke was calm, but wasn't displaying the prickly arrogance often seen in the likes of him. A polished sociopath, Winter thought.

He suddenly felt very weary, much more weary than when he'd lain down on that far-too-soft bed. Helander had never seen Bielke before. It could be a mistake. It happens, and it's not good, but we're all human. What's Bielke?

He thought about Molina, the prosecutor. They had to have more evidence if they wanted to keep Bielke in custody. Five hours to go. Custody or freedom, temporary freedom for the man from Långedrag. He wanted Bielke kept inside. That would give them room for manoeuvre until the court made a decision about remanding him. He wanted Molina to agree that they had adequate grounds for pointing the finger at Bielke. And he wanted the adequate to grow into probable. But precisely what was Bielke suspected of doing? Involvement in the abduction of Fredrik Halders? The murder of three young women? The rape of his own daughter? What Winter had seen of Bielke didn't exclude any of those possibilities. Bielke is a key to something vital. I mustn't make any mistakes now.

He needed a witness. A piece of evidence. A link. Bielke would deny everything. He had the strength.

Winter thought about Halders again. Halders' head that was as well trimmed and sharply outlined and hard as the rocks at Saltholmen where people were sunbathing at this very moment.

The first thing they'd done was to look for Samic, and Samic wasn't there. Not at his dance restaurant, not at home, not with people they knew he was acquainted with. I'm not really surprised, Ringmar had said. He's wherever Halders is, Bergenhem had suggested. Did he mean in the realm of the dead? Winter hadn't responded, merely continued searching in the morning light, gazing out over the glittering streets of Gothenburg.

*

Bergenhem went to Bielke's house with his colleagues Johan Setter and Sara Helander. I'm everywhere, she thought. Maybe it will be better here. She didn't want to sleep, not before they'd found Fredrik.

Bielke's wife said nothing, but stayed in her room.

'We won't go in there just now,' Bergenhem said.

'Where shall we go, then?' asked Setter.

'Where's the girl?' Helander said.

'Gone for a morning swim,' said Bergenhem.

'We can start with her room then,' said Setter.

'We've already been through there,' said Bergenhem. 'Pretty thoroughly.'

'That was then,' said Setter.

'Does she know?' Helander asked.

326

'Know what?' Bergenhem turned to look at her.

'Exactly why her father was taken in at dawn?'

'Do we?'

The house is smaller than it looked from the outside, she thought. Several windows were partly open, letting in the smell of sea salt and stone, dust that had dried, grass that had burned in the sun. There was dust in the air inside the house, like a mist.

'I'll go out to the garage,' said Bergenhem.

Everything in there was hanging in neat rows or packed in boxes. Bielke owned everything the owner of an oldish house needed.

There were two cars in the double garage.

Bielke had gone to the house on foot. Helander hadn't seen a car. It could have been in the garage all the time. They would soon know.

Bergenhem went from box to box. It had to be done. Routine work produced results. The most unlikely things, such as a suspect hiding something compromising in an . . . ordinary place at home, were often not only likely but true. A revolver replaced in its rack next to the elk's head. A knife hung alongside all the others on their magnetic strip. A dog lead over a chair in the hall, as usual. A lamb chop put back in the freezer. A blunt instrument.

Dog lead. The Bielkes didn't have a dog. It would be excellent if we could find a dog lead or something else that could be used for throttling a victim.

He stood next to the smaller car, a compact estate, and tried the front door on the left. It wasn't locked. The keys were in the ignition. Locking the garage door was good enough.

He'd soon have to decide when they should call in the professional vacuum cleaners from Beier's unit.

Bergenhem opened the car door, wearing his white gloves, and quickly searched the glove box, the floor and the seats. Paper, crumbs, dust, a road atlas of Europe. A piece of dried chewing gum in the ashtray. No smell of tobacco.

He took the keys and opened the tailgate. A collapsible chair, a blanket that seemed to be scrunched together rather than folded, a wicker basket, a pair of working gloves stained with oil, a few old newspapers that were starting to turn yellow, a beer crate with no bottles, a single slipper split at the toe. Chewed by a dog, Bergenhem thought.

He pushed the objects carefully to one side and opened the compartment in the floor of the luggage space. He could see an unused spare tyre, a case with a jack, a case containing several screwdrivers. Nothing else. He put back the lid.

He was about to close the tailgate when he noticed the faint outline of another compartment to the left, not much more than a shadow on the side of the luggage space. It had a little symbol on it. He pulled at it, but it didn't open. He pulled harder and it came loose with a sighing noise. Inside was a place for the folded warning triangle and for a flat first-aid box. He took both objects out. Nothing else there. He put his hand inside and felt something right at the back, to the right, something hard. He knew what it was even before he saw it. He took it out.

The camera was dusty but quite new, small and compact and easy to use. What the experts call an idiot camera, he thought.

There was a film in it, partially exposed.

A secret place for keeping a camera. Next to the

warning triangle. Look out, Lars. There's a warning here.

He heard something behind him.

'What's going on?'

Bergenhem turned round and saw the girl standing there with her bicycle. Shorts, T-shirt, sandals, tanned, pretty, sunglasses pushed up onto her forehead, basket with a bath towel and a bottle of mineral water.

'Are you from the press?' she asked.

Bergenhem glanced at the camera in his hand.

'The police,' he said. He'd never met her before. He went up to her and introduced himself: 'Lars Bergenhem, CID.'

'Why don't you lot move in?' she said.

It's better that your dad moves in with us, he thought. She seems surprisingly calm.

'What are you doing with my father?'

'We have a few questions we want to ask him,' he said.

'It's always just a few questions,' she said.

'Is this yours?' he asked, holding up the camera.

'No.'

'Your dad's?'

'Where was it?'

'In this car. The Opel.'

'That's Mum's shopping trolley, you might say.'

Bergenhem nodded.

'I don't recognise that camera, though,' she said. 'I have a similar one, but it's in my room. Or was earlier this morning, at least.'

*

It was impossible to get any sense out of Bielke. Questions and counter-questions. Winter had taken a break and tried to get something more out of Andy, Anne Nöjd's friend who'd come to the station when they'd asked him to.

He knew nothing more. Winter was as convinced of that as he could be. Andy had been totally overcome by grief and made a catatonic impression.

Then Bergenhem phoned.

'The family here doesn't recognise it,' he said. 'The girl still has her own, and there's another one in the kitchen that they say belongs to the family, as it were.'

'Take them all and come straight back here,' Winter said.

'The wife and daughter?' asked Bergenhem.

'I mean the cameras.'

*

The only camera with a film in was the one Bergenhem had found in the car. Half the film had been exposed. They had the pictures within forty minutes. Winter, Bergenhem, Ringmar, Helander and Djanali were in the conference room when the photographs were delivered.

Nobody spoke as Winter put the pile on the big table and picked them up one at a time. Bergenhem broke the silence when he saw picture number two.

'For Christ's sake, that's Angelika Hansson.'

Her black face shone as brightly as the golden sun that coloured everything round about her as she stood on the sands close to the water. A lot of sand, Djanali thought. No camels and no camel shit, but a lot of sand.

There were four pictures of Angelika Hansson on that beach, all taken from about the same angle. The usual wasted snaps, Djanali thought. A solitary young man smiled, from the same place that Angelika had been standing.

'That's him,' Winter said. 'Angelika's boyfriend.'

'He's in this one as well, taken at the edge of the trees,' said Ringmar.

'It looks familiar,' Helander said.

If Fredrik had been here, he'd have said 'The west coast', thought Aneta Djanali.

'You can see the football pitch in the background of this picture,' said Bergenhem.

'Hovås bathing beach,' said Winter. 'That was taken at the Hovås beach.'

'What's this?' Helander asked.

'Angelika's home,' said Winter. Nobody outside the house. The photo was taken in the afternoon when the shadows were long.

'And this is where the Bielkes live.' Bergenhem looked at the next photograph. 'And this is another one of their house.'

Winter turned over another picture, like a blackjack dealer in a casino. It was good for the concentration to do it like this, good for everybody's concentration. There were only a few photographs left.

He found himself looking at another picture of a house, but a different one, north of Angelika Hansson's home, south of Jeanette Bielke's.

'What the hell . . . ?' exclaimed Ringmar.

'This is where Beatrice Wägner's parents live,' Winter said.

'What is all this?' Helander said.

'Where Beatrice Wägner lived,' said Winter in a tone that tried to change the atmosphere, break the spell.

No people here either, another summer picture, late, long shadows. Winter looked at the remaining photographs in his right hand. What was in store? He'd secured Bielke's remand, his arrest, but he didn't feel satisfied.

'Good God,' said Djanali.

'What's next?' Bergenhem leaned closer to see the next photograph.

Winter turned over the three remaining prints. They studied them in silence.

'Well, it looks as if we've got our man,' Bergenhem said.

'But why?' asked Helander, voicing what everybody was thinking. Madness, they all thought as well. Madness explains everything yet nothing.

He studied the last three photographs again, starting with the one on the left.

The house on the other side of the river, where Halders had disappeared.

The cave-like hollow where Angelika and Beatrice had been found, and Jeanette attacked.

The place where they'd found Anne Nöjd. Where her final . . . no, not words, where her final . . . screams, screams of terror, had been recorded by her own answering machine.

All the pictures had long shadows. They'd all been taken when the area hadn't been cordoned off.

Ringmar said what everybody was thinking.

'Did he know what he was going to do? Had all these photographs been taken . . . before? Did he take them *before* it happened?'

Good God, thought Aneta Djanali for the eighteenth time. The only thing missing is a picture of a place we don't recognise and that will be where we find Fredrik. Good God. Just think if we'd had these pictures . . . before. Before the crimes were committed. Murder will be committed there and there and there and if you can find the locations quickly you might be able to strike a blow for peace.

The camera was upstairs with Beier.

Bielke was sitting in a cell, or maybe lying down.

'We have jobs to do,' said Winter.

The shadows were lengthening outside. It would soon be evening. We'll soon be there now, he thought.

34

Winter went to Yngvesson's studio. It had a dry smell, as if from another year. Dust was dancing in tunnels of light over the computer. Tapes spun round emitting their dead screams. It was hard to breathe.

When this is all over I'll give up smoking. We'll buy a house by the sea and I'll take a year off work, and then we'll see.

'Still just bits and pieces,' Yngvesson said.

'Shall I come back another time?'

'This afternoon.'

'So far it hasn't been possible to recognise a voice. Really *recognise*. Do you think it will be possible? A voice we've heard before?'

'I'm trying to get as close to the voice register as possible, Erik.'

*

Kurt Bielke was staring at a point somewhere above Winter's head. The camera was on the table between them. Beier's forensic team had finished with it. There were several fingerprints on it, corresponding to others, as yet unidentified, found in Bielke's home. They hadn't taken Bielke's fingerprints yet. Soon, though. Winter had spoken to Molina about putting him on remand. Give me an hour, Molina had said. No. You spend another hour with him. Then phone me.

After that we'll take blood tests. Then it'll be over.

Bielke was still staring.

'I'll ask you one more time: do you know who this camera belongs to?'

'I've never seen it before.'

'It was found at your house.'

Bielke didn't respond. Winter looked at the tape recorder.

'I'll repeat what I've just said: it was found at your house, Kurt Bielke.'

Bielke shrugged.

'Why was it there?'

'Where?'

'At your house.'

'Where in my house?'

'We found it in one of the cars in your garage.'

'I've no idea.'

Winter thought. The air in the room already felt too hot and too scarce.

He wanted a confession. Now. Everybody wanted to go home. It was summer outside.

'You have been identified at the scene of a crime.'

Bielke said nothing. He could have said 'What scene, what crime?', but he said nothing.

'Talk to my family,' he said now.

'I beg your pardon?'

'Talk to my family.'

'Why?'

'They know where I've been.'

'I'm asking you.'

Bielke didn't reply to that. There was no answer in his eyes, nothing. His eyes were a blue reminiscent of over-washed jeans, blue going on white and soon destined to fade away altogether.

What happens if the fingerprints and DNA and the whole bloody shooting match don't turn up anything? Winter thought. If we have to let him go?

He asked again, kept on asking. Bielke answered intermittently.

*

Winter phoned Molina after an hour, and was granted the extension he asked for. It meant that he gained time, a maximum of four days to prepare a charge.

'Be sensible about this, now,' Molina said.

Winter hung up without comment. He felt a degree of relief. As that feeling drifted away with the smoke from his cigarillo out of the window and over the river, he thought again about what Bielke had said.

The family.

The man was mad. Everything he said might well mean something, but only to him.

He called the SOC team. Beier answered.

'Are your boys still at Bielke's house?'

'Not just at the moment. Why?'

'I'm going there.'

'Have you nailed him?'

'I don't know. When will we hear from Linköping?'

'About the glass, you mean? They're working overtime on it, I can promise you that. But you know how it is.'

They had vacuum cleaned Bielke's shoes and clothes one at a time and found some very small pieces of glass that would be compared with the broken glass they'd found after the Hanssons' house had been broken into. It wouldn't necessarily tell them anything, but they could measure various properties of the shards and establish if it was the same type of glass they'd found in the shoes, or in the breast pocket. It might be a pointer, no more than that. There were an awful lot of panes of glass. But one thing could lead to another, and then to another.

*

Yet again a hot afternoon with no promise of cooling down as evening drew in. The sun was still strong as it started to sink down to the horizon he was driving towards. All growing things were shrinking in the heat, starting to die and emitting the same dry, acidic smell that permeates old folk's homes as the bodies of ancient inhabitants dry out with the onset of death. The same smell of decay mixed with pungent disinfectant.

Winter turned into the Bielkes' drive.

There was nobody on the verandah. He noticed that Jeanette's window was wide open.

The family.

Bielke's deranged eyes might have indicated something. Jeanette. Was she the key to the riddles? Her relationship with her father was complicated. A bloody silly word, given the context. He was standing at the front door, which was slightly ajar. Was she mad as well? Her mother? Was she normal? He pulled a face at his thoughts, possibly an ironic smile: what's the point, where are we heading, are there really any alternative routes to take, in which world does life weigh heaviest?

He knocked on the door, which opened slightly more as a result. He shouted. No answer. He shouted again, and went inside. On his left he could see the west side of the garden through a window in the room beyond the big, bright entrance hall. The shadows were now at their longest. The gulls were shrieking louder than ever as they hoped to find titbits in the gardens.

Something moved out there. A shadow shorter than the rest, contrasting with the long, recumbent giants that would soon be swallowed up by the ground.

A movement. As if somebody had run over the lawn. Winter charged out of the door and raced along the gravel path that surrounded the house. Tried to look in all directions at the same time. Why on earth am I doing this? Because somebody's been here and it has to do with what's going on inside this house. Has gone on.

The gulls laughed at him as he stood there. No sign of anybody else. The shadows were everywhere now, as if a black blanket had been lowered over the scene. He approached the hedge separating the garden from next door: there were gaps big enough for somebody to scramble through.

What now?

He turned back, towards the house. No sign of movement, no voices, no shouts, no faces, no bodies. There ought to be a reaction. The door open.

Winter went back into the house. He couldn't hear a sound from inside, only the birds outside and the faint hum of traffic; no radio, no dishwasher, no extractor fan, no clinking of cutlery on crockery, no mixer, no telly, no voices, no laughter, no weeping, no screaming, no blows.

'Hello? HELLO?'

He stood stock still, but there was no answer.

'HELLO?'

He went upstairs. It was darker on the landing. A half-open door. Jeanette's room.

He could hear a faint humming noise now, a soft buzz that seemed to be creeping over the ceiling, slowly.

'HELLO? JEANETTE?'

Winter strode purposefully across the landing and into Jeanette's room. The window was still wide open and he looked out over the garden and the hedge and the trees and noticed a movement behind one of them and a pale . . . object that was there and then not there, a sort of sphere in the twilight, and Winter stayed put, watching movements in the bushes and among the trees, but he couldn't go racing downstairs again until he actually *saw* something; nothing happened, and he waited, but the face didn't return; it had been a face, or the outline of a face, but he hadn't recognised it, not from this distance.

He came to life again and heard the noise, still faint but louder than before, louder, it sounded like . . . sounded like . . . and he turned to look at the alcove on the right where the bathroom door was and . . . Jesus, he could see a trickle of water stuttering out from under the door and onto the parquet floor that was gleaming in the fairytale light of evening, and he could hear the sound now, a waterfall splashing down inside there and he flung himself at the door which was locked, he rattled the knob, pulled at it, shouted her name, took two paces backwards then kicked at the middle where the resistance would be lowest, three kicks and then a fourth and the bloody thing split open at last and he kicked his way into the bathroom that was overflowing with water and blood and he slipped and fell heavily and felt something give way in his elbow and scrambled to his feet with the pain affecting somebody else and his fancy khaki gear was now soaked in blood and water was still overflowing from the bath where Jeanette was sitting with her eyes closed or maybe open, he couldn't tell which, all he could see was her face and her neck sticking up out of or perhaps sinking down into the red sea and he glided over the ice towards her as if on skates, bent down and lifted her up. LIFTED a body that was heavier than anything else he'd ever lifted and the pain in his elbow was like red-hot needles in a wound.

*

It was past midnight when he got home with his arm in a sling and a pain that seemed like a caress compared with what he'd had to endure before. Angela gave him a hug, looking even paler than he did. She'd arranged for him to be treated far more quickly than he'd have been able to manage alone – but that was her place of work, after all.

The childminder was hovering in the hall, was duly paid, and looked frightened to death when she saw Winter's face.

'Pour me a whisky,' he said, from his chair in the kitchen.

'It's not a good idea to drink alcohol in your state.'

'Make it a double.'

She poured him a glass from one of the bottles on the work surface in the kitchen.

'Aaagh!' he said after the first swig.

He felt the alcohol penetrate his body, his head, down as far as his elbow. He took another drink.

'You should have stayed in,' she said. 'They'll have to put you in plaster once the swelling's gone down.'

'She's still alive,' said Winter, holding out his glass: Angela poured him a miserly measure. 'And another.' She filled him up, and he drank. 'She made it. She's still alive.'

'Only just.'

'But she'll make it.'

'It looks like it,' said Angela. 'She'd lost a lot of blood. Too much really, if she'd hoped to survive.'

Winter could still see the floor, the water in the bath. The pain, the pressure. The girl's naked body on the floor as he fumbled for his mobile that he'd dropped in the nasty, foaming water pouring out of the taps. He'd given up, slid into her room and used the telephone by her bed. He'd used his belt and a strip of curtain to bind her wrists. He'd tried her pulse, and maybe just about heard something. He'd given her mouth-to-mouth, but she hadn't responded. He'd checked her wrists, and looked for other possible injuries. Done whatever he could until the ambulance blasted its way to the door.

'Erik?'

'Hmm . . . What?'

'Time you were asleep.'

'Eh?'

'Let me help you.'

She leaned over him. She was strong.

She's stronger than I am.

'You saved her life.'

'I was too late.'

'If you hadn't got there, she'd have died.'

'She was more or less dead anyway.'

'Come on, Erik.'

He let her help him. Sank back into the pillow, and fell asleep.

The first thing he knew was the smell of coffee. He heard Elsa asking some question or other, using the new words she'd just learned. Angela answered. He tried to sit up, and felt the pain from his elbow.

Elsa was in her high chair in the kitchen.

'DADDY, DADDY!'

Winter went to see her, and stayed there for ages.

*

He'd phoned the hospital. Now he was sitting on the blanket in the living room, trying to protect his arm from Elsa. Angela lifted her up, and whizzed her through the air like an aeroplane.

'The crisis is over,' he said. Again.

'Hang on,' she said.

She came back alone.

'She's my baby. Goes to sleep at the drop of a hat.'

'Mind you, she's the boss,' said Winter with a smile.

'Stay at home now,' Angela said.

'She's awake,' he said.

'No she isn't.'

'Jeanette.'

'So you're going there?'

'Bertil and Lars are there already.'

'Is that your answer?'

'Can you help me on with my clothes?'

35

Jeanette Bielke had been drugged into unconsciousness again when Winter arrived at intensive care.

'The risk was too great,' said the doctor.

'When will she come round?'

'When will we bring her round, do you mean?'

Winter shot the doctor a look to concentrate his mind.

'In a few hours.'

'I'll be back exactly two hours from now.' Winter looked at the watch on the wrist that wasn't swathed in bandages and in a sling. 'I only want a couple of pieces of information.'

'I can't promise anything.'

*

Winter directed the patrol car to the square in Frölunda. The driver was young, and Winter didn't recognise him. The heat haze over the huge car park was reminiscent of a firestorm. The wind was picking up from the south. The thermometer display on the roof of the shopping centre was nailed down on 39. People crouched beneath the canvas sheets over the vegetable stalls, or they retreated into the shopping arcades where sweat made their bodies stiff and the chill set many of them coughing.

Nobody answered when they rang the bell of Mattias' flat.

He hadn't seen Mattias at the hospital. Had anybody phoned him? Did he know? Was it his face he'd seen in the garden? Mattias had been hanging around the Bielkes' house like an abandoned dog. Refused to accept the fact. Had Mattias spoken to Jeanette before she'd made her suicide attempt? Attempt? She might yet have succeeded.

He rang again, heard the sound echoing in the room behind the veneered door. Windows were open on all floors, irrespective of whether people were at home or not. There was a smell of fire in the stairwell, caused by the dry air inside.

It was better outdoors, but only just. The police constable was standing under a tree, contemplating his gaudy patrol car.

'I'm going across the square,' he said. 'Wait here.'

He passed the Arts Centre and continued to the building beyond.

The missing boy's gloomy flat was just as empty and unfurnished as before. They'd soon have to hand it over to the owner. The riddle it contained would be hidden by new furniture, curtains, pictures, colours, voices, signs of life.

The swings outside were moving, but only in the wind. Children would melt if they tried to sit on them, he thought. There was no sound to be heard. The birds had fallen silent. The southerly wind was stronger now, but still soundless, it set the swings swaying back and forth, and soon their ropes would become entangled. Clouds were building up to the south, thanks to the wind. Black clouds that as yet only covered about a fifth of the sky. He stood in the entrance. The wind was audible now, as if somebody had just turned up the volume of the drama being played out. Clouds raced over the sky at the speed of rockets. He retraced his steps. The drunks outside the Arts Centre staggered to and fro in the thundery wind.

Suddenly, it started raining, and stopped just as quickly. The sky turned blue in the south and it spread rapidly. All around children were jumping into puddles of water that would dry out in less than an hour.

He walked back to the square. Bergenhem waved from the unmarked car he'd driven up to where Winter was standing. They took the lift up to the flat where Mattias lived, but still nobody was at home.

'Something nasty could have happened to the lad,' Bergenhem said.

'Anything's possible,' said Winter. 'We'd better seal off this place.' He phoned the Frölunda police station. When their colleagues arrived they went down to the street. Bergenhem drove back to the city centre.

'Take the route past the park,' said Winter.

They parked the car and stood in silence by the pond, under the trees. The hollow was gleaming after the rain.

There was nobody walking up and down with a dog lead in their hand. Only he and Bergenhem had returned to the scene of the crime. I could stand here for a while every day for the rest of this summer and half the autumn, he thought. But I don't need to. We'll soon nail Bielke.

Nevertheless, something inside him raised doubts.

'I think of Fredrik all the time,' said Bergenhem as they resumed their drive to the city centre. Winter could feel the pain growing in his arm. He tried raising it, but that only made it worse. Perhaps it needed putting in plaster. But not now.

Jeanette's face had more colour than the pillow, but not much. He could see that she had difficulty in turning her gaze towards him when he entered.

'I won't stay long,' he said.

She closed her eyes.

'How do you feel?'

'It hurts.'

Winter sat in his office. He was forced to make time to read up again now. The pile of documentation was as high as a house. Night was setting in outside.

They had left Bielke for the time being.

His daughter's face had sunk deeper into the pillow as they talked. No, as Winter talked. He had asked her questions but she hadn't answered. There was a band of silence surrounding everybody he'd been in contact with. A dog lead, a belt.

He needed to go back to the paperwork. It was all there. It always was. It was there all right.

He read until his eyes gave up.

He was back a few hours later. He hadn't had enough sleep, but he was thinking more clearly. I shan't sleep any more until this case is solved.

Their priorities had changed, he could sense that in everyone. The most important thing was to get Halders back. The most important. No, just as important. One led naturally to the other.

Winter had phoned Vennerhag and Vennerhag had promised to put all his fellow gangsters on the case. Your most important task so far, Winter had told him.

The phone rang.

'I've got something interesting for you,' said Möllerström.

Winter waited for the call to be put through.

'Hello . . . ?'

'Detective Chief Inspector Winter here.'

'Er . . . we've seen those articles in the newspaper . . .'

The man and his son arrived an hour later. They were five years older now, and Winter guessed that could be seen most in the son, who would have been no more than ten at the time.

Winter had read about them again three days before, in the cold case notes, and then again only a few hours ago. They'd been standing there for ever, always packing their car next to the park, never again to be seen or heard. Until now.

'It's been a long time,' said the man. 'But here we are. Whatever it is you want us for.'

'How's your memory?'

The man smiled, or tried to. The son looked as if he wondered what the hell he was doing there.

'Why didn't you ever contact us before?' Winter asked.

'Well . . . we were going on holiday when it happened . . . and it was a very long trip that lasted well into the school term,' said the man. He looked at his son. 'I was given permission to educate him myself while we were away.' Perhaps that was a mistake, his eyes suggested. 'Anyway . . . we eventually came back home and there was nothing about that . . . murder that I would have linked with . . . us, as it were. Do you follow me?'

'But now there is,' said Winter.

'Well . . . the articles about that murder five years ago seemed to be appealing directly to us.'

'But I don't remember a thing,' said the boy, speaking for the first time. 'Except that it was hot that night. And I was tired.'

'It was late,' said the man. He looked round. 'Anyway . . . what can we try to help you with?'

We'll see, Winter thought. Several studies of the psychology of memory suggested that people are especially good at remembering faces. Even after a long time. There is a separate system inside the brain for storing faces, for working on faces. Winter had often thought about that. It fitted in naturally with the way humans had developed: it was important to recognise other people and their faces if you were going to survive. You had to be able to read emotions in other people's faces.

It had been of help to him, a part of his work.

Children learn to recognise faces at an early age. It has nothing to do with language. I can talk to the man and his son until the cows come home, but it won't do any good, he thought. What he wanted from them was a specific memory, an identification memory.

Five years had passed. He'd like them to confront Kurt Bielke in an identity parade, but it would be difficult to identify him conclusively, perhaps impossible. The passage of years was a big obstacle, now they'd be confronted with a face in a different light, at a different angle, with a different haircut. A different setting. Besides, had they even seen anybody that night?

'Did you see anybody?' Winter asked.

'Well . . .' said the man, 'I've been thinking about that, obviously. It's not easy. But that was a memorable night . . . I remember it because I had a devil of a toothache and we were going to have to start our holiday, later that same morning in fact, by looking for a dentist in Skåne.'

Winter waited.

'Anyway . . . it makes it easier to remember, if you follow me. I do actually remember somebody coming out of the park because I'd put down a suitcase and thought maybe I ought to go into the trees and look for a lump of resin to chew, because my grandma always used to say that was good for toothache, and I was sort of looking right at the trees and somebody came walking out.' He looked at Winter. 'I don't know what time it was.'

'We do,' said Winter.

36

They had the line-up ready by three o'clock: a classic
identity parade with the witnesses behind a one-way
mirror and the suspected murderer on the other side
together with various odd bods who had been wandering round the police station with nothing important
to do.

Bielke looks normal, but he's tired, thought Winter.
Bertil looks chirpier. Chirpier and more dangerous.
Ringmar was staring straight at the mirror, two places
to the left of Bielke. There were eight of them on the
podium.

The man and his son were standing next to Winter.
The boy looked as if he thought he was in a movie.

Winter knew his forensic psychology: a witness who's
seen the murderer should have it made as easy as possible for him to recognise the individual in the identity
parade, but at the same time it should be impossible
for a witness who has never seen the suspect to work
out who it is.

'Take your time,' he said.

'Er . . .' said the man.

Bergenhem and Djanali were standing next to Winter.

'Er . . .' said the man again, 'the light was sort of
different then.'

It was sort of a different time, thought Aneta Djanali. How many times had she seen Fredrik standing on that podium? Nine times out of ten, witnesses who were unsure would, after a brief pause, pick him out as the criminal. Witnesses who were sure would pick him out with no hesitation.

Winter gave a signal for the light to be dimmed. Let's imagine a warm summer night in a park in the centre of a big city. Somebody emerges from the bushes. Dries his hands after committing murder. Returns home and goes to bed.

'It's something to do with his hair,' the man said.

'I beg your pardon?'

'His hair was standing up a bit just as he passed under the street light.'

'Who?' said Winter. 'Who was under the street light?'

'Er . . . he had his head bowed towards his chest, if you follow me, and that meant you could see his hair more, sort of.'

'Who are you talking about?' Winter asked.

'Him over there,' said the man, nodding towards the mirror as if his eyes were emitting a beam of light. 'The bloke who looks as if he isn't enjoying it very much.'

Ringmar, thought Winter. He's playing his role too well. 'The third from the left?'

The man hesitated.

'Er . . . no, not him. I mean the one on the other side. The third from the right.'

'The third from the right?' Winter checked to make sure.

'Er . . .'

'Take all the time you need.'

'I can't be a hundred . . .' The man looked at his son, at Winter, at Bergenhem, then back at the podium.

At Bielke. He looked at Bielke. Bielke looked at Winter through his own reflection.

The witness nodded, as if to emphasise what he'd said.

It was a small step forward, useful for tomorrow morning when the application for the remand order was made in the cramped little court room over the corridor. Remanded in custody, of course. Fourteen days in which to bring charges, with the possibility of an extension.

'I remember now,' said the boy, whose voice seemed unnaturally deep for one so young.

The man turned to his son. They were the same height. Winter waited and felt his pulse racing.

'I remember what happened now,' said the boy. He was still looking through the two-way mirror. 'Funny, ain't it? I mean, it's funny. You shouldn't do something like that, should you?'

'Er . . .' said his father.

'What?' asked Winter. 'What do you remember?'

'What happened. And that it could be the same bloke as my dad said. Third from the right.'

Maybe he just wants to show his father what a good boy he is, Winter thought.

'Anything special?' asked Winter, gently.

The boy didn't answer, couldn't take his eyes off Bielke.

'Is there anything special about him that you recognise?' Winter asked.

'What he hasn't got,' said the boy.

'What he hasn't got.' Winter echoed him, still speaking gently.

'I remember it clear as day now, in fact,' said the boy.

Winter smiled encouragingly.

'The dog lead.'

Winter's heart skipped a beat.

'He had a dog lead, but he dropped it as he walked away, or ran, or whatever. I remember it sort of rattling on the gravel, and then he picked it up. I remember clearly standing there, thinking it was odd that no dog appeared.' The boy turned to Winter. 'I thought it was a pity the dog didn't come. Where was his dog? Yep, I remember thinking that before. Afterwards, I mean. Where was his dog?'

*

Winter was driven to the Bielkes' house because Irma Bielke had asked to see him – only him, nobody else would do. It was just as hot as before the thunderstorm. He played Halders' Julie Miller CD, just slotted it in, smelled the sea air after two kilometres, a scratchy but clear voice, like low-grade sandpaper.

She was waiting on the familiar verandah. Winter held out his left hand for her to shake in greeting.

'What's happened?' she asked, and broke down before he had chance to answer.

'How long's this going to go on for?' she asked ten minutes later. They were sitting on the tropical-looking furniture at the far end of the verandah.

What? Winter thought. Tell me what.

She looked at him. There were lots of tears still to come.

'I went . . . I went to see Jeanette today.' Tears burst forth. 'For God's sake.' She looked at Winter. 'Why wasn't I here?'

'Where were you?'

'Out . . . driving around.' She blew her nose and put the handkerchief in a pocket in her calf-length skirt. 'I've been out driving around rather a lot recently.'

Winter allowed it to seep away, down through the garden that would never be the same again for this family.

'We're getting divorced,' she said out of the blue.

Winter waited. More was to come.

'I've spoken to an estate agent. About the house.' She turned to Winter. 'Would you want to stay on here?'

'What does your husband say?'

'Huh.' She said it in a neutral tone, no exclamation mark.

'You visited him yesterday, didn't you?'

'That's why I wanted to . . . to talk to you.' She took out her handkerchief again and carefully blew her nose. Winter didn't move and she looked at him as if she couldn't see him sitting on the bamboo chair with the flowery cushions. 'What should I do?' she said. 'It's so hopeless. So awful. What should I do?'

'Tell me about it.'

She said nothing, seemed to have forgotten.

'Fru Bielke? Irma?'

'Mattias is Kurt's son,' she said, staring straight ahead.

'I beg your pardon?'

'Mattias. Jeanette's boyfriend. Or ex. He's Kurt's son from another relationship.'

Winter's mind was racing. Was Irma Bielke just as sick as her husband?

'You're telling me that Mattias is Kurt Bielke's son?' Winter asked.

'Everybody knew apart from me,' she said.

'Everybody knew?'

'He told Mattias when he found out that . . . that he and Jeanette were seeing each other. They were seeing each other . . . long before we knew anything about it. And then . . . then he told her. Jeanette.'

'When?'

She shrugged.

'Just before she told him. It must have been,' she said.

'She? Who's *she*? The "she" who told Kurt. Mattias' mother. Who's she?'

'No, I mean that Jeanette told Mattias.'

'But surely your husband had told him?'

She looked Winter in the eye.

'Neither of them believed it,' she said.

'What's the situation now, then?' he asked.

'Evidently he could prove it,' she said.

'How?'

'I don't know.' She looked Winter in the eye again. 'You'd better ask him.'

Winter heard a lawnmower starting up. He heard a helicopter and looked up to see it flying westwards, out to sea. He tried to catch her eye again.

'When did he tell you?'

'He hasn't told me,' she said, lifting up a book lying on the table. Underneath it was a handwritten letter that had been folded then smoothed out again thousands of times.

'Hasn't told you?' said Winter, looking at the letter.

'I took this with me from your police station yesterday,' she said. 'It's from Kurt, and I smuggled it out.' She looked at Winter. 'He said I shouldn't show it to anybody.'

'Go on.'

'He knew full well that I would.'

'Why . . . now?' Winter leaned forward. 'Why tell you now?'

'Haven't you noticed what he's been like since he heard about . . . about Jeanette? When he heard about her attempted suicide?'

We've been trying to exploit it, Winter thought. Now we've succeeded, it seems, just a little bit. Everything's collapsing for the Bielke family, and we're exploiting it.

'Do you know where Mattias is now?' Winter asked. She didn't reply, seemed to be gazing into other worlds that could mitigate the disaster her life was turning out to be. 'Irma. Where's Mattias? It's extremely important that we find him.'

'He's where she is.'

'What . . . what did you say?'

'He's done what she did. He's done the same as my little Jeanette diiid . . .' She screamed, sobbed, her head on her knees, bared as her skirt worked its way up.

'Do you KNOW that?' Winter asked, leaning over her, trying to help, holding her shoulders.

'What else could he have done? How could he li . . . live with that . . . ?'

'Jeanette isn't dead,' said Winter.

She said nothing. Then mumbled something he couldn't hear.

'I couldn't hear what you said.'

'My little girl,' she said.

'I have to ask you,' said Winter, 'if you know what your husband has done.'

'What has he done?'

'Don't you know?'

'I can't believe it,' she said. 'I don't want to live with that man any more, never again, but I can't believe that. That he's killed anybody. He might have gone to some

356

porno club or whatever it was, but not the rest.' She shook her head. 'But it's enough for me even so.' She shook her head again. 'Jeanette and I are going to move.'

'May I read the letter?' Winter asked.

'It's there.'

He picked it up and read it, handwriting that flew over the page like black seagulls. It said no more than she'd told him.

Could it all be lunatic fantasies?

'Who's the mother?' he asked.

She didn't answer. Winter repeated the question.

'I've told you, he hasn't told me anything.' She looked up. 'He kept that secret between him and her all these years and I don't know who she is. I DON'T WANT TO KNOW. I could . . . I could . . .' But she let it drop without explaining what she could do to the woman who had shared her husband all those years ago.

Winter needed to get back to the police station, to Kurt Bielke before he sank into eternal silence.

He took out the photograph from Angelika's graduation party. Irma Bielke looked away.

'You must look,' said Winter.

She looked at the woman's profile. Winter could see the relief in her face. Note how important it has been over the whole span of our evolutionary history to be able to recognise other individuals and to read intentions and emotions in their faces, he thought.

'I've never seen her before,' said Irma Bielke, turning to Winter. 'I don't know her. Who is she?'

'I don't know. So far, it's just a face we've got. We don't yet know where it fits in.'

'There's something I've forgotten all about,' she said suddenly. 'Good Lord. That was really *why*.'

'Why what?'

'Why I wanted to talk to you. Or why I wanted to meet you.'

Is there more? he thought. The floodgates are evidently not yet completely open.

'Thank you,' she said.

'I beg your pardon?'

'Thank you. You saved her life. OK, I know she's not yet out of danger; but she's still alive and she's going to live. I'll make sure that she lives.'

Winter didn't know what to say. She reached out and put her hand on his right shoulder. He gave a start.

'You're a good man.'

A good man in the right place. He could feel the pain in his elbow. It had started again, at this very moment. Time for another Voltaren.

She dried her eyes, blew her nose, stood up. Something was over. Over and out, but there was hope there. He could see it. There would be something else after hell, something cooler and stronger.

'You must have something to drink before you go. And your police officer waiting outside as well.'

His mobile rang on the way back. His elbow was aching something awful, even though he used his other hand to answer the phone.

'I've managed to produce a few more words,' said Yngvesson. 'The same voice, more words.'

'What words?' Winter asked.

'You'll have to come here and listen. I've got about as far as I can go.'

'I'm on my way.'

He hung up and found himself having to squint as the sun suddenly shone straight into his eyes. One more hour, maybe two. One day. He could see Halders' damned face in his mind's eye. There was no other face. I'll be seeing you.

37

The APB on Samic had gone out several days ago. The headlines on the news placards filled all the available space, black on yellow, like dark clouds obscuring the sun. There were reporters everywhere. Winter tried to ignore the media attention as something that didn't affect him, had nothing to do with him, with *his* world. He wanted to think his way into a world that was bright and full of summer, evenings spent in pavement cafés where the buzz of activity increased then declined as darkness set in. Playful dips in the sea with salt left in your eyebrows afterwards on the rocks when the water had dried on your body. All that kind of thing.

A group of reporters was waiting in the newly renovated foyer. Notebooks and pens and large and small cameras. Winter walked straight past them, staring fixedly ahead. It was like a film, only worse.

Yngvesson's tape was spinning round like the course of time. Winter remained standing. There was a scraping noise in the loudspeakers. Yngvesson had added an extra pair to amplify the roaring. He looked tired, or worse.

'Here it comes,' he said.

Winter was now able to make out words from what had previously been an atonal cacophony:

'I XKXKBL BEFORE! BEFORE! XBLBSFF HAVE TOGLCXBL BEFORE! BEFORE! AAIII!'

Yngvesson stopped the tape.

'Is that all?' asked Winter. He could feel something in the back of his head. Something inside.

'All? It's quite a lot, I'd have thought.'

'I didn't mean it like that,' said Winter. 'I was just asking if there's any more.'

'No.'

'Play it again.'

Winter listened. 'BEFORE! BEFORE! AAIII!'

'Before,' said Yngvesson. 'He's said something to her before.'

'Or to somebody else.'

'Or done something before.'

'Sounds like an old codger,' Yngvesson said.

'What did you say?' Winter asked.

'It sounds like an elderly man.'

Winter had heard it before. Before. Jesus, he'd heard it before. No, READ it before. It was in the cold case files.

He went to his office and phoned Möllerström, the invaluable officer in charge of computer files. Everything was on the hard disk. Run a word search. Möllerström had gone home early for once. Children's party.

'Get him on the phone.'

Sorry about that, Mölli.

Bergenhem was still around. Winter filled him in. Bergenhem didn't recognise the words.

'What are you doing at the moment?' Winter asked.

'Setter and I have started that check on Samic's business interests. Names. Old business contacts.'

'Addresses?'

'Masses. But we can't go checking to see if he's with every one of his old contacts, Erik. We have made a start nevertheless.'

'Bielke?'

'Well . . . his name's there as well. Some property deals. Co-ownership of some third-rate diner. But we knew that already. And at least we know where he is at the moment. And also where he lives.'

Not for much longer, thought Winter, and he could picture Irma Bielke, crushed and yet unbroken at the same time, on her way to the estate agent's.

She wasn't mad.

He'd offered to go with her. He could help her to move into a hotel. Or to a relative's, or a friend's. She'd declined. She was already on her way to somewhere else, somewhere better.

Bergenhem stood up.

'If that's all . . .'

Winter thought about Halders. About Angela and Elsa, and how he ought to stand in the window and have a smoke and turn up the sound of Brecker's *Time is of the Essence* that was spinning round in the Panasonic, in its usual place on the floor.

He thought about the paternity claim. As far as he was concerned it was just a claim, there could be hidden intentions behind it. Bielke hadn't made any such confession to him.

He stood by the window. Long shadows again, black spears floating along the river on the other side of the park lying silently below his office. The park, park, park, park, park, park . . .

He put his cigarillo in the ashtray, returned to his desk and dialled Mattias' number. No reply. The boy might have hanged himself from a tree or be at the bottom of a river after all. Or he might be wandering around the baking-hot houses.

Winter stood up, went to Möllerström's computer and started the search. The telephone rang, but he let it ring. As he was searching he remembered, suddenly remembered. It wasn't just the word. It was the voice as well.

Bergenhem drove. They had to weave their way cautiously through the mass of pedestrians and the pavement cafés. Everybody was in the streets, which were glowing in the heat: children, teenagers, the middle aged, senior citizens, gigolos, tourists, newly-weds, divorcees, families with children, whores, pimps, drunks, police, junkies, the Salvation Army, lunatics, all on their way from nothing to nowhere.

The park was the city's lung, and masses of people were wandering down the cycle tracks or over the lawns.

'Pull over outside,' said Winter.

Bergenhem found a space in one of the little side-streets. They entered the park from the north.

'I've been here every day, almost,' said Bergenhem. 'Discreetly.'

'Hmm.'

'I expect the same applies to y—'

'Shh.'

They were standing by the pond. A group was picnicking quietly to their right. Some one-legged flamingos were viewing the scene. Winter could smell grilled meat from the pavement café behind them, heard a single peal of laughter gliding over the water. The shadows had lain down now, as if the trees in the park had been taken down for the night but would be put up again the next day.

'Let's go a bit closer.'

'I'll stay here,' said Bergenhem.

Winter took three strides to the next tree. It was ten metres to the hollow near the big rock, opening up like a black cave. The vegetation round about was swaying gently, a final rustle before settling down for the night.

Winter heard a loud engine noise from somewhere and a souped-up moped with a madly grinning teenager on board came racing over the grass. Winter turned and saw Bergenhem shaking his head. The moped made a U-turn on the other side of the pond, came back making the same racket and disappeared along the road a hundred metres away. All was quiet again, quieter than ever before now that the commotion had subsided. Winter stood still as if he knew, really *knew* that so much had led up to these seconds and that everything might come to an end here, not absolutely everything, but a lot would come to an end if he stayed here now, or if he came back tomorrow, or the day after and the day after that, and did all the other things one always did when looking for the answer to a riddle.

There was a rustling in the branches over there. Nobody emerged or walked past. No movement in the corner of his eye.

He stood still. Bergenhem would soon start moving and they'd return to the police station.

Something moved inside the hollow, in the darkness. A shadow deeper than the other shadows. Winter stayed put. It was now. Now. A figure moved, still a shadow. Moved again, made its way towards the exit. Winter could see the outline of a head, a body. Suddenly a face, only a blurred oval in the deceptive twilight. A pale impression of a face he'd seen through Jeanette's window.

Mattias emerged from the bushes and onto the grass. He was moving his head backwards and forwards, like a dog sniffing the wind for traces of people or other animals. He wore shorts and a shirt that was still black from the black light behind him. He took two more paces forward. His shirt suddenly turned white and flapped slightly in the breeze, unbuttoned at the bottom. The same shirt. A button was missing, and it's in Beier's office, Winter thought. The shirt flapped again, as if the breeze had suddenly grown stronger, but there was no breeze where Winter was standing.

He walked away from the tree trunk. Mattias gave a start and turned to face Winter. Winter took two paces. Mattias didn't move, his head up, as if he were still sniffing the air. Winter could see his eyes now, Mattias' eyes, there was no sign of recognition in those eyes, no longer, and Winter approached as if invisible and Mattias' head started moving again, backwards and forwards. His right hand was moving, as if following a rhythm. Winter was so close now that he could smell the acrid aroma coming from the boy who was swinging his arm higher and higher, and the dog lead he was holding glittered in the light like silver and gold.

*

When Winter had found the report he was looking for he'd read it and looked for the words. It was Halders' last conversation with Mattias. He could hear the voice behind the words as he read.

'Jeanette hasn't said anything, has she?'

'Why don't you let her go, Mattias?'

'What do you mean, let her go?'

'You know what I mean.'

'I did that ages ago. Let . . . everything go.'

Then Mattias had fallen silent when Halders showed him the picture of Angelika's boyfriend.

'Do you recognise him?' Halders had asked.

The conversation continued. Then Mattias said it: 'It'll . . . never be like it used to be.' Mattias had repeated it, something different. A normal thing to say, but not now, not any more. And not what came next, after a short pause. 'It was different before. I've told you. I've told you before.' He repeated it again soon afterwards. Halders asked a few follow-up questions and that was all Mattias said, but it was enough. It was enough now.

Winter had finished reading, phoned Bergenhem and they had driven to the park. There had been no other place to go to.

38

In the back seat, Mattias said nothing. Winter could see the glow from the neon lights passing over his face without him blinking a single time. The glittering dog lead had been exchanged for handcuffs that gleamed in similar fashion.

They took him through the back entrance and up the stairs to a cell, then everyone assembled in Winter's office. Winter felt too nervous to move to a bigger conference room. He was smoking, drumming his fingers; he looked at each face and noted that Djanali's displayed the most worry.

This was not a moment to open the champagne.

'We'd better get going on the lad,' said Cohen, who rarely attended such meetings. The chief interrogation officer generally moved in his own circles.

'What are we going to do with Bielke?' wondered Johan Steer. He looked at Winter. 'Assuming it's the boy. Mattias.'

'It is him,' said Winter. 'But it's not only him.'

'In both cases?' asked Setter.

'No, he was too young when the first murder was committed,' said Djanali.

'He was sixteen or seventeen,' said Setter, 'and already about six foot, so we're told.'

'Bielke killed Beatrice,' said Winter. 'He hasn't admitted it yet but it's written between the lines of the letter to his wife, and if we ask him again he'll tell us.' He puffed at his cigarillo then looked round the room again. 'He'll tell us now. Once he's heard what happened tonight.'

'Why?' asked Setter, playing the role of interrogator, trying to find out how and why. 'And how?'

'We know that Bielke took part in the . . . activities at the house. We haven't found anybody there, but we know. We've seen.' He thought about Halders again, could see that Djanali was thinking about Halders. Halders must have seen. 'We know that Beatrice was there. We don't know why, but we can guess. More than guess. Beatrice was there five years ago, shortly before she died.'

'But why did Bielke kill her?' Setter asked again.

For Christ's sake! thought Djanali. Tell us why people kill one another so that we know once and for all and the world becomes a paradise. Bielke killed her because he's an evil person, or a sick person, perhaps there's a link. It wasn't enough to see her behind a pane of glass. He wanted more than that.

She heard Winter answering Setter's question.

'Maybe that wasn't his intention. Maybe one thing led to another. The man's sick.'

Like his son, if it is his son, Djanali thought. Like father, like son.

But the most important thing was Fredrik.

'As far as I can see there's only one reason why we're all sitting here now, and that's finding Fredrik,' she said. 'So: what is there about what has happened now that can help us to find him?'

'That *is* what we're talking about,' said Setter.

'Oh yes?'

'It's all interlinked, surely? What did Halders see in that house that was so compromising that he had to disappear?'

'And Samic,' said Bergenhem. 'Why has he disappeared?'

'There's another big question,' said Winter with a glance at Djanali, possibly slightly apologetic. 'Did Bielke rape his own daughter? Or did Mattias do it?'

'Raped his own sister?' said Sara Helander. 'Or half sister.'

'He might not have known at the time,' Ringmar said. 'Presuming that *is* what happened.'

'If Mattias murdered Angelika and Anne, he could well have done something like that,' said Setter. 'But I say it again: why?'

A punishment, Winter thought. Mattias was punishing them for something. For something they'd done. What had they done? Danced, perhaps. Possibly more. How did Mattias know about that? Had somebody told him? Why should Mattias bother about it? Had he been there himself? *Had he been there himself?* Had he seen Kurt Bielke? Had he seen . . . his daughter? Had she been there? No. Or . . . been there without her father knowing? Had Bielke done something that resulted in his daughter being raped? Somebody who was punishing *him*? Via his daughter? Somebody who had a . . . hold on him. Who knew what he'd done.

Beatrice five years ago. Beatrice who'd been there. Others who'd been there. Samic had been there. Samic. Where else had Samic been? With whom? There was a woman involved. Was *she* Mattias' mother?

Mattias had suffered in various ways. He was seeking attention and . . . he was seeking the ones who were involved . . . in the sinister game. The girls were involved in the game. Perhaps he thought they were responsible for what had happened to Jeanette and what had happened between the two of them. The girls . . . but also Kurt Bielke. Did Mattias know what had happened to Beatrice? He hadn't murdered her, couldn't have done.

Mattias put the camera in Bielke's car. Mattias broke into the Hanssons' house looking for something that could expose Bielke. No. Somebody else. Samic? Had Samic known about the photographs of the bar?

Mattias could have killed Angelika's boyfriend because he might have known Mattias and started to suspect something.

When they searched Mattias's flat they would find the camera that had taken the pictures of the girls sitting in the bar, a camera with a damaged lens. They'd also find Anne Nöjd's mobile phone.

All this flashed through his mind in the space of a few seconds.

Mattias might give them all the answers, or just add a few more questions. Bielke would talk, maybe too much.

Somebody said 'Samic'.

'What was that?'

'If we can find Samic, we'll find Fredrik as well,' Djanali said. Samic, Samic. Samic. Winter thought, thought, like everybody else.

*

It hadn't been possible to talk to Mattias. He was in a silent world of his own that Winter had not been able to break into.

Bielke had not yet confessed, but he would. He did talk, however. Asked about his daughter, never about his wife. His madness came and went in his eyes. Cohen and Winter tried to concentrate on what had happened in the house on the other side of the river the hour after Halders had entered it.

'I know nothing about that.'

'You were there after all,' said Winter.

Bielke suddenly looked him in the eye, and held his gaze. Bielke's forehead was throbbing as if his thoughts were about to burst out of it and spurt all over the table. Winter waited.

'You were there after all,' he said again, as calmly as he could.

'Yes,' said Bielke. 'Yes.'

That was the first time he'd admitted it.

'Where were you?' Winter asked.

'I was in the house.'

'Where in the house?'

'I was in the basement.'

Bielke's eyes had glazed over, or were in the process of doing so. He stumbled over syllables in a monotone. Weariness was setting in now that it was all over.

'Who else was in the basement?'

'Eh?'

'Who else was in the basement?'

'Her.'

'Who's her?'

'I dunno.'

'What's her name?'

'Dunno. A girl.'

'What did she do?'

'Eh?'

'What did she do?'

'Dan . . . danced.'

'What did she dance?'

Bielke didn't understand. That was the only dance as far as he was concerned, and he didn't think of it as a dance anyway. It was just a name, an expression.

'What kind of a dance was it?' Winter asked.

'Dunno.'

'Was she dancing alone?'

'Alone.'

'Who else was there?'

Bielke didn't answer. He seemed to be looking for somebody who wasn't there. There was only Winter and Cohen and a tape recorder and a video camera.

'Where's the boy?' asked Bielke out of the blue, raising his head.

'What boy?'

'The boy.'

'Mattias? Was Mattias there?' Winter asked.

'He's my boy,' he said.

'We know.'

Bielke nodded.

'Was he there?' asked Winter.

'I don't know.'

'Who else was there?'

Bielke said something that Winter couldn't hear.

'What did you say?'

Bielke muttered again.

'Can you repeat what you just said?'

'She was there as well.'

'Who's she?'

'She's been with *him* for ages. She took the boy with her. I didn't know at first.'

'Was Mattias in the house?'

'He used to help a bit. I saw him sometimes.' Bielke stared at the wall behind Winter. 'He didn't know then. Yet. About me. Who I was.'

'Did he see you?'

'Eh?'

'Did he see you?'

'No. I don't think so.'

You think wrong, Winter thought.

Bielke said something under his breath.

'Can you repeat what you just said?'

'Drove off with him,' said Bielke in a voice that once again sounded monotonous, flat.

'Drove off?' asked Winter. 'Drove off with whom?'

Bielke mumbled something but seemed to be thinking as well.

'Drove off with whom?' Winter repeated.

'Him who came.'

'Who came?'

'Him.'

'Who's him?'

'Dunno.'

'Who was driving when they left?'

'Eh?'

'Who was driving?'

Bielke looked as if he were thinking again. Looked as if he were making up his mind.

'Johan,' he said.

Johan Samic, Winter thought. Samic, Samic, Samic.

'He was the one who did it,' said Bielke in a louder voice, as if he was breathing out forcefully. 'Samic did it.'

'Did what?'

'My little girl.'

Bielke burst into tears.

Winter waited. The tape recorder spun round silently. Cohen looked at Bielke who now looked back. He dried his eyes with the back of his right hand.

'Hurt my little girl.'

'Jeanette?'

Bielke nodded.

'Can you repeat what you just said?'

'He hurt my Jeanette.'

'Why?'

Bielke sobbed, wiped his eyes again.

'He knew.'

'What did he know?'

Winter could feel something cold in the back of his head, like a chilly draught.

'He exploited it,' said Bielke. 'Me. And . . . us.'

'What did he exploit?' asked Winter. 'What did Johan Samic exploit about you?'

Bielke seemed to drift away again, disappear into another world.

'What did Johan Samic know about you?' asked Winter.

'What I'd done.'

Bielke looked at Winter, his eyes a mixture of alertness and fog.

'He said he could do whatever he liked,' said Bielke.

'Why?' asked Winter.

Bielke muttered again.

'Why?' Winter repeated the question.

'Because I killed her.'

Bielke said that with his head bowed. His hair was the same pale colour as the walls of the room.

'Can you repeat what you just said?'

'I killed her.' He looked at Winter and Cohen. 'I didn't mean to. I just followed her. I didn't mean to. You know that. Everybody understands that.'

'Did you kill Angelika Hansson?' asked Cohen.

'Who?'

'Did you kill Angelika Hansson?'

'No, no. That wasn't me.'

'Did you kill Anne Nöjd?'

'Not me.'

Another snuffle from Bielke.

'Pardon?'

'He . . . away. He was there later. Ask him.'

'I didn't get what you said just now,' Winter said.

'When they drove away. Ask Samic.'

'Ask what?'

'And Benny,' said Bielke. 'He was driving.'

'Be . . . Benny?'

'Benny.'

'Benny who?'

'Benny. Benny boy.'

Winter was standing outside the interrogation room. His face was burning. He'd got to his feet immediately and left the room. Cohen stayed with Bielke.

Winter took the lift up to the room where Setter and Bergenhem were sifting through documentation of Samic's business transactions, past and present.

Bergenhem was there.

'I need a name,' said Winter. 'Benny. Benny Vennerhag.'

'Vennerhag?'

'Has Samic had any dealings with Benny Vennerhag?'

'I don't recognise the name.'

'Then look, FOR FUCK'S SAKE!' Winter yelled.

'Hey, calm down, calm down.'

Winter grabbed at the keyboard in front of Bergenhem.

'What the HELL are you doing, Erik? Give me a

chance.' Bergenhem was tapping into the register of all the names they had so far.

'Yes,' he said. 'We've got the name here. I can't say if—'

'That's good enough,' said Winter and strode to his office. He met Ringmar. 'Come with me,' shouted Winter over his shoulder.

Ringmar followed Winter into his office and saw him picking through a pile of photographs.

'What's going on, Erik?'

Winter was holding the photograph taken at Angelika Hansson's graduation party. Lars-Olof Hansson behind the camera. In front of it: the woman in profile. He knew he would never meet her. Unless she came here now that Mattias was here.

The boy next to her.

A dark face that might be Johan Samic, might not.

For Christ's sake, it was Samic all right.

A fair-haired man, almost alongside him, with a beard and dark glasses. Lars-Olof Hansson hadn't recognised him either. There was something familiar about him. The beard looked a bit odd, the glasses . . .

Winter looked at the other photograph, taken at about the same time by Cecilia, Angelika's friend who knew nothing about the house on the other side of the river. Couldn't have known about it, wouldn't have been able to cover it up unless she was out of her mind. They'd have another chat with her.

The woman, taken from directly in front. The boy wasn't in Cecilia's picture, he might have taken a step forward. That would explain it. The dark man was no longer there, but there were more people in this picture, more faces. He'd noticed that before.

He scrutinised the picture. Took out his magnifying

glass again. Turned to the enlargements they'd made. Examined the first of them through the magnifying glass. Now he knew what he was looking for. That was the key difference. The photograph opened itself up as he looked and as he focused further into the mass of people, at the back, he could see a fair-haired head in profile, only the upper part of his face, a forehead, eyes, nose and nothing more, but he didn't need a magnifying glass to see who it was in the background, under a cloud of balloons. Benny.

He was wearing a false beard. Samic had a wig. An arrogant joke, or something much worse.

Samic. The woman. Vennerhag. They hadn't been at the party for Angelika's sake, not in the first place. She was leaving school, but so was Mattias. He'd gone to the same school, but hadn't been in the same class. Winter was certain now.

They'd been there for Mattias' sake.

The woman was Mattias' mother. Benny and Samic knew that Angelika would recognise them from the club.

Ringmar drove, up the hills. Winter directed him through the deserted streets. Somebody was having a midnight barbecue in his garden. Winter could see a flame leaping up.

The crack in his elbow was burning like fire.

'Shouldn't you have that plastered?' Ringmar asked.

Winter didn't reply, merely smoked, gazing out into the night.

'Isn't Fredrik's house up here somewhere?' Ringmar asked.

'On the other side. Over there.'

They drove past it. No lights in any of the windows.

'Down here then turn left,' said Winter. He was rocking backwards and forwards, holding his elbow.

'Calm down now, Erik.'

'Are we going to find Halders or aren't we?'

'Yes, but—'

'Put your foot down, then.' He inhaled deeply, released his safety belt as Ringmar pulled up outside Vennerhag's house. There was a light in each of the windows.

'He'll be at the back,' said Winter. 'I'll find him.'

Ringmar followed and came to the lawn behind the house. A man in swimming trunks was holding a glass. A naked woman glided smoothly up to the edge of the pool.

The man saw who it was approaching and put his glass down on the table under the parasol. The woman had clambered out of the pool and had crossed her arms over her body, which was slick from the water. Ringmar saw how Winter accelerated. The man in the swimming trunks started speaking.

'Erik, it was—'

Winter's skull crashed into Vennerhag at chest height. The woman screamed. Vennerhag emitted a sound like air escaping from a Lilo. He staggered backwards. Winter held his right arm as if it were still in the sling lying on the lawn at the side of Ringmar, who seemed to be screwed down. The woman screamed again. Vennerhag staggered forwards and Winter kicked him in the crotch. Vennerhag spluttered. Winter kicked both his kneecaps. Vennerhag collapsed to the accompaniment of sounds like the cracking of dry twigs, slid backwards and into the water. Winter jumped in after him and forced his head under the surface with his good arm, then pulled it up again. Ringmar registered

Vennerhag's gaping eyes, reflecting the lights over the pool.

'WHERE IS HE?' Winter yelled. He forced Vennerhag's head under the water again, pulled it up once more. 'WHERE IS HE, YOU BASTARD? WHERE IS FREDRIK HALDERS?'

Ringmar saw Winter head-butt Vennerhag over the bridge of his nose. Vennerhag gave vent to a rattling sound. He'll kill him, Ringmar thought. I'll have to dive in.

Vennerhag's head was dipped under again, then pulled up. Blood was pouring from his nose. The water hadn't managed to wash it away.

'I'll kill you, Benny, you know I will,' said Winter, aiming a kick at Ringmar, who had dived in. 'Fuck off, Bertil. Keep your distance.'

'Steady on, Erik.'

'STAY WHERE YOU ARE,' Winter yelled. Ringmar did as bidden and wondered what to do next.

Winter pulled Vennerhag's face up to his own. 'This is your last chance before I drown you. Where is he? Where is Halders?'

Another rattling noise from Vennerhag.

'WELL? WELL?'

Winter thrust his head under water again. 'Aaagh' came from Vennerhag. Winter raised his head. Benny's face was disfigured by the blows and the blood and the light that seemed to be drilling its way through his head from underneath.

'WELL, WHAT DO YOU SAY?'

Ringmar saw Vennerhag's lips move, saw Winter lean forward to listen, saw Vennerhag's lips again, saw Winter stand up straight, cast Vennerhag's body aside and wade away with water up to his waist.

Ringmar pulled Vennerhag out of the pool. He looked dead. The woman had her face in her hands, shuddering violently. Ringmar felt Vennerhag's pulse and after a few seconds registered a faint beat. He could hear a voice from inside the house. Winter was calling for an ambulance and for the police.

Winter came back outside.

'God only knows where my mobile is,' he said. 'Let's go.'

Ringmar looked at the woman and at Vennerhag's body. She looked up, then hid her face in her hands again. She was a stranger.

'COME ON, Bertil. You'll have to drive.'

'Where to?' asked Ringmar, but Winter was already on his way.

39

Ringmar drove west, past the funfair. It looked to Winter as if the roundabout was spinning, a circle of false light.

Another light started to appear over the horizon behind them, a new day. Winter could feel the pain like sledgehammers pounding away at the right-hand side of his body, from the top down. He had Vennerhag's blood on his knuckles, and could smell his own wild animal-like scent. He was shivering in his wet clothes as Ringmar accelerated on the motorway and the wind rushed in through the open windows.

Have I gone out of my mind? Is this what being mad is like?

Ringmar was talking over the radio.

'They'll have to wait,' Winter said. 'We can't go storming in with a whole battalion.'

Ringmar carried on talking to Bergenhem and whoever else was there. Winter ran his hands over his shirt.

'There's a sweater on the back seat,' said Ringmar, turning to look at him. 'How many of them are there?'

'I don't know.'

'Didn't he say anything about that?'

'No.'

'What did he say?'

'What we needed to know. Where Fredrik is. Turn right at the next exit,' said Winter, staring straight ahead. 'It'll be quicker.'

He watched an aeroplane climbing into the morning sky, like a dark bird. The flashing lights on its tail sent a message down to earth. Now he could hear the engines, a muffled rumbling.

They crossed the bridge. The sea looked like a field.

It was darker again on the other side. The light was behind them, over the open water. There were no cars on the road, which was narrower when they came to the island.

'This must be it,' said Ringmar. He turned off and it grew even darker in among the trees. Ringmar glanced at Winter, who was making sure his SigSauer had survived the dip in the pool. 'How are you feeling, Erik?'

'Be patient with me,' said Winter.

'We must stay calm when we get there,' said Ringmar. 'We'll see.'

Winter leaned back in his seat and pictured the boy's face.

*

Cohen had phoned while he was examining the photographs earlier in the day, a day that never seemed to end.

'Mattias wants to say something,' Cohen had said.

'What?' Winter had asked, holding up a photograph that seemed to be mostly filled with brightly coloured balloons.

'I think he wants to tell us the whole story.'

Mattias ignored him when he came into the room. He was sitting quietly on the chair in front of them.

'You wanted to tell us something, Mattias?'

He didn't answer.

'Do you want to tell us something?'

'I might.'

Winter could see the similarities with his father, now that he knew. The eyes were the same, had that same inner darkness.

'What do you want to tell us, Mattias?'

'Where's my mum?'

Winter had expected the boy to look at him, but he continued staring down at the table.

'I want her to come here,' he said.

'What's your mum called, Mattias?'

'Eh?'

'What's she called?'

He said nothing.

Have I made a mistake? Winter wondered.

Mattias looked at Cohen now, then at Winter.

'Where is my mum?'

'We don't know,' said Winter. 'We're looking for her as well.' He leaned forward. 'Why can't we find her, Mattias?'

'How should I know?'

'When did you last see her?'

'Dunno.'

'It doesn't seem as if you live together.'

Mattias didn't respond.

'Where does she live?'

He didn't answer.

'Where is she, Mattias?'

'She lives with him. Samic.' He looked at Winter. 'It's a long time now. It's been a long time.' He stroked his hand across his mouth. 'They've been living together for a long time.' He rubbed his forehead. 'I've told her I don't like it. I've told her before.' He

383

gave a sudden, short laugh. 'I showed 'em. I showed that bastard! Now it'll never happen again . . . never again!'

Winter waited. The boy seemed animated, but only for a few seconds.

'I showed him as well,' Mattias said. 'Just like . . . them.'

'Why did you kill the girls, Mattias?'

The boy was in a different world, seeing things only he could see.

'Th . . . they shouldn't have been there,' he said.

Winter listened to the sound of air circulating round the room. He could feel the sweat on his back. His arm had started to hurt again, badly.

'Th . . . they had no business to be there. I . . . I told them.'

He stared at the wall behind Winter where so many had stared while being interrogated.

'It was their own fault,' said Mattias. 'If they hadn't been there, it wouldn't have . . . been like that.'

'Why was it their fault?'

'Jeanette.'

'Jeanette? Was she there?'

'Sh . . . she went with th . . . them once.'

'Was Jeanette at the club?'

Mattias nodded. Winter didn't know what to believe.

'What did she do?'

The boy nodded again. Perhaps he hadn't heard the question.

'What did she do there, Mattias?'

'She was outside.'

Winter could see the house in his mind's eye, the street, the lights, the door, the hall, the stairs, the wall.

'Outside?'

384

'Sh . . . she was only outside but th . . . that was enough.'

'Enough? Enough for what?'

'Fo . . . for him to follow her. Follow her and d . . . do wh . . . what he d . . . did.'

'Who? Samic?'

Mattias nodded.

'Th . . . they won't do it again. Never again.' He looked at Winter now. His body was crumpled up, as if it had no bones. 'He did it.'

'Johan Samic?'

The boy shook his head.

'N . . . not that. The other thing.'

'Kurt Bielke?'

The boy nodded. There was a glint in his eye, as if he'd just shared a secret with Winter. There were spots of red in the whites of his eyes and saliva in the corners of his mouth.

'What did Kurt Bielke do?'

'I heard him and Samic talking about it,' said Mattias in a voice that suddenly sounded loud and clear. 'He'd done it and could do it again.' His voice was lower now. 'H . . . h . . . he . . . it was his fault as well. That . . . Jeanette.'

'Could do it again? What do you mean?'

'He'd done it once, hadn't he?'

'Why—'

'It could have been him the other times as well, couldn't it?' He interrupted Winter's question.

'But it was you, Mattias.'

'It could have been him.' Mattias raised both hands in the air. 'It could have been him.'

'Do you know who he is? Who Kurt Bielke is?'

'He's a shit.'

'What else is he?'

'They say he's my dad, but I don't believe that.'

'What does your mum say?'

'I haven't got round to asking her,' said Mattias, and he laughed.

She didn't know what her son had done, Winter thought, and when it eventually dawned on her she was scared. She left him in order to get help, but there was no help forthcoming from where she turned to. It was even worse there.

And then we arrived. Halders arrived.

Cohen looked at Winter, who hadn't followed up with another question.

'Where is Angelika's boyfriend?' Cohen asked.

'Who?'

'Angelika had a boyfriend, didn't she?'

'He's gone now,' Mattias said.

'What do you mean, "gone"?'

'He was the same as the rest of 'em.' Mattias looked up, stared past Cohen and Winter. 'And he came to me asking loads of questions. Same as you lot.'

Mattias was full of hatred for everybody and everything that had destroyed his life. Something inside him had snapped, and he had gone somewhere from which he could never return.

*

Ringmar was in third gear and worried about the headlights shining so far ahead.

'I'll switch the lights off,' he said.

'Watch out for deer,' said Winter.

Ringmar couldn't help smiling. He peered into the faint, uncertain light hovering between day and night over the trees.

'Samic raped Jeanette,' Winter said.

Ringmar didn't respond. He was too busy trying to keep the car on a road that was no more than a black line between the fir trees.

'He'd had a hold on Bielke for all those years, a big hold. He exploited it.'

'How do you know that?'

'Bielke told us during the latest interrogation.' Winter turned to face Ringmar. 'The boy said so as well.'

'There are a lot of villains in this story,' said Ringmar.

'And victims,' said Winter. 'Most of them are victims.'

'Hmm.'

'They're all victims in their different ways,' said Winter. 'That never ends.' He tapped the dashboard. 'Stop a minute.'

Ringmar pulled in to the side of the road and switched off the engine. The silence was more distinct in among the trees and stones and bushes. Winter consulted the map again, as he'd done before they left town, once his pulse rate had fallen a little. He shone the torch down at the floor.

'It was only a name,' he said. Vennerhag had mumbled the name of the cottage and the direction. He'd managed to do it twice.

'One kilometre, maybe a bit less. There's a fork in the road there, then it's another five hundred metres.' Winter dropped the map. 'We'll walk from here.' He opened the door. 'Park the car sideways on so that Lars will understand what's going on when he and the others get here. It'll make a road block as well.' Winter could see that there were deep ditches on either side of the road. He stood up, lost his balance slightly and automatically supported himself on the side of the car with his injured arm. The stab of pain shot all the way up into his scalp.

'We'd better wait for the others,' Ringmar said.

That was the only right thing to do, of course. He could see that. But there was something inside him that said there wasn't enough time.

'There isn't enough time for that,' he said, feeling the intense pain seeping out of his body. 'I'm sure of it.'

'We're only talking about half an hour, Erik. Max.'

'It's not only that. There'll be too many of us later. All at once.'

He set off walking alongside the ditch. Ringmar followed suit. There was a smell of water full of weed, of plants that hadn't yet shrivelled up in the sun. The sun didn't penetrate very far into here, and Winter detected smells that seemed to be hundreds of years old.

When all this was over he would go walking in the woods with Angela and Elsa, creep under the trees and dig up some moss. Mushrooms in the autumn. Wellington boots through damp undergrowth. He shivered again in the thin, knitted sweater that was irritating his shoulders. His deck shoes were sticking to his feet as if glued.

They'd gone as far as the fork. Winter pointed right. He crossed over the road and walked through the trees, which were less dense there. He could hear a great northern diver calling in the distance. He knew there was a lake behind the house they were heading for. The bird called again, a lonely cry through the early morning light that was starting to scrape out shapes and contours. The bird sounded close now. Winter could feel the ferns and bracken brushing his shins, and once a sting. His wet shorts clung to his thighs and backside.

'I can see it,' Ringmar whispered.

They paused. They could just discern the outline of the house, the pointed roof. They moved closer and paused behind the fir trees. The house was bigger than Winter had expected. There was a car outside, looking as if it had been hurled against one of the walls. An estate car. The house was dark in all its windows.

So Halders is supposed to be in there, thought Ringmar. Or under. Under the house, in the ground.

'This is Samic's hideaway,' Winter said.

'How long had he intended hiding here?'

'Until we came.'

'And he has Halders for company?'

'Where else would they put him?'

There are ten thousand burial plots round Gothenburg, Ringmar thought.

People would soon be up and about. The sky was grey and blue now.

Halders saw everything, knows everything. Now we're coming so that you can tell us. He knew that Ringmar didn't think for a moment that Halders was still alive. Probably not that he was in there either. But Winter knew Vennerhag. Halders was here all right. He had beaten up Vennerhag because he thought there was still hope for Halders.

Now, standing in front of the silent house by the lake, hope had faded away like the stars over the forest. There was a red shimmer beyond the lake that could be seen glinting in places on both sides of the house. Why go in there in a couple of seconds when they could wait for the army of police officers that would encircle the place and shoot their way in?

'Let's go,' said Winter.

Ringmar nodded and set off. It was nothing to do with loyalty. He's not trigger-happy. Bertil thinks like me. Now's the moment. He hasn't come with me to wait for Lars and Aneta and sunrise.

They crept between the car and the house. The grass brushed against their knees, but silently. Winter didn't listen for any noise from the grass. A roller blind was pulled down behind the window to the left of the verandah. A hat was hanging on a hook. A pair of boots stood by the door. There was a tool on the bench to the right, a screwdriver.

And now? Winter tried the door handle, pressed it down and pushed gently and the door slid open a few centimetres without creaking. He looked at Ringmar, who was ready. Winter pushed and the door opened and they walked quickly and quietly inside, finding themselves in a hallway with the outline of a staircase straight ahead and the pale rectangles of two doors. I'm too old for this sort of thing, Ringmar thought.

There was a dark hole to the right that might be the entrance to a cellar. Winter took another step forward. Another table along one of the walls with some items of clothing on it. Two chairs. There was a mirror over the table and Winter looked at it and saw the eyes staring at him from the side of the room opposite the entrance and he could see the knuckles in front of the face at the end of the outstretched arm, holding something: a gun, a bloody big gun, and he didn't move a muscle, he heard nothing, no barked command, no breathing, nothing from Ringmar who was also motionless and staring at the same thing but not through the mirror. Winter waited for the impact of the bullet that would pass right through him and smash the glass and wipe out the picture of Samic who was pointing the gun at them and waiting for the movement that would come and—

The shot broke the odious silence, another shot immediately after the first, Winter was still staring at the mirror, which hadn't been shattered, *he* hadn't been shattered, Ringmar was just as immobile with his eyes fixed on something Winter couldn't see, he couldn't drag his eyes away from the mirror and the world inside it.

Samic's arm started sinking. Winter could see his eyes, still open. There was no longer a pistol in Samic's hand. It was lying on the floor in front of him. Samic grasped hold of the hand that had held the pistol, but he didn't seem to be injured. He fell, slowly, revealing the woman standing diagonally behind him with a gun in her hand. Possibly Halders' SigSauer. She had shot the gun out of Samic's hand. Samic whimpered. She dropped her own weapon onto his body.

Winter had seen her face before, in profile and full face.

'That's enough,' she said. 'That's enough now.'

Winter finally dragged his eyes away from the mirror. She was wearing a nightdress, angel-white. Winter took a step towards her.

'Yes,' she said, 'I'm Mattias' mother.'

Ringmar started moving.

'He's upstairs,' she said. She knew they knew who she meant. She was looking straight at Winter.

'Is there anybody else here?' Ringmar asked. 'Apart from . . . our colleague?'

'What do you think?' she said, looking down at her gun lying between Samic's legs.

Winter rushed up the stairs. All at once he saw a searchlight through an upstairs window. He could hear Ringmar downstairs talking into a mobile telephone. He could hear car engines outside, doors opening, the rattling of a helicopter in the sky.

There were two doors, both of them closed. He opened the one on the left and saw a double bed, unmade. There were clothes on the floor.

The door on the other side of the landing creaked as he opened it. There was a bed in there too. The beam from the helicopter was swinging round and round as if at some funfair, sending circles of light into the room. There was a figure in the bed, its head tied down with straps of some kind. Winter bent over it.

Halders' face was patchily lit up by searchlights, or maybe it was the rising sun. Winter could hear footsteps downstairs now, voices, car doors slamming.

Halders opened his eyes.

BY ÅKE EDWARDSON
ALSO AVAILABLE FROM VINTAGE

☐ **Sun and Shadow**	9780099472056	£6.99